I0635161

Emerilia

Book 4
New Horizons

MICHAEL CHATFIELD

Cover Art by Luciano Fleitas

Interior Layout & Design by Caitlin Greer Paperback

ISBN: 978-1-9995411-6-3

Hardcover ISBN: 978-1-989377-54-3

eBook ISBN: 978-1-989377-44-4

OTHER BOOKS BY MICHAEL CHATFIELD

Ten Realms
Two Week Curse
Second Realm
Third Realm
Fourth Realm
Fifth Realm
Sixth Realm P1
Sixth Realm P2
Seventh Realm P1
Seventh Realm P2
Eighth Realm
Ninth Realm
TenthRealm

Four Horsemen
Four Horsemen Series
Planes of Etera
Ilus Found

Emerilia Series
The Trapped Mind Project
Benvari Mountains
For The Guild
New Horizons
This Is Our Land
Stone Raiders' Return
Time of Change
Beyond All Expectations
Of Myths and Legends
The Pantheon Moves
Empire Burning

Free Fleet
The Recruitment:
*   Rise of the Free Fleet*
Coming Home
No Rest For The Wicked
From The Black
From Furies Forged
War's Reward

Builders Legacy
Connection Unknown
Sliding Reality
Existential Threat

Harmony War
Sacremon Masoul
Osdal Fernix Earth

Maraukain War
The Tenth Awakens
The Vanguard Emerges
An Empire is Born
Enemies on All Sides
On The War Path

The Death Knight
Skeleton With a Heart
Possessor of the Heart
A Skeleton and a Lich
A Skeleton's Duty
A Lich's Love

Other Languages by Michael Chatfield Die Zehn Reiche

Der Zwei-Wochen-Fluch
Das Zweite Reich
Das Dritte Reich
Das Vierte Reich
Das Fünfte Reich
Das Sechste Reich: Teil 1

Das Vermächtnis der Erbauer

Unbekannte Verbindung

THE CHATFIELD CONNECTION NEWSLETTER

Sign up for exclusive offers, original stories, events, and more.
https://michaelchatfield.com/pages/newsletter

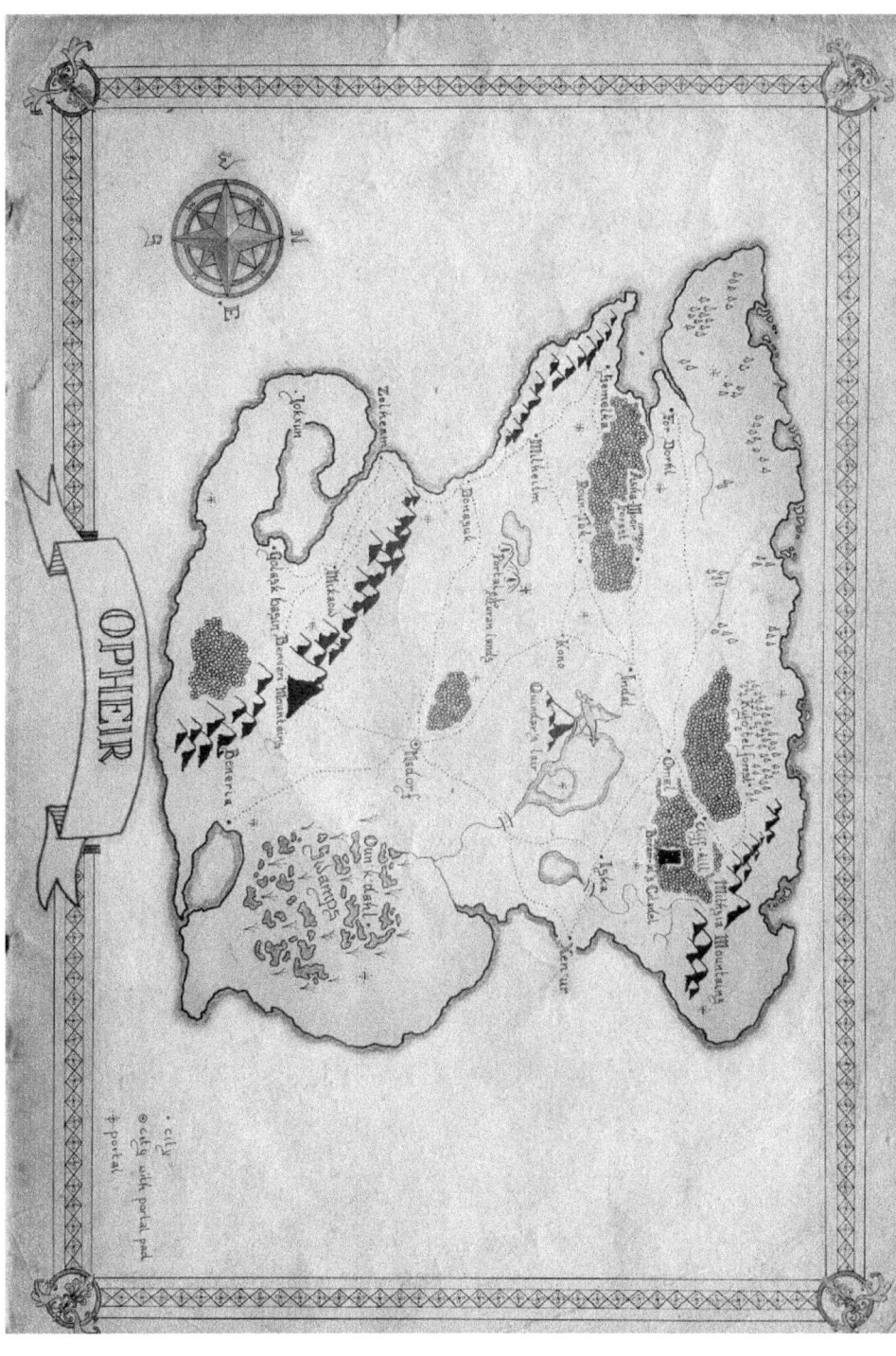

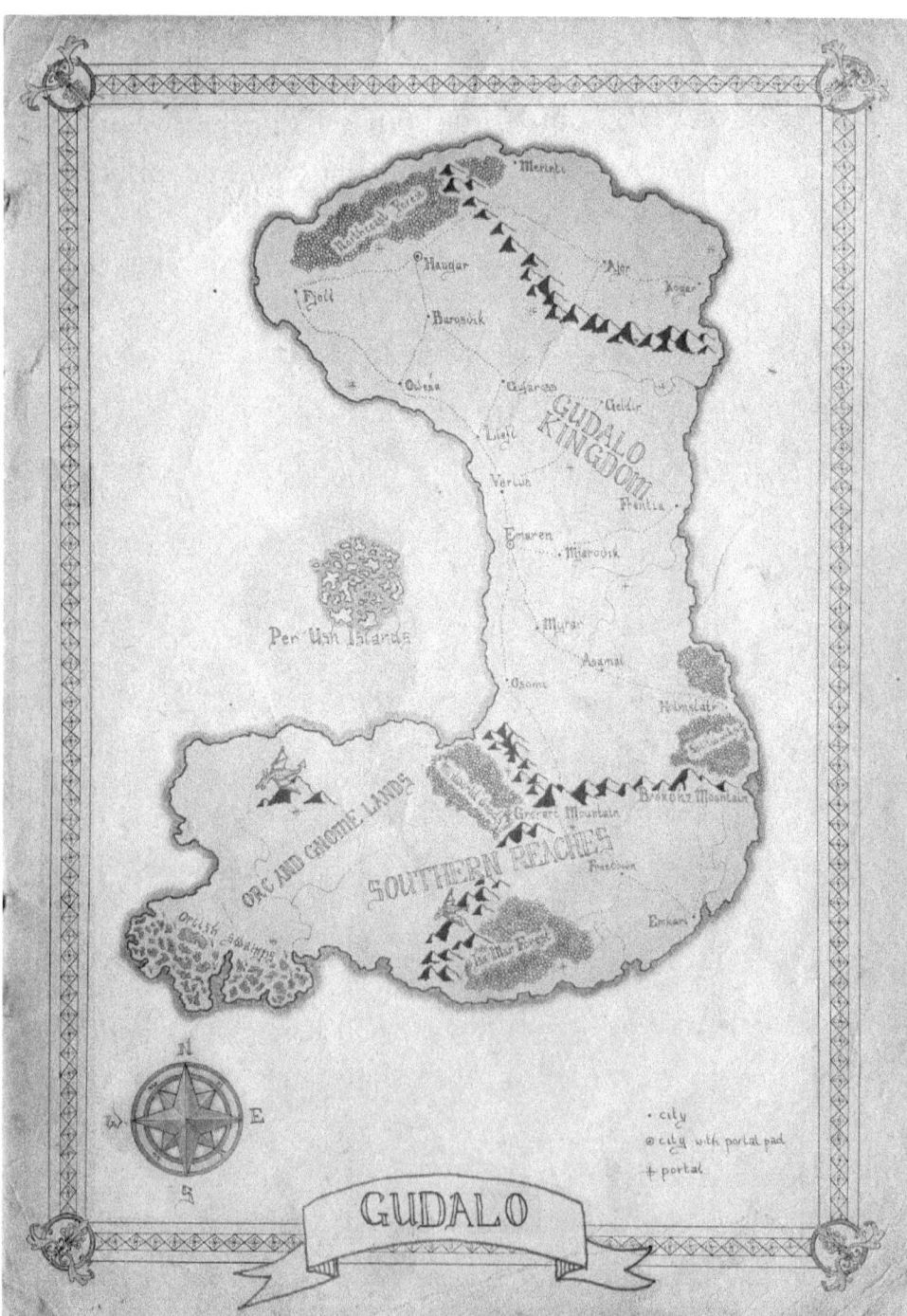

GUDALO

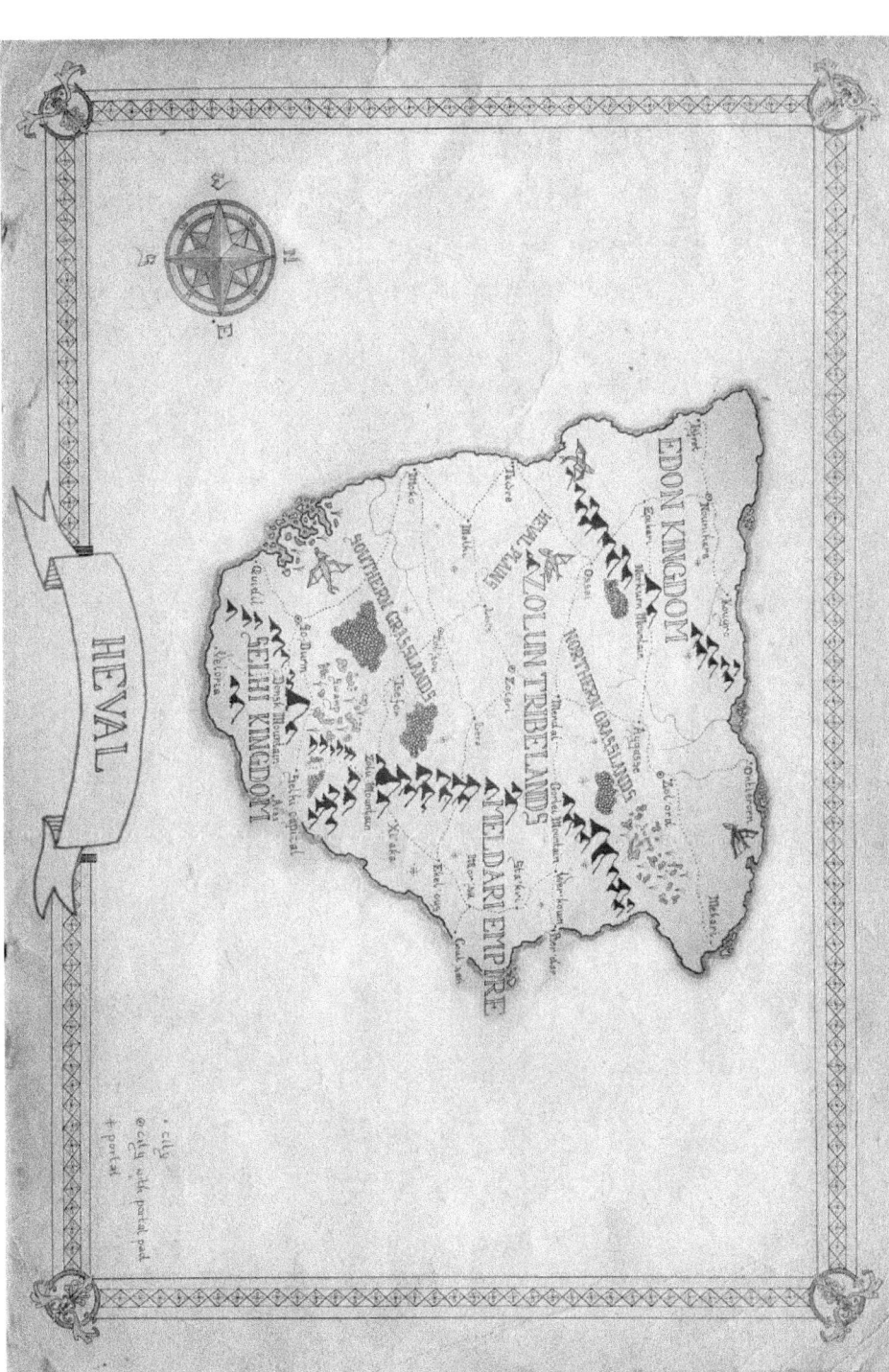

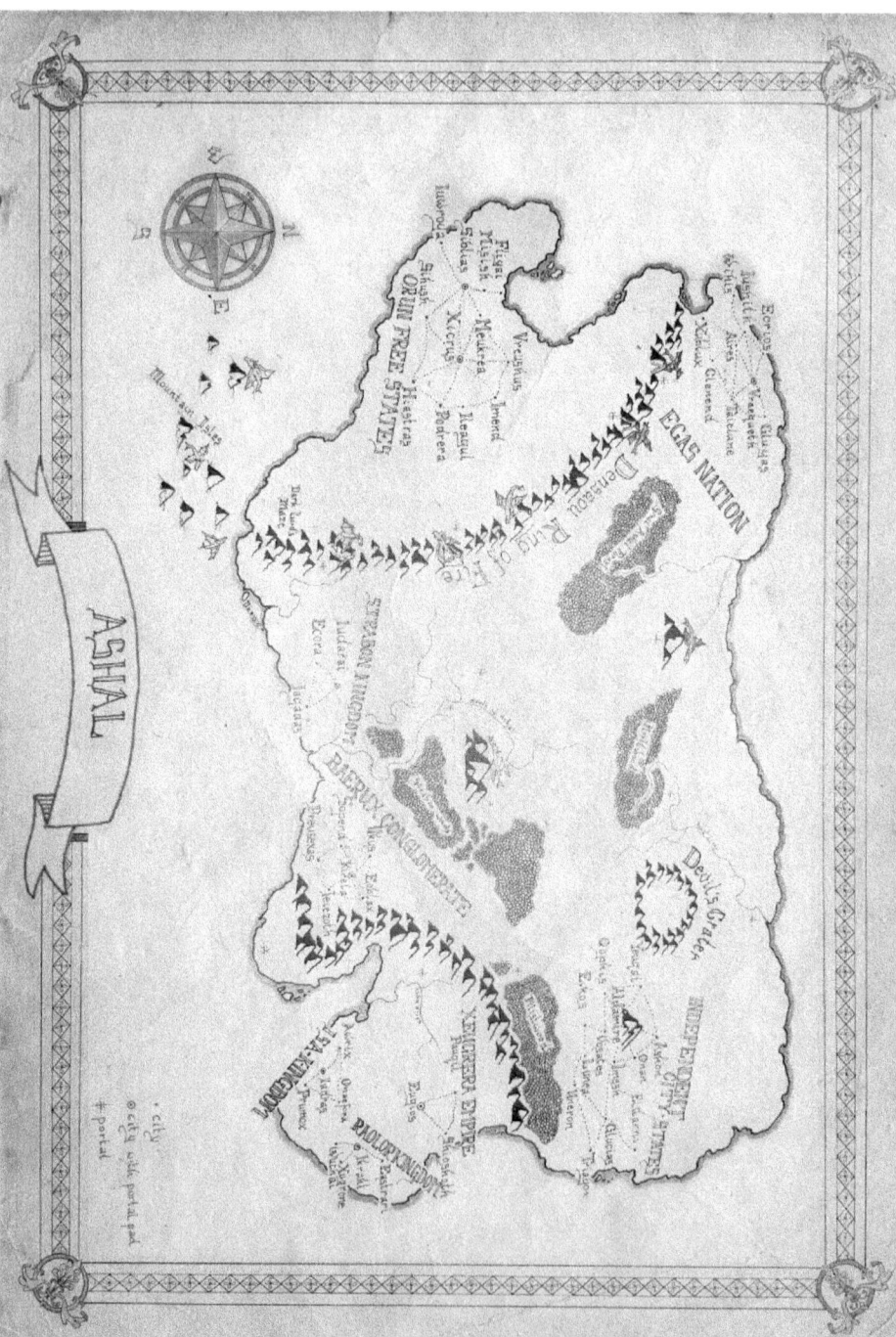

MARKOLM

MARKOLM RANGE

- city
- city with portal pad
+ portal

Want a bigger map
of Emerilia and the continents?
Check out
http://theeternalwriter.deviantart.com/

Character Sheet is located in the back
of the book for reference.

Table of Contents

SIX MONTHS

Anna looked out of the keep's tower and saw Devil's Crater. She had been there nearly every other week, with Induca or Malsour coming with her to speed up the travel time between the Aleph's hidden teleport pad and the Demons' home.

Malsour and Fornau had started the basics of the valley. Fornau had marked out an area for the city that would rest in the middle of the crater. Fields had been created and a lumber mill sat in the middle of the northeastern forest, with a number of mines opened. Homes made of polished stone had been raised near the farms, the hunting forests, and the lumber mill.

While Malsour had repaired all the keeps, Alkao's was still the only one which had been covered with metals.

He'd also built an eighth keep to distance them all apart and watch over the surrounding lands. Unless you knew where the keeps were, they were hard to see; Malsour's work made them look like part of the cliff they grew from.

Anna looked into the crater, watching as farmers were working their fields. Fornau had been gracious enough to bless the ground, ensuring that it would remain fertile for a long time to come. His touch could be seen across the crater and while he had to return to Quindar and their hatchlings, he promised to return.

Anna heard a flap of wings. She looked over to see Alkao swoop down toward the balcony she stood on.

He landed easily, walking as soon as he touched down. Wearing simple clothes and caring less about appearance and more about form, he wore the weapons Dave had gifted him with pride.

"Anna, I did not know that you would be here today." Alkao smiled.

Her chest tightened. Over the last six months, they had worked long nights and longer days to make sure that Devil's Crater would be ready for the return of their people and to make sure that their alliance would work.

She had come to see him as not only a brilliant warrior, but a man who was coming to understand his shortcomings and was looking to do the best by his people. She saw the stress that wore on them both and they'd become close. Often, Anna had thought about becoming even closer. She put her feelings down to the stress weighing on them and pushed them aside.

"I was able to get the day off from raiding," Anna said.

"One day, I hope that you tell me how you get here so fast," Alkao said.

"Maybe one day." Anna shrugged, continuing to look out over Devil's Crater while watching Beast Kin and Demons who were working together at the lumber mill and checking on the growing orchard and planting fields. They had been getting reports, sent through the incoming villagers and supporting Demons and Beast Kin, on the progress of both sides.

As the stigma of being a non-combatant disappeared, several demons had left the Army. Having been shown by their Beast Kin allies that a farmer was a necessary component for any community. The Beast Kin had shown them that a farmer was as useful, if not more useful, than fifty Demon warriors.

They had taken the Demons and turned them from a fighting rabble to a semblance of a military. Order was created; duels for advancement were banned; medical treatment and fighting tactics were adopted. Although on Emerilia, six months had passed since

Kala and her Beast Kin had started to teach the demons, it had been nine months for the nameless planet Bob had placed them on.

"It is almost time," Alkao said after a few minutes.

Anna looked at her friends list. A number of names of her Beast Kin friends were there, but she couldn't call them up directly. The distances were too great for her private messaging system to reach.

"I'm looking forward to seeing how the Demons have changed," Anna said.

"So am I." Alkao paused, as if thinking something over. "After they arrive, will you continue to come back?" He looked to her, his face stony. While he was prepared for her to say no, he really hoped she wouldn't.

"I will." Anna smiled at his relief.

"Good. My brothers might be good Demons, but there is something *refreshing* about having a female member on the council."

"I will take that as a compliment." She laughed and moved for the keep's door.

Alkao followed her into the barely furnished command center. The Devil's Crater map had been updated and there were also maps and information off to the side, detailing the advance of the Dark Lord's Demon Horde. They had decreased in numbers as they moved toward Devil's Crater. In-fighting and their constant hunger made them more rabid after a few weeks of not killing.

By their rate of advance, they would arrive in two months. It didn't seem that the Dark Lord knew that his rebelling first Demons had already returned to the crater.

Something that Alkao and Anna were going to take advantage of.

Anna and Alkao stepped out in front of the keep and looked over the expansive interior. A handful of DCA guards kept watch. Alkao had requested villagers and non-warriors first to give the warriors more time for training and allow the Beast Kin to beat more information into the Demon warrior's heads.

Anna and Alkao stopped at the entrance, Anna took the opportunity to check her interface's clock. She looked to the open area once again.

Five hundred Demon and Beast Kin warriors appeared, their leaders standing in front of each square formation.

Anna's hand went to her blade at the suddenness of it all and the eerie quiet of the five hundred men and women in front of her.

A big bear-human walked out of formation and came to stand in front of Alkao and Anna. "Captain Kala. Prince Alkao, I present the First Regiment. The other regiments are being moved to the different fortresses with their commanders. The rest are being placed down within the city. We await your orders," Kala said.

Anna and Alkao looked out over the forces in front of them. They wore a variety of weapons and clothes, looking like a rabble. However, the way they were formed up, the look in their eyes—it spoke of hardened fighters who had been formed into a singular disciplined fighting force.

"Captain Kala, have two companies remain here to take over duties of the keep. As for the rest, we have a number of fields that need labor." Alkao's eyes flickered to the battalion behind her.

"As you command." Kala nodded her head slightly before she turned and headed back to her battalion to issue her orders.

A slow, hungry smile passed over Alkao's face, seeing that not one of the Demons looked annoyed or voiced their anger at being used to help on the farms.

"Something funny?" Anna asked.

"No. I'm proud—proud that my people were able to come this far. If they can handle being treated like simple farmhands, then they'll have the discipline in battle to fight together. I thought that two months might not be enough time to get the crater ready. Now, I don't feel so nervous. I feel excited. In two months, we'll show the Dark Lord and his minions the true power of the Demons and Beast Kin." Alkao looked at her with a proud expression.

Anna turned to watch as four hundred Demons and Beast Kin turned and marched out of the keep, headed into Devil's Crater. The remaining companies came together for a quick briefing before heading about their newly assigned duties.

Kala walked back over to Anna and Alkao. "I was thinking at the rate Bob was going, it would be two years before he told you he had us out of the ice." Kala clapped forearms with Anna before they brought each other into a deep hug. They hugged for a moment before pulling away.

"It was only a few days, you big complainer." Anna laughed. "He didn't tell you?" Kala scratched her head awkwardly. "What?" Anna asked.

"Uh, well, we've been awake for a few months longer than the Demons."

Anna closed her eyes and rubbed the bridge of her nose. "Daaaad, you damn forgetful Gnome!" Anna yelled at the sky.

"So you must be Alkao." Kala ignored her outburst and clapped wrists with the Demon prince, one of the few people who was taller than her.

"Captain Kala, I have heard good things from my brothers and so far, I have been impressed with how you have turned my Demon Hordes into a true fighting force. I think it is about time we talked about getting them proper weapons and armor," Alkao said.

"I like him—can we keep him?" Kala looked at Anna, who was muttering to herself.

"Kala, he kind of rules this whole place." Anna waved at Devil's Crater.

"Seventy percent," Kala countered. As per their alliance, Alkao was part of the ruling council, which was made up of the seven Demon princes/princesses and three representatives of the Beast Kin, Anna, Kala and Edwin. Alkao, Malkur, Kino, Lena, Ishox, Efri, and Goula made up the Demon side. Lena was Vrexu's new wife. Both Vrexu and Lezar had become generals, each leading fifty thousand soldiers. Malkur, Efri, and Alkao were also generals. Kala had denied the rank of general, but Anna had been named as the sixth general.

"Congratulations are in order!" Alkao said.

"Oh?" Kala asked.

"On your new promotion," Alkao said.

"Well, I've been a captain for a while now," Kala said dryly.

"But now you're a major general, General Anna's second in command."

Ignoring Kala's glare, Anna said,"Look, you're the best qualified for it. I don't know why you didn't take the damned position already. So shut up and take the second spot," Anna said.

"Well, you get to go off and deal with other matters! It'll be like I'm in charge of it eighty percent of the time!"

"Well, it's a good thing that I have such a competent second-in-command," Anna said, making it clear that there was no way Kala could get out of this.

Kala snorted, still not happy but going with it. "Fine."

"Good. Then you can take over talks with Alkao about kit and weapons. I have somewhere I need to be," Anna said.

"Just saw each other for the first time in centuries and you're off again?"

"Lots to do, not much time to do it in!" Anna smiled and hugged her friend. "I'll be back soon enough, then we can start seeing what this lot are capable of." Anna nodded toward the demons and Beast Kin.

"I think you'll be pleasantly surprised," Kala said with a confident smile.

"Hmm, feels like someone is cursing me." A shiver went down Bob's spine.

"What would make you think that?" the Lord of Water asked as they sat in the Mer capital, playing three-dimensional chess.

"No reason." Bob made a quick move to get past the comment. "So, how are your people liking the mage's guild and Emerilia in general?"

"I was not sure if Fire would accept my alliance. I also thought that she would have used the power to improve herself. I did not think that she would feed it right into the Mana pools of the college and mage's guild. The more my people and I interact with her, the more I realize how blind I was. I knew that we were conditioned from birth to become the lords and ladies of the Affinities, yet each of us comes to the task in a different way. Dark and Light crave power above all else. Earth demands respect from all. Air wishes to create mischief, while I just wish to see my children thrive as Fire does with her dragons and those who attend her schools. My anger and drive for more power made me hide under the seas and create the merpeople. Over time, they changed me more than I changed them. I didn't wish for more power; I wished to help them grow." The Lord of Water moved his piece. "Checkmate." He smiled.

"What have you been doing down here, playing chess the entire time?" Bob complained, using the Gnome form he'd started using nearly two years ago.

"Among other things." The Lord of Water smiled. It was hard for him to find a good opponent. Fire was his best by far, but Bob was also rather good at the game.

"So, what do you think of Fire's offer?" Bob pushed his king over and admitted defeat.

Water looked thoughtful as tendrils of water moved the pieces back into place. "Become a teacher within the mage's college? I must say I am interested and after a brief look at what information they have, I must say that I am interested to read more of their books."

"If you are to join the college, then you will have to accept the contract. It will bind your power to the mage's guild as well as the merpeople. You will no longer be able to access your divine pool that holds the mana devotions made by your followers. With only your personal power, your power will be greatly limited. The knowledge the mage's guild has will assist you, but you will need to work on your levels and stats to increase your strength," Bob warned.

"It is only recently that I have come to realize how much of a father you are." The Lord of Water smiled, making the first move.

"Yeah, with some of the biggest and most powerful brats in the universe." Bob sighed and moved his pieces out.

"I still haven't decided yet. I would like to, but I fear for the safety of my people and my person. Fire takes a great risk with walking across Emerilia. If one of the other affinities' paladins found out where she was, they could kill her. It would be hard, but it would also be possible," the Lord of Water said.

"Well, at least you recognize that you can die," Bob said. "Few in the Pantheon believe such a thing is possible after living for so long."

"They have never left the Pantheon or their various hidden strongholds. They don't know the affect their games have on Emerilia. To them, it is a game, though recently I have felt new forces at play on Emerilia." Water moved his pieces, watching Bob closely.

"Things are changing in a way that even I can't predict," Bob said, following up Water's move.

Water moved his pieces in silence. Bob had given him much to think on.

2

END IN SIGHT

"You damn cart!" Dave yelled. The wrench in his hands doubled in size, looking nearly as large as Steve's axe, and used it to hit the cart. It jumped slightly as Dave shook his head, seeming to give up its fight and shuddering slightly before moving backwards."

"Hah! Take that!" Dave let the wrench go. It turned to smoke, revealing two rods that flew back to either side of Dave's belt.

He tiredly rubbed his head. It had taken them two months to clear out the first phase/stage of the facilities and three for the second, leaving them with just the final one to be completed. Based on the difficulty of getting the previous facilities working, Dave knew it was going to be a challenge.

Deia walked through the refinery's catwalks, finding Dave sitting at a nearby empty workstation.

"Hey, babe." Dave looked to her with a weary smile.

"What did the poor cart do to you?" She smiled, making Dave feel a little less tired as she gave him a side-hug.

"Got stuck." Dave shrugged.

The other crafters who had been sent to learn from the impressive Dave snorted and shook their heads, working on the varied maintenance issues that plagued their latest forge facility.

"So you hit it with a wrench?" she asked, exasperated at her fiancé's antics.

"No, I hit it with a *bigger* wrench." Dave smiled, clearly pleased with himself. "First lesson of engineering" Adding quietly to himself, "although that's more mechanical than rocket…"

"So other than beating the forge's carts into motion with a massive wrench," Deia gave him a pointed look, the corners of her mouth twitching, "how are we looking on repairs?"

"Well, the main smelting furnaces are back online, thanks to my runers."

"Runers? Do you mean runners?" Deia said, giving him a confused look.

"No, Runers, I'm still working on the whole naming thing alright!"

Dave sighed.

He might have come up with a new way of making Magical Circuits by writing it out like lines of code instead of magical formations—it made the whole process more refined, increasing the effectiveness of the magical coding and also reducing the necessary size that a Magical Circuit took up— but there had been a number of real-life coders who had taken the idea and gone nuts with it. Dave had dangled his book of magical runes and now there were a number of them who tried to follow Dave everywhere to talk magic coding.

"I think I'll keep to magical coding for now," Dave said. "So, progress?" Deia asked.

"Those damn metal munching rodents messed this place up pretty bad. We fixed the metal plating that opens into the magma chamber, regulating the forge's heat. Fixed and filled the coolant tanks, which were either cold as hell or boiling hot. I actually gained Vitality points just for doing it!" Dave shook his head. Josh now only sent Deia and her party to where the worst damage or creatures were. Mostly, it was damage. With Dave's abilities, he could quickly diagnose and fix what would take several other people days or even weeks to do.

"The multiple different components on the factory side of the forge is messed up. We've put the repair bots on it and we're shipping most of our materials out to the other forges. I hear that we're having trouble with raw ore supplies?" Dave looked to Deia.

"Yeah, Shard and Josh have asked us to go and take a look at one of the mines. The crafters are having a rough time of it. There is a large concentration of those ore extracting machines in the mines' area. They've been extruding materials for decades but there hasn't been anything to cut it back. The mine looks like it's half caved in," Deia said.

"Awwweeeesome. I guess this is what I get for not needing that much sleep anymore?"

"Something like that," Deia said.

Dave snorted and opened up a flashing notification.

You have gained a Class Level: **Aleph Engineer**
Just making all kinds of things. For fixing Aleph tech—because it's confusing as hell and complicated (I'm surprised your brain could handle it)—you get a whole 'nother class! Seriously, you think these things are trading cards or something? Damn well racking them up.
Status: Level 2
Effects: +30 to Endurance, Willpower, and Intelligence

"Woo-hoo!" Dave laughed, doing a small jig with a giant smile on his face. Others looked over before they shook their heads and got back to work. They were used to the Dwarven Halfling's excitable manner.

Dave hummed out an upbeat song as he danced from side to side. Celebration over, Dave checked his character sheet.

CHARACTER SHEET			
Name:	David Grahslagg	Gender:	Male
Level:	10	Class:	Dwarven Master Smith, Friend of the Grey God, Bleeder, Librarian, Aleph Engineer
Race:	Human/Dwarf	Alignment:	Chaotic Neutral
Unspent points: 511			
Health:	12,100	Regen:	4.82 /s
Mana:	2,910	Regen:	12.95 /s
Stamina:	1,920	Regen:	9.35 /s
Vitality:	121	Endurance:	241
Intelligence:	291	Willpower:	259
Strength:	192	Agility:	187

Dave looked through his character sheet; it had all passed so quickly, going from one fight and fix to the next.

Active Skill: Archery
Level: Master Level 1
Effect: Critical Hit chance increases by 41%. Ranged targets take 22% increased damage.
Cost: 10 Stamina

Passive Skill: Dodge
Level: Master Level 2
Effect: 87% chance to evade objects. 10% faster when fighting more than two opponents.

Passive Skill: Perception
Level: Master Level 3
Effect: 91% chance to find hidden details. 15% chance at better loot.

Active Skill: Two Handed
Level: Expert Level 8
Effect: 38% armor penetration on target. Stamina costs reduced 15% while fighting.
Cost: 35 Stamina

Active Skill: Dual Wield
Level: Master Level 1
Effect: Attacks are 41 % faster. 5% chance of slowing target.
Cost: 15 Stamina

Active Skill: Inference
Level: Expert Level 3
Effect: 69% increased chance of using moves you've read in books.

Active Skill: One Handed and Shield
Level: Expert Level 9
Effect: Weapons damage increased by 39%. Defense increases by 15%.
Cost: 20 Stamina

Passive Skill: Night Vision
Level: Master Level 6
Effect: 95% increased night vision. 30% increased vision in magical darkness.
Racial bonus: Dwarves, even Half-Dwarves, are at home in the darkness of mines and their empires dug underneath mountains. +25% increased night vision (+5% in magical darkness).

Active Skill: Sprint
Level: Master Level 5
Effect: 93% increased speed. Sprinting costs 25% less Stamina.
Cost: 5 Stamina/second

Active Skill: Sneak Attack
Level: Master Level 2
Effect: When you are undetected in stealth, attacks will hit with 368% increased damage (Massive increase when hitting Critical area). May your aim be true. Ignores 10% of opponent's armor.
Cost: Attack 50 Stamina

Active Skill: Stealth
Level: Master Level 4
Effect: 91% chance to remain undetected (reduced in direct light). 20% easier to detect others in stealth (must be below your level in stealth).
Cost: 5 Stamina/second

Active Skill: Spell Formation
Level: Expert Level 7
Effect: You use 20% less Mana and your spells are 77% stronger.

Active Skill: Soul Smith
Level: Expert Level 5
Effect: 73% less soul energy necessary for crafting with soul smith.
Cost: Dependent on creation.

Active Skill: Builder
Level: Master Level 5
Effect: 93% speed and efficiency. Creations material cost is reduced by 25%.
Required: Tools

Active Skill: Smithing
Level: Master Level 4
Effect: 91% improved quality of smithing creation. 20% chance to imbue metal with skill. Able to analyze items made of stone, iron, steel, silver, malachite, gold, ebony, and Mithril, aluminum, titanium.

Active Skill: Soul Manipulation
Level: Master Level 3
Effect: Tools you make to manipulate souls and their energy are 89% stronger. Able to use soul energy to fuel spells. 15% increase to soul energies reserves (can only be used for spells, does not act as extra Willpower points).
Cost: Dependent on creation.

Active Skill: Magical Circuits
Level: Master Level 9
Effect: 100% chance of creating better Magical Circuits and understanding them. 45% reduction of cost.
Cost: Dependent

Active Skill: Maintainer
Level: Master Level 1
Effect: 85% chance to restore durability; at higher levels, possible to increase durability, quality, and gain 10% Sharpen bonus to items that have been cared for.
Required: Dependent on gear; sharpening stone, hammer, anvil.
Better maintainer's tools lead to higher chance of increasing stats.

Dave had to just look around him and see all the repair bots that swarmed the badly damaged forge to know that these levels had paid off. They had started with just a handful; now they had over a thousand of the creations rushing around, repairing different systems and speeding up their ability to fix areas. There were also guardian automatons that they could call on to fight with them, greatly increasing the effectiveness of a Stone Raiders' party.

Each and every one of them had gained an aura detection skill—a kind of sixth sense that came from fighting hundreds of opponents.

While the overall level gain might have been been barely thirty or so, the Stone Raiders were nothing like their old selves. Their new or improved skills, instincts, and training for fighting nearly every day for six months had made them a powerful force.

Josh was already joking about trying out Ashal's dungeons. "Dave?" Deia asked after a few minutes.

"Sorry, was somewhere else," he said.

"I noticed. First, you're getting some food, sleep, and *then* we can go to the mining facility," Deia said.

"I like that plan." Dave smiled.

Deia stood. The two of them held hands as they waved to the other Stone Raiders. Dave had worked as hard as any of them for two days straight. He had been the only crafter capable of braving the heat of the forge while he fixed the coolant systems and the heat regulators.

Malsour and Induca met them on the way, having taken the opportunity to change into their dragon forms.

Dave and Deia talked about different things. Deia sent messages to the rest of their party. They had made it through the honeymoon phase, supporting each other in their pursuits: Dave in his crafting and Deia in her leadership. They'd become so close that they found it difficult to think of living without the other.

"If I never see another metal-eating odo, I'll be happy!" Induca finished saying as she and Malsour talked.

They fell in behind Dave and Deia, deep in conversation.

"They are interesting beasts, using the planet's heat and Mana to survive. The metals down here probably tasted better to them than the unrefined ores," Malsour said.

"Did you really have one carted off so you could open it up?"

"Their ability to manipulate inanimate objects, but only for the elements that they have bands on their bodies, is amazing. Those bands must take decades to build up!"

"They're also highly refined and imbued with Mana. I can only imagine what the dwarves are going to pay for that kind of material," Dave interjected.

"What are you going to do with your share of the loot?" Suzy asked as they passed an automaton fighter that was sawing through an odo.

The odo had a massive maw, with eight clawed feet that jutted out like the points on a compass. They were meant to assist it through the ground as it consumed or pushed through anything in its path. It had a rigid body from its massive mouth to its only slightly smaller posterior. Inside, the bands had highly acidic linings that broke down the metals. The bands had different colors depending on which metals they had consumed. Each band was only formed of one singular metal. Some odo might have multiple bands of the same metals, or interspersed bands showing which metals the odo had eaten through over time. The odo could only manipulate the metal that they had bands of. The more bands, the more powerful.

"Looks like a rigid toilet roll that's been pinched at one end and has feet sticking out of it," Dave said.

"So kind of like a toilet roll, but not at all?" Suzy quipped. "I think the question is what to do with the loot," Deia said.

"Well, I'm going to keep it. I know that Suzy had been looking for a staff of some sort and I think that with the Mana attunement—if you two want it—I think I can make you magical weapons, as well as Induca."

They would also be getting a large portion of Mana-imbued Mithril, ebony, and other rare metals from the odos. No other party would be able to do anything but sell these expensive resources. With them, they looked first to improving themselves; anything else, they threw out. It was the Stone Raiders' way.

Dave already had requests from other Stone Raiders for custom work.

Anna's sword had made them all eager to get a Dave-crafted weapon.

"I would be interested in rings primarily. A wand capable of holding a higher level Dark spell would also be nice," Malsour said.

"I have been holding off on new blades, though these ones' durability has been dropping quickly due to the higher level buffs I am using with them," Deia said.

"I know I said a staff would be cool, but I'm more interested in heavy Mana-imbued cores, especially for steel, which takes so long to get it to retain any kind of Mana. It's the best metal to use for my creations," Suzy said.

"Heigh-ho party!" Steve said, waiting in the teleport room. "Hey, Steve." Dave waved and yawned.

"We off to the mining facility?"

"Nope, food and rest. Some of us need sleep," Deia said.

"Okay. Mind if I go off to do some hunting with Dwayne, then?" Steve asked as the teleport activated.

They stepped through without a second thought. The teleport pads had become familiar long ago.

"Sure, just don't get too banged up," Suzy warned as they walked out into an identical room. They waved to the Stone Raiders waiting in the different control rooms on the second floor. Trap runes lined the room. If someone needed to fall back and brought something with them, either the traps or the different Players would kill it before it could do much damage.

"Ah, I'll be fine." Steve waved, as if it would be an impossibility. "You said that before I had to replace your leg. Three days ago," Dave said.

"How was I supposed to know that the damn log with legs would try to eat my foot?"

"When we said, 'get out of the way, you idiot — it eats metal'? I think it would be around that point." Suzy nodded to herself.

"Sorry, can't hear you. Automatons don't have ears, you know? Hey, Dwayne!" Steve said, looking at the party that was organizing.

By their members and numbers, it looked as if it would be quite the battle.

"Hey, Steve." Dwayne looked to the rest of Party Zero. "Everyone else."

They greeted him as they headed out of the teleport room and into the central tower that had become their home. They headed into the mess, greeting different people before grabbing food and sitting down.

A large open window showed the rest of the city that had become their home base after they'd liberated it from an army of the undead, a few moles, and a Lich Lord. It was shaped like a hollow cylinder to increase the available living space, which was only possible by the centrifugal force created by a gentle spin and gravitational runes along the floor. When they had arrived, the city had been in darkness; only the tower that they had arrived in had any sort of power to it. Now, entire regions of the city were lit up as power stations, workshops, mining facilities, forges, and every major system had come online. Even with the lights coming online with different systems, the sheer scale of the city was still hard to understand. The lights barely illuminated the massive contained city.

They talked about this and that, their plans for the materials, and then what they thought could be their next mission after the mining facility.

"I think that it's going to be a combat mission," Malsour said.

"What makes you think that?" Suzy asked between bites of her burger. "We're finishing off all the maintenance issues and only going into the areas where there is little resistance. I think that there is a large concentration in one or more of these last few facilities we need to clear," Malsour said.

"I'm nearly at Master with one handed and two handed. I hope we can get in enough trouble for me to level those up," Dave said.

"Have you put thought into advancing to level 50 so that you can get another class?" Deia asked.

"Not just yet. I really want to try to go for the classes I know I can get on my own merits, though being level 50 does have its benefits. It'd take a lot more deaths before I lost my classes and the longer I stay at level 50, the more my body will get used to it. I think it's about time I started using those points. It takes me days of fighting just to get a few levels. How long is it taking you to get skills, Suz?"

"It's slowing down by a lot, but if I was to try out fighting, I think that my stats would still increase for a bit. I think you're reaching the realm of diminishing returns. It's hard for you to gain any kind of stat points by just training so you'll have to resort to using the stat points that comes with gaining a level to increase. What level are you, anyway?"

"Technically I'm level 10 still, but I've unlocked level 113," Dave said.

"How many stat points have you spent of your unlocked levels?" Deia asked.

"Fifty-four."

Malsour whistled. "That is a hell of a lot of stat points." Dave opened his interface and pulled up his level.

Level 113
You have reached level 113; you have **511** stat points to use.

"You could say that."

"How many stat points do you have already in your character sheet?" Deia asked.

Dave switched over to his character sheet, tallying it up. With his increased Intelligence, he could easily remember multiple things, his memory becoming almost photographic.

"One thousand, two hundred and ninety-one, which is the same amount as someone who is level 258." Dave took a moment for his brain to understand what he had just said.

"Damn," Suzy said.

"Looks like Josh might not have been joking about us being able to take on dungeons in Ashal," Deia said. "I hadn't realized how strong we had all become down here."

All of them sat, lost in their own thoughts.

Dave spread out his aura detection skill, checking the aura of all those around him. Few were trying to hide it; some did it unconsciously. He used Malsour as a reference point, knowing that his actual aura was ten times what he was letting out.

Damn, we don't look that much weaker. We're all about a tenth as strong as a dragon. Dave had to wonder how powerful Malsour was compared to his fellow dragons. Knowing that Malsour had killed the undead Xelur Demon Lord at Boran-al's Citadel made a hungry smile pass over Dave's face.

People and guilds had been arguing that the Stone Raiders were dead as they hadn't been seen in the longest time. They slowly grew in numbers and wealth but never showed themselves.

"Well, I think we're going to give the rest of Emerilia one hell of a shock when we finish helping the Aleph," Dave said.

Deia laughed and shook her head. "I don't think there has been a group of Players this powerful so soon in the Player's life cycle."

"I foresee an interesting future." Malsour smiled.

3

WELCOME TO THE GUILD

Lucy, Florence, and a dozen other guild members were having conversations about the supply and logistics situation of the clan.

Many of the people in the room weren't even using the same Mirror of Communication. They had taken them from the PKP, who'd had a bunch of them; being such expensive items, they targeted other Players who had them, using them as a status symbol.

Florence had, also, quickly bought a number of the smaller Mirror of Communications that were much cheaper than their larger and farther ranged mirrors, like the one Dave had secluded in his seeder. The Stone Raiders had discovered a large number of the mirrors wherever they were hidden and had the Exdar's Traders sell them off. In fact, a number of trade agreements had been advanced by offering a mirror at reduced cost to a governing person. Beyond just using them for their ability to safely meet face-to-face with their subjects and other rulers, they used them to display their wealth and power.

Josh came through the door, walking over to where Florence and Lucy were talking about the next food and materials shipment.

"We're going to need some more alchemy ingredients as well," Lucy said.

"How are you looking for meat?" Florence asked.

"We've got an agreement with some hunters for grade-A meat."

"Damn, that must be why that market terminal has been rating it as so expensive. Never had something so tasty." Florence sighed. "Which brings me to those terminals. If we were able to use them and put them into every city and village, then charged even a one percent tax, we'd make a fortune. It would also mean that we wouldn't need to use the wagons so much."

"Didn't you get the upgraded magical coding to improve their speed?"

"Ah, yes we have, though we're going to need better magical beasts to pull them. The quada are now too slow. I was thinking of heading to Ashal or Per'ush to see what manner of beasts they have in order to increase our delivery speed."

"You're by far the fastest distributors in Emerilia and you want to go faster?" Lucy looked amused.

"You should know — the faster we are, the better the profits will be upon reaching our destination. Oh, we had the arch mage come and see us the other day. It seems that they want to come into a trade agreement with us. Seems that we are the most reliable and consistent suppliers of fine materials that they have had the pleasure of working with. Most places don't sell as many high items as we do, or have such a stock of them."

"Is that so? I wonder if it has anything to do with the terminal you have in your guild headquarters and being able to get anything we're selling in moments?" Lucy said with a wry smile.

"It might have something to do with that." Florence tapped her chin in thought. "If I was to tell them that, they'd probably want to pull it apart! I know Bronx is always talking about the latest ancient artifact he bought and admired. He's getting a lecturer's spot at the mage's college because of his knowledge, did you know?"

"I didn't know that. Good for him."

Josh cleared his throat as he moved beside the desk the two ladies were talking to each other across. Their interfaces glowed white windows off to the side.

"Ah, Josh! How is it going?" Florence dismissed her screen.

"Not bad. Planning out how to retake a housing complex that is filled with shambling mounds, cultists, and possibly a paladin." Josh sighed, grabbed a chair and sat down. "So what did you need me for?"

"Well, Lucy and I have been talking," Florence said, as the both of them smiled as Josh looked between them.

"I know that the Stone Raiders and the Golden Sabres are looking to become an alliance. Our guilds have worked together for quite a while now and I've been thinking that we should make it official," Florence said.

"The proposal is that the Exdar's Traders becomes a part of the Stone Raiders. Florence would take over my position as quartermaster, allowing me to look toward my support of the Stone Raiders instead of the supply situation," Lucy said.

As well as your spies. Josh held his chin in thought.

There were a number of benefits. By removing the middle man, profits would increase. Some of the Stone Raiders had been training with the Exdar's or using their connections to get into places they wanted to train.

As time had gone on, the Exdar's had stopped being just regular Players and started to become another clan of E-heads. They were able to trade gold and other items directly for money, giving them a comfortable lifestyle on Earth, enough to afford pods. Hell, a number of them shared the same facility as Josh.

Josh's pensive frown turned to a smile. "Hell, I already think of you lot as part of the guild anyway. I'll leave it up to you two to work out the details." Josh stood and moved to Florence with his hand outstretched. Excited whispers and murmurs passed through the room.

Florence stood, finding Josh pulling her into a hug. "Welcome to the Stone Raiders!" he said.

"Thanks." Florence laughed as others whistled and cheered.

"Now, I've got a damned housing complex to clear out! Unless you have something else for me, I'll get going," Josh said.

"See you later. I'll get Suzy. She's better at this whole side of things," Lucy said.

Josh disappeared from the guild hall and went back to his bedroom.

He stood and stretched, waking up fully.

He sighed and rubbed his face. He had been in talks with Cassie about having the Golden Sabres join the Stone Raiders in an alliance, but it became clear that they hadn't recovered from the betrayal of so many within their ranks.

Josh knew that it would be just a matter of weeks until the guild would dissolve. He didn't know what they were going to do, but he did know that Cassie and her trusted personal friends were looking to join the Stone Raiders.

Guilds were falling and rising across Emerilia, many of them claiming to be the most powerful and Josh was looking forward to proving them all wrong.

A proud smile grew across his face as he moved to the shower in his room. His guild had grown. It wasn't massive like many other guilds—just under three hundred members. Nearly all of them were now E-heads. This had become their world in a way that Earth had never been.

He only had to look at Dwayne and Lucy's lieutenants, Jules and Esa. Jules didn't have legs back on Earth. Esa was barely making ends meet. Now they were both within E-head facilities, fully paid for and provided for by their in-game transactions. Emerilia had become their lives.

It was what had pushed Cassie and Josh apart. Being in an E-head facility, the pods they lived in would look after their bodies' needs, thus not needing to log out for weeks instead of hours. Cassie, however, just had the regular headset, meaning every eight hours in real life, or twenty-four hours in Emerilia, she had to log off. She was also supported by streams and her own brand she had built up with playing other video games, taking her to meetings and events away from Emerilia. She was one of the best fighters and people paid a ton to see her fight and ogle her. Josh just wanted to live his life here and be left alone by the world.

Cassie wanted to tell the world about their relationship but Josh didn't want to. He didn't want to be dragged away from his new life to go to the same conferences, banquets, dances, and events that he had become wrapped up in as an investment banker.

Cassie saw that coming to the Stone Raiders would let her keep playing in a powerful guild. Josh made it clear that although people could sell some of their videos, there would be times that things would be guild business only. The Stone Raiders were fine with this as they made enough from the loot that they were selling that they were well supported on Earth. Josh was not looking forward to talking to Cassie about not selling her footage because of the sensitive nature of the quests with the Aleph, Demons, and Beast Kin if she joined them.

The Beast Kin and Demons were stronger than ever but they still needed time to get themselves settled in to meet anything that might threaten them. The Aleph—well, the Aleph hadn't said a damn thing.

Dave had told Josh that they had returned, in a private message, but it seemed that they were content to keep to themselves as the Stone Raiders cleared out and repaired their homes. As they went along, they were given resources per clearing out each area.

Josh pulled up the quest log.

Quest: Aleph Homecoming
You have restored an Aleph City to full functionality and returned it to its original owners.
Other locations have been made available to you. Based on the power supplied to the teleport pads, you can travel to the following locations:
Aleph Portal Factory x1 (Ability to fix portals in different locations) Aleph Greenhouses x1 (Access to Herbs and Food)
Aleph Mining Facilities x2 (Repairs continue at faster rate)
Aleph College x1 (Knowledge on the Aleph areas you will be entering and different systems to repair)
Aleph Housing complex x1 (Increases in all areas)
Aleph Forges x3 (Access to weapons, upgrades, and automatons to buy for your own use)
Rewards: ???

Still, the rewards remained a mystery. The Aleph College was nothing that they had been expecting. The entire place was one massive scaled dungeon. It was half the size of the city Josh was standing in, but it had all manner of experiments that the Aleph had been working on and that had been altered with time.

He needed Dave to check over the remaining facilities since the repair bots would take weeks to finish the work. After finding out about the Aleph Engineer class, the crafters were pouring all their time into learning from Dave and working on the various facilities, yet there were still problems that they couldn't understand. Dealing with the portal factories was largely left to Dave and Malsour. Crafters went with them but the concepts were too advanced; only a few were able to understand the two as they worked.

To get the portal factories operational, they would need to clear out the college. Although Malsour and Dave could access a wide variety of information through their Librarian necklaces, there were some records and materials that were too valuable to be kept as anything but hard copies. Therefore, capturing the college was a necessity, one that would challenge them like nothing before.

Josh turned off the shower and dried off, looking at himself in the mirror. "Ah, looking good, mate." He made a pistol with his hand and pointed it at himself. His thin frame now had corded muscles covering it. He snorted at his own antics, putting the towel down. He hotkeyed his normal gear.

Leather clothes as black as night appeared. A hood that created shadows over the face, only allowing one's eyes to be visible—not dissimilar to the hoods that Party Zero wore—lay behind his head.

He checked the two Demon's blades in the small of his back and a familiar thrill filled him as his eyes turned black for a slight moment. The weapons were incredible, allowing him to cover himself in shadows. The more he killed with the blades, the faster he became. After a period of not being sated, the speed decreased back to normal.

It was one hell of a rush.

After checking his throwing blades and the modified crossbow on his back, Josh headed out of the room. The hall had Stone Raiders throughout it. They nodded and greeted him—some talking, others returning from their work or going out to it.

Josh meandered through, headed to where Kim was practicing different artillery spells with a few of her casters as well as showing other classes how to cast simple spells.

Emerilia rewarded those who focused on one class, but everyone was capable of casting magic and fighting with melee weapons.

"How are the trainees doing?" Josh walked over to her.

"Good, they're barely trainees anymore. Everyone has at least an understanding of magic. Most are using it for enhancing their fighting styles. Looks like we're going to have a whole bunch of spell swords," Kim said.

"Well, that is sure to scare the hell out of some people." Josh grinned. Kim rolled her eyes and the corners of her mouth lifted up slightly.

"So, when are we going to clear out that housing complex?"

"Once we have all of the other facilities cleared out, then we can deal with it."

"I'm guessing we're leaving the Aleph College for last?" Kim looked to Josh.

"Yeah, that place is huge and the scout guardians did not make it look simple." Josh shook his head.

"What made you think that? Was it the level 350 Arch Lich? Or his level 200 plus helpers? Maybe the fact that he has been inside the largest repository of magical artifacts and information outside of Per'ush for centuries?"

"That might have been a factor."

"Do we still have no idea where its damned soul box is?"

"You mean the phylactery?"

"Yeah."

"No, we don't have any idea." Josh sighed.

"I really hoped that Shard wasn't right this one time. How the hell could the Arch Lich make the *entire* college its lair?"

"Don't know, but it would explain how it is able to find even the scout guardians. I'm going to get some breakfast and then check on the other facilities. Make sure that everyone is rotating. I know we've been down here a while, but I want everyone rested and ready before we head into the housing complex."

"Will do. See you later." Kim waved Josh off as she headed back out into her training square to educate her trainees.

Josh shuddered, thinking about the housing complex. *I friggin' hate spiders.*

4

FUTURE CHALLENGES

Alkao looked to the two councils: the Leading Council of ten—with seven Demons and three Beast Kin members—and the Governing Council.

The Governing Council also had ten leaders, broken down into one elected leader for each region in the Devil's Crater (farms, city, forest, hunting regions, orchard, and crafters), then another for each military segment (magical, soldiering, and archer corps), with a final trading leader.

The Leading Council made the major decisions, much like a president or prime minister back on Earth; the Governing Council looked to support the people, make and uphold laws, and do the best for those they represented. There were six different brigades made up of 50,000 soldiers each, with nearly 200,000 Beast Kin and Demons who weren't in the Devil's Crater Army, or DCA.

Twenty people to try to guide the future of just over five hundred thousand Demons and Beast Kin. Alkao kept his nerves from showing as he opened the meeting.

"How are we looking with the farms' harvest?" Alkao asked. It wasn't official, but he seemed to have held the position as the leader of both Demons and Beast Kin. He saw more than one calculating look from both races. In their eyes, he still had to prove himself.

"The farms' harvest has been better than I hoped. With the aid of the army, we are well ahead of schedule. We're storing and preparing the foodstuffs but we're going to need to expand our storage facilities," a white tiger Beast Kin said.

"Good. If there are Earth or Dark mages and builders free, see if they can help. Food for the coming winter is our top priority," Alkao said, holding the Beast Kin's eyes.

"I will see to it, Prince Alkao." The Beast Kin nodded.

"Good. How about the orchards?" Alkao's gaze rested on a rabbit Beast Kin.

"We're going to need help bringing in our harvest. It won't be much, but it should help out. We've been building the greenhouses, but they are expensive due to the cost of clear glass. Some of the blacksmiths and other crafters have been working with glass silicate to try to make it cheaper. The way it looks, we might have one full-length greenhouse ready before month's end, when winter will really kick in."

"How many supplies will we need to get for the oncoming winter?" Alkao asked.

The Beast Kin representing farms looked to the rabbit Beast Kin who ran the orchards. "I'm not sure. We have enough for three, maybe four months with all of the supplies we have stacked up. I don't know what that would be like if we were to do army operations," the farms' Beast Kin said. The orchards' Beast Kin nodded in agreement.

"If I may." The Beast Kin trader raised his hand. Alkao waved for him to go on.

"We have two months for the Beast Kin and demon population, if we use the foodstuffs already stored and estimated to come in, *if* we are to fight. If we weren't, then we would have four months. This does not take into account how much meat we can get from the beasts in the hunting area or from clearing out the different areas of the crater," the trader finished.

Alkao nodded and turned away from the elk Beast Kin. *I wonder if he eats meat.* Alkao pondered his options.

"The going rate for the rare beasts we are killing in this area should help with the costs of foodstuffs. I will have a talk with Dave to see if he might have a way of making the greenhouses' glass. We need more wood for heating the homes of the different settlements and the keeps. I want to get a group of our scouts watching the oncoming Demon Horde. As they grow closer, we will start using the new tactics we have learned. Any forces that are not working with the villagers to harvest will be sent out in patrols to familiarize themselves with the area, gather herbs and edibles as well as start to make traps for the oncoming soulless demons. I want the forests and plains filled with physical and magical traps. I know that we can get weapons from the trading terminal, but I want our blacksmiths working as hard as possible to make weapons and armor. We're going to need our coin to buy foodstuffs.

"We should also get different units patrolling the untamed areas of the crater, clearing out unwanted beasts and looking for dungeons. They can be a great source of resources, and we're going to need them soon. I will be leaving Devil's Crater with the next batch of scouts to learn the area around the crater and about our enemy. I want every Beast Kin and Demon to know the terrain in and outside of the crater intimately," Alkao's eyes moved from the different generals in the room. "Some of you might be wondering why I am saying this to you all. In the coming months, we are going to face many hardships. We must work together, to know what one another is thinking, the various worries and issues of our people here. If we do not have enough food, then we will starve. If the army is not prepared, then we will die. We will survive together or die apart. Here in these coming months we can hammer out a home for our future generations or make it a pyre to the end of us all."

The room was quiet as hardened faces looked to Alkao, waiting and ready.

He looked back at them, nodding as he saw a resilience in them that made him proud to sit at this table with them.

Quest: Survival of the Fittest

Together—the races of Demon and Beast Kin have worked together, making a foothold in Devil's Crater. The Dark Lord who sends his Demon Horde, hardened by a long journey and countless fights, sends them unknowingly into your home.
He wishes to use it to grow his forces stronger. Show him your newfound strength. Rise from the history books that you were cast into and LIVE!
      Requirements: Defeat the Demon Horde
      Failure: Death
      Rewards: 1,000,000 gold to the Devil Crater Treasury

A collective gasp went through the room as people broke out into excited murmurs.

Alkao pushed the quest notification aside slowly, relieved. His eyes latched onto Efri as he saw his brother waiting to be called upon.

"What of the Stone Raiders?" Efri asked.

Alkao snorted, remembering his conversation with Josh. "They will fight as long as we let them use Devil's Crater later on when they do raids in the surrounding area,"

"That's it?" Malkur asked. "That's it."

Kala, sitting in for an absent Anna, let out a chuckle.

"Something you would like to share?" Lezar asked. The edge that might have been in his voice before he had started training with the Beast Kin was now replaced with dry humor as he had come to call many of them friends and learned from them.

"They were excited to get that deal. To them, Ashal is the final frontier. A land filled with the best loot, the greatest raids, and the biggest opponents. They live to fight, not too unlike some people I know in this room. But unlike us, they can come back time and time again. They live for battle, to prove themselves. Of course, they would want to fight the soulless Demons—what self-respecting warrior wouldn't want to put themselves up against an entire army of

Creatures of Power? They're *excited* to fight the soulless Demons and with our agreement, they get to be in the center of unknown and untamed lands of Ashal."

Alkao pursed his lips. He had not yet met the leader of the Stone Raiders in person. Anna seemed to have a great confidence in him. The way she talked of them was as if they were her equals. He had seen her training in the battlegrounds. He had matched blades with her.

Any force that she saw as her equal was a scary thing indeed. Alkao only needed to think of how their fight had gone. It had felt as if she were testing him. Playing with him and testing him out. At no time did he feel that she was serious in it all.

"The one piece of advice that Anna gave me concerning them was to not piss them off," Kala said.

"Anna has always given me sound advice." Alkao met Kala's eyes and nodded.

The big bear let out a hot breath and nodded.

"Well, we all have work to do and winter will not wait for us. I say we get back to work." Alkao rose. The rest of the combined councils also rose.

Alkao turned and made to leave the council chambers; his brothers followed him as he moved through the keep.

First he would protect his home and destroy the abominations made from his blood and the Xelur. Then he would become strong enough to tear the Dark Lord and Lady of Light apart.

Alkao's eyes flashed red as he pulled back his lips into a hungry smile.

"Where the hell are those bastards?" Gimel looked to the other guild members.

They were in the city Verdul. It had been a rather quiet place compared to most of the other cities that were located around the Per'ush islands. They supplied food and clothes and lived comfortably in the Gudalo Kingdom that controlled the north of Gudalo. The south of Gudalo was held by Orcs, Gnomes, Elves, Human settlements, and Dragons. The mountain range that linked the Grorart and Brokohz Dwarven Mountains served to divide the major groups.

Verdul was an interesting place, but it hadn't been of that much interest until the Player's guild called the Exdar's Traders set up shop. They had proceeded to put in massive orders for food and clothing, and all manner of industrial items that swarmed into the city or out of the newly formed factories that the mages and technicians of the Per'ush islands ran. In return, they sold materials that no other Player trading guild could meet in Per'ush and few POE trading guilds could compete with.

The overarching traders' guild had been called in a few times to review their practices as POE traders saw competition and became scared. They had tried putting pressure on the Exdar's from every angle.

They were not simply protected by hired guards through the adventurer's guild. Their guards were Stone Raiders themselves. Although the Stone Raiders' main force had disappeared, the Exdar's Traders had the largest group of them acting as guards.

As the Exdar's Traders' influence had grown, the merchants not competing with the Exdar's found business booming. Exdar's bought more than any other guild, while selling all manner of loot. The mage's guild and college had become one of their largest buyers of gear and rare items.

"Boss, don't you think it would be a bad idea to call them out, challenge them?" Penelope asked. "The last people who had a full-out fight with them were the PKP."

"We aren't damned assassins and we're not going to be challenging them to a fight in the streets or to the death. We're challenging them with completing an A-class raid. If we can complete one faster than they can, then we can show everyone else that we're the best," Gimel said.

"I've only heard some rumors about the PKP. What happened with them?" Jeremy looked up from his sausage and potatoes.

"They attacked the Stone Raiders in Selhi's Capital. It was a bloodbath. They killed POEs and Players alike—anyone they could. Heard that their leader Hevard even became a Champion of the Dark Lord." Penelope shook her head. "Anyway, the PKP had around six hundred members in total. They brought around five hundred into the city to take on the hundred and fifty or so Stone Raiders. The Stone Raiders were able to defend themselves and push the PKP back, but not before they placed a soul curse on them. Now, any member of the PKP who was there in Selhi Capital is marked. Always burning from the inside by fire. Some say that there is a tracking spell imbued right into their soul. Doesn't really matter. What does is that right afterward, the Stone Raiders disappeared after they were chased out by Selhi Capital's guard, the very people they fought beside and protected. While the main part of the guild is gone, there are Stone Raiders all over the place. Whenever they see a PKP who had been in Selhi, that PKP won't have to wait long until they get the white screen of death. Even leaving the guild isn't enough. It takes a full character reset, right back to zero, for you to remove the curse and get the Stone Raiders to leave you alone."

"So wait, where are the PKP now?" Jeremy asked.

"The guild was disbanded. If there are any people who didn't reset, I don't know. The Stone Raiders killed about a thousand PKP every two weeks, sometimes killing the same Players repeatedly and even camping altars of Rebirth. Sometimes, the Stone Raiders would just appear in cities with teleport pads to kill them before leaving again."

"Wow, that is one hell of a story." Jeremy snorted. "It ain't no story," Gimel said, stone-faced.

"How do you know?" Jeremy asked.

"I was there. When Fellox was just four parties, we were in Selhi Capital for the monster hunt. When we saw how the magistrate ran them out of town, we left. The monsters numbered in the thousands that year. Biggest season they saw in ten years. Many of the guilds and Player groups left, not caring about the bounty. There was fighting on the wall that year."

Gimel shook his head. "The Stone Raiders might have been at the peak and all mysterious, but they're honorable rivals. I wouldn't fight them head on. Though, I would challenge them. From the few beers I've had with Josh, he'd seem he'd welcome it more than anything."

"I hope they come back soon. I want to get back to raiding. I've been hearing that there are a few nice raiding spots down in south Gudalo," Jeremy said with a pleased grin.

"That's the spirit." Gimel laughed and clapped Jeremy on the shoulder.

"How are our Creatures of Power doing?" the Dark Lord asked the bowing Boran-al.

"The Demon Horde continues to march across Ashal, growing stronger as they kill one another and the beasts that they find in their path. By the time they reach Devil's Crater, they will be the strongest fighting force in all of Emerilia and they can hunt through the dungeons there to further increase their fighting abilities," Boran-al said into the floor.

"The others?"

"The Lich Lords have been sent out and the lower-leveled experiments. We have been having an issue. Our forces that were living in parts of the Aleph ruins that we located have been dying off. With the Aleph runes, we have been unable to view what is going on within their facilities."

"They were wiped out centuries ago. We saw to that—destroyed tens of their facilities, killed their rune-made master, Shard. What else could be down there?" The Dark Lord tapped his fingers against his throne.

"It might be other beasts. The Dark is known to hold some of the highest-level creatures." Sweat rolled down Boran-al's back.

"Well, they are just experiments. What of the portal guards?"

Boran-al, relieved, continued on. "The portal guards have been increased. The Dark Elves, Champions, and Creatures of Power have done their best to keep the locations a secret."

Boran-al hid his shiver as he felt his master's killing intent and hunger through his aura.

"Good. Remind the Dark Elves to not fail me."

"Yes, master," Boran-al said.

"Your cultists might have died, but their sacrifice will serve to raise us to the top of the Pantheon and all of Emerilia."

"You honor me, master. I only wish that I could assist in tearing apart those who dare think the other Affinities as more powerful." Boran-al looked up, his purple eyes flashing in anger.

"Soon enough, I will call on you. Prepare yourself."

"Yes, master." Boran-al once again bowed his head. The sigil around him flashed with black energy and shadows covered him. He disappeared from the great hall and reappeared in his experiment hall. Thousands of altars covered the room; the smell of rot, decay, and blood filled the air.

Boran-al smiled, thinking of the damage that his creatures would wreak on the People of Emerilia. His purple eyes seemed to flicker and dance.

"Those Elven mages thought that I was weak, that I was a blight on their race for being of a higher Affinity in Dark magics. They did not understand the power of it." Boran-al's face twisted into an ugly smile. "I will show them the true power of the Dark. I will rip down their homes. I will cast them out of their lands. I will kill their children, their loved ones, and I will end the Elven race, from Wood to High. I will watch them die, and when they have finally fallen to my hand, I will raise them as an army to kill their fellows."

Slightly crazed laughter left his lips. Dreams of death, pain, and servitude filled his mind.

5

LONG DISTANCE CONFERENCE

"Hey, Bob. How's things?" Dave asked as Bob connected to his Mirror of Communication. The two of them seemed to be sitting on Dave's porch back in Cliff-Hill.

"Not bad. I tried out those flasks you gave me a few months ago." Bob looked out over the land surrounding Cliff-Hill, sitting in his usual chair.

"How did it go?" Dave looked to him.

"It was interesting. If I was to use the contents and then destroy it before they made it all the way through my body, then it was like nothing happened — it was pulled from me. It was why I had you make the water ones and I tested them out on a number of crops. I grew them and harvested them. If I destroyed the flask once they were harvested, then they dried up. It seems that only what is in the flask is destroyed when you destroy the flask. If you were to give it to a person and they drank it, they would be hydrated. When you break the flask and the contents have been drunk by someone, then at whatever stage the created elements are in, they start to decay rapidly. The protons and neutrons that make up the elements go haywire; they go through radioactive decay. A person would need a minor healing spell and they would be okay," Bob said.

"So, once the power source is gone, then the glue that holds the conjured elements together dissipates and they pass through millennia of radiation decay in minutes?" Dave asked.

"Yeah, though it happens so fast that the nuclear decay of the elements is minimal."

"So, it's not bad as long as they have a minor healing spell or some kind of potion to cleanse them of the effects of the rapid decay." Dave tapped his lip in thought. "Okay, so, good for crops — not so good for people."

"Exactly — instant water at a moment's notice, but only for the non- living." Bob smiled.

"Now, we just need to find a kind of crop that it would be okay for it to go dry on," Dave said.

"Nuts!" Bob declared, pointing his finger in the air. "Uh, what?"

"Nuts, like peanuts, almonds…that sort of thing. They use a ton of water, but afterward if you were to take the water out, add a bit of salt, you've just got nuts still," Bob said with a big smile.

"So, just grow a ton of nut plants with flask water? Worth a try." Dave nodded.

"I gave it a go and it worked fine for me." Bob pulled out a bag of different nuts from his bag of holding.

Dave took some. "Taste fine to me." Dave threw them back. "So, how are things going for you?"

"Pretty boring right now. There's little for me to do but to see what happens. I've played my hand and now we wait to see where the chips might fall. In two or three months, the Demon Horde and the people at Devil's Crater will clash. In a couple of months, the tournament hosted by the dwarves will begin. After that, it won't be long until I have to start releasing the things I have locked up into events across Emerilia." Bob frowned, his voice becoming serious.

"These creatures are the kinds that would give an entire Jukal carrier trouble and I'm going to be releasing hundreds of them onto

Emerilia. I've tried talking to the Emperor but he's rather interested in it all. I haven't even been allowed access to know what the Affinities Pantheon are making for their Creatures of Power or who their Champions are. I know that they have bolstered all of their ranks. Their Divine Mana wells are lower than I've ever seen them before. I don't know what they have planned. Dark had to have been growing this new Demon Horde ever since the last one was supposedly destroyed. They're not loyal, but they're easy to lead and he's made it impossible for them to even think of rebelling against him. Damned walking mindless slaves and they don't know it." Bob sighed and shook his head.

"Well, I was one of those until you showed me the truth," Dave said. They lapsed into silence for a while.

"Do you ever regret it?" Bob asked. "What?"

"Regret knowing that Earth was destroyed and that Emerilia is real?" Bob asked, a worried expression on his face as he studied Dave.

"At times, yes, but not for the most part. I know what I am. I know why those things happened to me back on Earth. I have never felt more alive than I do right here. Sure, I built rockets and I sent people to Mars and around the Solar system. I loved it, but here, I get to find out new things every day. I'm not scared of being left alone. I know my friends are really there for me. I'm happy with what I have. Sure, it's not as relaxing as I wanted it to be, but I wouldn't have traded it for anything," Dave smiled, Bob shook his head a small smile on his lips.

Dave's eyes looked out over the fields around Cliff-Hill. "Here, I am making a difference. It feels like this is where I am supposed to be. I want to tell the others about what is really going on, but I know I can't. What was done to us was wrong. I know it wasn't your fault. You were just trying to keep the Human race alive in some small way. You didn't know we'd be turned into some mass entertainment with generation and generation killed off because the empire deemed it 'fun.' I don't know what the future holds or what will happen by the end of it, though I can tell you I'm going to live it to the max and do what I want."

"It's not going to be an easy path," Bob said.

"No, it won't, but it'll be mine and I'll do everything in my power to look after my friends and get rid of the Jukal Empire's control over our lives."

Bob patted Dave's shoulder. "Shoot for the stars and maybe you'll hit the moon?"

"Someone's been reading up on their Earth quotes!" Dave grinned. "Well, not much else to do other than just watch you lot run around.

Uggh, it's so boring dealing with just the Pantheon! Only Water and Fire are any fun. Air is annoying as hell. Light's like the definition of Machiavellian. Earth is a dumbass and Dark is a conniving and powerful arsehole."

"Well, I have some people that you could talk to." Dave smiled. "Who?"

"You know, that guy Sato? Well, him, as well as whoever else he connects us with. Also the Dwarves. They need more help with information and I know that you like helping them out. I was wondering if you might have a spare AI that I could hook up to them with information on different topics on Earth? You could also impersonate the AI and get in the middle of it." Dave smiled.

"Playing on an old scientist's weakness for progress and curiosity," Bob said in an accusatory tone.

"Possibly."

"Hell, yeah, I'll give it a go!" Bob smiled.

"Good, 'cause I have a meeting with Sato right now and then another one with the Dwarves right afterward." Dave's smile widened as Bob rolled his eyes.

"So, I'm going to have to step up an AI core in what?"

"Like fifteen minutes?"

"Sounds like a challenge." Bob laughed, some of the life coming back to him. Making plans and trying to give Emerilia a chance to survive was a tough job.

Dave knew that Bob just wanted to be a scientist, learning new things and being at the heart of discoveries. Give him a challenge and he'd excel; give him friends and nothing could hold him back.

"You've got ten more minutes," Dave said.

"Dammit!" Bob disappeared from the Cliff-Hill porch simulation, a big smile plastered on his face.

Sato started the recording device before he activated his Mirror of Communication. He arrived in a simple room with a fireplace at one end, flickering away with two comfortable chairs facing it.

"Hey, Sato." Dave already sat in one of the chairs and waved him over. Over the last couple of months, there seemed to have been a breakthrough every week as Edward's research division used the information gained from Dave and Shard.

Living conditions had improved. New ships were being proposed. People who had been accepted into the leveling program were showing increases in every area. Some had even been able to create spells.

"You look pretty tired." Sato sat down.

"Tell me about it. Lots of work to do, and not much time to do it. Need to be done within at least two months. I hope that we can make it in time." Dave looked into the fireplace.

"Edwards has a number of questions for Shard." Sato sent a file to Dave, who could forward it to Shard.

"And I have someone that I would like you to meet." Dave swiped his interface away.

"Who?" Sato asked.

"Me," an odd voice said from Dave's side. "Got it done in seven minutes — suck it."

Sato looked over. His eyes went wide as he looked at a true Jukal, with its purple skin and patches of fur and frog-like appearance.

"The hell is this?" Sato asked, ready to leave the conference at a moment's notice.

"I am Lo'kal, creator of the Trapped Mind Project. What you know as Emerilia." The Jukal changed, turning into a gnome. "Also, the guy who just stepped up an AI core in seven minutes." He buffed his nails on his jacket, looking pretty pleased with himself.

"I also modified the planet Emerilia and created the Earth simulation. I believe it was time that we had a talk. Oh, and please call me Bob." A chair seemed to rise out of the ground; Bob sat on it and faced Sato.

"What the hell is this?" Sato looked to Dave.

"This is Lo'kal, also known as the Grey God, Neutrality, and Bob. He made Emerilia to solve the issue of the aggressive species and keep Humanity alive, at least in some form. As you know, it wasn't long after Emerilia was created that Humanity started making strides in different kind of magical tech. The Jukal sucked this up and started watching Emerilia more. They started watching for entertainment. Millions of Humans died as they continued to watch, getting Bob to re-seed the planet twice. They stopped the Players from killing off the aggressive species as they wanted us to have more people to fight," Dave said.

"I did not realize how close I would become to those that I grew and placed across Emerilia. I no longer felt a connection with the Jukal. As my family died off, I was left here, never allowed to die, my one purpose to run Emerilia, to entertain the Jukal Empire. What was supposed to be a way to preserve the greatness of the Human race turned into a television show." Bob shook his head.

"What do you want from us?" Sato asked. Dave and Bob looked at each other.

"We don't want anything, dude," Dave said.

"You're enslaved on a planet that all of the Players think is a game, with a Pantheon that is playing power games with billions of Emerilian's lives and an empire that uses it all for fun," Sato said, not believing the two of them for a minute.

"We've got our own issues, that's right, but we're not going to let that stop us," Dave said, as if it was just a minor concern.

"See, I think this is why I came to be so enamored with you Humans. No matter what, you don't quit—you always strive forward. Also you're really argumentative, which leads to you making a lot of cool tech." Bob grinned.

"So, why are you giving us all this information then?" Sato asked. "Seemed like the right thing to do?" Dave shrugged.

Sato rubbed his temples. "So, you gave us all this advanced tech just because it seemed like the right thing to do and you're not asking anything from us?"

"Pretty much. And the stuff that you're figuring out right now is the kind of things that Players get used to within the first couple of weeks being on the planet. Or two years for the People of Emerilia." Dave tilted his hand in a rough approximation.

Sato kept his features straight as he took that in.

What kind of stuff are they using if this is what they have within the first couple of weeks? Dave has said that he has been within Emerilia constantly for nearly a year and a half.

"So, why did you want us to meet?" Sato asked.

"Well, Bob has all these plans and stuff, so I'm going to be busy for the next little while. I thought that between Bob and Shard, you would have most things covered. You know he was Jukal at one point so he knows how they think, where they are, and all that kind of information." Dave looked to Sato.

Sato looked to Bob, his eyes thinning. "Okay, well, we are always interested in more information. We have our own means of verifying it," Sato said. The information they had already provided was useful; even if Bob's information wasn't correct, at least they had it if they needed it. If it was, then Sato was not willing to lose it. That was how he had become vice- commander of Deq'ual's military forces.

"Sweet! This will be much more fun than hanging out with Denur or the Merpeople. Dragons sleep a lot and the Mer think of me as some all- powerful god. Getting really annoying. I should have kept a few of the Beast Kin and Demons around — they were pretty fun." Bob tapped his chin."'Bout time I had a vacation and started doing a few experiments!"

Sato felt as though he had been left out of the conversation. "So, what did you do before Humanity was killed off?" Sato asked.

"I was a scientist, worked with Humanity a lot. I was able to use my position to make this system. I have always been fascinated by how creative you lot are." Bob smiled, looking distant with a sad smile on his face.

Sato shook his head. *I would have thought this kind of thing impossible until a couple of months ago. Now I'm not so sure.*

Dave left Sato and Bob talking, skipping out and going to his second meeting that day. He entered the Dwarven conference.

"Dave!"

"Ah shit." Dave turned around and headed for the entrance he'd appeared in.

"You started this mess — you git yer arse to this table!" Kol yelled from the conference table.

Dave hung his head and turned around as he got mobbed by a dozen Dwarves at the same time, all of them asking different questions about the metals and elements he had sort of introduced to the Dwarves. Dave answered as many questions as possible. He had been joking about leaving as he started getting excited with all the ideas that the Dwarves were coming up with. Some ideas inspired fear.

"That will make a bomb—shouldn't do that, Keli," Dave said, as she explained a reaction she was working on.

"How big of a bomb?"

Dave stroked his beard in thought. "I'm not sure, but I have some equations that you can use to figure that out."

"Ah, I hate all this darned math. Used to be a time when you could just hammer metal into the right form!" Keli shook her head.

"You've got that high Intelligence—it's about time you used it for something." Kol slammed the hammer in his hand against the table. "All right, you delinquents, sit yer arses down and stop trying to touch Dave, ya bunch of bearded perverts!" Kol really didn't like being the head of the council.

There was a mass of grumbling, mostly from those around Dave as they moved to the conference table.

Kol hit the table once again as everyone sat down. "Council in session. We've got more materials to divvy up." Kol sent out messages through his interface. "That's done. We're also getting more shipments from the Stone Raiders with the rarer materials. Bob has been kind enough to lend us a hand in regards to the new information that we have. He has made a simple AI for us to talk to regarding our various questions on the new materials. Everyone, meet Jeeves." Kol waved to the side of the room.

An unassuming man wearing a butler outfit appeared, and bowed to the Dwarves.

"You can ask Jeeves whatever you need. He will do his best to gather information, formulas, and anything else you might need to know on the subjects you are studying. We are also running classes on magical coding. It's cheaper, easier, and shut up, Barry."

Barry crossed his arms, growling to himself.

"Quino has also had some breakthroughs with magical coding. You want to tell them?" Kol asked.

"Thanks, Kol. Okay, so as we know, if we have extremely complicated Magical Circuits on something, then we need a higher-classed material to contain that power. Same if we have two Magical Circuits operating as enchantments. With magical coding, we have been able to figure out how much power each metal can take. We're now working on different permutations of metals and densities," Quino said proudly. Knowing just how much power the magical coding could be on any given material would allow them to push the enchantments to the limit.

"Didn't have to use all my damned newly forged swords," Endur complained under his breath, not that many paid attention. Edmur, his brother, looked rather pleased himself.

"Okay, any other announcements?" Kol asked.

Dave raised his hand and received a nod. Dave might have been one of the new master smiths, but his actions meant that everyone listened to him.

"The Exdar's Traders and the Stone Raiders are working to become one guild. It will slow down deliveries slightly but we should be able to make up any difference. As the Exdar's will have access to more funds the greater buying power they'll hold," Dave said.

More than one Dwarf had an excited look on their faces. Dave had been refining multiple materials into different metals in the Aleph forges and then sending them out to the different Dwarven mountains. Each Dwarven mountain had a number of teleport pads, allowing them to take the material in any one mountain and then send it out to the rest. New refineries and processing facilities were being built in many mountains so that they could convert the materials themselves.

"Good. Even when the different facilities are up and running in the Dwarven lands, we're going to need other sources of the new materials. I know that the war council is already asking for more information on the titanium barrels. After the fire test that Jesal did, they want more. We all know that soon we will be embroiled in a battle of one kind or another. Keep in mind the different applications of the materials." Kol's covered eyes moved across the table.

"Anything else?"

No one seemed to have any good points so Kol hit his hammer on the table.

"Now git!" Kol gestured at the entrances and exits with his thumb.

The Dwarves grinned and laughed at his antics, taking their time in leaving. "Dave, a word."

The Dwarves had their talks; many moved to Jeeves, who multiplied into a dozen different avatars, ready to answer their questions.

Dave moved off to a private conference room behind Kol. The door closed as Kol took a seat.

"Well, when I taught you to be a Master Smith, I had no idea this was what you had in mind," Kol said with a rare smile.

"Enjoying being the leader of the council?" Dave grinned.

"Pain in the arse," Kol muttered. "Now, I wanted to talk about your smithy and the ceramics factory. Have you been reading the messages from me and Zel?"

"Yeah, I have and there is a reason I am putting more money into the companies instead of taking it out," Dave said.

"Boy, there is more coin there than I have seen outside of the Dwarven treasuries and we pluck gold from the ground," Kol said.

"I know, which is exactly why I don't need it. I just submitted another half-dozen patents and I'm making solid gold from those. I want the smithies and the ceramics factories to grow."

"We're producing as fast as possible, and now building warehouses. The traders buy up as much as they can, but we're isolated." Kol scratched his head.

"Not for long," Dave said.

"Well, you going to tell me what your damned plan is or am I going to have to drag you out of where you and your guild are holed up?"

"I want us to buy a teleport pad," Dave said.

Kol was silent for a few moments. "You want to buy a teleport pad for Cliff-Hill? Do you know how much that will cost?"

"Quite a bit, I know. It's why I haven't been taking any money from the companies or the patents. In a few weeks, we should have enough to buy one."

"Damn boy, you don't have simple plans, do you?"

"Think big or go home," Dave winked. Kol let out an amused grunt. "Well. Gurren and Lox still talk about you and Deia all the time.

They're going off on some dungeon raids with the Stone Raiders they've trained up. Could never keep them in one place for too long." Kol laughed.

"They'll be fine. They could kick my ass any day." Dave laughed. "But you can come back from the dead—they can't. It makes things a lot harder," Kol said.

"I know, but dying is not our aim. We'll be beside the best trained Stone Raiders. All of us have been working on our skills. The Stone Raiders might act like idiots when we're in town, but when we're on a raid, things change. Players always go first; if we die, we can come back. The People of Emerilia are some of our strongest fighters. They don't want to be a burden so they train harder than anyone. Which makes us Players get off our asses and try to outdo them." Dave shook his head at his guild's ways. "We really are a bunch of idiots."

"Can say that again. I Still remember a little incident with a certain guild master throwing weapons in my smithy, or a certain student turning decades long practices on their heads," Kol said, but Dave could see the corners of his old teacher's mouth lift up in amusement.

"Thanks, Kol," Dave said dryly.

Kol chuckled. "Well, I've probably taken up enough of your time. What do you want us to do once we have the money for the teleport pad?"

"Place it somewhere in the town, with defenses around it. You never know when someone might get your codes and be able to come through the damn thing. Set up a power grid like the one that was around Boran-al's Citadel. Charge the equivalent cost of soul gems plus five percent for the time it's open per person. Get with Zel and figure that out. If you have any issues, send me a message and I'll see what I can do about sorting it out," Dave said.

"Fine, sounds straightforward enough. It will also open up a lot of places to sell our wares. Having a smithy that takes on applicants from across Emerilia and can repair the highest-tier armor — Cliff-Hill is going to expand just because of that. Zel was complaining about the clay and other materials he needs for different projects. Damn, I'm only just starting to realize how much this is going to change the two businesses."

Dave just smiled. Having the teleport pad to help out the two businesses was one reason; the other was so that he could get to the seeder whenever he wanted to. The Dwarves and Elves were reinforcing the area. If the Stone Raiders ever needed to retreat somewhere, then Cliff-Hill was the place to do it.

6
MOVING FORWARD

Shard looked over his people. When they had escaped Emerilia, they were being hunted down by creatures made by the Pantheon, their numbers pitifully low compared to their original strength.

They were a group that had come together in adversity. Even as they came back to their homes, feeling as if only hours had passed when it had really been centuries, they didn't let it play on their minds. Already, they were working to pull together their cities. They brought new life to the growing areas and assisted the automatons Shard was using to continue the repairs done by the Raiders Alephir was a massive city. Party Zero had worked tirelessly to get the different power generators and stations online. The city was once again able to spin with that power, but the Aleph were rebuilding homes that had fallen apart, planting gardens, growing food, and returning the city to its former glory.

It will take time, but once again the Aleph will rise.

They were keeping their return a secret from the guild as they built up their strength. The Stone Raiders had helped them, but they didn't know them. There had been many cycles of Players while they had been gone.

Shard was interested in the various simulations he had run to see what might happen with the Stone Raiders and Aleph. *It is my role to give the council and my people choices of what to do.*

Shard had been an immature AI when they had all left; now, he was something of a guiding elder. The council paid much more attention to what he said instead of just thinking of him as a convenience.

Hamdir looked away from the windows that overlooked Alephir. As more and more of their people returned from where the Grey God had kept them, lights could be seen everywhere, greenhouses were once again creating food and factories were barely able to keep up with all the demands. The lights were back on, the factories were working nonstop, and Aleph walked through the streets once more.

There was over five million people just in Alephir.

"Something on your mind?" Ela-Dorn walked up beside him, also looking out the window at their capital.

Look at the consequence of our pride" Hamdir said "We are but a fraction of our numbers, all because we were unable to ask for help or accept it from the Grey God until too many had paid for that mistake."

"It still feels unreal. Many people are going through their mourning. Decades gone in the blink of an eye and we're left here," Ela-Dorn said her voice heavy with loss.

"We must look to the future, to what will come next. I have been thinking on the Stone Raiders."

"What about them?" Ela-Dorn asked as Shard arrived. "The meeting is beginning, council members."

"Thank you, Shard." Hamdir turned away from the window and headed into the council chambers. "All will be explained soon enough."

Ela-Dorn frowned, clearly wanting to ask more as they looked for their own seats in the council chamber.

There were viewing balconies that looked down on the council. These seats were given to whoever wanted to attend. The council sat around an elegantly carved table, natural scenes engraved into its mixed metal surface. "The Aleph Council is called to session," Shard said through unseen speakers as the council sat as one. Only Hamdir remained standing.

"Over the last couple of months, we have come far. We have brought our city to life and our people have been able to return. We are still weak compared to how we were before, but with time, we will regain our strength." Hamdir was met with applause by the council and those watching the meeting. "Though we must remember the lessons of what drove us from our homes. We were powerful, mighty, and proud. We lived in a time of prejudice and came together to create a society that did not care of your creed or your station in life. We took in all; we educated and we passed our knowledge on to those who were willing to work with us. We were proud of our society and we had every right to be. The Affinities Pantheon itself felt threatened. When they issued their threats, we stood together against them."

The hall was silent as his gaze looked to them all, races from all walks of life, from an age long passed.

"We fought the forces of the Pantheon; we slowed them and we declared that we would defeat them. Pride took us and we fought a losing battle even as we had been given another chance by the Grey God to escape the bloodshed. In the end, we took it, but taking that option was called the coward's choice. Pride blinded us, made us call one another cowards for escaping with our lives. Our pride made us weak, to admit that we were not as strong as we believed. With our knowledge and our open displays to the other races and the way we shut ourselves in, accepting so very few, we taunted and played with those who might have allied with us. When the Dwarves and Elves, years before judgment was brought down on us, asked if we would like to work together, to bring our races closer, we were brash and told them to worry about themselves. There were people all across Emerilia who wanted to work with us. Instead, we were too prideful. I hope that we do not make the same mistake. We have been given a second chance. A chance to return the Aleph to prominence. Will we once again shun those who wish to call us friends? Will we make walls when we could make roads?"

Silence had seemed to descend over Alephir, the meeting being broadcasted across the city.

"Shard protected our cities and homes as best as he could in our absence. We owe him a debt of gratitude. Yet, he had the wisdom to reach out to those who showed him friendship, who are right now fighting to reclaim *our* homes. You have all seen the videos of the Stone Raiders, seen as they charge forces that we could not fight with clear abandon. We are builders, creators, crafters, and I am proud of our achievements, but few of us are warriors. We created automatons to protect us, to care for us." Hamdir stabbed the table in front of him as he talked, holding the eyes of the council and the eyes of those watching this moment.

"It is only together that we might succeed or fail. We are not just the Aleph; we are the People of Emerilia. We have shown our strength together. Think of the possibilities if we are to work together with others. I have seen the things we are capable of and it brings a smile to my face. I hope that we as a race have matured enough to not shun those who have sacrificed so much in order to help us. I propose that we, the Aleph, extend our hand in friendship with the Stone Raiders, with the Demons and Beast Kin. All of us saved by the Grey God, all of us working together to try to look after our people and secure a future for tomorrow. To see a new horizon, with the suns of tomorrow shining upon us. Together, our four groups can build together. When we are ready, we can go out into Emerilia and hold our heads high. Not with pride, but with our hands extended in friendship."

Hamdir let the silence sit for a minute, feeling drained. His chest was tight with hope as the stony faces of the council looked back at him.

Hamdir didn't know who started it but a single clap rang out. The faces of those in the balconies and those in the council's chamber broke out into smiles and nods of agreement. Clapping sounds of agreement and whistling rang out through the council chamber.

Hamdir's eyes itched as he looked upon his people. They had come from the edge of oblivion and were now given another chance.

The Aleph, Demons, and Beast Kin had all defied the Affinities Pantheon; supported by the efforts of the Stone Raiders, they had been able to return. Hamdir smiled and looked to his people, hiding his shaking hands.

It took some time for the clapping to die down.

"We call for a vote," Shard said. The council's interfaces appeared.

They cast their votes, the room quiet.

"The votes have been cast. By unanimous decision, we will send out an envoy to the Stone Raiders, then to the Demons and Beast Kin to discuss terms of an alliance." Shard's words were cut off as Hamdir sat back in his chair, the applause and cheering of the Aleph filling the city.

They had taken their first step toward not only recovering their lost status but carving out a new future for themselves.

7

NEARING
THE END

Josh sighed as he sat down at the mess hall table.

"How's the forges going?" Josh asked Dave, who was shoveling food down his mouth.

Dave gave him a dirty look before clearing his throat. "In the six months we've been here, I've got all of the damned forges going, even modified a bunch of them to take the Dwarves' materials and turn them into different metals. We're cranking out carbon fiber, titanium, aluminum, and a dozen other metals and materials. Thankfully, no one has noticed the movement of materials because of the drop pads and using the Exdar's Traders. They part of the guild yet?" Dave looked to Josh.

"Uhhh..."

"They will be soon. We're in talks with them," Suzy said from down the table.

"Hey, Suzy, you had a look over that teleport pad stuff for Cliff-Hill?" Dave asked.

"Yeah. We should be good in a couple of weeks. Probably be a good idea for the Exdar's Traders in Verdul to get one as well." Suzy shrugged.

"I feel like I'm missing something." Josh looked between the two of them.

They both had just shoveled food into their mouths.

"Dave is going to buy a teleport pad for his smithy and ceramics factory. They're going to be putting it right in the middle of Cliff-Hill," Deia said.

"Ah," Josh said as Dave downed half a glass of orange juice. "Woohoo, that hit the spot! You guys ready to go mess with a mining facility?" Steve looked at the others with a goofy smile on his face. "You don't even eat food." Dave groaned.

Steve shrugged his massive shoulders, that goofy smile only growing. "There's a group out there with a bunch of destruction staffs and melee types. They should be able to clear it up and then the crafters there can get the machines moving," Deia said.

"All right, so what are you doing after breakfast?" Dave leaned over, giving suggestions with his eyes.

Deia smiled and shook her head at his antics. "*We're* going to do some extra training."

Dave put on his best hurt puppy-dog face.

"We're going to be working on how to actually shoot a bow."

"What do you mean by that?" Dave asked. The others seemed interested, too.

"Well, I have been doing a bit of research into Earth's history. Have you ever noticed how in ancient drawings, no one had a quiver on their back? The damn things are annoying as hell and well, you're going to drop a ton of arrows. Here we've got storage quivers that make sure we don't drop our arrows, though they're still not as good. So I went back to basics and I've been trying something out. I'll show you down in the training area." Deia smiled mischievously.

"How is it you know how to get me to go along with your training every time?" Dave sighed.

"Because you're curious as hell and it is so good seeing you working out." Deia winked as Josh choked on his breakfast.

"Proper pair of horndogs, them two," Suzy commiserated.

"Should we put in for that room change? I kept on hearing noises through the walls last week," Dave asked Deia.

"Nah, we'll just have to be louder than them next time." Deia gave Suzy a wide smirk.

Josh, who had been trying to clear his throat with orange juice, now had it fly out his nose.

Suzy turned an interesting shade of red.

"Cold season is coming along — good idea to get your vitamin C in," Dave said to Josh, who was spluttering on the table.

"Can we just go and shoot some targets please? I don't think my sinuses can take much more of your innuendos," Josh said.

Deia pulled three arrows out from her hip quiver, holding them between the fingers in her hand. She had three targets at different ranges in front of her, all of them armored.

"Okay, let's see this in action," Josh said.

A group of other archers had gathered. "Where did she get that quiver from?" one of them asked, confused.

"Shut up and watch!" another chided. Deia had proved herself to be one hell of a bowwoman and they were all interested.

"When I say, go," Dave said.

"Ready." Deia eyed her targets and brought her first arrow to her string. Another arrow appeared in the quiver of holding.

"Go!"

Deia fired at the middle target, pulling a new arrow from the quiver near her left hand, hitting the right target and then the left.

"Point two seconds? Probably faster," Dave said as Deia looked at the three arrows that had put holes through the armor and the targets behind them. The third target fell over as everyone gathered was silent.

"Damn, where can we get quivers like that?" one of the other archers asked.

"Most places. Just need to put the settings to one arrow at a time and then get used to the forward weight," Deia said.

"Makes a lot of sense—it's similar to the bow hand draw technique. Where people would hold the arrows in their hand, pulling them back and onto the string. Here you don't even need to hold them in your hand, just pull them out of the quiver draw them back onto the string and release. Much, much faster."

"Well, that just shot down the whole firearms thing," Josh said to Dave.

"Hell yeah. Think of how fast a group of ten archers can fire, all of them shooting arrows that could put a hole in an armored carrier back on Earth." Dave shook his head.

"Oi!" Steve slapped a troll with his axe, sending them into the wall. "Dick head!"

"Thanks." Dwayne slammed his shield into another troll, throwing them back ten feet even though they were twice Dwayne's height. "Sounds like you've been fighting with Josh a bit."

Steve's left hand transformed into a bolt thrower; a dozen arrows took down the troll Dwayne had pushed back.

"Hey! Kill steal!" Dwayne grabbed a spear from his back and hurled it into an advancing troll.

Steve's hand clicked back in place. A shield extended above and below his forearm, stopping a boulder that a troll had ripped out of the wall. "What? You're just slow! And Josh has good sayings!"

"Just have to be a bit faster," Esa chimed in, agreeing with Steve, slapping away another boulder with her shield.

"See! Nice block, Esa!" Steve said as Dwayne made annoyed noises. "Thanks, Steve!" Esa grinned as Dwayne sighed in frustration. "Sometimes, I wonder about my friends." Dwayne grunted as a troll punched his shield, letting out a howl as it shook its crushed hand.

Dwayne didn't give the shocked troll time to recover as he shoved his claymore through the troll's ribs, turning and ripping it out. The troll dropped to the ground.

"Fiddly dee potatoes!" Steve said. The trolls looked over as Steve threw four grenades into their midst.

The trolls caught them or juggled them, confused. Lightning, fire, and frost leaped out of the "grenades," removing half of the trolls.

Steve couldn't stop laughing. "Did you see that!" Steve stopped moving forward and slapped his thigh. "They were all like hot potato juggling them! Ah, fuck, I think I might break a rune!"

"Oh, stay down, will you?" Dwayne stabbed a troll that had been mostly torn apart.

"Dis is Sparta!"

"Watch out, Dwayne!" Esa yelled.

Dwayne flattened himself as a confused-looking troll flew over him. "Damn it, Steve! Let me know the next time you're going to punt a troll."

"Sorry, dude. Got all excited." Steve had a grin plastered on his face as he stepped up beside Dwayne. There were only a handful of the trolls left.

The Stone Raiders finished off the remaining trolls, all of them grouping together.

"Scout guardians, go out and see what else is hiding here. Send back one as soon as you find any more hostiles," Dwayne said.

The scout guardian automatons appeared before disappearing, headed through the partially cleared housing complex.

"Let's pull back for now. We've cleared out an area for the rest of the guild to come through. We don't want to antagonize the other beasts that are here," Dwayne said.

"I friggin' hate spiders." Esa shuddered.

"Why can't we just burn them out?" Steve asked.

"We got some of the guardians to try to clear out this place one time.

The webs are pretty resilient. We can burn it away but it shrinks rather than disappearing altogether. It also alerts the spiders—they'll track down the disturbance and destroy whatever came into its domain. We found out that when the webs shrink, they become conductive. If we can get to the middle of the nest, we're hoping to burn the spider webs and then feed a ton of lightning into the web to zap the bastards. We have to be in the center or else it won't work," Dwayne said.

"When they cut the webs, didn't spiders descend on them in just a few minutes?" Esa asked.

"Yeah, which is why we're bringing so much of the guild. We need to get into the center as quick as possible, then we zap them from the middle out and start preparing for the college."

"It sounds like it should be easy, but why is it that I know it's not going to be?" Steve said, as if mulling over the question.

"Because nothing ever goes as planned," Esa chimed in. Dwayne just grunted, agreeing with his two friends.

Dave's breathing was heavy as he circled Anna. She had returned the night before. After getting some sleep, she'd tracked down the rest of the party to the training area.

Deia had been mobbed by people wanting to know more about the quiver and where she had bought it from, so Anna took it upon herself to train Dave.

"You should just ask him out. Would hurt a lot less—well, for me at least." Dave blocked a screaming Wind blade with his shield and came in close with his sword. She caught the blade with her own, moving to kick his knee. He shifted his stance, pushing her out and to the side; his sword and shield came together, forming into a great sword as he swung at her, making her hastily throw her own blade up to defend herself.

"What the hell are you talking about?" Anna asked. "Alkao," Dave said, defending against a flurry of attacks. "What are you talking about?"

"Well, you like him, right? I don't know why you haven't asked him out yet. Has he asked you out yet?" Dave was rewarded by a slight whistling sound.

Dave saw several blue markers, his perception picking up Anna's Wind blades as he dodged, trying to fight them back and keep Anna pinned back at the same time. He was breathing heavier as he stared at her, holding his own blade.

"We both have our positions. It would not make sense if we were to 'go out' with each other. Things are not that simple."

"They are that simple if you stop trying to complicate them. Ya ask him! If he says yes or no, you at least know and you can go from there!" Dave smiled.

Anna charged in, beating back his defenses. He fought well, but his blade was conjured; it wasn't Mithril like hers. She cut through it as Dave edged away. She moved to attack him again, finding a gash on her side and his blade next to her gut.

She let out a snort and shook her head. "I think I'll take that as a win!"

"You've become faster at remaking your conjured items. I have no doubt that you would have been able to recreate your blade through my stomach if you wished. What are your Affinities now?"

"Avoiding the subject much?" Dave pulled up his Affinities.

Affinity Levels			
Dark	237	Light	173
Fire	193	Water	142
Earth	213	Air	139

"No avoiding anything if there is nothing there," Anna shot back as she looked over the information and shook her head. "You know that every time I see your stats, I feel a little chill run down my spine?"

"Cause he's annoying as hell?" Suzy asked from where she was fighting Induca and Malsour with her creations. They were the only things that were willing to go up against the two. They could actually use all of their powers and not try to hold back. Even against the Players, they were too strong and took them out too quickly for it to be much in the way of training. Deia was the only person who could kind of go toe-to-toe and Steve was a metal punching bag. He couldn't land a hit on them, though he could take one hell of a pounding.

"Malsour, she's not paying attention!" Dave said. Shadows seemed to spawn around Suzy.

"Dick!" Suzy said. Air creations clapped over her like some invisible armor, making her fly away from the shadows as she threw out a Fire creation, bringing light and destroying any shadows that Malsour might use to launch an attack.

"Why don't you fight Induca and Malsour?" Dave asked Anna. "What makes you think that I could fight them?" Anna raised her eyebrow.

"You are hailed as the famed 'Captain of the Wind.' You made the Beast Kin what they are and scared the ever-living shit out of anyone who came to annoy you and your people. You've been around awhile and I know my blades. I didn't make that thing weak and I can see that you're still handicapping yourself."

"Seems that someone is learning." Anna snorted and dismissed the Affinity levels. "The reason is because it is always good to hold something back. With Malsour and Induca, their true strength is hidden. What do I learn from fighting with all I have? I defeat my enemies fast, yes, but I don't learn anything new."

"I was wondering why you reversed the buffs on your armor," Dave said.

"What were you looking at my armor for?"

"Well, I want everyone to have the best weapons and armor possible.

I didn't know how to ask why you ruined my beautiful Magical Circuits and input your own crude code."

"It wasn't crude code!" Anna frowned.

"It was workable but it wasn't elegant, and the power wastage is annoying me to high hell. Can I at least put in a switch so that it can suppress you and then if you need it, you can turn it off or up the amount of power you have?"

"You can do that?" Anna asked.

"Sure, though I'm making Deia's twin swords first. Then the others' rings." Dave scratched his head, thinking of the other projects that he had in mind. "There just never seems to be enough time in a day or in a lifetime for all these plans."

"Okay, that would be useful," Anna grumbled.

"Good! And as a thank-you, you can go and ask Alkao out—see what the big bad Demon dude says!" Dave's goofy smile made Anna chuckle.

"Okay, if it gets you to stop pestering me, then I will!"

"Woohoo! Suzy, you owe me twenty bucks!"

"What?" Suzy looked to Dave, and got hit in the side by a Fire elemental that Induca had taken control of. It hit Suzy's Mana barrier and sent her flying across the training area.

"Made you look!" Dave laughed as her Air creations brought her back up into the air. Induca fired all manner of Fire attacks at her.

"What did you win?" Deia asked, coming up behind Dave.

"If I didn't have Touch of the Land going all the time, I might have just put a hole in the roof," Dave muttered, turning to Deia, who had a pleased smile on her face. "I just got Anna to agree to ask Alkao if he likes her and then onto a date if he says yes."

"I knew I made the right choice when I made you my fiancé. So when is your next trip to the Devil's Crater? I know that Malsour and Induca would be happy to take you there if you desire." Deia's smile was predatory, as Anna — for once — was the prey.

"Would we ever. Save my damn back from having to carry her to Devil's Crater so she can just stand there and pretend to study the craters instead of Alkao. If she looked sideways anymore, I would think that she was more rabbit than human and wolf!" Malsour said, getting an annoyed glare from Anna.

"I do not pretend to look at the Devil's Crater."

"Well, you face it while your eyes are running all over Alkao!" Induca chirped in, still fighting Suzy. The two of them flew through the air, using their powers to go head-to-head with each other.

"Well, hate to break this little meeting up, but we've got word from Dwayne. The first area is cleared in the housing complex. We're about ready to move the other fighting parties in and take on the spiders." Jules tried valiantly to hide her shiver, and failed horribly.

"What is it with fantasy worlds and spiders?" Dave groaned.

"It's pretty cliché," Suzy agreed. She and Induca gave up their fight as they lowered themselves down toward the rest of the party.

"Don't understand what is so bad about them though — just spiders." Dave shrugged and looked to Deia.

She just smiled and pat his back.

"Why do I feel like I'm missing something?" Dave leaned toward her. "They're *just* spiders." Deia continued to smile. Anna, Induca, and Malsour had either a smile or an uncomfortable look on their faces.

Deia elbowed Dave and gave him a look.

"Fine, we can go hunting, my dearest firecracker." Dave smiled.

Deia rolled her eyes and looked away as the corners of her mouth twitched upward.

"Hey you lot, heard that we're going spider hunting!" Lox said, approaching the group, a wide grin visible through his braided beard. Gurren at his side.

8

HOUSING COMPLEX

"So we've found out two things. First, the spiders are really adaptive. Once they are hit with one kind of magical attack, then they adapt outward and become resistant to it. Melee fighting will still tear them apart, though melee fighting isn't going to deal with the hordes that we're going to be facing." Josh looked out over the assembled Stone Raiders within the tower that they had turned into their base.

"Well, this sounds like it's going to be fun," Jason said.

"Dude, you're a necro. How do spiders weird you out?" Steve asked. "It's not the spiders—it's being *swarmed* by the little bastards!"

"Have you never played any zombie horde games?" Dave asked. "Well, sure, though I'm usually running away and screaming like a little girl."

Steve and Dave shared a look.

"Why the hell are you a necro?" Dave asked.

"Well, coz I want to make my enemies run away and scream like little girls, and they'll also put a barrier between me and any hordes." Jason looked at them as if the answer was obvious.

Suzy leaned over to Dave. "I know that there have been a lot of people saying that the Stone Raiders are weird. I never really paid them all that much attention until now."

"It's perfectly natural! Use what you hate the most to fight your enemies!"

"Sure it is, sure it is." Steve gently patted Jason's shoulder.

"We're going to be targeting the spider webs. We've found out that once you set fire to the webs then they change into a highly conductive material. Once we've got it in this state, we can electrify it." Josh ignored the Stone Raiders' byplay.

"How are we going to get them all? Are we going to go section by section?" Jocelyn, one of the combat mages, asked.

"No. We're going to set off massive Fire spells across the web and spread it throughout the housing complex. Once that is done, we're going to fight our way into the center of the web. Once there, we will electrify the web, zapping any of the spiders touching it, not giving them time to adapt to the lightning attacks," Josh said.

"Any and all electrical attacks must be held back until we start using them on the webs." Kim stepped forward. "All other spells can be used."

"The spider's venom can be partially cured by healing potions. The venom causes you to lose Health and Mana, and to be paralyzed. Multiple hits stack the effects. Only cure poison potions can get rid of the full effects. With the Health potion, you will stop losing Health from the poison and you will not become paralyzed, but you will continue to lose Mana. All mages will be given a supply of cure poison. Melee fighters, you'll get one extra cure poison per person. My support people will have additional cure poisons," Lucy said.

"We're going to hit with the mages first, then we're going to have them fall back behind the melee fighters once the spiders show themselves. Scouts and sneak types, you will be their bodyguards — any of the spiders getting past the melee fighters, you take them out before they get to the mages. We're going to plow through all the way to the center of the web. Support, focus on the Fire mages' buffs so that they can burn these bastards down and on the mages so that we don't get steamrolled," Josh said.

Stone Raiders started checking their gear and looking to one another. They had done this plenty of times. Now, they were just figuring out what they needed to deal with these different enemies.

"Dwayne is over there right now. We're going to rotate parties through to keep watch of the cleared-out sections of the housing complex. I want everyone good to go in two hours. Log off and log back on if you're not an E-head yet, so you get a full day of game time."

Headset VRs enforced a log-out on everyone who used them for more than eight hours. A number of aspiring entrepreneurs had made full-body VR pods that would look after a person's bodily needs and keep them in shape and good health while they played. There was no forced log-out after eight hours, but rather after weeks, where doctors would check on users before they went back into VR.

These places were populated by E-heads, but getting into a facility was expensive. The Stone Raiders, with their streams and the goods that they were selling, were able to meet the costs of these pods. Many of them were just a few feet from one another in real life.

The Stone Raiders took Josh's last words as their dismissal. Parties moved away to talk to one another and then the different groups that they would be fighting with for the raid. Others walked over to the board that showed the different positions that the forces were supposed to take, or looked at it through their linked interfaces.

"Well, I guess I'm going to take a nap." Dave stood and stretched. "That does sound nice." Deia looked to Induca and Suzy. "Please, keep it down, will you two?"

"What are you talking about? Have you heard you two going at it? I certainly have!" Induca grinned and looked at Deia.

"What are you looking at me for?" Dave complained as Deia shot him a look. "I didn't start this! Well, I don't think I did. I just want to take a damn nap!"

"You better. I swear, if you go off to one of those Dwarven conferences and spend the whole time messing around with your new projects…"

"You still get me as a comfortable body pillow." Dave smiled and pulled her close as they headed off toward their apartment.

"You think I just want you for a comfortable body pillow?"

"A good-looking body pillow?" Dave said with a roguish wink. She smacked his chest and their hands snaked together.

"Time to get up," Suzy said.

"Come on, I just fell asleep." Induca rolled over and pulled the sheets over her head to block out the light coming in from the now open curtains.

"Guild's orders, lazy butt!"

"You like my butt."

"Yeah, and the person attached to it is lazy as hell." Suzy jumped on the bed, sitting on Induca's butt.

"See, now I can't get up, even if I wanted to," Induca purred with a pleased smile.

"Up, you get." Suzy's fingers found Induca's sides.

Induca laughed and bucked, trying to get away from Suzy's terrorizing hands. Finally, she rolled Suzy over, now the one on top.

"Look, you're up." Suzy laughed.

A cruel smile passed over Induca's face as Suzy's eyes went wide. "Don't even think about it!"

"It's only fair!" Induca's fingers tickled Suzy's sides, making her squeal as it was her turn to try to get away from Induca's tickling torture.

Finally Induca gave up, pinning Suzy's hands back, and slowly kissed her bare stomach.

"We've got a raid to do," Suzy pouted, looking at Induca.

Induca pressed her thigh forward between Suzy's legs as she moved her mouth beside Suzy's ear. "That's a shame." The heat built between Induca's legs as she kissed down Suzy's neck.

"Sto-op," Suzy stuttered, her enjoyment of the moment warring with their responsibilities. Her legs and hips moved on their own, her body wanting more of Induca's attention.

"Well, now we have something to look forward to later." Induca nibbled Suzy's earlobe, her tongue flickering over her ear before she gave Suzy a quick kiss.

She rolled off the bed, now truly awake with longing in her loins as she pulled her clothes on.

"Damn, I was the one waking you up and now I want to stay in bed all day." Suzy pushed off the bed.

"Well, you've just have to find the proper way to *motivate* someone after they wake up." Induca winked and pulled her pants on.

Suzy slapped Induca's butt and then pulled it tight to her. Her hand snaked down the front of her pants; her fingers stroked through Induca's panties, finding them damp.

Induca made to return the favor.

Suzy slipped away, licking her fingers. "Seems someone is *very* awake."

Induca smiled, changing out of her sleeping shirt and stretching like a cat so that Suzy could take in the full view of her curves before she pulled on her underclothes and armor.

"I am so happy that I took this assignment from Grandmother," Induca purred, kissing Suzy.

"Who is your grandmother?"

"The Lady of Fire. She made Denur and all of the Dragons."

"So, what did she send you and Malsour here for?"

"Well, it was supposed to just be one of the Fire Dragons. I was excited to meet her daughter and I wanted to go see the world. Malsour just kind of tagged along. Mostly, because I went to sleep for so long that I'm not the strongest of the Dragons and well, he has a soft spot for me." Induca gave a wide smile as she pulled on her leather armor and cape and took out a staff she had looted.

"Her daughter? The Lady of Fire has a daughter? What would that make her? Like some kind of Demi-God?" Suzy asked. "Why are you still with us? Shouldn't you be with her?"

"Uh, well, umm, I've said more than I was supposed to." Induca realized too late what she had revealed.

"But then the only person we know who has…"

Induca could only wince as Suzy put the pieces together. *She's too smart for her own good. But I love her for it.*

"You're telling me Deia is the daughter of the Lady of Fire?" Suzy hissed, lowering her voice as if Deia could hear her from her room with Dave.

"Well, uh…" Induca scratched her head. In the end, she couldn't lie to Suzy and she had all the key points anyway. "Yeah, but you can't tell her!"

"Why not?"

"Cause Grandmother should be the one to do it. I was going to watch over her to make sure that she had good control of her gifts. Then, we became friends and all of this happened. The Lady of Fire doesn't mind, but having people know that you have a kid when the Pantheon is filled with people who would do anything in order to get some more power over you? I don't think it's exactly something she wants to broadcast to the whole world."

"But this is Deia! She deserves to know who her mother is!" Suzy hissed.

"Look, if we go to Per'ush after this, then we can set up another meeting between the two of them. I know that they met before but it wasn't the best time." Induca winced at Suzy's glare.

"They met before and the Lady of Fire didn't say anything?"

"Well, she has only loved one person, that person being Deia's father. She didn't want to draw attention to them both, especially as she knew that Deia was going off to fight at Boran-al's Citadel in just a few short weeks."

"Ugh,!" Suzy groaned, flopping onto the bed.

There was a knock at the door. "You two coming? Deia and the others are waiting for us down in the teleport room," Dave yelled through the door. "We're coming—keep your armor on!" Suzy yelled back. "After we're done here, we're going to Per'ush. Then the two of them can have a much-needed talk." Suzy looked to Induca.

"I want the same thing." Induca smiled.

"Why is this place so darned complicated?" Suzy stood up.

"Makes things more fun." Induca squeezed Suzy's hand; she gave a reassuring squeeze back as they walked to the door.

It opened before them, showing Dave flipping his conjuring rods. "Let's go clear out that final housing complex!" he declared, turning and heading for the lifts.

"Going on a raid, we're going on a raid." Dave hummed along his tune as he met up with the rest of the party. Already, the teleport pad was working, linking the city with the housing complex.

Dave smiled, seeing everyone ready. "Shall we?" Deia asked.

"After you, milady." Dave bowed and waved for her to go ahead. "Why, aren't you the most chivalrous of men?"

"Only the best for my girl." Dave walked beside her. The rest of the party followed, combining with the other parties heading through the door.

As soon as they were through the teleport pad, the atmosphere seemed to change, going from joking and playful to serious as everyone moved into their different groups, broken down by class.

"Look after yourself and remember to work on your two handed and one handed," Deia said as they moved apart for their different groups.

"I'll do my best," Dave said, being pulled in for a quick kiss.

They just looked into each other's eyes for a few moments, no words needed to express what they were feeling.

"Let's go burn some spiders." Dave smiled.

"Look after him," she said to Anna and Steve, who waited for Dave off to the side.

"Ah, he'll be fine. His head is harder than mine!" Steve grinned. "I'll do my best—you know how he is," Anna said.

"Indeed, I do. Don't make things harder for Anna!"

"Thanks for the faith," he said sarcastically, walking over to the others.

They grouped up and headed to join the front lines. Dave wasn't the best fighter, but with his passive skills and his conjuring ability, he could overcome this weakness.

The other Stone Raiders, Anna, and Deia, were looking to turn his decent fighting skills into something that could be truly terrifying.

It's good to have friends like these.

Anna was their best fighter by far. It never seemed difficult for her in a fight. Steve had all of the gadgets Dave had given him and was so big and armored that he was a moving tank.

The three of them would make the tip of the formation, with Dwayne and Esa beside them.

It wasn't long until the teleport pad to the city closed; the housing complex became darker and more foreboding.

"Let's move out!" Josh called. The Stone Raiders moved forward. Dave conjured a shield and a sword, as he looked for anything that might try to kill him. Dwayne and Esa did the same. Anna held her great sword over her shoulder while Steve deployed his left forearm shield, his axe also resting on his shoulder.

"Heigh-ho, Heigh-ho, it's off to work we go," Steve said.

"That is just offensive to Dwarves everywhere," Dave said in an offended tone.

Silence reigned for perhaps two seconds before the two of them chuckled, breaking the ominous mood of their advance somewhat.

9

FIRE AND LIGHTNING

"I'm mel-l-l-ting!" Steve said as the Fire mages blasted through the webs. Flames flew down the webs, making them shrink as they lit the housing complex. The webs closest to the Fire mages had been burned away.

They were advancing from the lowest level of the housing complex, where several teleport pads were located. They worked their way up a large hallway that had different working and living areas off to either side before they entered the housing complex proper that split off to the left and right into different living areas identical to the wing that the Stone Raiders were advancing up. The other wing's teleport pads were covered in webs already.

The center of the spider's web was located in the middle of the housing complex.

"Smartass," Dwayne coughed. "Move forward!"

"You're a massive metal man, not the freaking Abominable Snowman," Dave said.

"You say something, Dwayne?" Steve said, ignoring Dave's "facts."

"Move forward? You getting deaf in your old age, Steve?"

"Jackass," Steve coughed.

"Say something, Steve?"

"No, just an itch in my throat."

"Dude, you're a fourteen-foot-tall metal man. You don't have a throat!" Dave said.

"Ah, c'mon, Dwayne was about to believe me!" Steve complained, swinging his axe lazily as he cut through a bunch of web strands that had melted together.

The Fire mages were in the lead, Induca and Deia out front. Elementals ranged far ahead, spreading out and spraying fire everywhere. They marched through what had been webs. At first, the spiders had charged the Fire mages, being burned down in the dozens. The survivors had retreated back up their webs and hadn't shown themselves for some time.

Dave shifted the sword in his grip. The hairs on the back of his neck were straight up, as if he was being stalked by a hungry wolf.

The melee fighters walked on either side of the Fire mages, everyone watching for more of the red eyes.

Dave extended out his Touch of the Land. He could pick up a lot of the housing complex but the place was massive. The webs, heat, and all of the Stone Raiders made it hard to see where the spiders were hiding. Instead, he limited himself to focusing on the hundred meters ahead of the mages, looking for any signs of the spider horde's return.

Flames had reached the center of the web. With elementals burning everything they could, about half of the web had been set on fire. More started to burn every second. Elementals were set upon by spiders here and there.

"What you seeing?" Dwayne kept his voice low as he stood at Dave's side.

"Got a shit ton of spiders but they're…" Just then, Dave sensed something that he had thought was just a thick part of the web shifting. "I think the queen just woke up."

"Why does that not sound good at all?"

Dave didn't say anything, but continued to walk as he watched the queen and her minions.

Hundreds of spiders turned from the queen and headed for the Stone Raiders.

"They're coming," Dave said.

"Ready yourselves! Fire mages, as soon as it looks like the spiders have a resistance to your fire, pull back and start using Fire elementals if you have them! Fighters! You better be ready!" Dwayne bellowed.

"Archers, get those arrows out. Mages, remember—only use spells if you *must*. We don't want them building up resistances before we even get to the center!" Kim yelled.

"Protect the mages, boys and girls," Josh followed with after.

"You know your jobs. Jules, you're in charge of medical. Get those buffs ready. Dave, tell us when they're within a hundred meters!" Lucy called out.

"Woohoo, Human radar." Dave licked his dry lips, his words half- hearted.

"You're half Dwarf," Anna said.

"Only on my good days." Dave moved his shoulders and arms, loosening them up as he checked to make sure his hood was up.

"They're within a hundred meters!" Dave yelled out. He couldn't count all of the spiders that rushed them. His Dwarven eyes could make out their glowing red ones in the darkness.

It was enough for him to get his analyze skill working.

Mana Permeated Spider Hatchling Level 78

Mana Permeated Spider Worker Level 103

Dave was close enough to Deia and Induca that he could influence their spells. He used his Touch of the Land on their spells, using his spell formation skill to alter their attacks, making them more powerful as they focused on not only clearing out the webs but also the spiders that were now charging them from all sides. Dave didn't see it but his wrists where his tattoos lay glowed while his gray eyes lit up like twin searchlights.

The spiders announced their presence with their angry chittering to one another. The spiders were a furry and chitin covered wave as they were slowed, the living crawling over the dead. More of them learned how to resist the Fire attacks as they climbed over their fallen brothers and sisters. The spiders screamed and squealed, collapsing in on themselves like ants under a magnifying glass.

The Fire mages slowed their advance.

"Fighters, pick up the pace—cover the Fire mages!" Dwayne yelled. Dave and the others moved out around the Fire mages.

Spiders rushed toward them as the Fire mages focused on the spiders coming in from above. Spiders started to sprout arrows as the archers took aim over their heads. Others gained bolts, using the bolt throwers that Josh had bought from the Aleph and armed anyone who didn't have the skills for archery.

Dave created a spear in his right hand, expanding his shield out to cover his entire body. Shields came together to cover one another's weak spots. Buffs started strengthening the fighters, different auras covering them as the support mages went to work.

"Brace!" Dwayne's voice cut through the spiders' screams.

The spiders slammed into their shields. Their legs pulled at the shields, trying to get to those who were hiding behind them.

Dave stabbed forward with his spear; it came back with orange ichor. "Hold!" Dwayne's voice carried over the battlefield. Fire, arrows, and bolts continued to fly overhead.

Dave grunted, holding his ground. The fighters' weapons flashed forward, stabbing into the spiders' ranks.

Finally the spiders and the Stone Raider fighters came to a standstill. "Come on, Stone Raiders! Forward!" Dwayne called out.

Dave changed his spear for a sword and slammed his shield forward. With his newfound Strength, he turned two spiders into mush, cutting through two more with a swing.

His shield turned into a halberd, catching a spider trying to jump over him and tearing through them. Dave dodged to the side; his sword lashed out and caught a spider hatchling in the face, cutting it in two. His sword and halberd changed into a greatsword as he swung, cutting three spiders back.

Slowly the Stone Raiders moved forward. Here and there, spiders got through the fighters' lines, only to be dealt by those behind them.

"Send out elementals. The spider's Fire resistance is too high!" Kim's voice came over the guild chat.

The Fire attacks reduced and mages changed to their bolt throwers or bows. Those with a high enough level and the Mana left spawned Fire elementals. They sped away from the Stone Raiders, looking for any web that had not been melted into the conductive strands that the Stone Raiders' plans depended on.

"We've got bigger spiders coming!" Dave called out as he saw another wave of the spiders coming in behind the rear of the first.

"Prepare to brace!" Dwayne called out.

The fighters adjusted their stances, but kept on moving forward, cutting down anything in their path. The spiders weren't hard to kill, but their sheer numbers meant that the Stone Raiders had to work together or be overrun by them.

Dave altered his greatsword, mimicking Anna's blade. Weaker Air blades stretched from its edge, cutting into the spiders and making the floor slick with their ichor.

A Mana bolt hit Steve's shield.

"Spider mages and fighters. All over 150," Lucy called out.

"Well, this just got more interesting." Dave talked to himself as spiders started throwing mana bolts. Blue lines of mana surged across the spiders as they hit the Stone Raider's guild members at the front.

New buffs fell on the melee fighters, increasing their magical resistance.

"The Spiders have a poison in their fangs! It reduces Mana pool size and regeneration," Kim warned.

"Fighters coming in," Dave said to Dwayne.

The bigger spiders walked over their smaller brethren. These ones didn't have the simple legs of the workers and hatchlings. These ones had twin scythe legs as big as a short sword and fangs as large as daggers.

Along their weapon-like legs there were lines of Mana tracing through them and along their edges.

"Brace!" Dwayne called out. Shields slammed down; Stone Raiders looked to protect one another as their weapons continued to lash out at their eight-limbed enemies.

The Dwarves' training paid off as the Stone Raiders worked like a Dwarven shield wall, tirelessly, holding their shield wall as their swords or spears darted out to attack, the ranged Stone Raiders firing over them to slim the Spider's numbers.

The Spider's forward momentum was halted, the two forces stuck in tight quarters.

The spiders spat Mana ichor and bolts, the fighter's weapons highly effective against magical barrier and enchanted weapons, draining them of power.

"They're breaking through our barriers!" Dwayne yelled.

"We're giving you everything we've got!" Kim said through clenched teeth.

Dave felt it more than saw it as the Stone Raiders started to lose their momentum. Mana barriers failed armor and weapons dissolving as the venom made it through, reducing its durability and armor value.

"Clean the shields!" Lucy ordered. Her support people moved to do what they could to help those whose shields had been affected.

"Support the Mana barriers!" Kim yelled.

Spells were called out, coming together in a large barrier that allowed living creatures through but only attacks outward. Buffs and supporting spells were forgotten in the face of defense.

The venom hit the barrier, falling to the floor and dissolving it. "Uhh, guys, the spiders are on the roof," Steve said.

"Ranged, get those bastards!" Dwayne yelled out. Spiders that couldn't make it to the front were scuttling up the walls and moving to the ceiling, firing their Mana bolts, trying to get close enough to use their powerful venom.

Spider fighters rushed through the Mana barrier, climbing over or crushing their brethren to engage the Stone Raiders. Now they weren't spitting that much, but they were at point-blank range and could use their fangs and forward cutting legs.

"Acid and venom resistance buffs!" Lucy called out.

The Stone Raiders' armor started to bubble and melt. A few panicked, but most took the pain on instead of screwing over their friends.

"We're three-quarters of the way there!" Josh yelled.

The Stone Raiders took heart in this as the support mages buffed and healed like no tomorrow. The stealth types and scouts worked to kill the ever growing amount of spiders that leapt from the walls, and ceiling, or climbed over one another and the Stone Raider front lines. Kim's mages were openly using their attacks to make sure they wouldn't be overrun.

Dave felt the battle changing. They were no longer moving forward; they were at a standstill. They had the skill and the organization, though the numbers that the spiders had and their skill set made it near impossible.

"Josh, we need to go with Plan B and soon," Dwayne said.

Hearing those words, Dave conjured a bow with his rods, drawing and releasing arrow after arrow. It was hard to miss the spiders that seemed to crawl over every surface, charging forward without a care for their livelihood. They only cared to destroy those that had entered their territory.

"All right, Shard — your people ready?"

"Ready to go," Shard's voice said from overhead. "Tell me when you need us to move," Dwayne said. "Starting the charge," Shard said.

"Artillery spells ready!" Kim yelled.

Mages moved into groups, working together as everyone else worked to cover them and their work. Balls and runes of energy started to make the very air in the large hall they were in shimmer.

"Fighters, be ready to split!" Dwayne called out.

The Stone Raiders fighters used any buffs they had remaining, wasting their Stamina in order to keep the spiders back for just a few more seconds.

Dave felt the floor vibrate beneath his feet, as if he stood in front of heavy cavalry.

"Coming through!" Shard called out. "Split!" Dwayne yelled.

The Stone Raiders' front line pulled back to opposite sides. The spiders that had been so tightly packed before spilled out into the now open corridor, right through into the Stone Raiders' group.

They turned, ready to rip them apart from the inside.

"Fire!" At Kim's command, artillery spells that the spiders hadn't been able to build up resistances to yet drove through the opened area one after another, cleaving a path through the spiders and down the hallway.

As the last spell hit, flashes of silver and steel rushed past the Stone Raiders' front line.

Fourteen behemoths charged through the spiders with abandon. The spiders fell into the opened corridor, closing in behind the charging automatons.

"Reform!" Dwayne yelled.

Dave and Steve stepped up next to each other again. Dave watched as the behemoths used their mass and speed to crash through the spiders.

The spiders fell on the behemoths, their venom making the automaton's armor bumble and dissolve.

Dave winced as the first went down.

Another fell and then another. Spiders that Dave felt through his Touch of the Land spell left the center of the web, charging forwards. They were almost three times the size of the spider fighters.

The massive spiders slammed into behemoths, tackling them to the ground as their limbs tore into them.

Shit, our behemoths aren't going to be able to get to the center of the web. Dave thought to himself. There was nothing he or anyone else could do. There were too many spiders, they were low on Mana and Stamina. Their confidence with their other battles had made them confident and now Emerilia was showing them once again to never underestimate their enemies.

"Pull back!" Dwayne said.

The Stone Raiders did so, giving them some room to move and fight for a few seconds. The spiders filled it in and hammered on their shields within seconds.

Before the spiders seemed to attack with some kind of sense and tactics. Now, they were in a frenzy.

Stone Raiders cried out, falling to the spiders' attacks.

Some screamed as fighters tore them from their positions in the line.

The Mana barrier spell failed as the front lines turned into chaos.

The behemoths that had been taken down, ignited their Mana cores, tearing holes through the spider ranks around them.

Dave held his hands out, trying to balance himself, watching in horror as unstable Stone Raiders were taken down by tens of spiders.

"Pull from the soul gems! Pull back to the teleport pad!" Josh yelled, it was clear that they had lost this fight.

"POEs, get a move on!" Lucy barked. "To the Bat Cave!" Steve yelled.

Josh's brain seemed to short circuit before shaking his head and glaring at Steve.

"How could I resist?" Steve said, smacking spiderlings back with his axe.

The Players could come back, but the POE's weren't as lucky; they turned and ran back, thinning out the Stone Raiders.

"Queen's Knights!" A scout called out as the corridor shook, the massive spiders had taken down the last of the behemoths and now charged the Stone Raider's lines. They were so large that only three of them could fit in the hall.

"Damn bastard spat on me!" Steve yelled out as venom hit his body.

There wasn't time to reply. Everyone was using whatever spells and weapons they had to try and stave off the spiders for just a few more minutes as they pulled back towards the teleport pad.

Anna's Air blades cut lines in the ceiling, but the spiders moved so fast that she couldn't stop them.

Red traces of fire imbued arrows hit spiders, exploding on impact.

Deia's hands moving in a blur as she moved from target to target. "Lox, Gurren! Get out of here!" Deia yelled.

"We're not leaving without you!" Lox barked back, grunting as he stopped a spider knight's charge with his shield.

Gurren leaned over cutting off the spider's leg, yelling as he stabbed into its head.

"We're staying right here," Malsour said, speaking for himself and Induca, spears of metal taking a dozen spiders down from the walls.

Induca floated up, taking a deep breath, as she released it, flames rushed forth turning the walls red hot, causing the stone to crack and explode here and there with the overwhelming heat.

Knowing it was a failing argument, Deia focused on firing her arrows instead as they pulled back. The spiders didn't give them time to catch their breath as they continued to hammer on their shields, pulling them open in places and attacking the Raiders behind.

Dave stepped over Stone Raider bodies as he cut, slashed, and stabbed at the writhing mass of spiders in front of him.

"Make sure you're not touching any of the webs," Shard said. Dave checked around him.

"Big step back when Shard says so!" Dwayne said. Dave tensed himself at Shard's words.

"Jump back now!" Shard yelled to all of the Stone Raiders.

They rushed backwards, everyone making sure that they weren't touching a part of the web.

Three remaining behemoths destroyed the soul gems that supported their cores, converting it into lightning mana.

Lightning ran through the now conductive webs and rushed through the hallways, right through the spiders. Electricity arced through the webs, causing the spiders to fry from the inside out. Some even exploded and painted the walls blue.

Dave winced at the noises the spiders made as they died in the thousands.

It lasted for a few seconds but the spiders around the Stone Raiders were either stunned or dead.

"To the teleport pad!" Josh barked.

The Stone Raiders turned and ran. The behemoths hadn't even made it to the center of the web and they'd only been able to burn around twenty percent of the webbing that made up the spider's territory to make it conductive.

Spider screams cut through the halls as the facility seemed to shake with thousands of legs rushing to meet the intruders.

Dave glanced backwards. Past Steve, he could see the spider knights that had been advancing were now rushing forwards. Smoke rose from some of their bodies, but their injuries only seemed to enrage them more.

They got to the active teleport pad, rushing through as fast as possible.

Dave made it through, moving out of the path of the pad's event horizon as more people charged through.

"Make sure none of them make it through!" Lucy yelled.

Those that had made it through now faced the event horizon, watching as spiders covered the walls, floor and roof of the housing complex they had been in. They were like a living sea.

"Well that's nightmare fuel," Steve shivered.

"Come on!" One of the Stone Raiders yelled to the last members who were running with all their might for the teleport pad.

The Stone Raiders yelled out their encouragement. Ranged attackers fired spells or weapons through the teleport pad to support them.

The last three made it to the teleport pad just as a spider knight jumped through the teleport pad and into the tower, crushing one of the last Stone Raiders.

"Shut the teleport pad!" Josh yelled, spiderlings rushed in and a few fighters before the teleport closed, cutting some of the creatures in half.

"Focus on the small spiders first!" Dwayne yelled.

Using their soul gems, the mages supported the melee types as they charged forward to greet the spiders that made it into their base.

The fighting was furious and desperate. The knight's limbs hit hard enough to throw the unlucky Stone Raiders that found themselves in its path.

The fighters and Spiderlings were quickly killed off.

"Focus on the spider knight! Speed and strength debuffs!" Josh said as he appeared behind the spider, his blades cutting deep into the spider.

All of the Guild was focused on the spider knight. It was so large that hitting anything vital was hard.

Rogues and assassins flittered around behind it. Mages threw down debuffs on the spiders while healing their fellow Stone Raiders as they could.

Support pulled out fighters that had been too wounded or tossed by the Spider.

As one melee fighter was thrown or pushed down, another took their spot.

Steve cut through the spider's leg like a lumberjack cutting through a tree trunk.

The knight's eyes turned to focus on Steve as it let out a pained screech.

"Damn thing's a tank!" Dwayne yelled.

"No, you don't!" Steve barked. It was one of the few times Dave had see the large metal man being serious. The Spider Knight slammed a leg down on top of Steve.

Steve stopped the Spider's leg with his axe, his metal body groaning with strain as the floor cracked beneath him.

The spider's attention was all on Steve as more limbs came in from either side.

"Huaahhh!" Lox and Gurren yelled out, bracing themselves and their shields, stopping the twin mana imbued scythe legs that were meant to tear Steve apart.

Rage built within Dave, he was too weak to do what they were doing.

Any help he provided would be in the way.

He called on his mana reserves, draining out from his armor. With the venom and Mana bolts, he was dangerously low on Mana.

His bow came apart as he held his twin rods in his hands. He planted his feet; the engraved runes along his skin started to glow as grey circles holding runes formed in front of Dave's hands, connecting to the rods.

Another magical circle formed under his feet.

Identical magical circles formed on Gurren and Lox's shields, while a circle appeared under Steve's legs.

Through the magical circles, he boosted their Strength and Agility, reducing the strain on them.

They pushed the spider back.

The spider knight, alarmed at their small creatures ability to push it back, let out a screech of anger. Even as it was hit with different spells and weapons, Gurren, Lox and Steve had earned it's aggro.

It spat out a glob of Mana infused venom right at Gurren, Lox and Steve.

Panic and fear ran through Dave as he felt cold fear grip his body. Time seemed to slow as his higher Intelligence focused on one thing, saving his friends.

His mind was under such strain from fighting, amplifying people's spells and barriers that he wasn't sure that he could properly form a complex spell, definitely not a spell that could stop the Mana venom.

Dave let out a wordless yell as Gurren, Lox and Steve seemed to move in slow motion as they covered themselves with their shields, trying to overlap their coverage with one another.

Even facing their demise, they were protecting one another.

Mana seemed to surge through the air; it was familiar as it was powerful.

Deia's fuel air bomb! The thought raced through Dave's mind. Deia's spell ignited the air before the trio. Dave added in what weak amplification he could. Anna fed it more Air and helped direct it and Induca followed it up with another if the first didn't work.

Time seemed to come back to normal.

The first fuel air bomb spell went off; the very air in the room seemed to explode as pressure built up and release faster than Dave could comprehend.

The pressure wave of the fuel air bomb, pushed the venom back in the direction it had come from.

The second from Induca was much more focused, where the venom's forward momentum was stopped by Deia's attack, Induca's turned it into a lance, back at the spider knight.

The accelerating venom hit the knight, piercing its carapace.

It screamed out in pain. While it had made the venom it had stayed in venom sacs, never being ingested.

The Mana imbued venom tore at Mana constructs, working on a creature that had spent so much time around Mana that it had become part of its physiology; the Spider Knight's health plummeted.

Some of the Venom hit Stone Raiders, but it was nowhere as concentrated as it was before.

They moved back as the knight spasmed, hitting and killing people out of accident rather than in any kind of coordinated attack.

It took it nearly a full minute before it collapsed to the ground, its hit points finally reaching zero, speaking to its massive health pool.

Josh stabbed the creature, making sure that it was indeed dead. "Check your wounds! Badly wounded to waypoint one! Anyone poisoned or burned by venom, to waypoint two!" Jules called out. Two new waypoints appeared on the minimap as the supporting Stone Raiders looked to their guild mates.

Gurren, Lox and Steve sat down on the ground where they stood.

After a few moments, the three of them started laughing and shaking their fists in the air. They knew how close they had been to death.

Dave felt as if his guts uncoiled as he stumbled slightly. The strain of his low Stamina and Mana pool making him feel light headed and nauseous. "You good?" Dwayne looked Dave over for burns and signs of wounds.

"Good." Dave had slight cuts on his arms and legs, but nothing that was life-threatening. Dave looked over Dwayne. "You feeling okay?"

"Yeah." Dwayne shook his head. "Damn, that was one hell of a raid! Damn risky! If we didn't have those behemoths, I don't know if we could have held off all those spiders."

Dave tapped him on the shoulder. "I don't see any wounds — you're good. Yeah." Dave hooked his rods onto his hips and pulled his hood down. He was covered in sweat, his arms heavy from the constant fighting. "If the rest of the spiders got here, we would have been fucked."

"There were more of them?" Dwayne asked.

"This was just the tip of the iceberg." Dave waved to the spiders that filled the control room and the housing complex that had been on the other side of the teleport pad.

"How many more were there?" Dwayne's voice dropped so no one else could hear.

"You don't want to know." Dave shook his head to try to forget the number of spiders that littered the housing complex's hallways.

"Do you have any ideas of how to deal with them?" Dwayne asked. Dave thought about it for a moment, looking at the spider knight. "Smoke them out," Dave said seriously, looking to Dwayne.

"Dave, honey how are you?' Deia asked, moving to Dave's side to check him over.

"I'm fine, are you okay," Dave said, studying her for injuries.

"I'm okay," Deia said with a weak smile; it was clear that the Spiders had put the love of creepy crawlies into her.

"Quick thinking with that spell," Dave said.

"I didn't know if I could make it work," Deia admitted, running a shaky hand through her hair.

"It was a close call," Dwayne agreed looking around at everyone. Stone Raiders were sprawled over the ground; wounded were being carried to the different waypoints as others recovered from their ordeal.

"If we can help it, I don't want to have to go into that housing complex again. If you figure out someway to clear out those spiders, let me know. I'm going to check on if anyone got perm'd," Dwayne said, his tone sad.

Perm'd was a term that the Stone Raiders used when talking about POEs that died. Unlike the Players, there was no coming back from death for them.

Dave and Deia nodded to Dwayne, not jealous of his job. He wandered away.

Dave put an arm around Deia, the two of them looking over the battlefield that the control room had turned into.

If Deia and the rest of Party Zero wasn't there, then Gurren, Lox and Steve might not have made it. I've been focused on increasing my own strength to protect everyone instead of realizing their strengths.

Josh sat down heavily, looking to his lieutenants and Dave.

He hadn't washed since going to the Housing Complex filled with spiders.

With the information that they had gathered, they hadn't thought that they would fight such a tenacious and powerful enemy.

Five Stone Raider POEs had been perm'd, with several more which had been seriously injured but had been saved by the healers. Twenty three Players had also needed to respawn.

Even though they're just NPC's, its hard to think of them that way. I talked to them, saw them in the halls, fought beside them and they followed me. Now their code is gone forever and I can't get them back.

Josh let out a heavy sigh. In other games, he had seen NPCs under his command. In those games, they had been two dimensional characters that he saw as nothing more than resources to be used. Just like gold or weapons.

In Emerilia, thinking of them as NPCs just didn't make sense. They were POE, the sentient forces of the game.

"Dwayne said that you have a plan Dave?" Josh asked, trying to distract himself.

"I think so," Dave said seriously. "Okay, what is it?" Josh asked.

"I can enchant a bunch of items that we can chuck into the Housing complex. They'll be enchanted with fire circuits. They'll burn up all the energy in them, creating flames that will use the air in the Housing complex to fuel them," Dave said.

"Burn all the oxygen up and they have nothing to breathe," Kim said with a nod. Even her normally playful mood was subdued by their recent losses.

So close to the end, it hurt to lose people.

"Lucy, see that Dave has everything he needs. We'll try it out. I don't want anyone going to that Housing Complex. There are just too many powerful and high level creatures there," Josh looked around, his people agreed with his assessment.

"Dave, let me know when you've got something that works," Josh said.

"Will do," Dave agreed.

Dave wiped his brow, looking at the half dozen fire bombs. "Well that was fun," He muttered to himself.

Deia snorted, shaking her head.

"Yes, playing around with pieces of metal that have been magically coded to burn up as much oxygen as possible is always an exciting time."

They had been working together, Deia showing Dave different magical spells, layering them so that they could figure out the best way to burn up the oxygen in the housing complex. Once they found the right spells, Dave had memorized them, playing around with magical coding to get the required effects.

Deia had watched; with her intimate knowledge of Fire, she was able to troubleshoot issues easily.

She could also control the Fire coming off of the metal plates so that it didn't melt Dave' workbench or take his head off.

"Tell that to my eyebrows," Dave muttered, waggling them at Deia.

She giggled at the odd sight. With his regenerative abilities, they were coming back, but they were just two black lines of fuzz right now.

Kim wandered into the room that Dave had claimed as his workshop, mostly because it was the furthest place from the tower that the Stone Raiders were staying in.

"I heard that you were done with the bombs," Kim said.

"Yep!" Dave gestured to the bombs. They weren't pretty, each was simply a large metal plate with runes engraved on it, attached to a greater soul gem.

Kim looked over the plates.

"You sure this is going to work?" Kim asked.

"Well unless they don't breathe oxygen to live, I'm pretty sure it'll work," Dave said.

"Well, worth a try in my books!" Kim smiled. "The others are waiting at the teleport pad."

"I'll just bag them up," Dave said, grabbing the six plates and throwing them into his bag.

They jogged to the tower. There was a somber air in the tower. Losing a battle when they had been so close to winning grated on everyone's nerves. Other guilds might have people leaving the raid in frustration. The Stone Raiders instead redoubled their efforts.

All of them were armed and armored. As Dave made it into the control room, ranged attackers were on the second floor, watching the teleport pad with mages behind them. On the bottom floor melee types formed lines, ready for whatever might come through the teleport pad.

"Steve, going to need that arm of yours," Dave said.

"Knew you liked me for more than my good looks," Steve said, doing some flexing poses even though his metal body didn't change at all.

"Okay, everyone ready?" Josh asked, looking out over the assembled Stone Raiders.

"Connect us!" Josh said.

Dave stood beside Steve, pulling out a fire bomb.

"I'll hand them to you, you just need to get them on the other side of the teleport pad," Dave said.

"Can do!" Steve said, taking the fire bomb. Dave had conjured a trigger into the fire bombs, as soon as he destroyed the conjuration then the fire bomb would go off.

The teleport pad activated.

Spiders that had been standing on the opposite teleport pad were torn apart, others fell in.

They looked around in shock, mana lines covering their bodies flaring in anger as mages and archers let loose.

Steve hurled the fire bomb, just as it was about to clear the teleport pad, it hit a spider Fighter that was charging through.

Dave passed him another fire bomb, this one being grabbed out of the air by a spiderling that rushed forwards "Come on," Dave muttered, passing another to Steve, seeing two spider knights rushing for the teleport pad.

The third sailed through the spiders that were now coming in from every direction, covering the floor, roof and walls of the teleport pad like some black and blue lined plague.

Dave activated the fire bomb.

It flared to life. It was so hot that it passed through a spiderling, cauterizing the wounds as it passed.

The ground around it blackened in seconds as flames erupted around the bomb.

Spiders rushed away from the out of control fire bomb. With most spells and magically coded constructs, they had something to manage the power output and the elements used.

Dave had removed the part of the magical code that would synthesize oxygen, turning the spells to pure heat and fuel as well as the controlling part of the spell turned enchanted metal plate.

In seconds, the area around it was hundreds of degrees, burning out its soul gem as fast as possible, giving about five minutes when activated.

Steve grabbed and threw the remaining three, all of them making it into the housing complex.

The stream of spiders abruptly stopped, just being within a few hundred meters was enough to burn the spiders.

They started running away, trying to escape the heat and the carbon monoxide.

The Stone Raiders let out a ragged cheer as they finished off the spiders that had made it through the teleport pad.

The remaining fire bombs that didn't make it into the housing complex were grabbed and thrown through the teleport pad's event horizon.

"The best spider is a crispy one!" Josh yelled, the Stone Raiders yelling their agreement.

"Shut down the teleport pad," Josh signaled to the controllers.

The six fire bombs made the other side of the teleport pad look like the inside of an oven; anything that was remotely combustible within a few hundred meters was burning.

"Damn, there's probably some decent loot in there," One of the Stone Raiders complained.

"Think about that experience, I'm nearly level two hundred I could get a new class," Another complained.

"You're welcome to try it, though its going to be a damn oven in there. I sure as hell don't want to fight all those things on their home turf," Dave said.

The two made to argue but they closed their mouths instead. Even if they had got all of that loot and experience, they could have been fighting for days. There was simply too many of those spiders.

10

IN SEATS
OF POWER

"The Queen Mendari Selhi has arrived!" a servant told Magistrate Houn, who had been at her office table, reviewing the documents that lay on it.

"What? Why was there no word? I thought that we were just changing over the military command of the soldiers here?" Houn said.

The servant didn't answer as Houn slammed her papers down.

"Tell the rest of the staff. Send word to the advisors, nobles, military officers and get me the captains of the guard now!" Houn said. There was nothing to do, but try to make the best of an already bad situation.

"Yes Magistrate!" The servant hurried off as Houn looked herself over in a mirror. She tried to make herself look as presentable as possible.

Why is the queen here? Without any announcement or anyone warning me of it? Houn's fears played in her mind as she quickly left her offices and moved to the front of her residence. She could see over the city and the snaking procession of soldiers, officers, their beasts and supply wagons heading into Selhi.

It was only forty minutes later when the queen of Selhi stepped out of her carriage. She was a symbol of beauty and power. The queen of Selhi was a brilliant lady and one of the few female leaders on Emerilia who had gained if not the respect, the fear of the men around her.

"My Queen." Houn bowed deeply in front of her queen. Her personal guard saluted their monarch. Advisors and nobles had flocked to the castle in order to greet the queen properly. They all bowed behind their magistrate. "Rise. We have much to discuss. Take me to your offices." The queen walked past Houn. Her royal guard moved in around her, their ebony and gold armor shining in the sun.

Houn shuddered at the auras of the queen's personal guard.

The nobles parted before their queen. Sensing the tense atmosphere, they kept their tongues instead of trying to increase their station through pleasantries and compliments.

Houn followed the queen, an uneasy feeling in her stomach as she felt like a stranger in her own home.

Everywhere they went, the staff bowed to the queen. She paid them no attention as she drifted through the halls, finally entering the magistrate's office. Two guards stayed outside; the rest moved inside. Four checked the room over quickly, one clearly a mage. With a nod to their queen, all but two left. The queen sat in the magistrate's chair, dominating the room with her presence. Her two guards stood at ease in front of the desk.

"Sit." There was no denying the command or the anger in the queen's voice.

Houn's stomach plummeted as she did as commanded. The tense silence spread out as the queen stared at Houn, a dark frown on her face. Houn averted her eyes as cold sweat broke out across her back.

Finally Queen Mendari Selhi shook her head and rubbed her temples. "You've made a right fine mess, Houn."

Houn didn't dare to respond and waited for the queen to go on. Houn's mind worked to try to figure out what the queen was talking about.

"When I made you the magistrate of the capital, it was with my expressed writ as I took up my seat in Veloria. I trusted you to do what was not only in the best interests of this city but for all of Selhi. When the assassination guild PKP started a war in our city against the Stone Raiders, the Stone Raiders worked to fight against them and with your guards. The destruction was great, but the PKP were killed or driven from the city. You saw the Stone Raiders as being weak, having just been in a battle, and looked to blame them for the battle. As they were the only one of the two groups that were here, you used them to hold the blame of defending themselves. They had to flee the capital with you ordering the army to hunt them down and kill them within a few weeks. Then they disappeared into thin air. What do you think that makes Selhi look like?" The queen's voice was conversational, almost curious sounding, but Houn could hear the cold steel in her tone.

"It would not look good." Houn kept her eyes averted.

"It makes us look like backstabbing, disrespectful cowards who are looking for a scapegoat even if they are a potential ally!" the queen erupted, fire in her eyes as she slammed her fist down on Houn's desk.

Houn jumped and sat back in her seat. "Look at me, Houn!" Mendari demanded. Houn met her queen's gaze.

"They were the victims. They didn't have to protect our people, yet they did. They were even aiding in fixing our homes, then you ran them out of the city like savages. The MOST POWERFUL PLAYER GUILD ON EMERILIA!" The queen took a moment to get her composure back. "The same guild that just added the Exdar's Traders to their ranks, the very traders who have the ear of the Arch Mage himself, as well as the royal court of Gudalo. The ones who are refusing to sell or buy anything from Selhi and have a trade agreement with the Dwarven mountains!"

Houn paled and squeezed her hands in her lap, so that they didn't tremble in the open.

"No one knows where the Stone Raiders are, but what is for damn sure is that they have not been idle. While they were gone, they have built a guild—the kind that has not been seen this early on in a Player cycle. They are becoming a cornerstone guild."

Cornerstone guilds were the kinds of guilds that all others were compared to. They were either the strongest or the oldest of the Player guilds that rose at one time or another. It usually took nearly three years for these guilds to start forming.

"I sent you here to keep the snakes here sated, so that I could focus on Veloria. Now, I see that it looks like you've become one of the snakes. Guilds started staying away from us after you chased the Stone Raiders down. It would have been bad enough to use the city guard, but you used *my* troops. Turning it from a simple issue between a town and a guild to an issue between a guild and Selhi." The queen sat back in her chair.

"I'm sorry. I never meant for things to turn out this way. I was hoping to use their items to allay the costs of the damages," Houn said.

"Players are a resource in and of themselves. They can go out and do the seasonal monster hunts, so that we don't lose people to them. They can come back from death, while our people can't. I would give them Selhi Capital if they were to do the monster hunts and keep our people safe! Our people are our greatest resource, not our money." Queen Mendari Selhi deflated, a tired expression on her face.

"I hoped that you would have been able to deal with Selhi Capital in my stead. I take from you all your responsibilities, lands, and titles as given to you by the crown. Do you understand this?" The queen's voice was calm and cold as she passed down the sentencing.

Houn heard the sadness in her queen and old friend's voice, which hurt her more than her cold tone. "I understand," Houn almost whispered, holding her head in shame.

Fire's head snapped upward as she felt an aura she would know anywhere. It was calming and gentle, much like a small Fire to keep away the chill of the night.

"And can turn into a raging inferno in a second." She smiled and sat back in her chair.

There were thousands of auras all over the mage's college campus. The strength of the mages there were the highest in all of Emerilia. They came from all walks of life and all different places. Most hid their auras, so that they wouldn't stifle the students.

An aura could be a terrifying thing to someone who didn't know what they were dealing with. Most of the third-year students of the guild gained the ability of aura detection and everyone was trained in the art of aura suppression.

To gain the skill, you needed to be around people over level 150 who had a strong aura, something that was a daily occurrence at the college.

Fire pinpointed the location of the aura. She pulled out a scroll and placed her hand on it.

Her eyes shone with blue Fire as she stopped looking inside her office, instead finding herself looking through one of the thousands of mage lights. A melancholic smile spread over her face as she looked at a face she saw every time she went to sleep.

"What are you doing here, Mal?" she said to herself, changing to another mage light as Mal walked into an ornate office.

"Hello, I am Oson'Mal, here to see Arch Mage Jelanos."

"Do you have an appointment?" the secretary asked.

"No, sorry. I was off wandering and I didn't send him a message. You know how he is if I give him a reminder. With all the Merpeople, I didn't send one to Alamos either. Thought it would be best to make it a surprise." Mal smiled.

The secretary smiled back, enamored by Mal's smile. Fire's eyes thinned as she glowered at Mal and the secretary, who was slightly blushing.

"Well, I can send them a message," the secretary said.

"Would it be okay if I surprised them?" Mal pulled a sigil from a pouch on his hip and passed it to the secretary.

Her eyes flashed green with her mage sight, a shocked expression on her face as she looked at Oson'Mal.

Fire giggled to herself. *He doesn't look over thirty, but to have that sigil he must be a few hundred years old. Ah, loved playing that trick on everyone we met.*

"Certainly. I will tell them that someone is meeting with them. It's just Jelanos and Alamos in there." The secretary handed back the medallion.

Their fingers touched, the secretary's cheeks reddening as Mal smiled. "Thank you." He turned and headed for the door. Mal knocked on the door. As he walked in, Fire changed to one of the lights in the room. Jelanos looked at it for a moment before he looked to the door.

"Come in," Jelanos said, trying to look official, knowing that the Lady of Fire was watching the meeting.

I'm going to have to figure out a way to do this spell without him figuring out where I am. Fire sighed as Mal walked in the door.

"Mal?" Alamos asked as Jelanos leaned forward and squinted at the Elf.

"Hey Al, Jel. What you old bastards up to?" Mal grinned, greeting his old adventuring friends.

"Ah! You should have told us you were coming, you pointy-eared mutt!" Jel said. All sense of decorum he was trying to establish was gone as he wrapped Mal up in a hug.

"Are you sure you're the Arch Mage? Looks like you just escaped from the damned fighting pits of Akapore!" Mal laughed.

Jelanos set him down after a few moments. "You look good!" Jel declared.

"Friggin' Elves." Alamos shook his head before he snorted and shook Mal's hand vigorously. "So, what brings you to our humble abode? Last we heard, you were off in the Kufo'tel forest with your daughter. Where is she?"

"Humble abode? You're living on nearly fifty islands. Your memory really is going, or could it be your sight?" Mal laughed.

"Hey, listen here, you ornery old bastard, you've got to be like two hundred years older than us!" Alamos said.

"Jenny, could you see if we could get some food sent up?" Jelanos asked, sticking his head out of the office door.

"Yes, Arch Mage." She nodded and opened her interface. Jelanos shut the door and sealed it with magic.

The three old friends sat down, relaxing as they talked about times of old. Fire watched, smiling and laughing at the tales. Fire heard tales from the time when she had lived with their party—from escaping Earth trolls by jumping into the Efadel rapids or trying to run out of a haunted crypt with a master phantom chasing them and Alamos got a cramp, so they had to carry him, throwing him out of the crypt's entrance as Fire had set off an explosion behind them, sending them cartwheeling through the air, collapsing part of the crypt and blasting the phantasm in the face with pure sunlight, killing it.

It was a number of hours later when they stopped talking about their stories, a pile of sandwich remains to the side of Jelanos's large desk.

"So, you looking to get the band back together?" Jelanos looked to Mal.

"I'm here to learn as well as catch up with a few people." Fire swore that Mal's eyes flickered to the mage light she was looking through.

"Learn? You're one of the strongest Fire mages I have ever seen anywhere. To this day," Alamos said.

"I remember a time when you would have made a sexual joke out of that instead." Mal sighed.

"Melanie made me stop doing that when I had my first kids." Alamos sighed.

"Been beaten out of him." Jelanos wiped an unseen tear. "I have to go down to the magical arena to just live the old days now, though they're nowhere near as inventive as our dear Alamos."

"For a man who doesn't swear, he is rather good at getting the point over regardless," Mal mused.

"I wasn't *that* bad." Alamos looked to the two of them. "Right?"

"Remember Lord Fontane? Or that knight from that Ashal kingdom who tried to attack the Dwarves? Hell, that Dwarven king of the Xendur Mountains?" Mal asked.

"The look on his face when he realized it was the king of the mountain range!" Jelanos slapped his desk, laughing. "I thought you'd shit yourself! Damn, everyone shut the hell up, just in awe of your abilities. Thought we were dead for sure. No Mana left, tired, and just finished fighting off hobgoblins and a troll infestation!"

Mal was laughing too. "Then you remember what the king said?" Mal said, having trouble with the words.

Neither Jelanos nor Mal were able to speak coherently as a smile crossed Alamos's face.

"Well, slap me sideways and call me a hobgoblin. If that ain't the finest chirping I have ever received! This lot can't even put two words together—like you can string a whole sentence. Lads—we're going DRINKING!" Alamos couldn't help himself, laughing with his two friends.

It took some time before they all calmed down. "God, I miss the old days." Mal wiped tears away. "Don't we all," Alamos said.

"So, what you looking to learn and what do you have to trade?" Jelanos asked.

"More Fire magic. I offer information and applicants," Mal said. "What information?" Jelanos opened his desk to try to find his pipe. "Information about the coming wars," Mal said.

Jelanos and Alamos looked to Mal quizzically.

"Which wars?" Alamos asked. The mage's guild and college did not get involved in wars. Members were allowed to do as they wished in defending their homes, but they were not to involve the college or guild in any way. The one thing that the mage's guild did do was put a stop to war crimes: killing innocents, treating those who have surrendered outside of the laws that had been passed down. The mage's guild kept all of the kingdoms and fighting groups of Emerilia in check.

Mal opened up his private chat; the other two opened up their own interfaces to accept it. They talked among themselves. No words came from their mouths and Fire was unable to read their lips.

She waited, watching their facial expressions.

Alamos and Jelanos looked to each other. Their faces ranged from shock and confusion to regret, then determination and finally resolve.

It was awhile before they canceled the private chat.

"I believe it is time that we ran readiness checks on the battle mages and those contracted with the guilds. Many of these forces are already in Emerilia and we must be ready to deal with them when they surface. The next three years are going to be hell," Alamos said.

"It shocks the mind, but we must be prepared and vigilant. Very well, you may peruse our libraries as you desire and attend classes. Would you be interested in a teaching position?" Jelanos asked, his demeanor brisk and business-like, a side that few rarely saw.

"I will think about it. I'm not sure about teaching. I like being in the field a lot more. I have a number of students who would do well to substitute for me. I've spent too long hiding away in my forest. Now, it's time to fight for my home and protect my daughter's future," Mal said.

Fire didn't need to imagine anything as Mal looked directly at the mage light that was on the wall.

Damn, he has gotten stronger if he's able to know that I'm spying on him. I can't leave right now. There's too much at stake for me to get away. Guilt followed Fire's thoughts.

Why am I always running away from him when I see him? Fire felt a wave of sadness. *What must he think of me as I just continue to run away? It would be nice to see him in person again.*

11

ENVOY

"Dave?" Shard appeared as Dave put down a smoking destruction staff. "Holy! Damn, dude! Think I just blew a heart valve, scared the hell out of me!" Dave held his chest.

"Seems that people can still sneak up on you," Shard said with some pride. Since Dave had his Touch of the Land, no one had been able to truly sneak up on him.

"Just you, Shard. Have you been testing out the applications of that graphite? Damn stuff is pretty useful back on Earth." Dave slumped into a chair, pulling out a waterskin and drinking from it.

"I have. The material is indeed interesting. I even applied it to the soul gem projects. I have high hopes." Shard's excitement was getting ahead of him.

"Going to need to boost the power output by like forty percent if my next plan works out." Dave's eyes shone as he thought of the applications of the new metals and discoveries.

"What are you thinking of making?" Shard couldn't help himself. "Some true artillery. It takes too long for it right now. So complicated with all the chanting and then the Mana distribution. Going to speed it some. Taking an idea from the Dwarves and my own armor."

"Before we get sidetracked even more, there was another reason that I was here." Shard sat across from Dave.

"Okay," Dave said, feeling the atmosphere tense between them.

Shard didn't say anything for a while, as if not knowing how to put his thoughts into words.

"Will you spit it out? You look like dial-up. All we need now is that annoying ass tone and I'd swear you were crashing."

"What's dial-up?" Shard asked.

"I don't think that is the reason you're here."

"Ah, no, it's not. I am here to extend an invitation from the Aleph Council. They wish to show their gratitude to the Stone Raiders for all that you have done and extend their hand in friendship." Shard studied Dave's reactions.

"Well, you know that Josh, ah, no, probably Lucy is the person you should be talking to?"

"I know that, but I wanted to field the idea to you first. You have a lot of sway within the guild and I wanted to know your thoughts on it," Shard said.

"Huh, well, personally, I like the idea. The Aleph are powerful allies to have. Just for the trade opportunities. My first question would be to ask if the Aleph are going to reveal their return to the rest of Emerilia." It was Dave's turn to look at Shard, who seemed to be a statue except for the blinking eyes.

"Well, remind me to never play poker with you. If the Aleph want to stay in the dark, which I think would be their best option, I know that the Stone Raiders would be happy to help out, being sent on different quests to help your people. More quests, more fun. We're already hoping to set the same thing up with those living in Devil's Crater. That way, your people can gain strength. We get resources, show our friendship, and grow together. If you do choose to come out and show yourselves, then the Stone Raiders would also reap benefits for being the people to aid yours. It will show that we are the guild that different POE kingdoms and empires want working for them. Other Players will want to join up like no tomorrow and we can show the pesky other guilds who think they are as strong as us their place."

"Interesting. What would you like to be the reward for helping the Aleph?" Shard asked.

"Going with the easy questions, huh?" Dave chuckled and ran his hand through his hair. Dave thought for some long minutes before he stared into Shard's eyes.

"Friendship with the Aleph," Dave said, thinking back on all the agreements and alliances that the Stone Raiders had made with those they had helped out with various raids. There was always a clause for the Stone Raiders and the other party to help each other, to open trade and teleport pads between the two.

"Want to read all of our books, do you?" Shard teased with a small smile.

"While I do want to read your books, I am only halfway through that apprentice book on portals yet. Damn, those things are hard to make!" Dave shook his head.

"You are crossing possible light-years of distance through them," Shard pointed out.

"Well, yeah, but books are not the reason I would like your friendship. Friendship has to be earned between two people, yet it is one of the strongest bonds that people have. Family you are born into. If you are lucky, your family will be awesome and it will feel like they are your friends. Friends are the people who have stood by your side, know the most about you and they're still willing to deal with you. Friends are there for one another no matter what. I can get all the materials and items that I want through hard work. The possibility of becoming friends, or at least the mutual trust between the Aleph and the Stone Raiders, so that we might become friends in the future—if all we get is that opportunity, then I would say it was worth it."

"That was not the answer I was expecting," Shard said.

"Plus with all the stuff we've sold off, we're rich as hell." Dave laughed.

"I now see why Deia always calls you a smartass." Shard's dry tone made Dave laugh more.

"Get used to it. He might be smart as all hell, but sometimes he acts like a right dolt." Suzy walked into the forge, hearing the tail end of their conversation.

"So, how is the staff?" Suzy looked to Dave.

"It's cooling!" Dave whined, as if sensing that he would need to do more work.

"So, want to tell me what this staff is going to do?" Suzy asked.

Dave tried to pout, but his excitement won through. He stood and clapped his hands together.

"So, this thing is a bit experimental," he started, moving to where the staff lay on a workbench. Every one of the nine main materials, as well as veins of others that had been "discovered," twisted together to form a grip around a sphere. Each face of the sphere was made from a different chemical.

"What I did was gather every element from the periodic table and contain them into the top of the staff. That way you'll have a greater resonance with any of your creations down to the elemental level."

"There's so many sides to that damned thing it's almost a sphere." Suzy studied it.

"Yes, well, my thought is that with every single element known to humanity that you will be able to create items from all manner of substances—from ice to sand, to helium and radon—each contained within a non-reactive crystal matrix."

"You've got radon in there?" Suzy stepped away in alarm. "Well, it's an element." Dave shrugged.

"And it's radioactive!"

"What is radioactive?" Shard asked, confused.

"Don't worry—it's all contained. Trust me, I checked with my Touch of the Land. Even if you were poisoned, a bit of healing magic or just respawning and you'd be good." Dave shrugged, ignoring Shard's question. "I don't want to have to get myself killed just because your staff poisoned me," Suzy growled.

"Hmm, do you think it would be possible to harness pure radioactive isotopes and convert them into Mana? Just like they do with the coal in the city power stations?" Dave said out loud.

"Math and numbers here, not chemical reactions." Suzy raised her hands up in surrender. Shard and she shared a look before she looked back at Dave, who was in full thought fugue.

"Hmm, definitely something to think on. Imagine if you were able to store all the power from a kilogram of radioactive isotope. Could be completely clean as you're taking all the available power from it."

"Dave, staff," Suzy reminded him.

"Ah, yes, sorry, another experiment, I think." Dave shook his head, looking back to the staff. "Okay, so, we've got the major materials throughout the rest of the staff as well as magical coding. Everything that is included in this staff you will have greater control over. We've also got a boost in Willpower and your range will be extended. I've added in a last resort phase as well. Only activate it if *absolutely* necessary. So, that this staff won't explode the soul gems that are inside it, it will only release a charge as it is used. The staff doesn't hold the charge like other weapons but leeches it. If it didn't leech, then it'd turn into one big ole bomb. I'll tell you how to change things so you can do that." Dave laughed to himself. "Guess there are *two* last resorts with this thing. So, anyway, the one that doesn't blow up in your face. Well, shouldn't. It will cast the control orb up into the sky, acting kind of like a signal booster. Your range will increase dramatically. The fail-safes will be removed and your control over your creations will soar. You will need to have a high amount of soul power stored in your armor to use this, or else it will be wasted. You might die from the feedback of it all, though with respawn that isn't too bad. If you do somehow survive, you're going to be out for days with your body messed up."

"So, if I use this then I'm going to increase in power a lot and I will hopefully die afterward, so that I'm not useless for a few days," Suzy said. "I still don't understand how you Players talk about this all so easily.

Dying seems to just be a reason to use some kinds of magic that no one should dive into." Shard sighed.

"Well, it's an advantage that I'm willing to use every damn time. Suzy will possibly double or triple her power if she uses that last resort on her staff."

"Have you named it?" Suzy asked.

"Yep! Everything has to have a name. Don't worry, you'll find something to name in the future." Dave smiled.

Suzy rolled her eyes. "Well, what is it?"

"Staff of Hecate."

"Huh, well, it isn't horrible." Suzy looked at the staff.

"I must be going. I will talk to you later. If you could keep our conversation to yourself?"

"I will, but all of the Stone Raiders know that they're back."

"How?" Shard frowned.

"Bob told me and then I told everyone else. With us, it's best that everyone knows what's going on around them. The more information we have, the less blind we are going into different situations."

"This is interesting, but I will still ask you keep our conversation a secret."

"You have my word. Just tell them to hurry up and make a decision. Also, any help we could get for the college would be appreciated. I am not looking forward to going up against that Lich and his creatures." Dave shuddered.

"I will try to have an answer as soon as possible." Shard nodded. "See ya, Shard." Suzy waved as Shard disappeared.

"So, you going to pick it up or just stare at it?" Dave looked at the staff.

"Fine." Suzy picked up the staff. A screen appeared in front of her; her eyes widened as she read the screen. Dave smiled, knowing what it said.

Staff of Hecate
Forged by Dave Grahslagg, this item has been made for his dear sister, Suzy. With it, the very gods themselves shall fear her wrath and accept her judgment. **Quality:** S **Abilities:** Increased command of all elements making up the staff (+10%) Increased range of Creations (+20%) Wielder's Willpower increased (+15%) Grows in power through use. Summoner's Bastille **Charge:** 100,000/100,000 **Durability:** 314/314

"Damn." Suzy looked at the staff with new eyes. "Only the best for you." Dave smiled.

"I'm your sister now?" Suzy laughed.

"Ah, no one I'd rather have." Dave winked.

"Well, thank you, big brother." She smiled, her eyes becoming misty.

Dave wrapped her up in a hug and pat her back as she cried. "Quiet down, you—making me all misty-eyed."

Suzy just laughed before she broke the hug, the two of them wiping their tears away.

"Now, go, and show off to Induca. I still have Deia's blades to work on and then the Dracul's ornaments." Dave waved her toward the teleport pad out of the forge.

"Don't overwork yourself!" Suzy glared. "I wouldn't dare."

"You always say that and you always do way too much work. You've got two hours, then I'll send Deia down to pull you out of your workshop," Suzy said.

"Spoilsport," Dave muttered.

"Got to look out for my idiot bro." She laughed and walked away. Dave smiled. Despite all they bugged each other, he truly did love Suzy. He would do anything to protect his little sister. The staff had only put into words what they had both been thinking for years.

Dave pulled metals out of his bag as he accessed his notepad for the sketches he'd pulled together. "Now, better get Deia's blades done first. Malsour and Induca are crazy assed powerful as it is."

Ever since the reversal of the raid in the housing Complex, Dave had been striving to do everything in his power to increase the strength of his party.

He wasn't alone and he could rely on their strength as well as his own. A notification popped up in his vision.

Quest: Aleph Homecoming
You have cleared an Aleph Housing Complex.
Rewards: Increase all power and resources gained by 5%.
205,000 EXP
Increased standing with Aleph people

Level 114
You have reached level 114; you have **516** stat points to use.

Dave breathed a sigh of relief, they had been throwing fire bombs into the teleport pad for a few days. After their recent losses, they had agreed to take some time off between the next raid.

With the spiders dealt with, they could focus on the next job they had. Other than the repairs on various facilities, that the automatons could mostly fix, except for the portal factory, there was only one location they needed to clear of mobs.

The Aleph College and the undead that walked through the mini-city.

12

FACE OF
THE ENEMY

Alkao glided down onto the rise that Krenua had secured.

"I hate flying in trees," Vrexu said as they moved through the forest and up the rise, staying low. Their guards watched for any possible threat.

"Better than alerting our twisted descendants that we're here." Alkao knelt in the muck and took his time through the forest. He dropped down to his stomach as he found Krenua past the forest and up a steep incline, lying on his stomach and watching something intently.

Before, Alkao would have never knelt, let alone crawled; doing so was seen as a sign of weakness. Now, his Demons didn't give a second glance as they were doing the same. They took their time in reaching Krenua and his second.

The second moved over to Vrexu as Alkao moved up next to Krenua. "Well, looks like we're in the right place." Alkao saw signs of destruction in the distance. Wisps of smoke rose up into the air, thousands of fires set ablaze. Krenua handed him a pair of binoculars. Alkao used them and his natural eyesight to look into the ragtag camp.

Demons of all kinds lay around — fighting, dying, eating, sleeping, and copulating. They were pure savages. Alkao watched as one leaped straight through a five-meter-tall bonfire to tear at the

Demon on the other side with their claws and teeth. Strength was the only thing that was respected in the camp. The scent of death and blood drifted on the wind.

"Your commands?" Krenua asked.

"Gather some of their dead. See what has been done to them. Strengths, weaknesses—see if we can bring them to our side." Alkao lowered the binoculars. "Bring the most intact bodies to the crater for the healers and others to have a look."

"Yes, my prince," Krenua said.

"We either bring them into the fold or destroy them before they have a chance to harm our people. Vrexu, I want you to drive the creatures in the area away. The more things they have to kill, the stronger they will become. After we drive the beasts of the area out, they will only have one another to kill. Have scouts watch them and pick out their strongest. No direct action except picking off the stragglers tomorrow and bringing them to be examined. As Malsour says, the battle starts well before we meet our enemies in combat. When we fight, it is just the end of our battle. This here, the information we gather, will allow us to cripple them before they ever reach our home. It's time we put our training to use." Alkao looked to the leaders of Vrexu's battalion. Multiple races of Demon and Beast Kin looked back at him, united in their one duty: defend those they loved and cared about—defend Devil's Crater.

Alkao nodded to them, accepting those hard gazes.

Each had seen blood spilt and looked death in the eye on multiple battlefields. United and with their training, Alkao was secure in the thought that they knew what they were doing.

He shimmied back down the rise, his guards and officers following him. Alkao grabbed one of the Beast Kin; the other Demons grabbed their fellow Beast Kin or wingless Demons. Their wings pulled them into the air as they moved toward Devil's Crater at their best speed.

Hamdir and the rest of the council sat in thought of Shard's words. The session was a closed one. The council had a meal as they discussed the future. Lately the council's work had taken up most of their time.

"The possibility of friendship," Hamdir said, echoing Shard's words. "Yes." Shard smiled, sitting in his seat on the council.

"Not resources or information, but the possibility to come to know us and become friends?" Councilwoman Sela adjusted her glasses that rested on her Gnomish features. Slowly, a smile spread across her face as she shook her head, cackling lightly. "These Players are an interesting bunch! I wish we met more of them before!"

"Most of them were off killing whatever they could find and disregarding us," Frenik said.

"Only in the first year or two. Then, of course, there are the ones who just kill all over the place, though many more of them start to become Champions of Emerilia. They would then look out for the people, unless they get some twisted quest by the Dark Lord or work for the Dark guilds," Sela said.

"I think that the best course of action is for one of us to meet with their leaders. They have asked for help with destroying the creature that prowls our college. It is a good opportunity for us to show ourselves and ally ourselves with them. I also think that we should keep to the council's agreed prize for them. Except, we allow our people to go and visit them," Ela-Dorn said.

"You want to let our people meander through an area under their control?" Koza said.

"They are our people, but they must make their own decisions. Taking options away from them is the same as taking information and training away from them," Sela interjected.

"Koza, we know how you care for the people and their protection. However, does not a good parent allow their child to experience the world instead of hold them chained to their home with words and emotions?" Hamdir asked.

"Fine, I don't like it, though! I ask that automatons be on the ready to attack the complex if our people are threatened," Koza said.

"I see that as an acceptable addition." Frenik looked to Hamdir.

The others didn't look as though they agreed fully, but none voiced a dissenting opinion.

"Shard?"

"I will add it to my contingency plans." Shard bowed his head. "Done. Might I say that the Stone Raiders are nothing if not resourceful. They have been betrayed in the past and every time, they have come out the victor. They, too, believe in giving people a chance, but verifying that trust."

"Emerilia jades all who live on it." Hamdir's voice was sad but accepting of that simple truth. "If that is all, I will be on my way to the Stone Raiders' lodgings in order to pass on information about our opponent."

"No, you will not!" Ela-Dorn's eyes were fierce as she looked to Hamdir. He made to speak, but was cut off. "You are the head of this council. We will not be putting you into the middle of a bunch of extremely powerful fighters. It has been some time since you were last in the college. I am the administrator of the facility; I will go and talk with them."

Hamdir made to argue but seeing the glares from around the room, he cleared his throat. "Very well. All in favor of Ela-Dorn representing the Aleph people and meeting with the Stone Raiders?"

Hands shot up in favor.

Ela-Dorn stood. "Well, no time like the present." She bowed slightly to the rest of the council.

"See if you can't get them to agree to leave some of the housing complexes. We can move more of our people into them and start the different growing areas there," Meda, a Dwarf-Elf, added.

"I'll try my best, Meda!" Ela-Dorn said. The doors to the chambers opened before her and closed behind.

"Watch over her." Hamdir looked to Shard.

"She's going to one of the safest places in Emerilia, as long as she doesn't go to the test range...Dave's damned inventions." Shard muttered the last part to himself.

Hamdir smiled, his ears able to pick up the AI's mutterings.

"She's Orcish!" one of the Stone Raiders guarding the teleport pad said as an Orcish woman wearing flowing robes with an infinity symbol hanging over a circle of seven X's stood just on the edge of the teleport pad. "No shit, Sherlock! Was it the tusks or the green skin that gave it away?" The woman beside the yelling man rolled her eyes.

Ela-Dorn snorted but didn't make to move forward. All of the Stone Raiders were relaxed, but she had seen them fight. In a moment, they could draw their arrows or release their spells in her direction. The real thing that stopped her moving forward was the mass of trap runes that covered the floor. The first ones promised to immobilize her. The ones deeper in were meant to kill.

"What is it? This better be good!" A woman, with her brown hair pulled back, holding a magical staff and a battle mage's armored robes, entered the second floor and looked at Ela-Dorn. "Hello, who are you?"

"I am Ela-Dorn. The council has sent me to talk to you. What is your name?"

"Kim. Which council?" She scratched her head and yawned. "The Aleph Council," Ela-Dorn said.

"Ah, okay. Was wondering if you lot were going to send someone to talk to us. Was kind of thinking that Dave had gone a bit loopy talking about gods and whatnot. Rosie, turn off the traps for a minute. Everyone, battle stance." The words were light and Kim yawned again as the runes deactivated.

Within seconds, mages held balls of energy in their hands. Blades were in warriors' hands and bows were pulled back with an arrow on the string.

Ela-Dorn's eyes bugged out as she looked at the display.

"I'll take you to meet the others." Kim floated down from the second floor and waved for Ela-Dorn to follow her.

She did so, crossing the runes quickly. As soon as she had passed, the runes came back on.

"Stand down." Weapons were put away and energies dissipated, and the Stone Raiders went back to acting as though nothing had happened. Most of them cast glances at Ela-Dorn as she followed Kim deeper into the tower.

These auras — they're suppressing them well, but I am able to see past most of their efforts. She had seen them fighting and their abilities. Ela-Dorn was a level 279, but many of the Stone Raiders were a lower level. However, her gut feeling was that they could cut her down in a moment. They weren't a higher level but their skills and training made them opponents to be respected and feared.

The Players were from every race. None of them seemed to care about their outward appearance. Most talked battle tactics, or about the kinds of food they were going to get once they were done with the Lich. Others were talking about the planet Earth, where they hailed from, and different things, like television. Oddly, those last few were in the minority; most of the Stone Raiders talked about Emerilia as if it was their home.

They entered one of the cafeterias. Kim led her to one of the tables, where people were eating and planning at the same time.

"This is Josh and that's Dwayne." Kim pointed to the two men in the center of the table huddle. They looked up, breaking their conversation. "Lucy is off dealing with something. I'm going to go see what the hell Dave is talking about with magical artillery. This is Ela-Dorn; she's with the Aleph Council." With that, Kim turned and left, grabbing a cup of Xer on her way out.

"Clear a seat. You want something to eat?" Josh asked. The Stone Raiders moved to either side, so that there was a seat opposite Josh and Dwayne.

"I'm good, thank you." Ela-Dorn sat down.

"So, what do the Aleph need from us? We're currently working on the college. We're hoping to have it done in a week or two. Finding that damn Lich's soul box is going to be a big pain in the ass. Once we've got that, then Dave is pretty sure that he can fix the portal factory up," Josh said, digging into his dinner.

They think that they can fix the portal facility? It takes years to train someone to be able to make even a part of the system. This Dave is more than he appears to be. He might just be overstating his abilities, though. Ela- Dorn kept her thoughts to herself.

"We were wondering what kind of assistance we could be to help you with the college. I know that we have tried to keep our presence a secret.

After being attacked on all sides by the races of Emerilia, we are a bit paranoid."

"Makes sense. Nearly anyone is willing to screw another over for what they want or don't have. Especially where the Affinities Pantheon is involved," Dwayne grunted, and the Stone Raiders agreed.

"Quite. We also hope to become closer with your guild and your people. You have helped us out in a time of need and we are thankful for that. We know that you are also helping two other races that have come back from the Grey God's care, just like us. We wish to come to know you all more and hopefully become allies and friends to face what might come."

"That suits us just fine. Always good to have friends." Josh smiled. "Though first, we need to clear out that college for you. I'm going to have to ask if you have any solid plans on the facility and how many scouts you could lend us. We need to find the Lich's soul box and, while we're pretty good at sneaking around, that Lich has made the entire college its lair. It knows the minute that we step into it and he sends his minions to hunt us down. That or he uses the natural creatures of the college to trap and kill our people."

"Natural creatures?" Ela-Dorn cocked her head to the side and frowned.

"It seems that there might have been creatures kept in the college at some time. Instead of killing them, the Lich has them holed up in different areas. They create a barrier around the areas that he must be using. We've got shambling mounds, weeping sirens, goblins, and hobgoblins. There are also undead versions that the Lich directly controls. Nothing has died in that place in many years, corrupting the very ground," Dwayne explained.

"What is a Lich?" Ela-Dorn asked.

"They are creatures that have attached their soul to a box and then destroyed their old bodies, turning them into immortal beasts, so long as they feed their soul box other creatures. The process requires them to make a contract with a Dark force. Well, that is what we know of Lichs at least," Josh said.

"It's a phylactery," Dwayne sighed. "Soul box is easier to say," Josh retorted. "Fine!" Dwayne shook his head.

"So, what do you want these scouts for?" Ela-Dorn asked.

"We're going to take a ton of them, shove them through every friggin' portal in the place and send them to find that soul box. Once we have it, then we can destroy it and bye-bye Lich," Josh said.

"I will see how many we can give you." Ela-Dorn nodded. "Thanks!" Josh smiled and turned to Dwayne. "Wanna show her around? She's probably seen it all through the different mage lenses around the place, but it's usually better in person."

"Fine. I was just going to check on the training grounds anyway." Dwayne rose to his feet. "Would you like to accompany me, Ela-Dorn?"

"Certainly." She rose and followed him.

"Is there anything you are interested in specifically, like different magics and such? Watching people swing weapons around is not always the most interesting thing," Dwayne said as he cleared off his tray.

"Kim said something about Dave using magical artillery."

"Well, some things I can't show you. One of them being what Dave's inventions do. That stuff we try to keep under wraps. I can see if he's free to talk to you, though he's probably going back to the forge after his demonstration. He's working on weapons."

"That is fine. Shard is enamored with him and I would like to understand why."

"With all the ideas he's spouting and tests he has Shard running, I would think it would be because of their shared interest in making the impossible and things that would scare the Pantheon." Dwayne snorted.

"Interesting." Ela-Dorn doubted that anything Dave could come up with could make the Pantheon pay the slightest attention to a mere mortal. She felt it was best to keep that to herself. "Kim said that Dave told you that we were back on Emerilia. I was wondering how this is possible. We do like to keep our privacy."

"Well, his friend Bob told him." Dwayne stepped into a lift. Ela-Dorn followed him. "Bob?"

"Well, you might know him as the Grey God…uhh, Neutrality? Balancer? I'm not sure what his titles are, but apparently Dave caught the eye of the game's AI and became friends with it." Dwayne snorted and shook his head. "Never know what that guy is going to do next."

There was a loud thump and smoke started to come from somewhere in the tower.

"This way, please," Dwayne said as the lift stopped, guiding her away from the explosion.

"I told you to *not* set it off inside!" an angry male voice yelled. "Well, you didn't tell me it didn't have a safety!" Kim yelled back.

"The safety is *not* channeling your Mana into it and then giving it coordinates!"

"Whoops, though on the plus side, I'm awake now. Can't hear shit, but awake."

"What asshole just tried to blow up a side of this damn tower while I was sleeping!?" Another female voice joined into the fray.

Ela-Dorn didn't know whether to run for safety or laugh at Dwayne's pained expression.

"It was Dave?"

"What? I can't hear, 'cause someone blew my eardrums out!"

"Kim, no more touching shit that goes bang inside!"

"But it wasn't me."

There was a massive surge of Mana as Ela-Dorn felt her blood go cold. "Ow! Fine, no more using things that could explode inside!" Kim said. "Good. Anyone else wants to wake me up, I'll kick their ass into the Densaou Ring of Fire myself!" There was a loud bang as a door slammed shut.

"Lucy isn't a morning person. Hasn't got much sleep recently. Makes her a bit cranky," Dwayne said as they reached outside, where people were sparring. Their attacks left dents and furrows in the ground.

"O-okay," Ela-Dorn said, giving a weak smile.

They might not have been that strong when they came here, but now they're becoming monsters. Lucy's attack was that of a Master level mage of thirty years, not someone who has been around for less than two! These Players learn and grow so fast! I must figure out how they do it!

Excited by the new challenge ahead of her, she listened to Dwayne as he talked about the fighting skills of the Stone Raiders, happily answering any questions that Ela-Dorn might have.

They stopped to watch Steve as he fought against four other behemoths. He whistled out a tune as he moved with the kind of seamless actions one would never think of seeing in a creature as big as him. He'd weave out of attack range, and fire a lightning bolt from his right hand, or change his left to hurl three-foot-long bolts into his opponents.

"We're teaching him better control. He's big, strong, and well-armored, so he was lacking many of the basic skills. Had to get Anna to pound it into his metal head that there is always someone bigger and more powerful. So, he trains just like the rest of us," Dwayne said, following her eyes.

She nodded, unable to form words at it all. *It was just…surprising? Awe-inspiring? Exciting?* All these thoughts and more ran through her mind. *These Players are something else. I wonder what the other groups are like?*

13

OPERATION FETCH

"Commence Operation Fetch!" Josh said.

"Seriously, we're going with Fetch?" Kim asked.

Lucy just gave her a look that seemed to ask "what else did you expect?" as she read a book on her magic carpet.

Scout guardians flooded through different teleport pads all across the city, and different facilities that the Stone Raiders controlled. They were connected to every teleport pad in the Aleph College. Hundreds of scouts appeared in the college, turning invisible and spreading out as fast as possible. Many met various creatures waiting at the teleport pad control rooms.

A number of scouts' signals disappeared as they rushed through the facility. As one was captured, they would set off a grenade hidden within them, clearing the way for more of their brethren and taking out the creatures within before the real fight started.

Josh watched the map in the command center as it updated with information on all manner of threats, from rune traps to creatures.

Everyone watched as the scouts were cut down faster and faster. They had forty percent of the college mapped out.

"Where are you? Come on." Josh held onto the side of the table that showed the college's map.

Even Lucy had put down her book to watch the scouts' progress.

They got to seventy percent when one of the scouts found the Lich. Its clothes and body were barely holding onto its bones, rotting off. The Lich let out a hellish scream and activated its Legendary attack.

The attack was like a wave of destruction. Shadows seemed to spread out from the Lich, flowing through the halls of the college and wiping out any of the scouts it saw.

"Well, mates, got some good news and bad news. Good news, we're going to go and fight the Lich today because it doesn't have that attack anymore and it should take quite awhile for it to get it back. Bad news, we're going to go fight that Lich today. We, also, have no bloody idea where that soul box is. So, now, let's pull a plan together to kill the creatures in the library, hold that Lich down in one place, and send people to find its damned "phylactery"." Josh said doing air quotes in the air as if he was some super villain in flashy silver spandex.

For a moment, nothing happened and then people started to talk to one another and discuss what the hell they were going to do. Some of them shaking their heads at Josh's antics.

"No? Nothing?" Josh said moving in his seat looking to everyone. "Well there goes the two hundred times I've watched Austin powers,"

He muttered to himself.

Just got to kill an Arch Lich — no problem, easy as pie! Josh thought to himself, finding that he was more perturbed that no one got his reference.

He shrugged giving up on it and started to help planning how they were going to kill an Arch Lich. Even if they died a dozen times, they'd clear out the college and grind the Lich down to nothing.

It was just a matter of time and planning.

"And that is the plan," Josh said three hours later.

"Rush the college, kill anything in our way. Teams go off and try to find the phylactery while the rest kill creatures or pin down the Arch Lich," Dave summarized.

"Quick version, yep." Josh grinned.

Dave shook his head and cracked a smile.

"Sounds like a fine plan to me. Why did you ask me and mine to come in here for a private briefing?" Deia asked.

"You have some of the highest magical sensing skills out of any party. I want you to be spearheading the different groups that are going out to find that bloody box."

"You do realize this is a college, right?" Suzy asked. "I told him," Lucy said from in the corner.

"What? So, it's going to have a few magical objects in it." Josh shrugged.

"The whole place is filled with magical objects, not including different runes and whatever traps and different magical items the Arch Lich has created," Shard said through the command center's speakers.

Josh scratched his head. "Okay, so it's going to be a bit difficult, but it is the best shot we've got."

"Sounds like fun! When do we leave?" Induca asked. "Two hours and we start."

"Well, I don't know about all of you, but I have some things I need to do. Never killed me an Arch Lich before." Dave sounded thoughtful before a big smile crossed his face. "First time for everything, right?"

"These are for you." Dave pulled two blades from out behind his back and presented them to Deia.

Her eyes went wide as she covered her mouth, appraising them.

Firecracker's Blades
Forged by Dave Grahslagg for his beloved, these blades hold the passion of the heart.

> **Quality:** S
> **Abilities:**
> Increased Affinity for Fire (+10%)
> Increased Agility (+20%)
> Increased Willpower (+35%)
> Forever sharp
> Grows in power through use.
> Fire Dancer
> **Charge:** 20,000/20,000
> **Durability:** 351/351

"Dave." She smiled as she read the words and gave him a great big kiss.

A goofy smile spread across his face at her reaction.

"You shouldn't be wearing yourself out before a battle, making all of these items." She looked at him with concern, looking for signs for fatigue— scared that his fatigue might mean him dying again.

"It was worth it and your blades right now couldn't take more than a half-dozen Fire-imbued slashes before falling apart. You've become too strong for them." Dave held the blades behind her as they looked into each other's eyes.

"Well, thank you, but next time, get some rest instead of being tired right before a battle." Her concern was clear in her eyes and voice.

"I'll do my best, babe." Dave smiled and leaned forward.

She eagerly met his lips. "Now, what is this Fire Dancer ability?"

"Well, I kind of got something I wasn't expecting with that one. I was trying to modify the blades so that they would be able to handle you imbuing them with your Mana, so that they would work together. The magical coding worked well, but the metal was not supposed to handle the kinds of heat that you usually use. So, I kept on heating it up as hot as it could go and reforming it to try to get the blade to temper the metal and strengthen it through its ability to grow with the user. I used the Master skill of Smithing. The metal gained the skill Fire-resistant. Combined with the magical coding, it should be able to take on your Fire-based sword attacks. The more you use it and use Fire Dancer attacks, the stronger it will become and you can use more powerful Fire attacks." Dave's pride was clear.

Deia pulled the blades out of their sheaths. They were curved slightly like a katana but without its hilt. Their razor-sharp edges glinted slightly in the light. They were the perfect blades for her. She moved with them, practicing her different forms, flowing from one through to the next.

She held them out, studying the magnificent weapons. "It looks like you were not just getting your ass beaten when you were fighting me." She smiled.

"Hey, I only got my ass beat because my teacher's beauty stole my attention the whole time." Dave grinned and gave her a wink.

She laughed and wrapped her hands around his neck.

Others had been scared by her tendencies to fight and because of her desire to be a ranger. Men from Kufo'tel had said that she would calm down eventually to become a lovely wife, sitting at home. Dave never nursed those hopes and dreams. He might be an inventor and a man pulled by his curiosities, but Deia knew that he was a warrior as well.

She kissed him, looking into his eyes at the laugh lines around his eyes and the way those eyes looked at her. She kissed him again, pulling his head to hers, as if pulling him tighter would make the moment last longer.

"All right, Stone Raiders! Let's raid!" Josh's voice reverberated through the entire city as whistles and cheers responded, weapons held high in excitement for the coming battle.

Dave hotkeyed his armor, pulling his hood down so others couldn't see his face. He moved in it, jumping up and down a few times to make sure that it was comfortable.

Deia added her blades to her outfit and then hotkeyed her armor as well. She, too, pulled down her hood, her hair pulled back into a ponytail at the back of her head and tucked into her hood. "How are your one handed and two handed?"

Dave pulled up the skills.

Active Skill: Two Handed
Level: Expert Level 9
Effect: 38% armor penetration on target. Stamina costs reduced 15% while fighting
Cost: 35 Stamina

Active Skill: One Handed and Shield
Level: Master Level 1
Effect: Weapons damage increased by 41%. Defense increased by 20%. Can use two-handed weapon in one hand with 50% speed penalty.
Cost: 20 Stamina

"Two handed at Expert nine, one handed just made it into Master.

Almost got everything I need for Weapons Master."

"I have a feeling you'll be able to get that two handed in this next fight," Deia said.

"Me too," Dave said.

It wasn't long until the rest of their party was gathered together. "Well, this is bound to be interesting," Suzy said.

"After that other Lich, I don't think this will be anything as mundane as fun," Malsour added.

"All right, everyone ready?" Josh's voice came out over the guild's chat. Everyone quieted down in their individual parties. Only once they found a big concentration of either enemies or the Arch Lich himself would they come together. Till then, it would be a mad dash toward the Arch Lich for the most part. The others would be heading into the areas that the scouts weren't able to check.

"Fire up the teleport pads!" Josh said.

Different locations with the least amount of creatures waiting at them had been picked. As soon as the teleport pad connected, the Stone Raiders surged forward in a charge.

Dave entered the teleport pad and entered the Aleph College. At one time, it had been a place of beauty; now it was barely lit, with rabid stone- worms rushing the Stone Raiders.

The front melee fighters engaged; their weapons cut deep and the worms screamed out in pain.

"Forget the fight. They've got it handled. We need to go find that box!" Deia yelled in the party's ears. "Dave, Anna, lead. Steve with me in the back. Let's go!"

With that, they headed away from the fight, rushing past the worms, Anna's wind blades cleaving a path through them. The following Stone Raiders opened the path out further before they spread out into the college. The place was massive, easily half the size of the city but without the rotating abilities of the Aleph cities. They passed dormitories, parks, libraries, training areas, fighting arenas, and laboratories.

It wasn't long until the other searching groups with them split off, heading for a different way to get to the area that the scouts weren't able to reach.

Dave ran over scout guardians that had been attacked, their bodies torn apart by the different types of magical grenades that they had been carrying. They weren't the only bodies on the ground.

"Looks like those grenades did work. Took out a few of the damn creatures 'round here," Malsour said.

"You find anything with your spidey senses?" Suzy asked.

"Nothing yet. There is a whole lot of college here and I need to be within a few hundred meters instead of miles to tell most of this magical stuff apart. There's just so much of it that it's hard. I'm trying to look for purely soul magic items, which does make it a bit easier." Dave made sure to keep his actual eyes open and looking for anything that might sneak up on them.

"Ah, shit. Looks like we've got a patrol of the Lich's undead moving toward us." Dave searched for a place to hide.

"There isn't anywhere that would be big enough for Steve to hide in.

We need to finish them off and quick," Deia said, reading his mind.

"Saying I'm fat?" Steve sounded hurt.

Dave and Anna looked to each other, nodding as they rushed forward.

Dave felt his buffs come into effect as they raced ahead.

The Lich's creatures snarled as soon as they saw Dave and Anna.

Inside their master's domain, there was no hiding from them.

Dave conjured and threw spears that exploded as soon as they hit their targets.

Anna sent Wind blades high and low.

Wolves, night terrors, and harpies fell before they could do anything. Deia fired an arrow between Dave and Anna, taking out the harpy.

One of the wolves, missing its rear leg, shambled toward them, its hollow and rotten eyes fixed on those who dared to come into its master's realm.

The night terrors seemed to expand around the lights that they used to lure their prey, like a deadly flower tentacles opened up, revealing a mouthful of teeth directly behind the light source.

They used their barbed tentacles to drag themselves forward. Their mouths were between their tentacles, making crunching noises as they moved toward their prey as fast as they could drag themselves.

Anna got the wolf as Dave hit a night terror with a spear. It exploded but the creature kept coming, even after losing a half-dozen tentacles.

Deia's arrows took out two more before the shadows lanced outward and killed the remaining four within seconds.

"Thanks, Malsour." Dave had already started to run forward, sensing the Mana that had powered the undead dissipating.

"We've got more of the undead coming to try to find us. Most of the guild are moving toward where the Arch Lich was seen last. He's still there—guess he likes whatever books he's reading." Dave shivered after using his Touch of the Land to study the Arch Lich.

He was able to sense his aura. The creature was a depraved soul that desired nothing more than death and pain. He had devoted his entire existence to finding new ways of making this possible. His corruption covered the creatures that he claimed as his servants. The magic and information of the Aleph had made him powerful.

"Induca, left side—weevils!" Dave said. A twister of fire landed in a hallway of laboratories. Massive weevils screamed out in pain as they were caught up in the inferno.

They were a mix between rats as big as a horse and beetles with a hard carapace. Dave had never seen or heard of weevils so big.

It didn't really matter when the damn thing was trying to rip your head off!

Suzy's creations started to range out as well. Malsour, Induca, and Deia dropped heavy magical attacks on everything that was trying to catch them. Dave barely saw any fighting as they rushed forward, entering the zone that the scouts weren't able to get into.

"This must be the grand library," Dave said as they ran up steps toward a massive building. Inside, Dave could sense all manner of magics and books.

"Can you find the soul box?" Deia asked.

Dave glanced back to see Deia sending fireballs into the skeletal creations, melting through them or causing them to explode from the impact. "It's going to be hard. There's a lot of books here on soul magic!"

Dave finished with the steps and started across the large open area before the library.

Harpies started their sorrowful singing that would make anyone listening want to go and comfort what looked like crying children. Bolts ripped through their thin bodies, cutting them short.

"Shut yer traps! Ain't got no ears!"

Dave shook his head as the harpies fell to the ground. Their true form appeared as their wings opened, showing the vicious beak and claws that rested underneath, ready to rip armor and flesh to shreds.

None of the Stone Raiders had to worry about the harpies. All of them had earplugs in and they were using their party chats to talk to one another.

More creatures started to appear out of the library and the buildings surrounding it.

Dave entered the library's door, Anna beside him, as they looked into a massive lobby with stairs curving up and unto the floors above. A creature jumped off the second-floor balcony and landed in the middle of the lobby. Its red eyes studied those who had dared to enter its domain.

Bone Lord
Level 234

It was a creation wholly formed from the bones of the Arch Lich's victims. Dave felt nausea overtake him for a moment, nearly making him throw up. There was no smell from the creature, but the disgust and rot at the very core of it had a more visceral reaction than any of the decomposing creatures Dave had fought so far.

"We've got incoming from everywhere!" Steve said.

"Malsour, seal off this door. We need to deal with this thing as fast as possible before those things get in here," Deia said.

Is it locked in here with us, or are we locking ourselves in here with it? Dave didn't like where his mind was going.

14

TAKING THE FIGHT TO THE ENEMY

With the Arch Lich and his forces knowing where the Stone Raiders were all the time, Josh and his stealth types were now acting like glorified bodyguards and supported the melee fighters as best as possible.

Josh weaved around Dwayne as he took aggro from a level 215 rock troll. Josh used his blade's abilities, melting into the shadows behind the creature before he plunged his blades between its rocky armor and through its neck, cutting its spine. The undead troll dropped to the ground as Josh felt a swell of energy fill him.

The daggers in his hand demanded more, demanded to be fed and to claim the lives of those who wished to attack the one who wielded them, to defeat those who tried to attack Josh and the Stone Raiders. Josh reeled in his control as he moved across the battlefield.

Although the Arch Lich might know where they were at all times, his creatures weren't as smart and they were liable to attack and focus on whatever had the most aggro. That left Josh plenty of openings to sate his daggers' thirst.

"Forward!" Dwayne yelled. The Stone Raiders, from support to melee fighters, let out a roar as they rushed the creatures in their way.

So far, they hadn't met anything that needed more than a party to dispatch. Most of the creatures were higher level than the Stone Raiders, but the Stone Raiders didn't care, working the creatures' Health down quickly and efficiently.

The parties had their roles down to a science, communicating with one another with just a few words. There were wounded, but no one had died so far.

The creatures were overwhelmed as the charging Stone Raiders smashed a path through them; their blades, spells, and chosen weapons claimed more of the creatures by the minute.

Josh found himself in an arena. Shambling mounds, three of them, rested in the arena.

"Throw the dead creatures into the arena! Once the shambling mounds have eaten, they go into hibernation!" Josh yelled over the guild chat.

A group of melee fighters hurled out a corpse into the middle of the arena. The shambling mounds that had been approaching the fighting now shot vines out from their body, playing tug-of-war with one another for the corpse in the air.

More corpses sailed through the air. The shambling mounds acted like a group of seagulls instead of terrifying creatures. Their vines shot out, pulling the corpses to them, pulling them into their maws. It took two or three corpses, but the mounds stopped moving and started to move into their hibernation state.

"Through the arena!" Josh appeared behind a forest wolf, his blades working between the wooden armor that covered it to pierce through its chest and into its heart. Josh jumped off, racing out into the arena after the other Stone Raiders.

Mages placed blessings on all of the fallen bodies, so that the Arch Lich couldn't revive them. Five parties raced across the arena, giving the shambling mounds a wide berth.

None of the living creatures dared to enter the arena, sensing the danger of the sleeping creatures. They instead started fighting one another now that their common enemy was gone.

"Undead!" Kim yelled out. Spells of Light rushed to meet the undead ranks. A number fell before they were able to reach the Stone Raiders. These creatures were a higher level than the living creatures they had fought.

Holy blades and blessed weapons tore into the creatures. A number of the fighters had changed their weapons. The effectiveness of the holy weapons against the undead was no joke. Just being close to them, the undead yelled out in pain.

Josh's mouth rose into a predatory smile. His blades were neither Dark nor Light; they were soul weapons, draining the very living essence and consciousness from his targets.

He had known that the weapons were powerful, but after they had been repaired in Zolun, he didn't know whether he could use another weapon. They fit his fighting style perfectly. When chaining kills together, he could take out fighters that were tens of levels above him. It was only through the high-ranked gear, buffs, and chain heals that the Stone Raiders were able to hold against the Arch Lich's forces.

Josh's blades, if fed with enough souls, would tear through the undead creatures. Josh ran into the fight, easily dodging past the incoming attacks, his blades' Legendary abilities now stacking his own to improve his Agility to unseen heights. As his blades hit the undead, he pulled the soul energy from them that animated them, turning them sluggish or ripping the Arch Lich's hold on the creatures.

As the first started to die, his weapons surged with power and a faint shadow started to spread from them across his body. Josh laughed, jumping out of the way of a bone knight and disappearing into the shadows. He appeared above the bone lord and stabbed between its shoulder blades; the chained kills and sneak attack fell the bone lord. Shadows seemed to envelope him again. Undead tried to cut at where he had been but found nothing but darkness.

He stepped out of the shadows, on top of one of the benches that lay above the arena, overlooking the entrance that the undead came from.

"Let them come to us!" Josh yelled. His body and his blades wanted him to drive forward, to feed and become stronger. However, he was first, and foremost, the guildmaster more than his blade; his guild needed his leadership. Getting himself killed because he wanted to strengthen his blades and achieve the heady rush of the power that came with using his opponents' souls was not his goal. Winning was.

The Stone Raiders broke into their different lines, turning from party fighting into guild fighting within moments.

Josh used his shadow ability to move behind his people. It drained a lot of the soul energy from his blades; with the reduced energy, he could focus on what was in front of him and clear his mind.

"We'll weaken their undead numbers here and then move on to the Arch Lich. I need a party with people capable of blessing to move back to the other side of the arena and bless the bodies of the creatures that are dying there. I don't want us to get hit in the ass. Jones, Kai—I want you two to go and watch the other two entrances into the arena. Let me know if anything tries to bite us in the ass." People rushed off to carry out his orders.

I hope the searching teams are able to find that damn box. It won't be long until that Arch Lich finds something big to send in our direction.

Josh pulled up his map to check on the rest of the guild. Scouting groups were headed into the regions that the scouts hadn't been able to enter.

Nearly half of them were dead already, finding resistance that they weren't able to overcome or being swarmed by the undead forces that knew exactly where they were.

Party Zero had made it into the grand library of the college. From the symbols, they were fighting off an undead bone lord as well as hundreds of other undead that were inside the library.

Josh moved to the next group he could see.

It looked as if the group with Kim were under attack by undead stone- worms. Lucy and the parties under her control, rushed through open areas and right up the central road that ran through the college.

"Dwayne, I'm thinking that we should move to link up with Lucy— nice open area, see where our enemies are behind us and ahead," Josh said. "Sounds good to me, boss," Dwayne said, fighting on the front lines against the undead.

Josh opened up a private chat to Mikal, who was running with Lucy's group.

"Mikal, I need you to scout a route from where you are to my position.

We're going to move to reinforce you."

"I'll see what I can do. Is it about time for the second wave? Lucy is asking."

"Five minutes, then send them in," Josh said.

The Arch Lich turned his head at the rumbling explosion in the distance. For centuries, it had been left in peace, building up his strength and gaining the knowledge that his fellow Aleph had kept from him. He had listened to the Dark Lord's apostle.

He had given up his fellow Aleph in order to be given everlasting life. To be left with the knowledge that the Aleph deemed him unworthy of learning, he had developed his own black arts and become the ruler of the Aleph.

He let out a dry noise as he went back to reading the book in front of him. He had experimented for generations on the creatures left within the college. He had created an army to deal with those he let run wild. All he needed was the college and the freedom to do his experiments as he desired. The Aleph called it the Dark arts, called it murder and torture.

The Arch Lich laughed, a noise that would make any living creature shiver in fear.

They had been so blind! They were not willing to push their magic and their abilities to their limits! Not him. He would do everything in his power to become stronger, no matter the cost. Through it, he had transcended death itself.

Another rumbling noise could be heard in the distance.

"Seems the experiments were not as strong as I hoped," the Arch Lich muttered darkly as he drifted through the main building of the college, up to the second floor and the laboratories. Magical tools were scattered around the room. Blood, offal, and dead creatures lay around the room. It was enough to make anyone gag.

The Arch Lich hummed to himself as he looked over a pile of yellowed bones. He held his arms up, infusing the bones with his Mana as he started to give the bones form. The Arch Lich's face contorted in anger as he felt an all too familiar magic. Necromancers asserted their will, tearing the controlling bonds the Arch Lich held.

"They dare take control of the creatures that I have made!" *They must have come for my notes, for my knowledge. I will reward them by making them one of my undead. I wonder if I could make a necromancer undead use their magical powers? Some of the experiments have shown the ability to use their old skills at a reduced level.*

The Arch Lich cackled to himself, excited for all the experiments he would be able to make in the future and the pain he would put them through as he turned them from living into his undying legions.

Dark strands of magic poured from his hands and into a pile of yellowed bones. Their aura was one of anger and uncontained fury. They had come from victims who had been put in mental and physical pain in the end, unable to do anything about their situation.

The heap of bones started to pile together, taking on a humanoid form.

The Arch Lich paused as teleport pads opened once again. He felt the automatons' stain as they ran through his halls.

The Lich screeched out in anger. *Those metal creations! Reminders of that dead race. I will remove all that is left of the Aleph. I will fill their cities and homes with my army of undead! All will know of Alastair Montgoa! The destroyer of the Aleph!*

Incensed, the Bone creations formed faster and faster; another bone pile came into a form, bones ripped from the dead creatures to fulfill their master's needs.

The Arch Lich cackled in glee and looked at his two new experiments. "I shall name you bone juggernauts."

Standing in front of him were two roughly humanoid creatures. Spikes jutted out from their shoulders and back. Their forearms were massive blades, with a spike where their hand would have been. Red eyes glowed in their empty sockets. The anger of the bones that made up their bodies added to their aura of death.

The Arch Lich touched the first bone juggernaut. Black shadows seemed to pour out from the Arch Lich's remaining robes and into the bone juggernaut.

It bellowed out in joy. Its eyes glowed brighter as black shadows seemed to spread out from its body and down the sharpened spikes and blades that covered its body. The juggernaut of death stomped out of the room, shaking it as the Arch Lich did the same to the second creation.

We will see how they do. Once I have more data, we can refine these creatures down. The Arch Lich made crooning noises as the second bone juggernaut followed the first.

It would have taken a normal level 100 necromancer weeks or months to create the bone juggernauts. The Arch Lich, with his knowledge and power over the undead, could make another twenty in as many minutes.

"Switch!" Deia said to Dave. Dave moved out of her way as she switched in. Steve had joined in the fight against the Bone lord, acting as a tank while Anna and Dave took his Health down.

Dave moved to help Malsour. Induca was supporting Suzy as her creations tore into the creatures that had been hiding in the library or had made it through Malsour's walls.

"How is it looking?" Malsour asked as Dave hammered two creatures back with his shield. His blade came low under his shield, cutting out legs. His two rods came together in a halberd that he swung across those in front of him, clearing out five meters in front.

"He's down maybe ten percent Health. Thing's hard as shit and fast somehow!" Dave followed his Inference and Perception skills flowing through the blue movements that he saw and pushed the undead back before Malsour's darklings once again descended and tore the undead apart.

Dave looked back to Malsour, a thin sheen of sweat on his face. He had been forming walls and fixing them for twenty minutes now. More and stronger creatures were trying to get in from all directions. It was a matter of time before Malsour's magic wasn't strong enough to keep them out.

"Start letting them in. Suzy and I can take more of them on. It will be less of a strain on your walls." Dave's halberd broke apart into two twin hammers.

"The main doorway," Malsour said.

Dave moved to it, setting his feet. Each of the hammers weighed twenty kilos but Dave no longer felt their weight after smithing for so long.

"Ready?" Malsour asked.

"Nope, but might as well try this out!" Dave felt Malsour's Mana stop channeling into the doorway ahead of him.

The wall that was in front of him started to crumble in a matter of seconds. It wasn't long until cracks formed. The wall disintegrated, the undead rushing in after it. Some were too fast, getting crushed by the crumbling wall as they charged.

Dave felt power surge through him. As he stamped his foot, spikes came up to pierce through the undead. Spikes continued to form and fall away, thinning the undead horde.

Dave spun, launching his hammer through the now open wall. It was like a cannon ball, slamming into a bone lord. Dave destroyed the hammer, creating a spiked ball within the bone lord. It grew shadowy spikes and dropped to its knees from the internal damage. Dave destroyed the spiked ball, recalling the rod as it transformed into a hammer. It crashed through another undead, bones and rotting parts exploding across the hall.

Dave met the first undead with his left hammer. Counting as a two- handed weapon, it was a wrecking ball. There was little need for piercing damage, but the blunt effects of armor penetration shattered those that met Dave's hammer heads. He grabbed the second hammer out of the air, bringing it across a minotaur and crushing its ribs, making it stagger.

Dave conjured defenses that tore into the undead. Thumping could be heard from above, coming closer every time. Dave leaped back out of an attack, letting his hammer go as a ball formed in his hand out of shadow.

"Watch your eyes!" Dave hurled the ball into the middle of the undead. A new sun lit the hall and the lobby as undead screamed at the onslaught of the Light grenade.

Dave drove his foot into the floor of the lobby, hurling himself forward. He recalled his hammer; catching it, he spun in mid-air, and brought it over the head of another minotaur. Its head rolled off as Dave used its corpse to propel himself forward.

He did everything he could to keep up his momentum, turning his axis and twisting his body for every ounce of power. Each kill and swing set him up for another strike as he turned, using the hammers to unleash his destruction.

Finally, the thumping from above stopped as a metal lance broke through the floors above and crashed into the undead piling through the front door.

It disappeared in a moment. A whistling sound came from above: one, then two — then three and more every second.

Dave could feel the bruises across his body, the growing headache from his Mana usage and the sweat that stung his eyes. He panted, looking at the advancing undead, undeterred by their loss in numbers.

We're not going to get out of here alive unless we find that damn box or someone kills the Arch Lich. Fuck, well, they're not going to get my life easily!

Now, without the worry about surviving or not, Dave ran toward the undead once again. His sledgehammers changed to swords, then a shield, and then a claymore and spear. They flashed from one weapon to the next as he dispatched undead.

They were on or below his overall level, including his skills. Although the undead were slow and had degraded skills after being reanimated, Dave had been trained into unconsciousness by weapons masters. His inference and perception skills allowed him to think of the right weapon for every fight and know how to use it. His dodge skill and perception allowed him to take the least amount of damage as the first of the whistling noises stopped, making it through several floors of the library before impacting in the middle of the hallway.

Four creatures were killed instantly in its impact area. Others were thrown away; dust and debris blew out through both ends of the hallway.

Dave used the distraction to kill any of the undead that had been left stunned around him before he backed away.

Whistling filled the air as a conjured spear of Light dropped from above. Runes glowed along its length, lightly at first and then stronger and stronger. It slammed into undead that were now charging toward him. The spear exploded into brilliant white. The undead cried out as the holy metal burned through their bodies, making them writhe in pain. Their Health dropped quickly from the status effect.

"That's what you get when you mix artillery shells, kinetic bombardment, and some good ole magically blessed metal!" Dave said as thirty undead creatures were turned into lifeless bodies.

Dave took a knee, concentrating as more thumping could be heard through the library. Dave sensed the floors and roofs above him started to dissolve.

Malsour, seeing what he was doing, was helping him out, banishing everything above where Dave was defending.

Whistling noises filled the air as Dave conjured lances to land among the undead masses that were trying to claw their way through Malsour's walls. He couldn't keep it up for long, but the toll on the undead would be high.

"Where is the biggest group of undead?" Suzy yelled.

"Over there." Malsour put a waypoint on one of the larger entrances into the lobby from the first floor.

Suzy and Induca moved to it. Suzy's creations moved into the hallway, moving onto the walls and floor.

"Open it up!" Induca said.

The wall disintegrated. Undead fell over one another just as the air in the lobby seemed to be dragged toward Induca and the cannon in her arms. Her plasma cannon bucked. Induca rocked with it slightly as the plasma round hit the undead, burning through them and turning it into a burning hell. A firestorm grew the length of the incoming hallway.

"Well, looks like Induca has this one. You have another hallway?" Suzy asked. A new waypoint appeared and Suzy moved her creations there.

Dave stopped calling down strikes on the undead. His mind nearly at its limit, he needed time to recover. If he overdid it now, then he would be out of the fight. The latest spear went off, the explosion clearing out as Dave moved among the undead. His weapons cleaved through them, knee-deep in undead bodies, as he fought.

Suzy watched her forces get into place, glancing at the fight happening in the middle of the lobby. Steve's Mithril was showing through in areas.

There looked to be actual scratches in it as Steve fought the bone lord. He wasn't as fast as the bone lord but he was the most armored of anyone in the party. If the bone lord started targeting his joints, then he would be fucked. But for now he was holding its attention, slamming his axe against it and yelling at it.

Anna and Deia's blades moved with controlled fury. Wind and Fire cut into the bone lord.

As she watched, the bone lord reached seventy-percent Health.

With a yell, it stopped on the ground. Steve was thrown back—stunned.

Deia shook off the effects as Anna, who had been out of the area of effect, charged in.

The bone lord was pushed back three feet. Its head turned to find Anna, the Fire in its eyes burning brighter in anger.

It was nearly three times her height, but Anna didn't seem to care. Suzy swore that she saw the wolf Beast Kin smiling as her movements blurred, too fast for Suzy to follow as the bone lord was rocked back on his heels. It tried to fend off Anna's attacks as the wind howled with her blade's fury.

They can handle it. Now I just have to get them the time that they need to deal with that ugly bastard.

"Come on, you lazy creations. Let's see what you can do!" She channeled some Willpower to Steve. He groaned and pulled himself to his feet.

"Well, seems that you're a pretty good opponent." Steve laughed. The lobby shook as he rushed forward. "Didn't you know! I love being the center of attention!"

Anna jumped clear as Steve, filled with new energy and power, smashed his axe into the bone lord. It didn't have enough time to recover from Anna's attacks and was hurled backward into stairs that led up and into the second floor.

Steve leaped after the bone lord, finishing the destruction of the stairs as it was the bone lord's turn to be stunned as Steve fought with newfound anger and vigor.

Anna and Deia raced in to help him as Suzy finished off her preparations. Air creations waited at the mouth of the hall. The rest of it was covered in various strong metals. Behind Suzy, her latest creations outlined her body. They were Light creations.

"Malsour! Drop the wall!" Suzy called out, holding out her staff. She had fifty creations at her call. The most that she could have, normally. With the staff controlling them, it seemed to turn barely contained chaos into precise destruction.

The Mana fled the area as Malsour used it somewhere else.

Suzy didn't need to wait long before the wall came apart and undead of all manner surged forward, baying for her death and the rest of her party's. They made it halfway from the now broken wall to the mouth of the corridor. "Blades!" Metals lashed out and formed themselves into destructive weapons that rose out of the walls and floor. The undead's natural movement drove them through these weapons and tore them apart.

The metal creations weren't done, forming into spears and other weapons, any form that could hurt or harm the undead that came through their domain cut outward.

Undead harpies rushed through. Their agile bodies escaped the tunnel, only to be met by the Air creations' blades.

All the while, Suzy watched over the destruction.

One of her Light creations fired, hitting an undead that was about to attack Dave's side.

"Thanks, Suz!"

"Just find that box!" Suzy only needed to give a glance to different undead for her creations to attack them. Having her consciousness linked to the creations made them similar to an extension of her body: she thought— they reacted. It had taken her some time to get used to it instead of just using word commands. With her higher Willpower and the staff, it gave her a larger range where it would work. Her spoken instructions would work over a larger area but it wasn't as controlled.

Her control now showed. As soon as she saw an issue, her creations rushed to solve it. It was like multiple minds working as one, thinking the same way, but able to act independently of one another.

"I think I might know where it is, but we've got some problems," Dave said.

"Where is it?" Deia panted as she jumped out of the way of the bone lord's sword. Multiple fireballs attacked its face, blackening the bones that made up its helmet and making it stagger as Steve landed a monstrous hit.

"All the way at the top of the library, and there are three more bone lords guarding it. Seems all the undead are down here with us, though!"

"Figure out a way to get us up there." Deia dodged a frantic swipe by the bone lord.

"How am I supposed… Okay, I might have an idea!"

"What?" Anna asked.

"Reverse underworld!" Dave sounded as if he were smiling.

"The hell is that?" Deia asked.

"We need to work on your movie knowledge! Malsour, I'm going to need your help." Dave crashed through four undead as Suzy shook her head.

Dave might be an inventor, but he was fiercely loyal to those he called his friends. He was always looking to become stronger and making those he cared for as strong as possible. Deia wondered whether he knew just how strong of a fighter he was as he fought off the most undead by himself.

Suzy and Induca could keep the undead at a distance but Dave was right in the middle of them, conjuring spears from the ground or slamming a shield into his opponent's face.

15

WATCHING FROM AFAR

The Aleph Council was silent as they watched the Stone Raiders fight their way through the college. There were the sounds of pain, of weapons clashing, and spells being unleashed. The Stone Raiders were deathly silent, their ears plugged and their mouths moving but nothing could be heard or read from their lips.

"How are they communicating?" Koza asked.

"They are using a system of chats, for their party, their different groups that they are part of when they come together to fight bigger groups, and the guild chat, where the guild leaders talk to one another, and important information is brought up and orders given," Shard said.

"Why so complicated?" Sela asked, a puzzled expression on her face. "Three reasons. First, so that they don't fall under the thrall of the harpies that are there. They also don't know how much power the Arch Lich has over his domain. If he can hear what they are saying, then he might be able to figure out their plan. Finally, because they're acting and reacting, having just one chat between people would turn into absolute chaos."

"Aren't they going to fall back? They've lost a third of their forces,"

Hamdir interjected.

"Within six hours, those forces will be back. Right now they are at their strongest. They might drive their way to the Arch Lich or pull back to a defensible position." Shard cocked his head to the side. "It seems that they have found the location of the Arch Lich's phylactery."

"Where is it?" Ela-Dorn looked to Shard.

"It is located in the grand library at the highest floor. Dave has sensed that there are three bone lords in the room with it."

"Are we sure that the Stone Raiders are sound in mind?" Meda shook her head, as if not believing what she was seeing.

"I have deemed that they are perfectly sane. Why do you ask?"

"Shard, have you noticed that most of them are *smiling*?"

"Councilwoman Meda, it is indeed hard to understand the Stone Raiders' mindset, but this is what they love the most. Say you have a problem in front of you. It looks impossible to overcome, yet you and your friends don't care how hard it looks. You've taken on a dozen other challenges; all of them seemed impossible at one time or another, but you kept at it. You drove yourself and your friends, so that you solved that problem. That is the same thing with the Stone Raiders. They're a group of friends who have done the impossible time and time again. They *know* that they're going to beat this Arch Lich. They have faith in themselves and in one another. They might die one time, or a hundred times. Each time they will come back, more powerful than the last, better prepared and ready to defeat their enemy.

"The Stone Raiders have two things on their side: trust and time. They have trust in one another to do their best and help one another to complete their mission. They have trust that they will complete this raid no matter what. They see this as fun. They're excited and happy because this is the most challenging fight they've had to date!"

"You said that they have time," Hamdir reminded Shard.

"Correct. They might die, but they come back every time. While this in itself is a huge advantage, death is no longer the end to them. It is an opportunity. It also makes their lives slightly boring. There is no fear of dying, but there is the fear of failure. They call themselves the Stone Raiders as they love going on raids with one another. Fighting the biggest things they can find for the sheer *challenge* of it. Death holds nothing on them, but failing — to them, it's worse than death."

Silence fell over the room, each of the council members lost in their own thoughts.

Hamdir changed the different views, looking at a different preset. His eyes went wide as he watched Party Zero fighting. Suzy, Dave, and Induca were hammering undead with everything in their arsenal. Malsour stood out of the way.

Hamdir changed views, looking at all of the walls that were keeping the different undead out of the lobby.

"How do they have that much power?" Hamdir talked to himself as he switched back to the view that looked over the three who were fighting the bone lord.

With its natural resistances, strength, and armor, it was already a hard opponent. Instead of having a full army to fight it, there were just three people.

Anna and Steve moved out of the way of Deia as flames ignited around her body; her eyes glowed with power as a dozen Fire lances erupted out of thin air and rammed the bone lord.

It stumbled backward with the impact. Some of them broke through its armor and made their way inside, leaving holes in its body.

Anna moved in first. It had crossed the fifty percent threshold and it looked as if she was going to do everything in her power to stop it from activating its powers. She wasn't fast enough. It pulled itself together and swiped at her, giving it enough time and room to complete an attack of its own.

A magical circle appeared under its feet as it let out a howl. The undead around it seemed to reciprocate the howl.

"Shut UP!" Steve's hit smashed the howling Bone lord into the ground. Anna and Deia were there to ravage it with their attacks as Steve hacked its leg off.

The bone lord's Legendary move took effect.

The undead redoubled their efforts, going into a frenzy, and pushed back Dave, Induca, and Suzy.

Hamdir's eyes found Malsour. His body seemed to distort for a moment. He let out a yell that seemed to pass throughout the entire library. The undead took pause at the roar that Malsour had let rip.

Hamdir's eyes went open. He had only heard his roar, but his blood chilled with the power in it. It seemed to cancel out the bone lord's yell as Party Zero redoubled their efforts, yelling their defiance.

"You. Shall. Not. Pass!" Dave yelled, before he devolved into childish giggling, while still killing undead.

Hamdir noticed fighting styles that he hadn't seen in years and others that had been imprinted onto him from fighting since a youth. Dave moved from reaping wheat to cleaving tree and bending willow through to morning rise, back down into dragon's wings and whirlwind's mercy.

The blending of the styles so completely was an art form in itself. Dave's weapons changed as needed to create the most damage, adding extra weight in the downstroke to get the most out of the attack and then reducing the weight while he pulled back, so he could counter-attack faster.

As the others of Party Zero did a dance of magic, Dave danced with a multitude of weapons. He was second only to Anna and Deia. Each of their attacks were made to inflict the most damage: Their weapons an extension of themselves. Their powers an enhancement of their weapons and their movements. Their dance was a deadly one.

Steve was a brawler. There were hints that he was coming to learn more about fighting, yet brute strength ruled with him.

Hamdir couldn't even try to attempt to understand the powers or art that Malsour, Induca, and Suzy were using, but he could tell from his own adventures and experiences that they were no simple mages.

Hamdir found himself smiling, remembering how he had once seen such fights as a mere challenge. *I wonder, if none of my friends ever died from those adventures whether I, too, would have the same smile on my face?*

"Master, the Demons' progress is on schedule. There has been consistent fighting between the Demons. It seems that their aura has grown stronger than we thought. There are no creatures left in the wilds for them to fight." Boran-al's eyes focused on his master's back as the Dark Lord overlooked a glowing orb that moved and changed. It was showing a real- time view of Emerilia.

It specifically looked at Per'ush, moving from one area to another rapidly.

"What of their strength?" The Dark Lord's voice rumbled through the room. Although he was interested, it was clear he didn't care for the well- being of his creations.

"They have started fighting among one another more to sate their hunger for souls. They grow in strength by the day. A few have even shown a talent for magics. It is limited and uncontrolled but it is there."

"Good, so long as they have the strength needed. Once they get to Devil's Crater, then they can hunt the dungeons and creatures in the area. The surrounding towns and cities have forgotten their fear and their master. Send envoys to their cities, looking to convert them to our cause. Those who do, shall be spared. Those who do not, we will convince or destroy, so that no one else in the Pantheon might claim them."

"Yes, my lord." Boran-al bowed, taking that as his dismissal.

"I'm so BORED!" A woman swung her feet back and forth on her throne as she pouted. She had white hair and porcelain-smooth skin. Her lips were pink and her face would make many men and women of all the races lose their ability to think straight.

"My lady, you just played a prank on the King of Isa and made Queen Farun and Emperor Talis think that he was weak and start preparations to go to war," Venfik, her advisor said, not looking out over his scroll.

He was an Elf. His hair had long turned to white, while his eyes had been turned white by coming into the Lady of Air's service. She did not have Champions; instead, her Creatures of Power were dotted all over Emerilia, garnering respect for their power, or spite for their trickery.

"But that was last month!" She kicked her heels against her chair. "What about something with the mage's guild?"

Of the other lords and ladies of the Affinities Pantheon, most advisors held them in respect and even if they were about to make a bad decision, they kept their tone light, trying to convince them through other means.

Venfik's tone was like beaten steel.

"The Lady of Fire has made it clear that while you are welcome to come to her college and make use of her guild, if you mess with either of them she will destroy all of your Creatures of Power. It seemed she wasn't that happy when you started all those rumors of her return. Or sent the guild on a wild-goose chase for a magic well, in the middle of the Dark Lord's maze in Ashal while she was saying good-bye to her Dragons four hundred years ago. Add to that, she is, if not in an alliance with Water, at least on amicable terms, so it would be best to stay away from them."

"But we could always mess with the Lord of Water?" Air whined, much like a child might when asking their parent whether they could go outside to play, pretty please with a cherry on top.

"At times, you are the smartest lady I know. At others, I don't know what is going on in that mind of yours. Answer me this. Do you care for the People of Emerilia?"

"Well, yes, of course. If I didn't have them around, how would I have my fun? Also, it's not like my pranks hurt anyone. Like Farun is going to give up on her idea of a war because she wants to get her best people into the Dwarven tournaments next year. Talis might call himself an Emperor but he's really just got two cities and while he's an idiot, he's not stupid enough to attack Isa, without at least one more person in the fight. He wins by playing in the shadows and swooping in once victory is assured. Also, the Prince of Isa, and Aevstrra, the Princess of Raolor, daughter of Farun, are interested in each other." Air had a pleased smile on her face.

"I'm guessing that you had a part to play in that?"

"Well, of course. All that war is getting really annoying and I don't like Talis much. Having Raolor and Isa come together would join two decent-sized Ashal kingdoms. Also, might have given the two of them a Mirror of Communication after giving them plenty of time to talk to each other at one of the 'peace treaty talks.'" Air smiled at her own brilliance.

She missed Venfik's smile. It was not too dissimilar to the smile a parent might have when their child had done something to make them proud. "Well, then, how about instead of sowing chaos, we sow alliances?"

"Why would we do that?" Air frowned.

"There is a war coming, Air. Dark, Light, and Earth are massing their forces. They have more Champions than ever and if they don't have Creatures of Power out in Emerilia already, they are working on them as quickly as possible. If we are to sow the seeds of alliances, we could bring the People of Emerilia together. It is much harder to build something than it is to play a prank on them. I don't know if you would be up for the challenge," Venfik said in a dismissive tone.

"I see what you're trying to do, making me want to take it because I want to show you that I can do anything that I put my mind to and show you why I am the smartest of the Pantheon!" Air had an excited expression on her face.

"So, you're not going to do it?" Venfik asked.

"I didn't say that! This is my home as well and I'm not going to let those other lords and ladies get all the headlines! I accept your challenge/not challenge." She looked confused at her own words.

Venfik laughed and shook his head. "Very well, my lady, what shall we do?"

"I don't know! Let's go and ask Bob!" With that, the two of them disappeared from the room. The others who lived within the Lady of Air's hall smiled; a few laughed and rolled their eyes. For the most part, there was an anticipation and excitement in their eyes.

Much like their lady, they hated just lounging around.

Bob felt as someone entered his "hall." He turned from his seat. "This better be good," he muttered as he walked through the halls. It didn't take him long to reach the room where the two people had teleported into. He frowned as he recognized Air's aura and her minder, Venfik.

"What are you doing on my ship?" Bob demanded.

"We came to find out who are good people to make alliances with!" Air said, her usual excitable self.

Bob looked to Venfik.

"Hey! I'm the Lady of Air!" she complained, pouting and stomping her foot.

"When you act your age like you did three hundred years ago, I'll ask you the big questions." Bob knew that Air was as smart as they came. Instead of putting it to something useful, she used it to create pranks and make new Creatures of Power.

She might not have that much power, but even with what she had, she was a force to be reckoned with. Bob knew that half of her actions were a façade to get people to think of her as a teenager in goddess form. The other half was because she was lazy and it was easier for others to deal with explaining things. He knew the complexities of her projects.

They left his mind in twisters for it all.

"The Lady of Air is interested in making alliances between different groups. She sees it as a sort of challenge. As it is easy to bring the People of Emerilia to fighting, it is harder to make them make peace and fight together. We know that there is a war coming and we would like to see that we ally the right groups together. I think." Venfik looked to his lady, who shrugged.

"Pretty much."

"Why would I tell you about any possible alliances I have in the works? If I did tell you, what is to stop you from letting the rest of the Pantheon know, or to pull the alliances apart?" Bob asked.

"Oh, well, trust?"

Bob crossed his arms. His eyebrow rose as he tapped his foot. "You know, I am rather busy."

"Fine. Well, we could make a contract?" Air rolled her eyes.

"Do you think me an idiot? I know how you can get out of contracts like Air out of a balloon."

"Ugh, well, what else?" Air threw her hands down in defeat.

Bob studied her for a few minutes. "I will tell you something, something that only you might understand."

Air's eyes thinned for a second.

Bob saw through the teenager façade. "You've seen the limits of this planet, the rules that govern us all. The ones that I myself am beholden to and limited by. The forces that control me and all that goes on in Emerilia."

"And you say that I'm slippery with my contracts," she said with a sly smile, showing that she hadn't been just staring off into space through the meetings they held.

Bob returned the smile and chuckled. "Quite. Anyway, with this war, it will not just be Emerilia anymore. It could pull in forces much bigger than anything we have ever faced before." Bob held Air's eyes and saw his words hitting home. "The forces that will be visited upon Emerilia will be massive. The coming years will be like nothing this planet has ever seen in its entire history. It is not simply the alliances of one group against another anymore." There was only the odd thrumming of Bob's hall as Air and the Grey God exchanged looks.

Venfik shivered, overwhelmed with what Bob was saying.

A smile spread across Air's face. "Well, then, it seems that we have two people to meet first if we want to get these alliances started. How interesting—uniting Emerilia." She made an amused noise. "Now, that will be exciting!"

She disappeared from the deck, taking Venfik with her.

Bob looked at the space where they had stood, his features unreadable. "I hope it's for the best." He turned and headed deeper into his home. He still had a lot of work to do and Shard had patched him into the Aleph College's feeds to see the fight between the Stone Raiders and the Arch Lich.

16

REGROUP

"All right, everyone follow the route and we'll pull back to Lucy's location!" Josh said for the fifth time.

All of the Stone Raiders tensed, ready for the run. "Move!"

As one, the Stone Raiders' melee fighters pulled back and away from the undead. The mages unleashed their biggest spells and legged it.

The undead were slowed as the Stone Raiders ran because their lives depended on it. They exited through another path into the arena. Waiting support mages sealed it up with dirt, metal, and stone.

Josh looked on his mini map. All of the other parties that were split off were also pulling to Lucy's location. Only Party Zero was unable to run. Josh didn't have anyone he could send to them and help them escape. He knew that the phylactery was in the library with them.

I just need time to pull the guild together, get them organized. Then, I can send someone to help them. Hopefully, we attract enough attention from them that they can escape and meet up with us.

Josh checked the time.

They had been in the college for five hours already. They were at fifty percent of their fighting force. In just over an hour, more of the Stoner Raiders would respawn and could join back into the battle.

They ran between different buildings that looked similar to the college that Josh had gone to. They were better made, with the Aleph's mix of natural aesthetics and functionality.

Josh looked toward the loud noises that could be heard in the distance. He laughed as he saw the magical firepower that Kim was putting out, laying waste to anything that got in her way. "Well, I guess this is what we get for stopping her experiments inside! Now when Kim gets outside, she tries to blow up someone else's buildings!"

The Stone Raiders laughed, excited to be alive, to be on the raid, and confident in their skills and power.

"Watch out!" Deia called.

Anna jumped away from the bone lord as Steve threw himself out of the bone lord's range as it reached twenty-five percent Health.

"Fuck, scratched the paint!"

"Come on, dude! You know how annoying it is to fix your heavy ass!" Dave complained as he fired out a lightning orb into the center of his undead opponents. As time had gone on, he had gotten used to fighting the undead. They were higher levels and harder targets, but it was easy to tell what their basic attacks were going to be by their rough form.

The undead weren't that smart and kind of robotic, which led to Dave's hallways being a mass of slowly dissolving bodies and tombstones waiting to be looted.

The bone lord raised its hands up. Bones from the undead in range, both animated and not, were ripped out of their original positions, and swarmed around the bone lord to repair its wounds. Its eyes glowed in victory as it looked at its three main opponents, all of them tired and low on energy.

"Dave, cut the damn feeds. I've had enough of this prick," Malsour said, his voice growing deep.

Dave closed his eyes, conjuring items into the Magical Circuits that formed recording devices that could see into the lobby. "Done! The Arch Lich is probably going to sense whatever you're doing!"

"Let him." Malsour's voice grew deeper as his body elongated. His tired and sweaty expression faded away in relief as black scales spread across his body. He shook himself, his legs growing claws as wings sprouted from his back.

"Much easier." Malsour's voice was deep and powerful as he looked at the recovering bone lord. Malsour let out a powerful bellow; black flames came out in a stream.

The Bone lord let out a painful screech.

Deia watched the power of a true Dragon.

Malsour walked forward. His flames made the bone lord's sixty percent Health plummet. The bone lord continued to try to regenerate. Suzy, Induca, and Dave stayed back as their opponents were torn apart to fuel the Bone lord's need for new bones to stay together.

Malsour slowed his burn as hundreds of creatures were torn apart. The bone lord consumed all of its allies as its repair skill was active. It finally gave up. The bone lord sunk to its knees as Malsour's flames intensified.

Malsour's flames disappeared. There were ripples in the ground from their impact and intense heat. Different inanimate objects had grown in odd ways under the pure Dark Mana flames.

There was only a tombstone to mark where the bone lord had been. "And stay down. Fucking thing was doing my head in." Malsour's voice got deeper and more powerful as he shook his majestic bulk.

"I can't hold the walls much longer in my other form. I suggest someone grabs that bone lord's loot and we go group up with the others? Oh, and has someone got a Mana potion?" Malsour asked.

"Don't fuck with a Dragon," Dave said. The creature that they had taken hours to whittle down, Malsour had torn apart in mere minutes.

"Words to live by," Induca said.

"Malsour is right—we're all tired. Dave and I will lead. Anna, Steve at the back. Rest of you in the middle." Deia looked to Anna and then the tombstone.

Anna clicked it and opened a prompt. She took all the loot from the tombstone, which disappeared moments later.

"On the road again! Dun-nuh unhuh road again!" Steve said.

"Well, you just ruined one of the great Willie Nelson's greatest songs." Dave sighed.

"What is with you gamers and damn music lyrics all the time? If it's not 'another one bites the dust', it's 'let the bodies hit the floor,'" Suzy said. Her different creations jumped into her bag of holding; her Air creations held onto her, Light creations attached to them.

"Well, you're a gamer too, should get to know the lingo," Dave quipped.

"Well, what about that big lummox? He's a damned AI in a big metal box with arms and legs. Anna, what the hell did you teach him?"

"Well, he always had a great interest in Players. He picked up a few things, I think. It was half the problem with why he was a pain in the ass to control. Always wanted to go on adventures like Players," Anna said.

"Am I the only one thinking that this might not be the best place to talk about this?" Malsour asked.

"I just usually wait until they run out of steam." Induca and Deia shared a knowing and sympathetic look.

"And we're running!" Deia jogged for the door Dave had been defending.

The rest of the party followed. Malsour turned into his human form, a look of strain on his face for a few moments before they exited the library and back out onto the stairs that led up to it.

Dave closed his eyes, allowing the video feed to reactivate. Immediately, Dave sensed someone using the video feed to study the library. *I wonder what they think of our renovations.*

Deia let out an angry cry. "Fire plow!" A plow shot out in front of her, accelerating as it went. It didn't kill many of the undead that were rushing up the steps, but it did throw them out of the way as the party moved forward. The plow ran out and Suzy took her turn; a half-dozen beams of light projected out of her Light creations. Undead screamed in pain as they looked upon the light or were found in its path; their bodies erupted in flames with the holy light.

Steve just hummed tunelessly and swiped his axe as if he were going through a field of grass, cutting down the stunned undead.

Anna hurled out her wind blades.

Whistling came from overhead. Dave's artillery spears of Light landed in the biggest groups of undead and turned them into flying bits.

"Ah, I do love a nice mid-afternoon jog," Dave said, loud enough for everyone to hear.

"It's three in the morning!" Suzy said.

"Well, it's mid-afternoon somewhere, right?"

"If there is a god, please, for my sanity, make him shut the hell up."

Even though they were heavily outnumbered and charging through a horde of undead, Party Zero laughed together. It might have sounded tired or relieved, but still they laughed.

17

MUCH-NEEDED RESPAWNS

"We're not going to be able to get through here!" Deia said as they looked along their fourth route. It was filled with undead.

Deia looked over everyone. They had been fighting for just over six hours, most of it fighting in the library or running away from undead and various creatures in the college. Even with their high Endurance, their fights had taken a heavy toll on their bodies.

"Pull back to the teleport pads!" Deia yelled.

Dave grunted as he was hit by an undead and flew back a few feet. He got to his feet, clearly wobbly.

"I've got him." Steve grabbed Dave. "Let's go!" Deia said.

They turned from the undead. Deia cast her Fire plow as Induca let loose a plasma cannon shot into the undead swarming behind them.

"I can't do another shot in this form," Induca said. The strain of casting so much magic was clear in her voice.

"I've got maybe a few more shots," Suzy added. "I'm okay for a bit," Malsour said.

Deia felt the anxiety in her stomach as she charged after her plow. Anna ran up next to her. The two of them cut down anything that got in their way.

"How you feeling?" Anna asked.

"Got some still left in the tank. Head's hurting like hell and I'm tired and hungry," Deia admitted.

"We've got this," Anna said.

Deia gritted her teeth and plowed on. She was covered in bruises and she'd gained a concussion from something hitting her hood. Her armor's Mana barrier stopped her from getting her head caved in but the shock was still partly transmitted to her head.

She blinked fiercely. The sudden light of her Fire attacks made her brain shudder in pain. She drove on, keeping up her attacks. As much as it hurt, she didn't dare to slow them down.

"Where are they going?" Hamdir watched Party Zero.

"Looks like back to the teleporters. Seems that they can't break through to the main group of Stone Raiders and the Arch Lich is sending a lot of his forces to try to hunt them down." Shard sounded almost nervous.

"Will they make it?" Hamdir asked. "I don't know." Shard shrugged.

"Smart move—go back to the teleporters and then come out at another location," Frenik grunted.

"They'll most likely group up with their respawned forces," Shard said.

There were looks of confusion. Shard changed the main viewing screens that were in the center of the council's chamber.

Around forty Stone Raiders stood in a teleport pad room. Stone Raiders entered through one of the teleport pads, opening their soul bound bags of holding and equipping any gear that they had lost on their dead bodies in the college.

"Where are they coming from?" Sela asked.

"Our very own Altar of Rebirth." Shard changed the view. The Altar of Rebirth blazed white before a Stone Raider practically leaped off the altar and rushed through rooms and the teleport pad that linked the Altar of Rebirth in Alephir to the city that the Stone Raiders were living in.

"Is there not an issue with them possibly running through Alephir?" Koza asked.

"I asked Josh to make sure that no one goes through areas that they are not allowed access to. Few have deviated from the direct path from the Altar of Rebirth to the teleport pad. While there is a fight going on, I wouldn't think any of them would try to search Alephir. All they want to do is get back into the fight."

Hamdir sat back in his chair and looked over the fortress that the Stone Raiders had made in the middle of the college's main street. A five-meter by ten-meter trench ringed their defenses; metal spikes sprouted from it, ready to claim anything that tried to get close. Priests and mages with a Light Affinity blessed the metals. Just being close to them, the undead felt pain.

By the minute, the trench grew wider. Battlements stood above the trench, walls of earth. On the first floor, melee fighters fired bolt throwers or used their spears to keep anything from making it to their walls. On the second floor, there were archers. The third floor held casting balconies for the mages.

It had taken minutes for the fortress to take form. From the speed of its creation, it was a structure that they had practiced making dozens of times. It was simple, inelegant but functional.

Mages grouped together inside the fortress on raised platforms. They conjured artillery spells. The mages on the walls guided the spells into the undead. Bone lords and larger undead creations like the shambling mounds caused trouble but the Stone Raiders were figuring out a system to deal with them as time went on.

Hamdir leaned forward as he looked at a crafter working on the wall with a chisel and mallet. "What are they carving into the walls?"

"It is code runing, a refined form of Magical Circuits. It should make the walls stronger or give them different attributes depending on what the coding entails," Shard said.

"I've had a look at it. Formulaic but simple and easy to understand. A certain refinement to it that makes it alluring," Frenik said.

"They've built a fortress in a matter of minutes and now they're runing the damn walls? What kind of monsters are they?" Koza said breathlessly.

"They've adapted to being the weakest in any situation. It is why they are never confident in their own skills and their defenses. They will constantly work on themselves and their skills to give them an edge."

"Party Zero is nearly at a teleport pad!" Ela-Dorn squealed. Anxiety, excitement, and hope mixed on her face as she balled her fists together, as if praying for the party to make it.

Hamdir changed screens.

Light blinded him as the Light creations around Suzy seemed to shine in brilliance. Dozens of undead were wiped away by the magical attack.

Induca made to grab her as she fell, but Malsour was there, scooping her up over his shoulder. Steve caught the now inert creation cores as they fell.

Induca caught others with Fire whips.

Deia and Anna tore through the undead. Their grace from before changed to mindless strength. They were too tired to do anything but react. They entered the teleport control room, and turned to cover the others.

Malsour and Induca ran to them, their own Dark and Fire magics tearing at those who tried to follow them. Steve crashed through a wall, covering Dave, so he didn't get hurt. He slammed shoulder first into the first floor and pushed himself up to his feet.

Hamdir didn't miss the look of determination on the behemoth's face. The normally joking AI concentrated on just one thing: keeping his friends alive.

The other conscious four let him pass, backing up as their magic and attacks made the undead and living creatures pay dearly for following them. Malsour and Induca passed through the teleport pad's event horizon.

Deia grabbed Anna and jumped into the air, holding her hand out as four plasma cannons appeared and fired. They were thrown backward and through the teleport pad that cut off before the explosion of plasma could follow.

They lay on the ground of the teleport room where the rest of the Stone Raiders who had respawned were waiting.

Deia passed out. Anna stayed on the floor, panting. Malsour groaned, laying Suzy down before he rolled onto the ground himself.

Induca checked Suzy over as the ground shook with Steve lying down. "Someone give me a soul gem!"

The Stone Raiders in the teleport room rushed to help their fellows, administering healing, as well as various potions to regenerate Mana and reduce fatigue.

Food and water was produced.

What are they going to do next?

Josh drank the sports drink concoction and let out a breath as he sat down heavily.

They had been fighting for six and a half hours. They'd been able to set up a camp of sorts, with the undead all around them. It was amazing what a few Earth and Dark mages could do with plenty of Mana and the right kind of motivation.

The undead kept coming, pushing one another into the growing pit ahead of the battlements or getting hit by the ranged weapons and spells.

Half of the seventy or so Stone Raiders who had made it so far were recovering, meditating, eating, drinking and caring for their weapons.

Lucy was running supplies. Jules, who had survived, was running medical. Esa was leading melee. Kim ran the ranged magical fighters. Mikal had the archers and the melee fighters armed with bows if they could handle it. Bolt throwers and crossbows if they couldn't.

Josh's purchases for the guild had made every member capable of fighting at distance. It had already paid off for itself as melee fighters plugged away with bolts.

A drop pad had been erected and powered up. Supplies came in from Shard, who had automatons picking up supplies stacked around the Stone Raiders' tower and pushing them through to the Stone Raiders.

"Okay, so, are we going to link up with you in the fortress, or do you want us to fight our way to the phylactery?" Deia asked.

"How strong are Suzy's Air creations?" Josh asked through the private chat.

"I'm not sure."

"Well, if they're capable of holding people up, then I have an idea."

18

FLY MONKEYS, FLY!

Deia finished talking to the Stone Raiders who were gathered back in the tower.

"Well, hell, sounds easy when you put it that way," Dave said.

Deia gave him an unamused look before she turned to Suzy. "Can you do it?"

"Yeah, I can, but it's going to make me useless after and I'm going to need to come with you. The distance is just too large for me to command the creations by myself."

"What if instead of flying the entire way, we just did till we got to the campus buildings on either side of the main strip? Then to cross the distance between the roofs and the grand library?" Anna interjected.

"That would help out a lot," Suzy admitted.

"We could also put drop pads at different locations so that even if this does get all messed up, then we'd at least be starting from somewhere closer," Malsour said.

"Agreed. Could you and Dave make the preparations or see if we have any spare drop pads?"

"On it!" Dave got to his feet. It had been an hour since they'd escaped from the college and although he had been largely healed, he was still weak from expending so much Mana and Stamina.

All of them were, but the longer they waited, the longer the Arch Lich would have to prepare.

"Okay, we've got an hour. Be ready!"

"What the hell is that?" Josephine asked her partner, Mikal, in close area chat. "Bone lords? Though they're so far away. Damn, it's hard to make out with the shadows."

Mikal held his tongue, using his natural abilities as well as a spell of far sight to see what they were talking about.

Two massive creatures of bone slowly made their way through the ranks of undead. The undead moved out of their way, a parting sea of bodies.

What is that on them? It almost looks like it's alive. Looks kind of like darklings.

"Jake! Get over here! I've got some weird ass undead that have arrived!" Mikal called out.

Jake didn't take long to show up, eating a vibrant bowl of salad, completely at odds with his own pale complexion. "Wha?" Jake munched on a leaf.

Mikal pointed to the two creatures.

Jake squinted. Mikal cast far sight on him as his fork stopped in mid-air.

"Well, holeee-shit. Those are bone creations alrighty, but they're imbued with Dark energy. How the hell did he do that?"

"Aren't all bone creations made of Dark energy?" Josh walked into the room.

"Well, it's the glue that holds them together. It would be better to say that they have been given corrupting energy. The Dark miasma that is leaking out of their bodies across their spikes and weapons is a *powerful* corrupting force. It's been attached and imbued into the creatures themselves. I wouldn't be surprised that if those creatures got within range of us, they would give off a corrupting aura that would harm all of those within its sphere of influence."

"So, it would be scary as hell?" Josephine asked.

"It would taint the air and the ground, damaging any within a certain range. Getting cut by one of those blades would not be fun." Jake shook his head.

"So, we keep it out of the fortress and hit it at range," Josh said. "Best bet, those things get in here, it's going to be a mess. They're level 207 but their natural abilities are going to make them scary as hell."

"Add in the fact that with their arms and spiked bodies, any attack we land is likely going to hurt the attacker..." Mikal trailed off.

"Kim! I've got a new target for you! Mikal, send a message to the Flying Monkey Brigade. They've got until those things start getting into range." Josh marched away from the wall.

"Get ready! There are two unknown mobs walking toward the fortress. Josh wants us to head out toward the library before they reach the fortress. You've got ten minutes!" Deia yelled.

Thankfully, all of those who had respawned came back with full energy. Party Zero were the only ones who had to gain back their strength the hard way. Stamina came back quickly due to their high Endurance. The same went for Mana, which they could all supplement with the four sets of Abscondita armor they could all draw power from.

There was a group of fifty, all of them staying off to the side. Those who had respawned, but had not been picked, armed themselves, either from the guild's weapons or used their own soul bound weapons. With their high levels and the amount of wealth they had, a number of them had been able to get soulbound weapons.

There were three crafters who could take care of the binding of the weapons. Still, the weapons were rare and expensive; only about five percent of the Stone Raiders had them. Most just had duplicates, all of them veteran raiders ready for the eventuality of their deaths.

They walked through the other teleport pad that was open, going right into the middle of the fortress to support the Raiders who hadn't died. The fifty or so fighters came together, ready for their mission.

Deia looked around, seeing that they were all accounted for. "Let's go steal that Arch Lich's soul box!" She turned to lead the fifty Stone Raiders out into the fortress.

They moved off to the third story that was closest to the buildings in the direction of the grand library. Air creations started to fly out of Suzy's bag; her staff glowed with power as they attached themselves to the backs of the fifty Stone Raiders.

"Good luck!" Josh called out. "Good to go!" Suzy reported.

"Let's go!" Deia yelled back over the sighs of the undead both alive and being put to rest as spells, bolts, and arrows screamed through the air.

"Fly monkeys, fly!" Steve took a running leap off the third-story magical balconies. His flying was more like slowly falling as the four Air creations attached to him fought to make sure he didn't go crashing through the buildings he was supposed to land on.

"This is not the land of OZ!" Dave shook his head in pain at another movie reference being lost on his hopeless friends.

Deia laughed despite the seriousness of what they were doing. Suzy's Air creation picked her up off the roof and flew with the other Stone Raiders, quickly crossing over the undead.

One was pulled from the air by an undead shambling mound's vines. Mages back in the fortress sent spell after spell into the shambling mound before it could bring the Stone Raider into its maw. The vines were cut and the Air creation tore the Stone Raider away from the shambling mound. It let out a keening wail as it succumbed to the mage's spells, crushing an undead minotaur at its side.

Deia landed on the buildings. No one needed to be told anything as they ran for the grand library. Steve already led the way.

She cast a glance back at the fortress. The twin bone creations that had scared Josh into action were now close enough to be analyzed.

Bone Juggernaut Level 207

"Pick up the pace!" Deia had a sense of foreboding when she looked at the two juggernauts. *If we don't deal with this phylactery, I think we're screwed.* The thought pervaded her mind. As much as she wanted to ignore it, she couldn't.

She picked up her pace and the Stone Raiders sprinted over the rooftops with ease.

19

FAILURES AND SUCCESSES

"Those conspiring creatures! What do they know of true magic! Using creations to carry them! Scared to even face my creatures! I will show them. I will make bone archers and draugr when I leave this place. Undead legions capable of shooting arrows and magic as well as tearing them apart on the ground!" the Arch Lich screamed. The room he was in looked as though it was rotting as his corrupting influence escaped his control in a fit of anger.

He was furious at the creatures that not only dared to kill his experiments, but then tried to escape his juggernauts as they were finally reaching the fortress the maggots had made. He wouldn't admit his own frustrations at not foreseeing the need for archers or ranged attackers. He had moved in more undead shambling mounds around the fortress, so that no more were able to escape.

The Arch Lich's attention was focused on his newest creations. He willed his lesser undead into the pit that had claimed so many of them. They howled in pain and anger at being unable to reach their opponents. The undead writhed and screamed on the blessed metal spikes, but more and more of them filled the pit. They advanced over the carcasses of one another, creating a bridge across the spikes. More and more undead accepted their deaths.

The fighters in the fortress focused all of their attacks on the juggernauts. One lost twenty-five percent Health. They focused all their attacks onto the one creature. It howled out and turned with speed that belied its size.

The dumb creature, not understanding where it was, followed its instincts to activate its Legendary action to cut down anything that was within fifty meters of it. That included the other juggernaut. It was thrown back, losing fifteen percent of its Health from the attack.

"Well, there are bound to be a few sacrifices. I will have to look at trying to making them smarter. It will be annoying to have them act the same way every time." The Arch Lich drifted over to a bookshelf and pulled off a book with his thin, skeletal fingers.

The juggernaut recovered from its Legendary attack, but the obnoxious living maggots had taken out a further seven percent of its Health, with status effects slowing the juggernaut further and stacking damage upon it. Even with the vicious spells, the juggernaut's massive Health pool was going down slowly.

It staggered under multiple magical artillery barrages, the undead around it obliterated. It took a step forward. The undead had to keep throwing themselves on the spikes that were now moving in order to keep their bridge.

The second juggernaut started to rise with difficulty. Its blade arms stuck into the ground, cutting through it. Its corruption seemed to melt the ground, making it slip and snarl.

The Arch Lich gave out a displeased noise as he sent some of his larger undead to help the second juggernaut to its feet. "They dare to wound my newest creations," his voice slightly crazed, his prior amusement turning to cold anger.

It was clear that his forces were taking heavy losses, but with time they would crush the Stone Raiders.

There were many more undead than Stone Raiders and they were unending. The Stone Raiders were burning through their Mana pools.

The Arch Lich turned from his research for the first time in forever. He had given up his body and his people so that he could learn more about the secrets of magic. To any, its anger would have sent shivers down their spines.

Drawing such a powerful creatures gaze could only mean one thing, death was coming for those that angered him.

"Skewer that fucker!" Josh yelled out. The first juggernaut was just crossing the undead bridge, while the second looked like a comedic skit, if it wasn't for the fact it could shrug off magical artillery and it was taking the biggest and strongest of the undead to get it back on its feet.

The first juggernaut made it three meters, its feet on the undead bridge that sagged underneath it. More undead threw themselves down to try to make sure it wasn't speared by the metal spikes below.

They'd forgotten one thing: the spikes had been pulled from the earth by Dark mages.

Spikes shot through the undead bridge and from its sides. As they slammed into the juggernaut, it cried out, making those nearest duck at its screams.

Its corrupting powers made the spikes dissolve with necrotic damage. As one spike was destroyed, another sped out of the ground in its place. Priests, healers, and Light mages could be heard giving out their blessings on the metal constructs and also covering the juggernaut in what looked like a cloak of golden light.

The corrupting forces warred against the power of the Light, eating at each other.

Josh laughed at it all, filled with pride and excitement at his own Stone Raiders. The power that they were throwing out sent shockwaves through the air.

"That's how the Stone Raiders do it! Get some of that, you pikey fuck!" The Stone Raiders stood on a precipice. If they worked together flawlessly, they might possibly defeat the bone juggernaut. If they didn't, then they'd fall apart and be killed. There was no time for second-guessing; they were reacting, working together—one guild, one group pulled together by their desire to be the best raiders in all of Emerilia. They yelled and screamed out different words, but if one was to see their faces, instead of cold fear, they held eerie smiles.

This was what they had come for; this was what they desired to do. If they were to pick one thing out of anything else that they wanted to do, it was this: to fight beside their friends against a supposedly unbeatable opponent. Here, they were in their element. All of their passions were realized, their hearts thumping in their chests. They had never felt so alive! Gamers were introverted people for the most part, but here, right now, they cried out for more bolts, called out weaknesses. They didn't care about their social anxieties and fears. All of that was swept away: they were their characters and nothing was going to stop them.

"That's right, you Arch Lich dickhead, you fucked with the wrong bloody people! Don't you know who the Stone Raiders are!?" Josh laughed. He grabbed a bow from his bag of holding and fired into the juggernaut that was slowly walking across its fellows that were trying to rush past it and cover the spikes before it. They had to replace their disappearing forces that had already sacrificed their bodies.

Josh's eyes lit up with the tombstone markers dotted over the battlefield.

Josh fired into the juggernaut again and again. The entire guild was focused on the big bastard. It reached fifty percent Health, but the guild didn't let up, hammering it for all it was worth, not letting it use its Legendary skill.

The juggernaut gave up as it approached forty percent Health; it staggered forward, as if it was almost drunk as it tried to reach the wall.

It got to thirty percent when it finally reached the fortress wall. Its bladed hand crashed into the wall, cutting through it and corrupting the metal, earth, and stone that made it.

"Eat this, dipshit," Matt called out as magical runes flared in protection.

The juggernaut was thrown back fifty meters, disintegrating as it went. The Stone Raiders cheered, yelling at the undead, some of which charged over their dead to try to climb the walls or get through the large hole the juggernaut had opened.

The undead that got their limbs through were cut apart as the walls closed on them. The ones crawling the walls forgot about the melee fighters; spears and staves tossed them off the walls and into the spike pits below.

The second juggernaut finally rose to its feet.

Josh hadn't needed to say anything. The Stone Raiders' attacks centered on the second juggernaut. The strongest of the undead had been needed to raise the thing back onto its feet. Now, they were wiped out by the spells and long range weapons raining down on the juggernaut.

It didn't have time to move as it hit twenty-five percent. The Stone Raiders stopped attacking.

The juggernaut sliced and diced its way through any of its remaining comrades that had allowed it to regain its feet.

"Focus on the other undead!" Josh called out. He looked to Jake, who rubbed his hands in anticipation.

Undead started to climb up the buildings, but they were too slow to catch the Stone Raiders. In the distance, through the low light and flickering mage lights, Deia saw the grand library and the mass of tombstones at its front entrance.

She heard a whistling in the distance as spears slammed into the dome- like structure in the center of the library. The spears were destroyed by a heavy Mana barrier. More and more spears rained down from the heavens. Their runes glowed as they hit the barrier.

Steve leapt free of the buildings, the Air creations on his back doing their best to extend the distance he traveled.

Stone Raiders followed him off the building, jumping off five-story buildings with complete faith in Suzy, as her creations carried them on toward the library.

Deia leaped; her attached Air creation guided her flight through the air.

A scream tore through the air, making people shudder and break out into a cold sweat.

"Keep moving!" Deia yelled as a murderous aura filled with killing intent seemed to erupt throughout the Aleph College's grounds.

"They dare! They dare to kill my juggernaut!" The area around the Arch Lich started to decay as Dark mana spread over twenty feet, looking like black flames, destroying anything in their path.

"I will show them their place as my test subjects! I will turn them into bones of malice and despair through decades of torture!"

The Arch Lich floated through an open doorway, his flames destroying the balcony below.

He waved his hand; a bone reaver stepped out of the library he had been studying in. The Arch Lich sat on the creature.

It looked like a mix between a wolf and a cheetah.

Its legs and body was made for speed, with blades for limbs and a wolf skull for a head.

Its bones weren't yellow but black from the Arch Lich using the creature and his Dark affinity and aura corrupting the bones further.

All around the Arch Lich Skeleton creatures stepped out of the building, their bones clacking against the surfaces as they let out tortured screams.

This was the Arch Lich's true strength, his skeleton army. One thousand strong creatures that he had sunk his power and time into making. They were the greatest of his weapons.

"Let us go greet your new comrades!" The Arch Lich rasped, his leathery old face twisted in crazed anger as his eyes glowed with a smoky green light that would make any shirk away in fear.

The skeletons raised their weapon, their screeching and pained cheers consoling the Arch Lich as his reaver rushed forwards.

The other skeletons mounted other reavers or faster members of the skeleton army, or simply ran forward.

He sent commands to his undead forces attacking the Stone Raiders.

They charged forwards letting out their cries while also making a path for their Master Skeleton Army.

"What the hell?" Dwayne muttered as the undead were now surging forth.

"They're making a push! Keep them back!" Josh yelled out.

The Stone Raiders' crude defenses lit up with magical spells, destruction staffs, arrows and bolts.

"To the walls!" Kim cried out, a note of panic in her voice.

Don't let what happened with the spiders happen here! Josh half thought, half prayed.

Anyone that could use a weapon got up to the walls.

People that were missing limbs grabbed what they could, dragging themselves to an opening.

There was no time for orders. People yelled out to one another, telling where undead were concentrating, pointing out higher level mobs that were an issue.

Most of the creatures were just reanimated dead, making them magical constructs, creatures that contained Mana, fighting against the barrier.

However, there were also soulbound undead, similar to draugr. These were creatures that had their souls forcibly molded and attached to their bodies.

They made it to the wall, clawing at it or trying to climb it.

They rushed into the spike pit with abandon even as Dark mages increased its depth and width. The undead filled the pit around the defenses, creating bridges for their fellows.

"We've got something approaching in the distance!' A scout called out, waypointing something. Josh cut off an undead's arms, dropping them down to the writhing mass of undead below.

He looked to where the waypoint was, using a far sight spell.

"What the hell?" Josh looked at the oncoming army of skeletons and bone creations; each and every one of the creatures gave off a corrupting aura similar to the bone juggernauts.

He felt a dominating presence among them.

His eyes locked with twin green glowing orbs of malice.

Josh felt his heart quiver as the Arch Lich seemed to look in his very soul and promise him unimaginable pain.

Josh was hit from the side, breaking eye contact.

Josh shook his head, a sense of dread filling him. He cut down another creature trying to scale the wall, dodging out of reach of a rotting vine.

"The Arch Lich is coming!" Josh yelled to the rest of the guild as he focused on dealing with the scaling creatures. The undead now covered the pit, turning it into a flat ground for them to cross.

The second bone juggernaut was getting closer. It was making good progress and its Health stayed the same as the Stone Raiders were focused on the undead at their walls.

Just then, several spears made of shadows slammed into the Mana barrier, making it quiver and turn an angry red.

More and more spears smashed into the barrier, coloring it darker and darker.

The spears' aura made Josh quiver in fear.

If they make it through the barrier, they'll blow the wall apart. I need to save the POEs; us Players can come back.

"POEs to the center of the camp! Support from there!" Josh called out. If it was any other time, the POE might argue about being treated different than the Players, but they understood. Right now, they could split their guildmates attention when they couldn't spare it.

The undead parted for their master and his skeleton army.

Josh glanced at the army; all of the skeletons and bone creations were of a high level, each exuding an aura of decay and maliciousness.

A truly massive Dark spear crashed into the barrier, two, then three followed afterwards, making the barrier shake dangerously.

Cracks formed as the barrier strained against the Arch Lich. Those that were near the runes for the Mana barrier pushed their power into it. The wounded that couldn't move altered their Stone Raider amulets to supply power to the Mana barrier. Even if they died, any bit of power they could put into helping the Stone Raiders get victory, they would give it.

It held for just a few more minutes.

It shattered under the constant and unrelenting barrage. Where the spears had impacted they had killed all of the undead around.

Spears careened off into the sky before the Arch Lich adjusted to fire more at the walls.

"Get back!" Josh yelled, turning as he saw a Dark spear appear around the Arch Lich and race towards the wall.

The world seemed to turn quiet as Josh saw some people trying to jump away from the section of wall that the spear was aimed at. Others were too caught up in battle to notice the spear or others' warnings.

The black spear crashed into the wall.

As it struck, the wall exploded like a bomb, people being thrown like ragdolls. Undead on the wall or near it were thrown back, killed by their master's spell.

Stone Raiders were killed by the explosion or torn apart by the raging Dark Mana that made up the spear, others were crushed or hit by the flying debris.

"Get down from the walls!" Dwayne called out. As time resumed its normal pace, blood fell from a cut on Dwayne's forehead.

The Stone Raiders camp was chaos as everyone tried to flee the walls as spears seemed to come in from every direction.

Josh leapt from the wall, glancing back at the Arch Lich that was now halfway through his undead army. Darkness seemed to cling to him like a cloak as a sea of darklings raced out of it, racing towards the defenses as fast as the spears that were cracking his defenses.

The darklings rushed through the undead, turning them to ash as they floated through the openings in the walls.

"Darklings!" Kim called out. "Blessed land!"

A golden light grew over the area that the Stone Raiders were pulling back to. Their strength had been cut down by a third and they were in a space half the size with the walls exploding, being pummeled into gravel as undead surged forwards in the new openings. Even if their fellows were cut down by the Arch Lich's magic, they continued their forward charge.

The darklings cried out as they entered the blessed land area of effect spell. The undead screamed, their dark bodies falling apart among their weakest members.

"Mages, focus on blessed land!" Josh yelled out.

"Darklings are only affected by magical weapons!" Lucy reminded everyone.

"With me!" Dwayne yelled, charging forward the few feet to the undead that had entered the blessed land, his sword and shield moving, taking down a darkling and an undead without pausing his charge.

Then, the skeleton army arrived.

Josh rushed forwards with his twin daggers, dispatching anything that came at him.

There was a commotion behind the undead as the skeleton army appeared.

They came through the openings in the walls, cutting down anything in their path.

Undead that were too slow to move felt the sharpened bones of their master's personal army.

The Arch Lich let out a screech, rising over the Stone Raider's broken walls.

Josh swore that the creature looked *pleased* with the chaos and death it saw.

It held out its hand, dark streams of light streaking out to crash into the blessed land's spell formation.

Spells and weapons were aimed at the Arch Lich, but it didn't even pay attention as they were eaten up by the Dark Mana that surged around it.

Its power was like a crushing weight on the Stone Raiders.

There was no way that they could survive against everything that was attacking them.

It's up to Party Zero now. The thought brought with it a sense of calm as Josh attacked with abandon.

He knew that he would probably die, so he was going to use everything he had to give those to either side of him a chance. He would die to give his guild mates the chance to live.

"Stone Raiders!" Josh yelled. His cry seemed to rally the guild. "Stone Raiders!" They cried out defiantly, even in the faces of creatures that had come back from the land of the dead.

Bone creations covered in serrated bone blades meant to tear and rip moved over the walls.

Instead of recoiling in fear, the Stone Raiders surged forwards, eager to greet these new opponents.

Dave dropped to the ground in a roll. He came up brandishing a sword and shield. A savage smile crossed his lips. When he'd been healed back to full Health, he'd glanced at his notifications to find that he had made it to Master level 1 for two handed.

It gave him the ability to claim the class Weapons Master, which gave him plus 20 to Vitality, plus 10 to Endurance, and plus 15 to Strength and Agility.

He laughed as he slammed the undead out of his way. Every hit with his sword put the undead to permanent rest.

They stormed through the front doors. What had been hard for Party Zero before was now easy for the fifty Stone Raiders fresh from their respawn. The Stone Raiders moved into a protective circle. Malsour's walls had been broken down in most places, but it didn't matter now.

Malsour nodded to Dave.

Dave looked up at the ceiling, making a square of metal in the roof above them. He destroyed it but the conjured item had cut right through the floor. It dropped to the ground as Dave continued to conjure boxes and then destroy them in the floors above.

It continued up for a dozen floors.

Dave dropped his arms, now thoroughly drained. "It's done!" he yelled.

"Pull back! Malsour, we ready?" Deia asked. The circle of Stone Raiders became smaller as they moved toward Dave and Malsour.

"As it will ever be," Malsour said. What looked like a gazebo made from metal seemed to grow out of the ground.

"Everyone on!" Deia yelled.

The Stone Raiders jumped on the thirty-by-thirty metal box. Walls erected around them as they shot upward and through the holes Dave had created in the ceilings above.

Sweat seemed to pour from Malsour's face. He hadn't yet recovered from the last time he had been in the library, only three hours ago.

The box stopped and the Stone Raiders poured out, finding themselves among bookshelves in a massive room.

Heavy footsteps could be heard, converging on their position. "Dave, go find it. Steve, Anna, Induca, cover him!" Deia yelled.

The sources of the loud noises appeared, three lumbering bone lords.

The Stone Raiders organized themselves, used to the dance between themselves and higher-leveled targets.

Dave and the others grouped together.

"Bye, dickheads!" Dave waved at the bone lords as Malsour pushed them through the library, closer to where they needed to be.

Dave shook his head as he got his bearings and started to run. He felt bad about leaving his guild mates, but he needed to find that box. If he got to it fast enough, then he could end the Arch Lich and his minions.

"We're nearly there!" Dave yelled. He used the bookshelves to get higher. He winced at what he was doing but between books and helping his guild, he'd pick his guild every time.

The Arch Lich's eyes filled with pure anger as he turned toward the grand library. He had felt faint life forces moving through his domain of death. Enraged with the loss of his bone juggernaut, he had not been paying attention to his most sacred treasure and close kept secret.

Now his alarm runes flared to life, living and breathing creatures had made it into the grand library and were heading straight towards his phylactery.

With a screech that could be heard through the entire college, he rushed toward the grand library.

The air exploded around him as he sped off in the direction of his phylactery, his source of life and continued survival.

He called on every spell he knew to increase his speed.

He had underestimated them. He had thought that they had run from the grand library in fear.

It was clear what their aim was. He tried to use all the trap runes that he had, but something was destroying them before he could. His screech of frustration pierced the ears of undead and living alike.

The skeleton army and undead forces turned as one, rushing towards the grand library to defend their master's most prized possession.

The Arch Lich's face was unreadable as he heard cheering in reply to its screams.

He would make them pay. He would bring them back to death again and again, until he bound their souls to their very bodies. They would be his first draugr — their souls twisted and shaped to serve him throughout eternity!

20

ROCKET
MAN

"Come on, you've got this," Bob said from his chair. He gripped the edges of it as he saw most of Party Zero rush through the library, leaping from the bookshelves. Steve just jumped from the floor he was on to the one above, his legs like jackhammers, leaving dents in the ground.

They tore a door apart by simply colliding with it. They'd made it into a domed room. At the very top, there were rare books lining preserved cases. Among them was the Arch Lich's phylactery.

None of the party slowed as they rushed forward. Bob gripped his seat tighter, warping the metal and the control panels, silently willing them on. Bob's eyes went wide as the glass window in the room facing outside exploded with the arrival of a screeching Arch Lich.

"No, come on! There has to be a way!" Bob yelled at the screen, pulling his armrests apart in frustration.

"Steve, send me right over there." Dave pointed at the top of a spiral staircase that led to the rarest of the library's books.

"I thought you said we shouldn't do that again. You know, the last time being when you got killed and everything?" Steve scooped Dave up as they continued to sprint through the room.

"Way to jinx it! Throw me before I start regretting this. I'll leave you a spot," Dave said.

The Arch Lich let out a scream. Dark-infused Mana surrounded his body.

Anna let loose with her wind blades, causing the very library to shake with their force. "Go!" she yelled.

Induca let out her own roar. A stream of flames poured out of her hands and her eyes turned brilliant red as the room heated up.

"Done!" Steve grabbed Dave, twirling once and then launching him. "Just put the Mana barrier up a little and then add a little safety." Gray smoke seemed to stream ahead of Dave, a metal casing wrapping around him.

The Arch Lich started to send out a tendril of Dark energy, the very library warping to try to stop Dave's progress.

"Well, fuck you too!" Dave yelled, placing his hands on the metal.

Bulbs seemed to form underneath the bullet-looking mass Dave was in before a rigid funnel formed underneath.

"Didn't you know? I'm a rocket man, motherfucker!" Dave yelled, the bottom of his capsule right next to Induca's flames.

For a second, it looked as if he was going to be burned by them. "Hydrogen saturation is high, nozzles are saturated," Dave said to himself, the words burned into his mind after years of saying the words.

Dave felt the spark ignite as a flame lit underneath the capsule he was in.

That torch had carried humanity's hopes, dreams, and people across the stars and beyond. Dave had made a rocket. About twenty feet from the Arch Lich's face.

"Don't fuck with a dude who makes rockets for a living," Dave muttered. He looked out over the control panels he had seen for decades as he had built his own spaceships.

"We've got rough combustion! Engine firing—looking good. These things are *sweet*. Okay, increasing the fuel consumption. Shit is costing a lot of Mana to make. Ugh! Fine, fuck it, jump-starting the engine." Dave opened the fuel valves on the rocket by simply destroying parts of them.

The Arch Lich had held on, and continued to pull Dave closer in his rocket as he had achieved engine start.

That was nothing to him firing the engines.

Cracks formed through the objects that held him. Dave let out a yell as he forced power into his construct, his mind and body wracked with pain from channeling Mana straight from his armor and through his body. The Dark Mana stopped pulling on Dave's rocket.

For a moment, everything seemed to stop, and then Dave was racing forward. He canceled the impromptu rocket. A big bouncy castle appeared in front of him, slowing him and allowing him to change his direction, right back toward the rare books.

Dave felt like a damned bobblehead from the shaking. Finally, he stopped shaking around, hearing only the sounds of his fellow Stone Raiders battling their opponents. Dave used healing on himself as he looked around. He knew the phylactery was up here because of the heavy warding. There was no need for it other than to try to protect something.

Being only made out of Mana with a high Dark Affinity checked all the boxes.

The screaming Arch Lich was also a big checkmark.

Dave cut through it with his spell formation and magical coding. He felt the Arch Lich recovering from receiving an impromptu rocket to the face just as he found the phylactery, hiding within a book on herb lore.

"Personal choices?" Dave broke through the remaining enchantments, rushing closer to the book.

Dave grabbed it, pulling it out, just as he fell to his knees. He looked at the Arch Lich, who seemed to be the epicenter of Dark Mana. *It called on a Legendary ability.* Fear pinned him to the ground.

Dave closed his eyes as the Lich moved toward him, taking his time— as if enjoying the torment he put Dave through. Dave coughed. Blood fell on his breastplate as he held the book to his chest. Pain seemed to come from everywhere. Dave's Mana barrier was failing as he worked.

Dave knew the coding of his armor explicitly. Which was why he knew he had one chance to win.

There was no time for anything fancy. He removed the fail safes power surged through his body. His gray runes shone so bright they seemed to be pure white. It made the Lich step backward as Dave stood.

His mind was crumbling, fighting the creature's aura, to be able to do what he needed to do: destroy his very body. The power that ran through his body—it was god-like. There was nothing he couldn't do within those few moments.

Dave laughed and jumped from the tall staircase and toward the bookshelves floors below. Dave activated a secondary rune and closed his glowing eyes. The darkness of the room turned to white.

Half of the stored power in his forward soul gem, nearly thirty thousand mana, exploded outwards like a bomb, pain filled Dave as the book holding the phylactery disappeared.

Malsour didn't know what spell the Arch Lich was using as it closed in on Dave, but alarm bells went off in his head.

Either Dave would destroy the phylactery or not, either way Malsour, knew that he would not come back from death like Dave, Deia, Suzy and the other Stone Raiders Players with them.

"Run!" Malsour yelled out, black waves of mana seemed to billow out from his body, magical enchantments and the feeds that the Aleph were using were overloaded as Malsour grew in power and size.

He finished his transformation, grabbing Induca with his right hand, Anna with his left and whipping his tail around Steve as his body broke through the library.

If there was a power ranking for Dragons the Denur would be the absolute peak, but after her would be Malsour. He didn't like to show off his strength, but in his Dragon form, he was a force of nature to be reckoned with.

His wings threw off the roof that was breaking over his back.

He used all of his strength enchantments, with one powerful flap of his wings he threw himself and his three charges out and away from the grand library.

The Library seemed to disintegrate, as if it was going through hundreds of years, crumbling and rotting from the inside.

It spread at an alarming rate.

Steve spread himself out, catching most of the spell while he was on Malsour's tail, sacrificing his material body so that they others wouldn't be as affected.

Anna grunted as she was hit by the spell that made it past Steve.

Then a massive white light seemed to ignite the very air, spreading over the Dark shadows of the Arch Lich's legendary ability, annulling any that was in the air.

Malsour glided downwards, landing heavily before the grand library, his belly and tail were being affected by the legendary ability.

He released his charges, focusing his Mana inwards.

The Arch Lich might have been a powerful entity that revelled in the Dark Affinity, but Malsour was much older with a much higher magical talent in his Dragon form.

He absorbed the curse, his mana destroying it easily.

"Steve!" Malsour yelled out, looking to the metal man that was showing large amounts of decay through his metal limbs.

"Looks like I'm a bit rusty at all this," Steve said, as distorted grin showing as rust decayed his body.

Malsour let out an annoyed sound. He breathed black flames over Steve, breaking the curse and the decay across Steve's form. Since he'd destroyed it in himself, it was easier to just stop the material eating effects on Steve.

"The others will need your help more," Steve said, his voice odd. His body had decomposed, gears, soul gems and his Mithril protective plates showing in places.

Malsour turned, looking to his little sister and Anna. Induca was the worst.

He stabilized Anna as much as possible, slowing the curse from hurting her as he worked to free Induca from the curse raging through her veins.

"Come to Daddy!" Jake yelled as a massive magical formation created from Dark Mana ignited under the second juggernaut's feet as it moved to step on the same bridge its ill-fated brother had used.

The juggernaut stopped, as if it was fighting through molasses. It tried to march forward, to try to follow its creator's bidding.

"Yeah, that's it. You're mine now! Mine!" Jake yelled out. Sweat poured from his face as purple and black swirled in his eyes.

The juggernaut seemed to shake slightly before it stopped its movement. All resistance left the Bone juggernaut as it turned around.

"Kill." Jake pointed at the undead around it. It started to cleave through them.

Another necro hit Jake on the back. "Dude, what did you do? None of the undead are moving," they asked.

"Stop," Jake said.

The bone juggernaut halted, looking out over the undead horde. It was eerily quiet as undead collapsed and fell over.

ting A pop-up blocked Jake and all of the Stone Raiders' visions.

Quest: Aleph Homecoming

You have defeated former Lord *Alastair Montgoa*, betrayer of the Aleph. His creatures and experiments have been destroyed.
    You have cleared the Aleph College.
    Rewards: Increase your technology advancements by 35%
Access to the Aleph Libraries
345,000 EXP
Increased standing with Aleph people

"Quick! Start claiming the best of the undead before they can be destroyed!" Jake said in a panic.

The necros rushed to obey as the rest of the Stone Raiders let out a cheer that filled the Aleph College.

The entire Aleph Council was in shock. All of them had seen Dave's final actions. The power coming off him had been like nothing that they had ever seen before.

Even dying through the Arch Lich's curse, he burned his very life force in order to carry out one last and final act. He dove from the hanging library of the Aleph's rarest works, like some kind of fallen angel. Brilliant light consumed Dave and the book he was holding as the Arch Lich raced toward him.

Dave's final act destroyed the phylactery. The Arch Lich disintegrated in pained screams.

Debris and Dave's floating tombstone were the only things to touch the ground.

Hamdir couldn't understand what the capsule Dave had been in was, or what grew from it. He had never seen such powerful magic in his life.

Black smoke spread through the area with the Lich's death. Everything it touched seemed to decay and wither in seconds. Old wards flared to life, trying to protect their books — only to be washed away in the destructive power. Half of the grand library seemed to be eaten from the inside. Stone Raiders fell down, the effect of the decaying spell making them writhe in pain in the remaining rubble.

The feed went dead, the council members leaned forwards as if willing it to come back.

With a flash it did, the Library now had a massive hole in its roof and was coming apart as structural members were disintegrated by the Arch Lich's curse.

Induca, Malsour, Anna and Steve were all laying on the ground outside of the library. Malsour and Steve had some bad injuries that seemed to be trying to eat through them. However while they were able to stop the curse, Anna and Induca were crying out in pain as it raged through their bodies. Power poured out of Malsour as he worked to stop the curse. Steve who was more parts than man, crawled over with one arm to help.

Hamdir's shaky hand wiped his face as he watched the Stone Raiders' own necromancers running through the undead horde as if they were in a candy store: picking out the best conditioned creatures, controlling them, and making them gather other undead for them to use. Creatures they had been fighting just minutes ago, they were now turning into their minions.

"I now know why people were so scared of making enemies of the Players." Hamdir's low and shaky voice carried through the silent room.

"Trust is rewarded with trust," Shard said, letting those words sink into their minds. There were only a handful of facilities that needed to be worked on before the Stone Raiders were finished clearing out the Aleph's beleaguered facilities.

We must become allies with them. They might not be the cleanest or know the proper etiquette but as I said: we must step forward into the future to see new horizons. With the Stone Raiders, they would give their lives hundreds of times, just to keep an agreement with us.

Hamdir felt assured in their final reward. It was not the largest they could give, but it was one that showed the Aleph's trust, thanks, and hope for both of their groups to grow in the future.

After what he had seen, he doubted anyone would argue it was too much when the Aleph people were just starting to get their feet under them.

Dave sighed and looked at the white that filled his vision.

You have died in Emerilia
You have been returned home.
You have 5:59 hrs (game time) until you can respawn at (Alephir)
Or
1:59 hrs in real life
Would you like to play a different game while you wait?

He sat up from the simple couch he was resting on. Dave sat up in a rush opening his interface, connecting to his party chat.

"What's going on? Is everyone okay?" He demanded.

Dave felt a thread of fear in his heart. Bob said that Deia was now a Player, but a part of him was still scared that she wouldn't respawn.

"Dave, what the hell is going on?" Deia asked, panic in her voice. "We died. That Arch Lich must have used one of its Legendary attacks. Want to come over to my home?" Dave asked, his hand shaking from the anxiety of possibly losing her.

"Is that what this place is? It looks just like your house," Deia said, her tone filled with interest instead of worry, making Dave laugh dryly, putting his nerves at ease.

"It must've taken an imprint of what you think of as home and turned it into reality. Send me an invite to join you," Dave said.

"Damn, I need to do some renovations," Suzy commented over the party chat.

"Everyone, go to your interface panel. Go down to home options. You should have the option to join friends. There should be an invite to the Stone Raiders' guild hall. Click on that and we can meet up with the rest of the Stone Raiders," Dave said, following his own instructions.

Dave appeared in the lobby of the guild hall.

Stone Raiders cheered as he and the rest of Party Zero and the Stone Raiders who had come with them to the grand library appeared.

Dave and the others laughed and smiled. Word seemed to have come back from the Players online. The Arch Lich was dead.

It took more of us than I would like to think, but we got him. Dave was just starting to realize how terrifying respawning was.

He grabbed Deia, bringing her into a deep kiss.

She tensed, embarrassed about kissing in front of so many other people. After a few moments, she stopped caring. She gave herself into the kiss and grabbed onto Dave. The exhilaration of the fight and the fear of death were a powerful aphrodisiac.

Dave checked his timer.

You have died in Emerilia
You have been returned home. You have 4:08 hrs (game time) until you can respawn at (Alephir) Or 1:37 hrs in real life Would you like to play a different game while you wait?

"What do you say if we go back to your place?" he asked, their foreheads together, sharing the same heated breath.

Deia's face lit up in a smile as she bit her lip. She pulled back and rested in his arms that were holding her. "What makes you think I'd invite you back to mine?" she asked playfully.

"Well, I can't very well be saying that in present company." Dave grinned.

"Good to know someone noticed me even if it was for the slight inconvenience that I present," Suzy said dryly.

Deia's eyes thinned, her teeth teasing her lower lip. Finally, she brought up her interface; after she punched a few buttons, they disappeared from the guild hall and reappeared in Dave and Deia's house in Cliff-Hill.

"Oh you beautiful lady." Josh fell onto his bed, still fully clothed. "Josh, we've got more people coming back from their respawns and the Aleph are asking if they can help in anyway," Dwayne asked.

After dying, he was now the section leader with the most energy. "Tell Lucy," Josh said, his face buried in his bed.

"Will do," Dwayne said.

Josh kicked off his clothes, wrestling with himself about having a shower. He marched over, luxuriating in a quick shower before he made his way back to his bed and pulled the sheets over himself.

There was still all of the college to sort out. The amount of loot was incredible and there were all kinds of drops over the place. There was still a mining facility and the portal factory to be fixed but they would be the last two facilities.

The Stone Raiders who had respawned were taking over the duties of those who had survived.

Josh pulled his cover tight, a pleased smile on his face. He'd deal with the rest in the morning. They'd taken on the strongest raid yet and won.

"So, what are we doing next? Helping the Demons?" Dave asked as Malsour cut down massive metal structures that seemed to have grown throughout the mining area organically.

"Once we have the Demons also able to build instead of just react to what is going on around them, we'll start to see them and the Beast Kin working together into a new force in Ashal.

"Few forces have really flourished in Ashal. The land promotes small kingdoms where people can control everything that goes on in it. They come for the highest-level dungeons and raids. The prizes they gain are more than Opheir earns in ten years. It's led to many people fighting in the area instead of coming to the table and talking of an alliance. The Demons are strong, but they are not as strong as those around them. Once they defeat the Dark Lord's forces, they will have the time to train, establish themselves and grow in strength," Malsour said. Darklings appeared and took away the pillars of metal and stone Dave had cut down by conjuring items into the pillars and destroying them.

There were other teams of Stone Raiders helping out with their Dark magics or their brute strength in other places.

There was a celebratory feeling in the air. They had defeated the Arch Lich and now they just had to do some repairs and they would have completed their quest.

"Do you think we would have defeated that Arch Lich if he was at full power and didn't underestimate us?"

"I don't think so—he was incredibly powerful. You only have to look at Jake's new juggernaut minion. He probably had a number of spells that could have defeated the fortress. He simply didn't think that we were capable of defeating him and even if we got close, his runes and traps were powerful. He should have had time to stop us if we attacked him. At least theoretically. With your abilities to destroy the magical formations and runes that protected the phylactery, we exceeded what he thought we were capable of. I think he got used to the low-level creatures and undead around him, just new fodder to be used in his creations. They had some differences between one another but the undead were largely the same. He kept back his strongest forces, using his weakest ones to swarm us and test their abilities."

"That's what I was thinking." Dave shook his head. "Let's take a break. I forgot to check my new notifications."

They wandered through the mining facility, watching as metal and stone was cut away to free the machinery underneath and the massive crushers that ate through the area. A teleport pad had been built into the rear of their moving drills. Materials were taken straight from the crusher and teleported to the forges, where it was refined out. Any waste materials were then teleported into the Densaou Ring of Fire.

There was no need for massive lines of carts to take the material from one facility to another: just connect the drills to whatever forge had space in its refinery and keep going.

Dave was pleased with their progress. Now that everyone was recovering, they had the guild members needed to free the crusher units and crafters were working on fixing any issues with them.

He opened up his notifications as they walked.

Active Skill: Spell Formation
Level: Expert Level 10
Effect: You use 20% less Mana and your spells are 83% stronger.

Passive Skill: Dodge
Level: Master Level 3
Effect: 89% chance to evade objects. 15% faster when fighting more than two opponents.

Passive Skill: Perception
Level: Master Level 5
Effect: 95% chance to find hidden details. 25% chance at better loot.

Active Skill: Two Handed
Level: Master Level 1
Effect: 41% armor penetration on target. Stamina costs reduced 20% while fighting. Can use two-handed weapons in one hand at 50% increased Stamina cost.
Cost: 35 Stamina

Active Skill: Dual Wield
Level: Master Level 1
Effect: Attacks are 41 % faster. 5% chance of slowing target.
Cost: 15 Stamina

Active Skill: Inference
Level: Expert Level 5
Effect: 73% increased chance of using moves you've read in books.

Active Skill: One Handed and Shield
Level: Master Level 1
Effect: Weapons damage increased by 41%. Defense increased by 20%. Shield bash is 5% more likely to stun opponent.
Cost: 20 Stamina

Active Skill: Soul Smith
Level: Expert Level 6
Effect:. 75% less soul energy necessary for crafting with soul smith.
Cost: Dependent on creation.

Active Skill: Builder
Level: Master Level 6
Effect: 95% speed and efficiency. Creations material cost is reduced by 30%.
Required: Tools

You have earned a new class: **Weapons Master**	
You've trained with every combination of weapons, earning mastery in all of them. For your perseverance, you are awarded the Weapons Master Class.	
Status:	Level 1
Effects:	+20 Vitality +10 Endurance +15 Strength +15 Agility

Level 119
You have reached level 119; you have **541** stat points to use.

Stat Increase
+1 Strength +2 Intelligence +2 Agility +2 Vitality +1 Endurance +1 Willpower

You Have Died
For dying you lose:
x3 levels and their associated points.
You lose your classes (you can gain them back by gaining level 10 again).
You have lost your equipment not already soul bound.
You have lost 130 gold, 7 silver, and 8 coppers.

You Have Claimed Your Tombstone
For recovering your tombstone you gain:
x1 level back
All items you were carrying, not including monetary losses.

Level 117
You have reached level 117; you have **531** stat points to use.

Dying at level ten isn't that bad except that the classes keep on resetting, not letting you get anything else. You don't lose too many levels but it still means every time I die, I have to put points back into my stats to bring me back up to ten.

Dave went to his status screen, putting his stat points back in, raising him back up to level ten once again.

CHARACTER SHEET			
Name:	David Grahslagg	Gender:	Male
Level:	10	Class:	Dwarven Master Smith, Friend of the Gray God, Bleeder, Librarian, Aleph Engineer, Weapons Master
Race:	Human/Dwarf	Alignment:	Chaotic Neutral
Unspent points: 531			
Health:	14,300	Regen:	5.04 /s
Mana:	2,930	Regen:	13.00 /s
Stamina:	2,080	Regen:	10.20 /s
Vitality:	143	Endurance:	252
Intelligence:	293	Willpower:	260
Strength:	208	Agility:	204

"I think it might be time that I started putting my stat points into my character," Dave mused aloud.

"Oh? Are you not gaining your stat points as fast naturally anymore?"

"Nope. It's coming down to the point where it's faster for me to level up than it is for me to get stat points through my actions."

Malsour nodded sagely. "Then, it does seem like it might be time for you to put those points to use. Remember to not overdo it like you did when making it to level ten. Don't need you running into ceilings and the like." Malsour laughed.

"Ugh, don't remind me."

Dave considered his character sheet. With his diminishing returns on stats by just straight training, he would have to look at leveling as well as gaining new classes in order to increase his power.

What are my quests for the different classes?

Dave went through his active quest logs to find the class quests. A pop-up jumped into his face.

Quest: Dwarven Master Smith Level 2
You have completed the level 2 quest for this class. Rewards: Unlock Level 3 quest +10 to all stats (stacks with previous class level) 200,000 EXP

Dave swiped it away, only to have another leap up.

Class: Dwarven Master Smith	
Status:	Level 2
Effect s:	Allowed access to all Dwarven Mountains and Smithies. Allowed to take on smithing apprentices. +20 to all stats Access to special quests.

"Okay, so the class tells me the overall gains I've made from the class. Kind of like a reminder of what I would lose if I was to die and drop below whatever level I gained the class at," Dave said to himself. He gained a +10 from the increase in class level, but his class window showed not only the rewards from the class level, but all the rewards that the class gave—from his access and privileges to the +20 from having both level 1 and 2 of the Dwarven Smith Class.

He checked the new quest that became available with the completion of the level 2 quest.

Quest: Dwarven Master Smith Level 3
You must craft 10 weapons of S quality with your Smithing Art (Currently 3/10)   **Rewards:** Unlock Level 4 quest   Increase to stat gain

Dave went to his settings, wondering why he hadn't seen the quests before.

"Dammit, turned off the class quests alert when I was trying to get all of the notifications out of my face when I first came here," Dave grumbled. He could have used those extra stats when he was fighting the undead.

"Something the matter?" Malsour asked. "Just pulled an idiot move."

Malsour made an understanding noise as Dave returned to the class quests.

Quest: Friend of the Grey God Level 3
Complete the Quest: Aleph   Homecoming **Rewards:** Unlock Level   4 Quest Increase to stats

Quest: Bleeder Level 2
Complete the Quest: Aleph   Homecoming **Rewards:** Unlock Level   3 Quest Increase to stats   (???)

"Damn, two class increase, I will take that!" Dave scrolled down to his other quests.

Quest: Librarian Level 2

Conduct research that allows you to understand how to create your own teleport pad.
    Rewards: Unlock Level 3 Quest
    Increase to stats

Quest: Aleph Engineer Level 2

Finish repairing all Aleph facilities mentioned in the quest: Aleph Homecoming
    Rewards: Unlock Level 3 Quest
    Increase to stats
    (???)

Quest: Weapons Master Level 2

Kill one hundred enemies with every weapon type. One handed and shield 13/100
    Two handed 41/100
    Dual wielding 46/100
    Archery 0/100
    Rewards: Unlock Level 3 Quest
    Increase to stats

Dave read the quests over again a few times. "What now?" Malsour sighed.

"Dude, I've got like four of my classes offering a reward for me to complete the Aleph Homecoming Quest," Dave said, his shock clear.

"It's not really that hard to understand. This quest is one of the hardest I have ever heard of. It needs a lot of people with different skill sets working together for a long period of time to try to complete it. We only won against the Arch Lich through mainly luck. The other facilities we've come to—had to have knowledge that was beyond us at one time or another. Right now, even you are stumped with what we have to do for the Aleph portal factory. You know several different runic languages and have refined Magical Circuits into magical coding. I don't know of any other group that would have been able to get this far. That said, I don't know if it will be possible to finish this quest. That portal factory is so complex that many people could spend years and not understand how to get it working."

Malsour's words sank in. Even if they cleared out all of the different facilities, the factory by itself would stop them from completing their goal.

A smile started on Dave's face, not one of nostalgia or defeat, but one of a man sensing a challenge, one that he was determined to meet.

"Malsour, get your reading glasses on. We're going to the Aleph College. It's time I put some of these stat points to use and we figured out how we can fix that Aleph portal factory!" Dave declared, walking for the teleport pad.

Malsour's lips lifted up as he saw Dave's inner curiosity and pursuit of knowledge rise to the occasion once again.

"What is it?" A light blinked on Ela-Dorn's interface, waking her up.

Her husband made an annoyed sound and rolled away as her interface bloomed into existence.

She rubbed his Elvish back, eliciting a pleased noise. She smiled at her husband as she accepted the chat invite with Shard.

"I thought that you would like to know that Dave Grahslagg and Malsour Dracul are within the grand library and are searching through the library for books that might help them on the portal factory," Shard said, his voice light.

"Huh? But it would take them years to learn that all," she muttered, still half asleep as she rubbed her husband's back, hearing the light snores as he drifted off to sleep.

"Maybe not. With their high Intelligence, and their skills and insights, it might be possible. Malsour has extensive knowledge on all things magical and has shown a complex mind capable of proving and disproving theories that have been stagnant for many years. Dave is largely focused on the materialistic items that he interacts with. He did not become a Dwarven Master Smith so quickly on just his good looks." Shard's voice was dry.

"Are you telling me that they could figure out how teleport pads and portals work?" Ela-Dorn's voice became serious as she ground her underbite and upper teeth together.

"I think that given enough time, it is possible. They do not need to sleep for extended periods of time. With their librarian classes, they are able to understand more. It comes down to Malsour, really. Dave can create most things he comes to understand. There are a bunch of theories and ideas that go beyond the normal thoughts, sciences, and magical practices that create the portals and teleport pads. Items that would take Dave a long time to figure out. But Malsour? He could very well put the pieces together."

"Can we stop them?"

Shard paused before responding, showing the debate he had in relating his words. "As you know, I overhear a great number of conversations. I trust Dave and Malsour completely, but my core programming made me pay attention to their conversation. Dave and Malsour have class-related quests that will be activated once they complete the quest Aleph Homecoming. I have been checking other keywords to other ongoing conversations. It seems that the majority of the Stone Raiders, if not all of them, have class-related quests that will be completed by finishing Aleph Homecoming due to its complex and difficult nature."

"Is there any way we can make the quest complete?" Ela-Dorn asked. "No."

"So, we either disrupt their quest to try to make sure that they don't get the knowledge of the portals and teleport pads, or we allow them to learn the secrets of the different devices." Ela-Dorn sat upright in her bed, grinding her teeth.

Her husband smacked her side. "You'll hurt your teeth doing that, love," he said sleepily.

"Sorry for waking you. Go back to sleep." She rubbed his back once again.

This is where we truly decide how much we trust them. To let them know our biggest secrets and the center of our power and society.

Ela-Dorn rose from her bed and closed the chat.

"You going somewhere, love?" Ela-Gal rolled over and looked at his orcish wife.

"I'm off to the college. It seems a decision must be made and warnings given." She had a grim look on her face.

Ela-Gal laughed at her expression. "I remember when we were in the college and we were the ones getting told to not look into matters beyond our abilities. I'm glad we did anyways. Wouldn't have figured out the new power plants otherwise." Ela-Gal's chuckle turned into a yawn.

He opened his golden eyes, finding her muddy brown ones. "Well, I have been looking forward to seeing the old place." He stood and stretched. His lithe body showed scars on his back, as well as a burn mark on his neck, the Elven symbol for heretic.

She smiled as he pulled his clothes on.

With her powerful magic, she had extended her life by possible decades, giving her more time with her love. He was a little less wild than when she had first met him, but his body seemed to have only aged years instead of the decades they had been together.

"I don't need you following me around like some wounded pup." She crossed her arms and put out her underbiting jaw.

"Aw, I forgot how cute you looked when you're trying to be all Arch Mage," he said, pulling on his shirt. He activated his hotkey set; thick silver clothes appeared over his undergarments, a sword at his side and a bow on his back. He looked every part of the warrior he was. His long, silver, almost- white hair was pulled back into a braid.

She frowned as he walked closer. "We don't both need to go," she tried to argue as he put his hands on her elbows.

After a few moments, she let her arms drop to her sides.

"But it would be much more fun if we did." He grinned, giving her a quick smile, and turned for their apartment door.

"You coming, Councilwoman Ela-Dorn? There's adventures to be had." He gave her a roguish wink.

For a moment, Ela-Dorn was once again a young Orcish maiden headed off on adventures with her friends, to reveal the magical truths of Emerilia and become the strongest mage of the Aleph, right beside her own Elven knight.

"Who made you the leader of this trip?" She smiled and caught up to Ela-Gal as he opened the door.

21

BREAKING SPACE AND TIME

"Okay, I've got the Inference skill," Malsour said. The spell he had been using died down.

"Good. I'm going to need to remake my armor," Dave complained. "Well, you did make it let out a surge of power into the phylactery to destroy it. How is it looking?"

Dave reached into his bag of holding and pulled out the breastplate of his armor. Holes showed through the steels and different layers; even the Mithril was heavily damaged. The under layers had been melted from the intense heat of Dave's magical coding, melting itself, so it could destroy the phylactery.

The front panel that formed a vault-classed soul gem had also been destroyed. Other than the front breastplate of Mithril, he only had his back plate—that was also pretty damaged, but had most of its coding intact and the soul gem hadn't been destroyed.

"By Fire." Malsour shook his head at Dave's pained expression as he held the Abscondita armor in defeat.

"Well, everything can be fixed." Dave put the armor away and grabbed a book from the ruins of what had been the secured books in the grand library.

A number of them had been destroyed by the fight that had taken place, but it was not as bad as Dave had feared. Most of the books were intact and they had access to everything up to Journeyman level through their relationship with Shard.

Here, they were cheating the system by going right to the source and getting the Master and Expert level books. With the Inference skill, it would improve the amount of information they would both retain. Their librarian classes would help as well.

They sat down among the wreckage and read the books.

"Okay, I think I have a rough idea of how the positioning system works. They make it really frigging complicated though." Dave pulled out a notepad, flipping through three books around him as he started to write out a Magical Circuit.

He sent it to Malsour, who looked up from his book to check it on his interface.

"Makes sense to me. The math is beyond me for the most part but it should work, in my mind."

"Good. Now, we just have to figure out how these things can punch a hole through the physics we both know. Simple."

"While it might not be simple; I think I am starting to understand a few of theories in these books. I will need some time to think about it, though." Malsour had a thoughtful look and returned to his book, making notes on his interface's notepad.

Dave looked to his stats. *Well, if I'm going to start putting stat points into my attributes, I might as well start now. Might help me out with this a bit. I'll take myself up to level 16.*

Dave had thirty points that he could put into his stats, being a single point under the level 17 threshold.

Right now, I'm a pretty balanced Player overall, but balancing my stats is just going to mess me up later. I'm going to get a massive boost to my stats by completing this quest. Also, I use my smarts more than anything else.

With my inference skills and magical coding, I'd kick my own ass if I didn't invest it into my own Intelligence.

Dave dumped all of the thirty points right into his Intelligence.

He took a deep breath as everything seemed to become clearer to him. He was able to recount information faster and with more clarity. He remembered his physics lessons from back in high school. Different articles he had read on possible space drives, possible wormhole theories.

He opened up his interface, knowing the exact locations of the information. He took pictures of the different stacks of information, reading hundreds of pages in the space of just a half hour, sending them to Malsour as he read.

He felt the need to read everything within reach, to consume all of the knowledge. With his higher Intelligence, the more he read, the stronger he would become. Unlike a normal human brain that had a hard time remembering what they had done the day before, or a week ago, Dave knew what he had eaten as a four-year-old.

All the cumulative knowledge of his childhood from Earth was just waiting for him to call on it. He took a breath, becoming tired from just remembering it all. He let out a sigh, getting used to his new level of Intelligence.

"Two people are approaching—Ela-Dorn and her husband." Dave stood.

"How do you know it is her husband?"

"They have similar compounds in the air around them. Two people of different races only get that if they have spent a lot of time together. They're also holding hands." Dave smiled.

"What did you do?" Malsour asked, studying Dave.

"I just put thirty points into my Intelligence. It's a rush." Dave laughed. He checked his character sheet and looked at his new information.

CHARACTER SHEET			
Name:	David Grahslagg	Gender:	Male
Level:	16	Class:	Dwarven Master Smith, Friend of the Gray God, Bleeder, Librarian, Aleph Engineer, Weapons Master
Race:	Human/Dwarf	Alignment:	Chaotic Neutral
Unspent points: 501			
Health:	15,300	Regen:	5.24 /s
Mana:	3,330	Regen:	13.50 /s
Stamina:	2,180	Regen:	10.70 /s
Vitality:	153	Endurance:	262
Intelligence:	333	Willpower:	270
Strength:	218	Agility:	214

Malsour whistled out a tune, putting his book into his bag of holding as they walked out of the restricted area of the library.

"I've got it," Malsour said as they got to the main lobby. A pillar of materials formed from the walls that had kept the undead at bay.

"Dude, as much as I get used to this place, this is cool as hell," Dave said with a stupid grin as they were lifted up off the ground and lowered down into the lobby.

Malsour laughed at Dave's almost childish excitement.

They stepped off, exiting the library's lobby just as Ela-Dorn and her husband reached the top of the stairs in front of the grand library.

"Ela-Dorn, what brings you and your husband here?" Dave asked.

Ela-Dorn's eyes thinned as she studied Dave. "How did you know we were coming?"

"A man must have some secrets of his own." Dave winked.

The Elf with Ela-Dorn was tense, but he looked amused at Dave's actions.

"I am Malsour. This is Dave. Good to meet you." Malsour offered his hand to Ela-Dorn's husband.

"I am Ela-Gal." The High Elf tilted his head slightly as they shook hands.

Dave brought his fist in for a fist pump. "Damn, I'm good. Was scared you were just going to be her boyfriend." Dave shook Gal's hand.

"So, it was a guess?" Ela-Dorn asked.

"Partly, but all things are in the end. Kind of like your damn teleport pads and the portal factory." Dave rolled his eyes.

Even though he wasn't looking at them, he could tell through his Touch of the Land that they had tensed up.

"So, what brings you to the grand library? Is there anything we might be able to help with?" Malsour asked.

"We were wondering what you are doing about the portal factory," Ela-Dorn said, diplomatically.

"Well, we're figuring out how the teleport pads that are made in the portal factory work, so that we can work backward from there to understand just what the heck the different machines are do... I'm an idiot." Dave slapped his forehead.

"What did you do now?" Malsour asked.

"My mastery of Magical Circuits! I don't need to know *how* to code it; that's the slow way. I can destroy one, then with my Intelligence, I will be able to understand what the heck is going on. I have the ability to understand whatever Magical Circuits I destroy. Sure, I might not know the science behind it. Give me enough time and information and I'll figure it out. Well, you'll probably figure it out before me—you're more theory smart than I am." Dave gestured to Malsour.

"How did we miss that?" Malsour slapped his forehead.

Ela-Dorn cleared her throat. "I must ask, what do you wish to do with the knowledge you gain about the teleport pads?"

Thoughts whizzed through Dave's mind as he held up a finger. "Sorry, one minute, brain's still going here," Dave said, feeling like there were only a rare few moments when he would gain the inspiration he was getting now. "Okay." Dave clicked his fingers. "So, you lot studied portals to make teleport pads. Portals have power sources that are just entirely massive. They tap into the Mana streams running through Emerilia. They are also set.

Which is why you had so many issues! I need to destroy a teleport pad right now!" Dave started to move toward the nearest teleport pad.

Gal made to block his way. "Could you please answer the question?"

"Oh, yeah, sure. I have about a hundred portals that are unlinked and under my control. If I can figure out what you did to make your teleport pads, I can maybe use it with the unconnected and untraceable portals and make them connect to not only teleport pads but portals on other planets. I would need the coordinates, but I could connect multiple portals together. Right now, we have point-to-point transference. You have one portal on Emerilia that connects to one portal in another area with creatures trying to kill you. Imagine if you could dial those portals up? Just like your teleport pads but in those hostile lands. Now that I have a higher Intelligence, I can see it now. I can compile all the information on the portals. They open at a set time and close at a set time. But if *we* have portals, we can go in whenever we want to, at *any* location, the portal on this side would be in locations of our choice. Supplies are a massive bottleneck when the portals start opening. You have all these vendors but they're looking for the portals where people are going through the most to make the most money. It might mean that in a new portal location, Players could come back to Emerilia and have to travel *days* before they can get their supplies! We would just have to change which portal we're connecting to. We could do what few have been able to do. We could farm entire planets!" Dave said, a massive smile plastered on his face as he saw his dream in his eyes.

"How is that possible?" Ela-Dorn looked to Malsour. "*Is that possible?*"

Malsour laughed. Dave was already writing notes down on his interface's notepad.

"One thing you're going to have to learn, Ela-Dorn. If Dave says that he can do something, he's going to do it."

"Do you really control that many portals?" Ela-Gal asked. "Dave does." Malsour nodded.

"How?"

"I built my house on them." Dave grinned, looking a bit crazed before he went back to his notes.

Ela-Dorn rubbed her face, as if she were developing a headache. "Do you know what kind of resource those portals are? Just having one in your possession, not to say hundreds of them, all of them unsecured and not linked to one another — do you know what we could learn from them?" It was clear that she was starting to think on her words for the first time and was surprised by the results.

"Ah, well, we already are Aleph Engineers. We do know quite a bit about you lot. Only makes sense that you know something about us. You know alliances work only if we both have shared interests and secrets. You are trying to make an alliance with us — signs are all there. I know that the rest of the Stone Raiders will be excited. You're kind of like an awesome myth." Dave's face scrunched up. "Though you're going to want to have us keep your existence a secret. Maybe tell the Demons and Beast Kin, make an alliance with them? Though that is a big step, if you ask me. You are a bunch of introverts as a group. Anyway, means we're going to have to keep this entire quest a secret, which is going to suck because who doesn't like to brag? Anyway, I can use a broken teleportation pad. I don't need to destroy one that is in working order."

"Have you been spying on us?" Ela-Dorn asked.

"Nope. Shard is a very loyal AI. He wouldn't allow us to do that, even if one of us were married to him. He literally can't. The Aleph come first and your protection is paramount," Dave assured them. "For right now, since I just upped my Intelligence attribute, my mind is going through a bunch of changes. Means that I'm making all kinds of things connect. Also, means I don't have much time till it slows down, so which teleport pad can I break? I'll make another one if this works! Promise." Dave gave his half crazed- excited smile.

The Elas looked to each other.

"If we lose a broken teleport pad, we can make it again. Having someone who knows how they work is rare," Gal said.

"Okay, on one condition. We get one unlinked portal to study," Ela- Dorn said.

"You're getting the better side of this deal, but fine." Dave held out his hand.

Ela-Dorn shook it.

"Now, which teleport pad can I destroy?" Dave rubbed his hands in excitement.

"I have a candidate lined up. It is broken and out of charge, but it should be intact enough for you to understand the teleport pads," Shard said from above.

Dave clapped his hands together, making Ela-Dorn jump.

"Lead the way, my finely runed compadre!" Dave took off at a run for the nearest teleport pad.

"Good meeting you." Malsour then chased after his friend, who was sprinting all-out. Their speed was incredible as they cruised through the street, both Malsour and Dave with wide smiles on their faces. The future was calling to them and it was filled with more possibilities than they had hoped for that morning.

Dave put his hands on the teleport pad. It was cracked in places and had been half eaten by something.

With his Touch, it seemed that most of the Magical Circuits were in place and although not functioning, he could learn what they each did.

Magical Circuits

You have detected (damaged) Magical Circuits. Do you wish to destroy them for the chance to learn their function?
    Cost: 1,000,000
    Mana Y/N

Dave moved up to the teleport pad, pulling out his burnt and disheveled back plate. "Yeah, let's see what secrets you're hiding."

The area around him lit up as the runes in his armor and on his body glowed with Mana rushing through him.

He tilted his head up, his eyes white with power as his Mana destroyed rune after rune, burning through the Magical Circuit. Information flooded his mind, faster than he could comprehend.

Ela-Dorn covered her eyes as Dave glowed with power surging through him. She gasped. She had *never* seen someone channel that much power through themselves before. Ribbons of colored light rose out of the broken teleport pad, weaving through the air and moving through his glowing white eyes.

It lasted for five or so minutes before the light died down and the teleport pad crumbled slightly, burn marks where runes had been.

"Ugh, that *sucked*. I think I'm going to pass out." Dave fell over. A shadow leapt up to grab him so he didn't smack his head on the ground.

"Well, that was one hell of a show," Ela-Gal said.

"Does he know how to make the Magical Circuits?" Ela-Dorn asked Malsour.

"I guess we'll find out when he wakes up," Malsour said as the shadows picked Dave up. "I'm going back to the grand library. Deia is not going to be happy about him knocking himself out, so it'd be good to keep him hidden for a while and I have some books I want to read." Malsour smiled. "Want to join me?"

"I'm interested in how much he now knows and I do have to check on my college. It looks like it's fallen into disrepair while I've been gone," Ela- Dorn said.

"That's fine. Just make sure you don't pick up any loot. We've got Stone Raiders going through and pulling the loot together to sell later."

"Fine with me. I have one question, though. What is this rune coding Dave was talking about?"

"I hope you have your notepad ready," Malsour said.

Ela-Dorn could see a familiar excitement in Malsour's eyes. Reading and gaining knowledge was half the fun of her work; teaching another about it and seeing the spark of understanding in their eyes was the other half. She wondered how much she would be able to learn from Dave, Malsour, and the rest of the Stone Raiders.

A sense of excitement replaced the one of foreboding.

Sato stretched in his chair. Using the Mirror of Communication in its conference mode could leave him stiff after not moving for so long.

Sato looked around the room, his mind focused on what his people had accomplished in such a short time. It was impressive to say the least. They were already in the process of working on a stealth scout ship to find Emerilia. The defeated and downtrodden looks of his people had now been filled with hope.

Sato activated the mirror and placed his hand on it, a smile on his face.

He accessed the conference function, waiting for Dave to connect.

"Hi, Sato. Sorry, Dave is currently passed out," Shard said after a few minutes.

"What happened?" Panic rose in Sato's chest.

"He consumed more knowledge than his mind could handle and he passed out. He should be good shortly, but right now he's being hidden from Deia, so she doesn't get annoyed at him for going overboard again."

Sato shook his head. "Well, do you mind if I ask you some questions?" Sato asked.

"Certainly." Shard smiled and moved to one of the seats.

Sato moved to the other. "So, we've been looking at making our own Magical Circuit AI and were wondering if you had any plans for it?"

"I do, but I am not allowed to give many of my plans out. It might be an idea to talk to Anna on that. Also, Magical Circuitry is not as versatile and efficient as magical coding that Dave has developed. It is my own hope that I will begin transferring over to a newly magically coded server instead of my current spherical connections. I am able to talk over a few points here and there that I am interested in developing for myself and might interest you?"

"Well, first of all, let me get my friend Edwards in on this call. He's the one with the most questions." Sato sighed, feeling out of his depth.

"Certainly!" Shard looked genuinely excited to talk about Magical Circuitry and coding.

"How is that possible?" Ela-Dorn asked.

"Well, it's about the understanding of the elements and the Affinities. See, when you increase in one Affinity, your body is altered on a very small level, so that you can increase your proficiency with whatever your Affinity might be. So, if you're working with Earth, you get larger and more nanites to allow you to move larger items of Earth. With Water, the condensing part of your nanites increases, allowing you to gather more water faster and direct it with finer control. However, one thing that few people take into account is environment. If you're trying to gather water in a desert, then it's going to take not more Mana, but more time to maintain the same spell to condense the water in the air and give you something to drink. Fire is one of the most robust as it is introducing stored chemicals within the nanites into the air in order to create the desired effect. Being angry and throwing out a punch is not going to be as effective as understanding the system that you're using and manipulating it. Mages, at most, are using about thirty to forty percent of their ability. Take Dave with his knowledge and understanding of the magic system he is using—he can get up to sixty or seventy percent understanding, which makes him rather powerful," Malsour said with some pride.

"So, coming to understand not only your element but the magical system of nanites and Mana can allow you to increase its efficiency. You can also do it in environments that are sympathetic to your Affinity. Water magic in the ocean, Air magic in the middle of a windy day, Fire in the heart of a volcano. Though, we don't usually see big changes in how magics work in these areas because we don't understand the magical system, creating a cycle of magical suppression as we aren't near to pushing our Affinities and magic to its limits." Ela-Dorn just sat there, trying to fully comprehend what Malsour was saying. Her mind made connections as the gravity of his words hit her.

"Teach me more about the magic system," she demanded, her attention wholly focused on him.

"Still having a discussion, I see?" Ela-Gal said, walking between the beaten bookshelves.

"With Malsour's knowledge, we could double the power of our magical output!" Ela-Dorn said.

Ela-Gal looked impressed as he looked to Malsour in confirmation. "I, too, was skeptical at first, but I had a very good teacher and she is something of a magical technology savant," Malsour said proudly, keeping away from telling them that his mentor had been the Lady of Fire herself.

Dave lurched up from where he lay on the floor. "Oh, ow." He promptly lowered himself back down to the floor.

"Dave, you okay?" Malsour moved to him.

"Uh, huh, just my head really hurts," he complained.

"So, do you know how teleport pads work now?" Ela-Dorn asked. "Yeah, kind of. Well, I know how the thing works. I just don't know *why*. Malsour, you figure out theories and laws of wormholing?"

"I have been able to understand a great amount of it. I still have a lot of information to go through."

"Well, I can get started on the portal factory. I don't think I should have too many issues in getting the place cleaned up. Then we can go over to Cliff-Hill and get a portal in payment for the Aleph." Dave made to get up, ending in a groan and him lowering himself back down. "Maybe after my brain has stopped ringing."

"That might be an idea." Malsour shook his head as Dave started to use his interface, adding to the prodigious notes he had been taking before he destroyed the teleport pad.

Ela-Dorn and Ela-Gal went off to see the rest of the library and show Malsour where the best books on wormhole theories and science were located.

Dave opened up a voice chat with Kol. "What?" Kol asked, sounding half asleep.

"When will we be ready to put in that purchase order for the teleport pad?" Dave asked, his mind still moving forward with his plans.

"Should be by the end of the week." Kol yawned.

"Okay, good. Should be done by then." Dave muttered the last to himself. "I'll talk to you later then."

"Was that all you wanted to know? What time is it?"

"Uh, about three in the morning for you." Dave held his breath.

Silence drifted between the two of them.

"Next time, I'll check what time it is. Sorry—had a kind of big development here," Dave said.

"Goodnight, Dave."

"Good morning, Kol!" Dave said with cheer, imagining Kol's face scrunched up in frustration.

Kol closed the voice chat.

"Good morning? What am I, six? Am I sure that this new Intelligence helped me?" Dave moved to his character sheet. Now that he had made the decision to start using his stat points, he needed to really start figuring out his total fighting style.

"Well, conjuring is my prime go-to; after that, Strength and Agility." Dave looked at the character sheet.

He dismissed it with a wave, his headache calming down. He pushed himself up. He wobbled on his feet, feeling unsteady, as if his natural rhythm was messed up. He took some test steps; his foot came down slower than he was used to.

Dave looked at his legs, deep in thought. "It's almost like those games where you go in slow-mo. Your limbs move so slowly as you do the same actions. There's like a heaviness to your actions. Wait? Did me increasing my Intelligence increase how fast I think? I might not feel it when my attributes were lower. Sure, I would gain a lot of stats in one go, but at those lower levels, it's not so much. At these higher levels, just getting an increase to a few attributes, you can feel a difference."

Dave pondered it for a minute and went to the Emerilia wiki. He headed over to people doing max-min spell casters. The wealth of information that had been added onto the wiki was incredible.

Dave kept bookmarking different things for later as he reached a post by someone with an Intelligence over 350.

Hey fellow Emerilians!

So, I've been max-min my character in Intelligence and Wisdom. I found that once I crossed the three hundred range, I started to get a lag spike. I reached out to the admins and they said that it was part of the game.

After about three weeks of me complaining, they finally came back and told me that it was an in-game mechanic!

Once you hit around the two hundred and fifty mark, you'll start to have rare moments where things seem to slow down for a second or two in high stress situations or when you haven't slept long. I didn't realize it until they told me (this game is freaking awesome!).

So, once you hit around three hundred, it's like a few bits of a second

off, but then it's a real pain in the ass trying to walk around. Once you get to around 350, it starts getting fun. Your casts are faster and your reactions are faster. It's weird cause it kind of feels like you think faster. I have no idea how they do this, but I tried it out with doing my work in the game and I got a month of work done in just a day!

Intelligence is the way to go!

EDIT: Increasing your Agility becomes almost necessary around the 400 mark. Otherwise, you feel like a fish in jelly. It sucks. With the increased Agility, you can actually move as fast as your slow-mo.

EDIT: Made a video of me fighting a lvl 230 fiend!

Dave clicked on the video.

The fiend was made of some black material that seemed to be formed in hard angles and lines. It was pitch black except for its burning eyes and flames that seemed to flicker across its back and make its chest glow.

The camera view was from someone up in a tree watching as a human wearing magical robes stepped out into the barren area that the fiend was moving across. It seemed to move in a black streak toward the mage, only to be hit with three spells before it had reached halfway.

It clawed at the mage, finding nothing but air. Instead it recoiled as five magical hits pushed the fiend back. Its black skin flashed red in pain as it reeled around and started moving faster.

The mage fired from their destruction staff and their own hands. The video was slowed down to actually see the Player and fiend's reactions.

The fiend's claws came across and over, and then under and up, two hits that would have turned the mage into a shredded mess.

The mage dodged to the side of the first attack, unleashing a lightning attack that hit the fiend's second arm, blowing it off as the fiend ran past the mage.

Dave watched in disbelief. The mage laughed as the video sped up again to real time. The fiend howled out in pain, trying to once again rush the mage. The mage seemed to be done with playing around. Magical attacks rang through the area. The trees that the recorder was in swayed as the fiend's rush was stopped.

Fire seemed to escape its body from different cuts. The fiend let out a bellow of flames, meeting an Air attack that cut through the flame and dispersed them.

The fiend tried everything, but two minutes later, it collapsed to the ground. The area around the mage and fiend was a war zone.

There was nothing that the fiend had been able to do against an attack like that.

Dave looked down at the description under the video.

> *Player: Maglidor*
> *Level for the video: 287*

Dave shook his head. The mage was much higher than the fiend but he was using lower-level spells to show off his crazy casting speed and his dodging ability.

"I bet that if he got hit just once, it would have been all over." Dave scratched at his scruff. "Though it shows me another use for Intelligence. Okay, so, increasing Intelligence is a must. Then Agility because when I'm fighting, I don't want everything to be slowed down so much that moving becomes a pain in the ass. I'd like to increase my Strength, but it's pretty good. With higher Intelligence working with my inference and perception skills, I should be able to hit vital areas a lot easier." He looked to Vitality and Endurance.

"Okay, I need to put something into Vitality so I don't get killed right away. Endurance, sure, every once in awhile. Needing to sleep less is great, but I have the healing ability of my armor, when I fix it." He frowned and stared at his Willpower attribute.

"Okay, I could put stat points into you, but my regeneration is pretty high and again, with my armor, I have a pool of forty million Mana points to pull from. Not including the other armor I'm linked to. Plus, I can store my Willpower as well, so that I can use it when smithing. Maybe, every once in a while, but not really necessary. So, that leaves Intelligence, Agility, and Vitality being my best attributes for me to put stat points into."

"Might be an idea to wait a bit before doing so." Malsour carried books in his arms. The Elas followed him.

"Yeah, might be an idea—don't need to pass out again! Should we go check on the portal factory? See if we can start working on it?" Dave rubbed his hands together.

"Excited to start putting up your portals?" Ela-Dorn asked.

"Be some time before I figure out how it all works, but got to have a plan for the future." Dave rubbed his head. His excitement might have gotten the best of him when he let those plans slip. He didn't even know if it was possible; hopefully Malsour could fill in the missing bits of knowledge.

"Well, let's go and see what you know, shall we? I'm excited to see a Dwarven Master Smith in action," Ela-Gal said.

Dave smiled, tilting his head in thanks for the compliment. "Shard, where we going?" Dave asked.

"Same teleport pad as before. I will have it linked to the portal factory. Also, Sato called; seems that his group has been rather busy developing the magical system. Malsour, you will be pleased to know that they have complete notes on their implementation so as to understand its functionality." Shard sounded rather pleased with himself.

"That is incredible. I look forward to hearing about it!" Malsour said. "Give you any scrap of information and you're happy as can be." Dave led the way to the teleport pad. "Malsour, when you increase your Intelligence, did you also increase the Agility in order to make up for the differences?"

"Ah, so, the time dilation effects started kicking in? I did, but then with training, you can still walk and talk normally, only using it in bursts when you need it. Having it active all the time wears on the mind and you need to then work on a high Endurance stat, so you don't need to constantly eat food or take a nap."

"You made it over level 300 for Intelligence?" Ela-Dorn asked. "Yep." Dave looked at her and her level 279. He studied Gal.

Ela-Gal High Elf Level 375

Dave's eyes went wide after reading Gal's level.

Ela-Dorn laughed at Dave's wide eyes. "While Ela-Gal looks younger than me, he is almost twice my age. He's also a much stronger mage than me. Though he hides it behind his weapon skills. Much like your Anna and Deia."

Ela-Gal shot her a look. "Their way of fighting is very interesting. I like how they have mixed their fighting styles with their melee fighting abilities. Both of them together increase their power—a smart combination." "He wants to see if they would be willing to teach him," Ela-Dorn said, getting a *don't-tell-them-that* look from her husband.

"Ela-Dorn is not one for secrets and I was interested in the fighting style," he finally admitted.

"Well, I can introduce you to them. I think they would be more than happy to show you their fighting styles," Dave reassured him.

The Stone Raiders and Aleph had just started to extend their hands in friendship to one another. Things like this were the best way to make their relationship work and truly bring them together.

Dave entered the teleport pad control room. "Well, let's see how much we really know about teleport pads!" Dave smiled and jumped through the teleport pad's event horizon.

22

THINNING THE HORDE

Krenua stepped out of the shadows, his footfalls silent as he followed behind one of his fellow mages. The mage grabbed a Demon taking a piss. There was a brief smell of ozone as the Demon dropped. More of the DCA wandered out of the darkness, knocking out the new Demons, others grabbing them and hauling them back.

Krenua moved into a caged area where meat had been stored.

A guard was eating a large haunch of meat, congealed blood on its chest and arms as it looked for other Demons trying to take its food.

Krenua made a quick run; he kicked out its legs and his arms wrapped around its neck before it could cry out. As the Demon fell into unconsciousness, more of the Demon Army seemed to creep out of the shadows.

Krenua let the unconscious guard down slowly. He pulled out a vial from a pouch on his belt and poured it over the meat in the cage. He hauled the unconscious guard over his shoulder, headed back out of the camp.

An owl let out a call.

The Demon Army melted back into the shadows. They had killed or knocked out around a hundred of the Dark Lord's minions. The horde was thinner as the Demon Army stole into the night.

"Good work." Lezar looked at their forces after a fifteen-minute sprint and thirty-minute flight.

"Now, let's see what information we can get from these bastards." Lezar stretched out his wings, letting out his full aura.

Krenua and the rest of the Demon Army stopped suppressing their auras.

The Demons sent by the Dark Lord, looked at them with wild eyes.

When they focused on Lezar, their bodies stared to shake with instinctual fear.

"Now, I want to know a few things. I want to know who's in charge, who are your strongest Demons, and what the hell the Dark shit stain did to you lot?" Lezar's voice pulled every one of the fifty or so demons that were bound, looking at their ancient ancestors.

"We will eat you!" The declaration came out in halting Abyssal. The Demon was punched by a Beast Kin so hard there was a dent in its skull as it dropped to the ground.

"Come on, Olivia. Fuck, he was the best out of all them." Lezar rubbed his face.

The Beast Kin shrugged. "Didn't think they were that weak. Sorry, General," Olivia, a mix of elk and Human, said.

"Apology accepted. Now someone put runes on them and we'll see what the hell they know," Lezar said.

Krenua nodded. Lezar would have given her a physical beating just a few short months ago. Krenua was pleased and proud with what his people had learned in their time away from Emerilia. They didn't use beatings to mete out punishments. Grueling physical feats and the knowledge that you had messed up and screwed over your friends were much more powerful motivators as they had become a second family to one another. Krenua had never seen the Demons more motivated to strengthen themselves, not even when the ranks were based on physical prowess.

Krenua watched as simple rune necklaces were placed around the captured Demons' necks.

"Take half of them back to Devil's Crater, as well as the dead we recovered," Lezar said to Krenua. "They're going to want your firsthand reports of what we saw in there."

"Yes, General." Krenua opened his interface and sent messages to his parties as he pulled out some of the prisoners.

Medics knocked the prisoners out again as they all grouped together.

Krenua looked over his people when they'd all arrived.

"Let's go!" Wind mages conjured Air around them as the Demons used their feet to grab onto their comrades who couldn't fly, or their unconscious burdens. They rose into the air. The air tunnel died and they started to glide and flap their wings, making their way to Devil's Crater.

Alkao looked to Krenua. The man looked tired. He had flown all night and most of the morning, dropping off his charges, who were now across the different keeps.

Now, he stood in front of the combined councils and Demon Army generals, finishing off his report of what he had seen in the approaching Demon Horde's sleeping areas.

"So, they're starting to form groups? Have we been able to get any idea of what their leadership is like from the ones with Lezar?" Alkao looked to Kala, who had been talking to him last through a voice chat.

"We've got a rough leadership forming. Lezar suggests that we attack it and take it out before it has time to fully form. I agree with him," Kala said.

"Before we get in there, we need some more information, like what the hell is wrong with these Demons." Malkur had a troubled expression on his face. His medical people couldn't figure out what was going on with them.

"Well, I think I might have an answer for that," Efri said. The tension in the room ratcheted up a few degrees at Efri's frown.

"If it wasn't for the information on Xelur's Demons one of my people has been researching, we wouldn't know what's wrong with them. It seems that somehow the Dark Lord has been able to make them hunger after souls. They can't absorb or use the souls like the Xelur do to power their own magic, though they still hunger after devouring them.

"Their minds have been imprinted with that idea. Add in a metabolism that burns through food at twenty times our own — they're mindless beasts in a constant state of unending hunger."

"Can we fix it?" Malkur asked.

"No. Their very bodies need so much sustenance that we couldn't break the cycle of their hunger to trick them into thinking that they didn't need to kill anything they see for sustenance, to try to get just a part of that filling feeling of devouring a soul." Efri shook his head.

"By the Grey," Kala swore.

Alkao's face was hard as he looked to the rest of the people in the room. All of their eyes were hard, but the thought behind those eyes clear. "So, we kill them all and we wipe their stain from Emerilia. I will contact the Stone Raiders and see when they will arrive. I want to see if we can't get some of our own people within the Demon Horde's camp. I think if we had a few of the Black Hands blend in with them and then start to make internal conflicts, it might be useful," Alkao said.

Kala nodded approvingly.

Krenua raised his hand.

"Krenua," Alkao acknowledged his second-in-command. "Another thing I noticed: they didn't use their interfaces." Alkao's stony face turned into a hungry smile.

"So, how long do you think this is going to take?" Josh asked Dave, who was hanging from a rafter that had multiple arms on either side of it. Before it, there was a cylinder of soul gem crystals. After the arms attached to the ceiling, there was a complex runed cylinder encasing the soul gem.

"Uh, well, we've got the soul gem extruder, which the repair bots are dealing with, then the small machine shop — those aren't bad at all. Mostly, it's this main assembly line and the rune engravers."

"With all of these working parts, they need some good ole maintenance on them and replacing a few sections down the line." Dave tapped his chin in thought. "Be about…two days? If you give me the repair bots, I can teach them most of this stuff and then I can focus on the full replacements and the engraving areas."

"Fine. You'll get them." Josh looked around the line in awe. "We're in the middle of a factory that makes wormholes. Ha! This game is awesome."

Dave hid his frown as Josh looked up and down the line. A cylinder was at one end; at the other, there were full teleport pads with their massive plates that lay on the ground. Underneath was a complex collection of runes and components that ringed down its length. Thick steel covered over these runes, engraved with their own forms that were made to hide the runes that made it up.

Although it had taken Dave a million Mana points for him to destroy the runes on the broken teleport pad, it would have taken ten million Mana points to destroy the runes in a working teleport pad.

He'd consumed the books on teleport pads and portals up to the Expert level. He didn't get it all because of the higher concepts that Malsour was hacking his way through, but he got enough.

"So, what's the plan?" Dave asked.

"After this? We'll go take some R and R—see the sights, get a tan. Maybe go see a few dungeons." Josh's tone made it clear he was making it all up on the spot.

Dave gave him a look.

Josh devolved into laughing, a big smile on his face. "Well, we finish this off, get our loot moved to where the Exdar's are and then I'm thinking Devil's Crater is interesting this time of year."

A smile spread across Dave's face. He had enjoyed fighting through the Aleph's facilities. He'd learned and grown a lot. Now he was looking forward to getting the hell outside. "Well, that is one hell of a way to show back up after being gone for so damn long." Dave grinned.

"Stone Raiders take on Demon Horde—does have a certain ring to it."

"You know the Dark Lord's not going to be happy. This will be the third time we've messed up something good for him. First with the citadel, then the Arch Lich, and now attacking his new massive army made up of Creatures of Power."

"He's just an archetype. There's no actual Dark Lord, just some AI, though if they did make one, be kind of interesting to fight him." Josh looked thoughtful.

"Want to fight gods?" Dave asked dryly.

"Well, sounds a little more interesting than your average weekend of gaming."

Dave couldn't help it; he laughed. Josh joined in a few moments after. *I was thinking about this all wrong. I was thinking that it was just on Party Zero to deal with what Emerilia really is.* Dave wanted to tell Josh and the rest of the Stone Raiders the truth. They weren't strong enough yet. Maybe if they could defeat a god, they might be ready to know the truth of Emerilia and capable of defending themselves against whatever the Jukal brought to the fight.

Dwayne and Kim walked out of the teleport pad that was hidden in a mountain range close to Devil's Crater.

The Stone Raiders who weren't needed for the final fixes to the portal factory moved around them. They'd become closer as a guild in the time that they had fought through Aleph. A few laughed or started to kiss the ground. The Aleph's homes had been dark at times, especially if their mage lights were out, though it hadn't been horrible.

All of them had big smiles on their faces, joking and laughing as they moved out of the silver arch that looked like a solid wall. They were greeted with a bright midday sun. They just basked in the sun for a while.

"Well, let's go see what this Demon Horde's all about!" Dwayne led them down the mountain range and off toward Devil's Crater.

Excitement was in the air, all the Stone Raiders ready for their next battle. It had been less than a week since they killed the Arch Lich and they were already starting to crave a battle to challenge them.

"Ah, I need a good beer and a city to drink it in!" Dwayne bellowed.

"Oh, I could just do with about three weeks of sunbathing." Kim sighed.

"Well, how about an entire Demon Horde?"

Kim's face turned thoughtful as she seemed to weigh the options in her mind. "Yeah, I guess I could." She laughed and broke out into a smile. "Would just be stones if not for the raiding part."

"Well, let's get a move on, Stone Raiders! Can finally see how fast we are!" Dwayne jogged down the weaving trail that dropped down to a large forested plain.

Dwayne whooped as he ran faster and faster; fighting in the Aleph areas, they'd been cramped in, unable to get in a large run, to reach their full speed.

There was something freeing about just running and testing one's limits.

"Prince Alkao, we have a group of people moving toward your keep," one of the scout commanders said as soon as they connected to Alkao.

"Bring our forces to full readiness."

"Yes, sir." The scout disconnected as Alkao opened up another chat. "Anna, I was wondering if I should be expecting anything today?"

"Well, a group of the Stone Raiders is heading toward you right now.

Most of our pure combat forces at least," Anna said.

"I think we just spotted them. Who am I looking for?" Alkao sighed. "Kim and Dwayne are the highest ranked two with them."

"Thank you. I better go say hello."

"See you soon enough. We're almost done here."

"I look forward to it." Alkao gave a small smile. He wasn't sure whether anything would come from his feelings, but even if not, he had become close to Malsour, Induca, and Anna over the last couple of months. *It will be good to see my friends in all the chaos that is about to come.*

Anna cut the chat and Alkao wandered out of his personal rooms, looking out over his keep, Devil's Crater, and the plains that lay around it.

He stepped off his balcony. His wings let him glide down to the parapets that watched over the crater's sides. "Where were they sighted?" Alkao asked. It wasn't long until his guards followed down from his balcony, watching for any possible threats to their master.

"Over there, sir," one of the watchers on the wall said.

Alkao pulled out a telescope and looked in the direction they pointed. Alkao saw colors moving through the natural foliage and the glint of polished metal. Something was definitely coming through the forest. He didn't know what it was but they were heavily armed.

Alkao watched for a bit, seeing the group pass through a clearing at an alarming speed. They seemed to be laughing and joking, though it looked like a group of brigands by their mismatched gear.

"It might be the Stone Raiders. Pass the word that all forces are to wait until engaging," Alkao said.

One of his guards who served to pass messages to the rest of his forces opened their interface and opened up the right chat groups. The keep was a mass of movement. People knew their positions after tireless drilling from one infraction or another.

It had just been minutes since the group of armed and armored individuals had been spotted but all of the Demons and Beast Kin on duty were ready. Those who had been off duty would be another thirty minutes or so.

It took three hours until the group started to slow down. Their pace was impressive. They ran nearly as fast as the Demons could fly.

A large man wearing about three different kinds of armor held up his hand, halting his people far enough out to give them time to start dodging if Alkao had bows.

Another thing that we're going to have to invest in.

Alkao had archers and many were trained in the art, but the problem was making proper bows. His crafters weren't of the highest quality. The Beast Kin were trying their best, but supplying an army as big as the demons' and Beast Kins' was a massive workload. Add in settling into a new home and it turned into a downright nightmare.

Even simple pikes were in short supply. Swords and shields were for training, with only Lezar's soldiers being anywhere near to equipped.

The man walked closer. Alkao saw the armor; even to his eyes, it looked as though it was expensive and powerful.

"Hey! We're the Stone Raiders. Was told that you were interested in hunting down a Demon Horde that's looking to mess with your home! The name's Dwayne."

Alkao focused on the one called Dwayne, waiting for his skill to kick in.

Dwayne Trebault
Human
Level 184

Alkao felt the tension fall from his back. "I will go down and check their identities."

His guard didn't have time to argue as he stepped off the parapet and glided down the road that ran up the cliffs through the keep and into Devil's Crater.

As he glided down with his wings, he heard excited murmurs from the group ahead of him. They didn't look organized at all, just milling about with smiles on their faces.

Alkao looked at their eyes. Although all of them might be smiling and laughing, their hands were next to their weapons. These were people who were used to being attacked at any moment and were ready to respond in any situation.

"Ah, you look like that Alkao fella. Party Zero is finishing up the last of the last quest and then they'll be on their way over. We thought it might be an idea to check out what we're dealing with and get to know one another." Dwayne extended his hand to Alkao.

He was a large tanned man with a big smile on his face. Alkao looked for Dwayne's aura; he couldn't figure out its size, making him raise an eyebrow in interest.

"Thank you for coming to help us." Alkao took Dwayne's hand and shook it.

"Seems we're in the business of helping races of lore come back from the brink." Dwayne smiled.

"Welcome to Devil's Crater," Alkao said.

"Thanks for having us. So, about this Demon Horde problem you've been having—they're about five weeks away, right?" A woman walked up. "Kim, introduce yourself—ya know it's the nice thing to do," Dwayne said.

"Fine." Kim held out her hand. "I'm Kim. I do magic stuff and raids like no one's business."

"Alkao, Demon Prince and General of the Devil's Crater Army." Alkao shook her hand.

"Ohh, snazzy, I like men with big wings and large armies," Kim said giving Alkao a sly wink.

Alkao shook her hand, the massive Demon unsure of how to respond as his mouth opened and closed.

"She gets like this," Dwayne apologized. Kim grinned at Alkao's confusion.

Alkao chuckled. "I have often thought the same thing; it is no worry. I do not know. I will bring it up in the next meeting. I think most of the soldiers are already calling themselves it. It would make them more identifiable."

"Having a name that's neither Demon nor Beast Kin brings you together. Calling it the Demon Beast Army, nah, but the place—the thing that connects you—perfect." Kim winked.

"She made up the Stone Raiders' guild name and we've never lived it down." Dwayne sighed. A few of the Stone Raiders laughed while Kim looked as though she were preening in the limelight.

"Well, please come in. We have much to discuss." Alkao indicated for them to follow him as they made the climb up the road.

He shot a glance at the Stone Raiders again. Nearly a hundred undying warriors who could come back time and time again, with more knowledge each time. *It's no wonder the Players hold so much power in Emerilia.*

"We have to do something about that damned Exdar's Traders branch!" Geswald, a balding human in flowing robes, said. A vein throbbed on his forehead.

"Agreed, but what?" Tommen, a stick-thin Wood Elf wearing an expensive and over-the-top purple suit with pink highlights, asked.

"We cut off their supplies. Take out their business. We put pressure on those who openly support them!" Geswald slammed his fist into the armrest of his chair.

"You want to try and pressure the mage's guild?" Lady Pina looked to Geswald. Her omni-chrome eyes and golden skin of a High Elf had captured more than one man's attention and not his mind.

"Of course not! I mean the other rabble around them selling food and their lesser wares," Geswald said.

"If we do something, then the traders' guild is not going to give us coverage on this. If we win, then they'll share in the profits. Otherwise, they won't lift a finger if this comes back on us," Orlani, the last person in the room, said. The overweight human sipped from an elegant wine glass.

"I know that!" Geswald let out a frustrated noise.

He was the chapter head of the traders' guild in the area, but even he knew his limits when it came to his power. The guildmaster himself made it clear — in flowery words — that they did not think going up against the Exdar's Traders branch in Verlun was a good idea.

"It all comes from that treaty that they have made with the Stone Raiders. It seems that somehow even with the raiding group seemingly vanishing from the face of Emerilia, they are still having the Exdar's fence their goods," Tommen said. "With it, they have become one of the largest trading guilds held primarily by Players."

"Something that we can use to our advantage." Geswald waved his finger at his companion.

"Oh?" Tommen asked. Everyone's interest was on the Chapter leader. "Players are a rather simple sort of people. They think that they are somehow in charge of what they do here. That they are doing quests, not being given them. They never think in the ways that the POE move and do things. The Players, while having an amazing amount of abilities, are no different than our normal customers. Give them the right incentives, show your wares at the right places, and you can make a sale. If we are to get the Players to attack the Exdar's Traders, making them think that the Stone Raiders won't be able to retaliate, it would only be normal. They have been gone for six months. We can get them to attack the Exdar's branch. We send in the city guard as soon as the Players are done finishing off the Exdar's and move in our own people to take whatever remains in the branch. One night and we will destroy their supplies and make them unable to supply the mage's guild and college." Geswald hit his hand on his chair in glee.

"You mustn't have heard about what happened with the PKP guild." Lady Pina's voice was light as everyone's attentions moved to her.

"Please continue," Tommen said.

"There was once a guild called Players Kill Players. They were one of the strongest guilds around. They went around, working under the assassins' guild. They would kill POE or Player — it didn't matter to them. Even when they were not working, they would kill anyone who looked to have anything expensive. They made holding the most Mirror of Communications a status symbol. They had some of the strongest and most powerful weapons from killing Players after they finished a hard raid. They had around five hundred Players. Till about seven months ago." She looked around the room.

"In Selhi Capital, the PKP hunted the Stone Raiders. Killed a whole lot of them, too. Then half the guild seemed to come out of the forest, cutting them down from behind. The Stone Raiders, outnumbered by nearly four to one in pure Players, pulled out a victory. They might not have been high levels but they could fight. They placed a soul hex on those who attacked them. A hex from the Lady of Fire. The Stone Raiders were run out of town by the magistrate and seemingly disappeared. Here and there, the PKP were killed off by the Stone Raiders. They were constantly being burned by the hex and the Stone Raiders could locate them, until the PKP messed up again and attacked an Exdar's Trader's caravan."

She sipped from her wine, hiding her emotions perfectly. Her eyes flicked up, looking to those in the room with anger in them. "They attacked, without warning, but the Exdar's knew. Stone Raiders poured out of their wagons — they had been ready and waiting. Still, it wasn't enough to kill off the PKPs amassed there. Until they started putting down a massive steel plate."

There were confused looks around the room.

"From this steel plate, dozens of Stone Raiders charged through. Don't know where they came from or what that plate was. The PKP launched their ambush, but they were outnumbered and cut down to the man. There were reports after that. Stone Raiders appearing in cities in the middle of the night, cutting down PKP as they found them and then disappearing again. The PKP couldn't stay in any city where there was a teleport pad. The PKP guild dissolved after two months of continuously being slaughtered across Emerilia. They had to reincarnate into another body to just remove the curse. I agree that the Exdar's Traders must be removed. We must make sure that this never comes back onto us. If it does…"

She left her words hanging in the air, a physical presence as the others' faces changed subtly, thinking on what had been said.

"Taking what Lady Pina has said, I believe it is best that as we carry this out, we first of all attempt some other possibilities to remove the Exdar's, saving the use of the Players and violence as a last resort," Orlani said.

"Agreed, Orlani. Lady Pina, would you be able to set that up? Tommen, I think that your skills might be put to use in influencing the people in the area to stay away from the Exdar's, from the mages to the locals. I can work my contacts to gather more information within the Exdar's, their practices and dealings that we might be able to use against them," Geswald said.

The others nodded. They were all well to-do business people but Geswald, being the local leader of the traders' guild chapter in Emaren, was the most powerful of them all in the room. In another land not connected to Per'ush, they could all own a small kingdom or city with their influence and power.

Here, they made deals worth kingdoms and dealt with an always shifting court. If Per'ush was the heart of Emerilia, they were the blood that kept goods moving to and from the magical college.

They had crushed countless other businesses that had tried to compete with them, from Player to POEs. To them, crushing Exdar's Traders branch was more of a source of entertainment. To show anyone else why they should never try to compete with them.

23

QUEST COMPLETED

Dave crossed his fingers and looked at the pop-up in front of him.

Aleph Portal Factory
Do you wish to start Aleph Portal Factory's main line? Y/N

"Yes," Dave said, his nervousness clear as lights started to blink and for the first time in decades, the line shuddered into life.

Arms and parts started to move and come together. "Woohoo!" Steve said.

Quest: Aleph Homecoming
You have restored the Aleph Portal Factory. Rewards: 345,000 EXP Increased standing with Aleph people

Level 118
You have reached level 118; you have **506** stat points to use.

Quest: Aleph Homecoming
You have restored the Aleph's facilities to their former glory. **Rewards:** 575,000 EXP Stone Raiders Guild is seen as Allies with the Aleph people Guild Hall

Level 120
You have reached level 120; you have **516** stat points to use.

Relationship Change
Your personal standing with the Aleph has changed to Trusted Ally

Quest: Friend of the Grey God Level 3
You have completed the level 3 quest for this class. **Rewards:** Unlock Level 4 quest +10 to all stats (stacks with previous class level) 300,000 EXP

Class: **Friend of the Grey God**	
Status:	Level 3
	+30 to all stats
Effects:	Access to hidden quests.
	300,000 EXP

Quest: Bleeder Level 2
You have completed the level 2 quest for this class. **Rewards:** Unlock Level 3 quest +10 to all stats (stacks with previous class level) 200,000 EXP

Class: **Bleeder**	
Status:	Level 2
Effects:	+20 to all stats

Quest: Librarian Level 2
You have completed the level 2 quest for this class.
Rewards: Unlock Level 4 quest
+10 to all stats (stacks with previous class level)

Class: **Librarian**	
Status:	Level 2
Effects:	+20 to all stats

Quest: Aleph Engineer Level 3
You have completed the level 3 quest for this class.
Rewards: Unlock Level 4 quest
+15 to Endurance, Willpower, and Intelligence (stacks with previous class level)
Gain access to Aleph College
resources 300,000 EXP

Class: **Aleph Engineer**	
Status:	Level 3
Effects:	+45 to Endurance, Willpower, and Intelligence Gain access to Aleph College resources 300,000 EXP

Level 124
You have reached level 124; you have **536** stat points to use.

Dave stayed very still as he slowly moved his fingers from being crossed. He closed his eyes, feeling the rush that spread through his body. His mind went a mile a minute. It seemed as if the gravity of Emerilia barely had hold on him anymore. He felt as though he could run for days and lift a tank above his head.

When he opened his eyes, he moved at a snail's pace to turn around. "Something wrong, Dave?" Josh gave him a peculiar look.

"Just trying to not fall over right now," Dave said, judging his steps. "What do you..." Deia turned, nearly falling over as if she had thought there was a step in front of her but she'd missed it.

"Looks like your Intelligence is over three hundred now," Dave said. "Ugh, so, I have to deal with the almost falling over stuff?"

"Yep! Welcome to the club." Dave smiled as he checked how he walked and such. With his increased Intelligence, his mind started to figure out the new inputs and outputs of his increased abilities.

The portal factory continued to work as everyone took time to understand the rewards they had received.

Dave opened up his character sheet, a massive smile on his face.

CHARACTER SHEET			
Name:	David Grahslagg	Gender:	Male
Level:	16	Class:	Dwarven Master Smith, Friend of the Gray God, Bleeder, Librarian, Aleph
			Engineer, Weapons Master
Race:	Human/Dwarf	Alignment :	Chaotic Neutral
Unspent points: 536			
Health:	18,300	Regen:	6.14 /s
Mana:	3,780	Regen:	15.75 /s
Stamina:	2,480	Regen:	12.20 /s
Vitality:	183	Endurance :	307
Intelligence :	378	Willpower :	315
Strength:	248	Agility:	244

"What does this mean by guild hall?" Josh muttered aloud.

"It is the gift that we thought best for you. Weapons, armor, resources, money—all of it you find in the places that you raid and although you have a base in Cliff-Hill and Verlun, you do not have a true base of operations which you can call home. It was the idea of the Aleph Council members to give you a self-contained housing complex that you could use as you desire. If you would like, I can send you there and have the Aleph automatons start bringing your gear from the city Anais you were staying in," Shard said.

His voice was loud enough so that all of the Stone Raiders could hear. "All right, all right, all right!" Steve said excitedly.

"Why couldn't I have got a creature that wasn't a complete metal-brained idiot?" Suzy said, holding her forehead.

"Well, don't worry. Soon enough you can get another one. With all this portal information I've got stacked up in here, we should be good to go." Dave pointed to his skull. "As long as Anna has some places that might be good to find some rare creatures."

"I know a few different locations that we could summon different high-level creatures from," Anna assured Suzy.

"All right, Stone Raiders, let's go and check out our new digs!" Josh led the way to the teleport pad.

They all followed behind, eager to see what they'd earned from their quest. Three of them promptly underestimated their newfound strength and slammed into one another, the third letting out a shriek as they tumbled through the air.

"Okay, maybe we should take a little time to get used to our newfound power," Josh said as the third returned to the ground with a thump and a groan.

Kim dismissed her notifications after reading over every exciting word. She found herself stumbling as if her body's timing was off and had to use the walls of the keep to make it outside.

Stone Raiders were chatting with one another excitedly. Others were showing off spells that they couldn't do without the extra boost to their classes or experience.

Kim stood at the doorway and watched the feats of her guild members. She glanced to the Devil's Crater Army, who were all looking at what the Stone Raiders were doing in clear awe. One melee fighter jumped a story and a half, grabbing onto the keep's wall before dropping back down. Others started to spar one another, a furious exchange of blades, shields, and magic. They didn't hold back, going full bore to test out their new improvements. A number of them started to blur in their actions. Kim wasn't able to keep up, finding her eyes were slower than her mind in processing what she was seeing.

"Well, this is going to be one hell of a Demon Horde hunt." Kim smiled and then frowned. "Wow, Demon Horde hunt? Seriously, that just sounds so wordy and dumb. Demon Horde battle? Display of magical might?" Kim made odd noises with her mouth and tongue, as if trying to get rid of the words she'd just said.

Dwayne leapt off the castle within the keep, falling into the training area and rolling up to his feet.

The Stone Raiders cheered in greeting.

"Bunch of idiots." Kim smiled and made her way across the keep's courtyard while trying her best to not fall over.

"I'll show you an entrance." Kim weaved her magic. She closed her eyes, muttering an incantation to stabilize her spell. Air whipped around, pulling itself into a shimmering construct of barely contained wind. More and more wind grew; four feet landed on the ground as a body, wings, tail, neck, and finally face was formed from the hurricane-like winds.

Kim wiped sweat away from her face as her Air dragon let out a screech into the air.

The Devil's Crater Army soldiers looked ready to make wet spots on their clothes as the Stone Raiders whooped and cheered at their guild mate's success.

24

LAYING THE FOUNDATION

The Stone Raiders exited the teleport pad to a familiar-looking teleport pad control room. Unlike the majority they had seen, this one was in near-perfect condition. The lights were on and it looked untouched.

Shard appeared before them.

"This is a self-contained housing complex unit. It currently has forty repair bots and ten scout guardians at its disposal. For rooms, there are two barracks with accompanying growing areas. It also includes one teleport pad control room, a mining shaft and two workshops. Power is supplied by the rune net that Dave showed me," Shard continued on as the Stone Raiders moved through the halls on either side of the control room and into the barracks. The barracks were identical to the main housing complex that the Stone Raiders had fought the kobolds in.

It was a cross, with four stories filled with apartments. In the center, there was a greenery area with plants and seeds. To the right of the intersection, there were workshops on the first and second level. The third and fourth were storage areas.

On the left side, there were four interconnected growing areas at the end of the living spaces. Straight ahead there was another barracks.

To the right intersection of that living barracks, there were stacked growing areas again.

To the left, the walls were bare, waiting for something to be placed there. Straight ahead, there was the back end of a mining drill. Ready to cut through the wall in front of it.

"The mining drill is currently at half power. With it, you can carve out different facilities." Shard moved to Josh.

Aleph Guild Hall
Shard, on behalf of the Aleph people, offers you this guild hall to do with as you desire. Do you accept? Y/N

"Yeah, hell, yeah, damn!" Josh looked around. This was nothing like he was expecting. With the teleport pad control room, Stone Raiders would be more connected than ever, moving from one place to another with ease. If some of the guild were under attack, they could rally here and go to aid them.

Just for that ability alone, it was incredible.

"This is your guild hall now. You can do with it as you desire. That said, if you desire, you can hire people from the Aleph or still purchase automatons from us, to use as protection, or keep your guild hall running, so that you don't need to. We have included some resources to get you started. You can also contact me at any time for anything at all. If you would not like me to listen in, call me up and change the privacy settings of the area you are in. We wish to extend unto you the rights and privileges of an Aleph citizen." Shard smiled.

Interesting how he never said anything about those privacy settings before. Seems that the Aleph have been keeping a better eye on us than I thought.

"When doing expansions, you can alter set plans as you desire, though there are set templates for all different areas, from forges to power stations. I will leave you with this. Let me know if you have any questions." Shard bowed his head and disappeared.

"Forge!" Dave shook his hand about in the air.

"I just got given all of this—I don't know what's going on," Josh said defensively. He looked through his menus. A new one called Guild Hall flashed green.

"Well, let's figure it out some then!" Dave conjured a table in the middle of the second barracks.

Josh laughed and rolled his eyes.

Stone Raiders were laughing and cheering, rushing off and clamoring to grab an apartment before anyone else.

Josh gave Dave administration rights to see the screens. There were three tabs: Map, Units and Resources.

The map was a three-dimensional representation of the guild hall. He could select anything from it, find out more information, or in the case of the automatons in the workshops and the drill, he could give them orders.

At the top of the map, there was a builder button that opened up a menu of different buildings, halls, walkways, and other areas to add to the guild hall. Each of them had upfront requirements. They needed a drill to carve it out, building machines to clean up the areas, as well as resources, which climbed up steeply for anything like forges or working areas.

The different facilities gave access to different items, just like when they were capturing Aleph facilities. More barracks, more sleeping areas. More greenhouses, more oxygen. More power stations, more power and so on.

There was also a running cost over time which related to the counters at the top of the menu. There was air and current power supply.

The Units menu had automatons listed on it, with numbers next to them. Clicking on them showed that they were all listed on standby status. From the Units panel, he could order new automatons from the Aleph, or he could commission more from his own workshops, though they were much slower than an Aleph automaton workshop.

There was also the option to hire people from the Aleph. They could look after things that the automatons couldn't, like the gardens, or look after the day-to-day maintenance, or increase the building speed of the Stone Raiders' guild hall.

The Resource tab made Josh's eyes go wide.

"Holy mother of resources," Dave said. He must've got to the same tab. He looked to Josh and then back to his sheet.

Resources
2x Teleport pad
1x Terminal
10x Vault Soul Gems (charged)
100x Steel ingots
50x Silver ingots
10x Ebony ingots
5x Mithril ingots

Josh pressed Teleport Pad, his finger quivering. Teleport pads were something that kingdoms gained. *Not a guild!*

Two options came up: [Place] and [Remove from storage]. Josh pressed [Place].

Place Teleport Pad
There are 2x Drop pads under the Stone Raiders' ownership that these teleport pads can be placed at.

Do you wish to place a teleport pad at:
[Verlun]
[Devil's Crater]

"Drop pads act as a beacon for the teleport pads to be moved to them, I guess," Josh muttered.

"So, where we going to put them?" Dave asked.

Lucy, who had been checking out the different areas, came and joined them. Josh sent her an invite without her needing to ask.

"Well, we need one at Cliff-Hill," Josh started.

Dave cleared his throat before he scratched the back of his head. "*Well*, there might be one showing up there soon." Dave looked a little embarrassed.

"What do you mean?" Josh frowned.

"Well, might have kind of made Kol make a drop pad and then put in a buy order for a new one, or will be in a few days, so, don't need that one. I'll let you guys use it for a discount." Dave grinned.

Josh stared at Dave as if he couldn't believe what he was hearing. "Fine. Okay, so, really then, we've just got Verlun, though having a place for us to use in Ashal and with the dungeons that are in the area, it would make sense to have a place there. It would also allow us to transport people and resources from Verlun to Devil's Crater," Josh said.

"Agreed. And with what Dave said about making a forge, now that we're not in Aleph, then they're probably going to be testing out those materials themselves, making us drop off in production and sales of materials to the Dwarves. We're raking in money for all of that, but with the guild hall, I think it will be pretty fast for us to start burning through it. Also, being one of the only Player guilds with the materials, maybe we can get a deal with the Dwarves for them to make us some special weaponry out of it all," Lucy said.

"What are you thinking?" Josh asked.

"We connect to Devil's Crater and Verlun as fast as possible. Keep goods moving. We'll be making enough in gold to get the resources that we need. Biggest thing is getting that drill mining. I say we put all of the guild's resources into building the guild hall. We're going to need to create a command area, dedicated mining areas, forges, power plants. Everything."

Dave nodded in agreement. "I like that plan, but I say we go a step further."

Josh, Lucy, and the other Stone Raiders listened in.

"We don't just make an extended housing complex. We copy the Aleph cities. Massive drills going all the time, expanding constantly as we build behind them. Power stations to keep them fueled up. Doesn't need to be a big city, like the Aleph, we can make it in the shape of a cylinder and spin it to maximize room."

Josh rubbed his face. "I like it, but it's going to cost a hell of a lot," Josh said. "Let me look after that. I'll leave the city designing to Dave and Suzy. First thing we need to do — Dave, see if you can detect any pockets of resources in the area and then we'll send the drill after it. We're going to need a ton of resources and room. We can expand out one end of the guild hall, widening it out with the drill and automatons. We're going to need a refinery, so that we can make use of the materials the drill is pumping out. Dave, you get with the crafters and start planning. We'll make this the ground floor and start building accordingly."

"I can supply you with designs of other Aleph cities," Shard added. "Great. We get that going at the same time. We're going to need Aleph people to help out with the greenhouses here and I can run that. For now, we don't need any more automatons for anything other than maintenance. The rest we can use for scouting the Demon Horde. Once we have the refinery up, then we need to focus on getting a power station. Going to need to find out where the nearest ley line is, so we can tap right into the Mana lines."

"I have a plot for the nearest Mana lines, but they are far away. You would have to do blind portalling to get near and then push in another mining drill to carve out the facility," Shard said.

The excitement in the barracks grew as everyone looked to one another. The guild hall was more than they ever thought it could be; the possibilities and hope to grow and thrive was a powerful drug.

"Well, we'd best get started. We can plan this out in a few hours and then leave it going before heading off to Devil's Crater. Be something of a surprise to come out of our *own* teleport pad." Dave smiled.

"That will be something else. I can already hear Kim complaining about how she had to walk all the way." Josh laughed.

Dave rubbed his face. It had been just a few hours since they had made it into their new guild hall. Already, they had a semblance of a plan for what they wanted to do. They'd use the Aleph automated mining drill to start cutting out apartment buildings and the taller structures of their new home. Automaton mining bots would carve out a refinery in that area before moving on to make a class C power station and the different areas that would need to be made to create a power collection system.

"How goes the planning?" Deia sat next to Dave as he and Suzy took a break from planning.

"It's mostly done. Really, we've just got to figure out what we want later. We're cutting out blocks that can be made into factories or storage areas. The main tower we're building will be laid out like the one we used in the city Anais. We're leaving tons of space for anything that we might expand into. With the Stone Raiders' resources and our people, this could be one of the biggest projects I've taken on." Dave put his arm around her and pulled her tight to him.

"Excited?" She smiled.

"Very," Dave said with a big smile.

Deia shook her head, passing him a bagged burger and fries. "Thanks, babe." He kissed her on the cheek as his stomach grumbled. "At least one of us knows when you forget to eat." Deia ate some fries from Dave's lunch. Dave would've argued but he had taken a bite of his burger. He made sounds of bliss as he chomped through the food.

"You didn't eat while you were working on the portal factory, did you?" Deia shook her head.

"Nope." He continued to devour the meal. They were in the second barracks. There were supplies and gear all over the place. Lucy's people were getting it organized while she dealt with the different Aleph people they were looking to hire. There were more applicants than Dave had thought there would be.

"So, I heard that you're having troubles with your plans?" Deia asked. Dave took a deep drink from his waterskin. "Well, we've got the city sorted. Well, it's just going to take time and power. The biggest thing is we need to have the refinery up and running, so that we can start processing down the materials and making them useful instead of just crap left behind by the mining drill. The power station is going to take a lot of materials to be made and to be burned, so that will help us lose some of the mass that we're pulling out of the ground. The thing is that we need to keep having the teleport pad active to get more air in here so we don't spread it too thin and make it unbreathable. So, as we work, we're going to have to make air locks everywhere, opening them when we open the teleport pad. It's going to be expensive having the teleport open for all of that," Dave said. "Sounds like a lot of work," Deia said.

"Oh, it is, but it also means that we're going to be designing this thing like a damned space station. Have air locks all over the place so that we can cut off one area from another. Stations are the coolest thing to build." Dave grinned.

"I keep forgetting all the things you did back on Earth, and how normal that sounds to you." Deia shook her head.

"Just another day at the office." Dave laughed, dusting off his fingers, as he finished off the remaining fries. He opened his interface, looking at the next set of tasks he'd put out for himself.

"Don't you want to sit with your fiancée instead of messing with all that right now?" Deia said.

Dave made to argue but stopped, shrugging and sitting back. He closed his interface and gave her a kiss on the lips.

"Mmm, burger flavor, gross," she said, unable to stop smiling.

She rested her head on his shoulder as he just took a step back from his work. Enjoying the feeling of having something that inspired him, ready to be worked on and taking a break. He had more than just work and the next thing in his life.

As Austin Zane, he'd always rushed off to the next project. There was always something that *needed* to be done. The real reason was because if he stopped, then he constantly felt lost; there were no real peers for him. He and Suzy would congratulate each other on a job well done, but the next day, they'd be working on something else. Work had become his everything, with no room for the small pleasures in life.

Here, he was doing stuff because he wanted to. When he stopped, he wasn't stuck wondering why he had no friends and lamenting over all the things he'd lost to get to this point in his life.

Instead, he was surrounded by people who would love to have a beer with him, were interested in hanging out, or just talk about random things. It was only when someone had no friends that they learned to appreciate them for all the small things they brought to his life.

Deia made him take a step back at times and think about what he was doing. Think about his plans and for the first time, he actually allowed himself to look over what he had done instead of charging ahead.

He'd always been proud of what he had done with Rock Breakers, but it had turned into his life, rather than just something he had done.

Deia pulled out two more burgers from her bag of holding. "What would I do without you?" He took the new burger. "Starve, probably." Deia laughed at Dave's grimace.

"Fair," he admitted. A big smile grew on his face as he picked her up and pulled her onto his lap.

She giggled like a little girl as Dave sat back, eating and looking at his girl and his guild.

"Dave, when are you going to make your new armor?" Deia asked.

He could hear the worry in her voice. She didn't want him to be without protection in whatever fight they found themselves in next.

"Well, there should be a teleport pad in Cliff-Hill in two days. Want to go on a little trip home?" Dave asked.

"I'd like that. Could we go to Per'ush? My father's there, learning." Deia stole some of his fries.

"Of course, be good to see him again." Dave smiled.

"And you've always wanted to see Per'ush," Deia added.

"Well, that is a part of it." Dave shrugged and gave her a wide smile. "I think he approves of you."

"Oh thanks, makes me feel like such a prized piece of beef." Dave smiled and rolled his eyes.

She shook her head, snorting at his antics as she grabbed more fries. Dave, enticed, started tickling her sides.

She sent the fries flying as she tried to fight back against his tickling attack. The other Stone Raiders smiled and shook their heads.

"St...stop! Ha-ha—it hurts! I can't breathe!" Tears came to Deia's face.

Dave gave her a kiss and wrapped her up in his arms to protect himself.

He saw a dark look in her eyes as she freed her hands; it was his time to giggle and laugh, trying everything to get away from her. After some time, they settled down, tired and flustered from the tickle fight as they just hung out.

"I think Steve is going to start climbing the walls, he's so bored," Dave commented. The behemoth carried goods around as Lucy directed him.

He seemed to have heard Dave and shot him a baleful look.

"Looks like Josh has news." Deia pointed at Josh, who had been off in the first barracks talking to various contacts and organizing things for the Stone Raiders.

"Everyone gather in!" Josh said. It didn't take long for the Stone Raiders to do just that.

"Okay, so, it looks like Dwayne will have a place for the teleport pad to move to in a few hours. Those who want to are welcome to join us at Devil's Crater. We're not expecting to do anything for a week or two. If you have anything you need to do, now would be the time for it. After this, we're probably going to have a pretty busy month kicking some Demon Horde ass!" Josh said to the hoots and hollers of the Stone Raiders. "It seems that everyone thinks we just walked off the edge of the world. With the Demon Horde, you can record and send as much video out into the world as you want once we're done! It's time we showed those people who have been missing us just why we're the best raiding guild in all of Emerilia!"

"Want to do Per'ush, then Cliff-Hill?" Dave asked Deia. "Let's see if the others want to join us," Deia said.

"I feel like I might know what Steve is going to say." Dave shook his head.

25

VERLUN

"What?" Florence said, in an almost screech. The door opened; her two guards walked in and looked for threats.

"Sorry, talking to Josh." She waved them out.

"I said that I have a teleport pad and I was thinking it would be a good idea to start making a trade network. I want to put one of the teleport pads within our branch at Verlun, though if you have a better location for it, I would be happy to go with that. Right now, Dave is putting one in at Cliff- Hill and we've got another going in at Devil's Crater."

After joining the Stone Raiders guild as a sub-guild, Florence and the others who were high up within the Exdar's had been told about the Aleph, Demons, and Beast Kin, as well as the coming war. Their excitement had been palpable, but they understood the need to keep things closely guarded. Having a teleport pad in Verlun would be huge. The next nearest teleport pad was fifty miles away, but the tax on it was incredibly high, just under the taxes that the mage's guild put on the goods coming onto their islands.

"We could make a lot off the teleport pad's fees and we have the drop pad already; it takes quite a number of soul gems to power it, but you can send us goods through it. Having the ability to send them back without having a week and a half lag time between our people taking them up to a hidden Aleph teleport pad would be nice. What kind of trade goods do the Devil's Crater residents need?" Florence tapped her lip in thought.

"First things they need are food, weapons and clothes. To survive the winter. Party Zero is going to Per'ush, then off to Cliff-Hill. I've sent them to look into these supplies as well. They can get high quality weapons and armor, though I need someone to buy it from them and then we can sell it to the Devil's Crater's Army. For clothes and food, we don't have many contacts, though I've heard that Verlun is a large agriculture community?" Josh asked.

"That it is. If I can't get the suppliers here, I can go through some contacts I've made to find out where they are," Florence assured him.

"Okay. Also, we're going to need you to send us some people to come and check out Devil's Crater and set up a branch location there. If we have our own teleport pad in Verlun, then we can send everything to you. If it doesn't sell there or if there is another location looking for items, you can distribute as the market dictates and gain a better return on it," Josh said.

Florence was silent for a while, thinking it over. There was a lot to do and she really didn't want to waste the teleport pad, though if she wanted to keep her current Exdar's Traders branch in Verlun, then it would make only too much sense to get it. Mages could just teleport from their islands directly into her branch to get their supplies instead of sending their aides every few days to gather it.

"Fine, yeah, it makes sense," Florence finally agreed. "Though we also have another problem. It seems that there is someone or a group of someones who are making things hard for us over here. I don't know what is going on, but I feel the tension in the air."

"Well, this will give you a lot more power to deal with them as you see fit. Take from the guild's treasury as you need to buy as much surrounding land as you can. If not, find a new location and building to put the teleport pad down. We will build a branch location around it if needed. If they even try anything aggressive, expect another Selhi. You're all Stone Raiders—you helped to deal with all the loot and such we hate dealing with. Stone Raiders look out for one another." Josh's tone left no room for questions.

"Thank you, Josh." A smile spread across Florence's face.

"Oh, and Lucy is also going to chew your ear off about what else is going on. She's in the guild's mirror hall. Talk later! I'm off to Devil's Crater!"

"As soon as I have this thing up and working, I'll get some of the traders to move to Devil's Crater and set up a branch there. Didn't think things would change this fast or in this way!" Florence laughed.

"Ah, way more exciting this way!"

Oson'Mal smiled as a group of five people walked out of the teleport pad.

Where have they been? Fire thought to herself, using far sight to see them all. She had a sad smile on her face as she saw Deia hug her waiting father. He laughed at seeing her, talking to Dave, who stood off to the side.

Fire tore her eyes from the scene before the need to run over and check whether Deia was all right overwhelmed her.

All of them seemed to be rubbing their eyes. It was only that she was trying to grab onto something else to distract her, her daughter being so close, that she even caught it. "Somewhere dark?" Fire tapped her chin in thought.

"Lady Fuego, I have one of the librarians having an issue with some traps that seemed to have activated by themselves," her secretary called from her office door.

"Very well, I will be right there." Fire grabbed the glasses hanging around her neck. Fire saw the group leave the teleport pad area and head off, being hidden by buildings.

Fire took a deep breath, putting her glasses on, and canceled her far sight. *A life of regret and missed opportunities,* she thought sadly, remembering the young lady who had run for two days straight to check on her father, one of the strongest Fire mages on Emerilia.

She smiled as she headed out of her office and toward the library. It wasn't far away and it took her just a handful of minutes to get there.

"What seems to be the issue?" she asked as she reached the desk. She was well known as a fair librarian who liked to spend the majority of her time reading and helping others find the resources they need to advance their studies. Many came to see her for her recommendations on different books to read. Most of the males came just to see her mousy beauty.

"This way. We had some of the runes get tripped earlier today. We've tried fixing them, but it hasn't worked. Not even using the different access cards that we have has worked so far," the older lady working there said, clearly frustrated.

"We'll sort it out, Yolinda." Fire gave her a reassuring smile and pat the lady's hand.

Yolinda gave a relieved smile as Fire entered the library. "It's in the section about high-tier Fire spells. Third floor, in the back where it's rather musty."

Fire paused mid-stride.

"Something the matter? Do you not know that area?" Yolinda asked. "Nothing. And I know the area rather well." Fire smiled to Yolinda and headed toward the secluded corner.

Of all days, what is the chance that it would be so close to the location where Mal and I snuck off to make out?

She pushed the thoughts from her mind as she passed through the library. She was delayed here and there by students asking questions. She got to the runes and studied them with her arcane sight spell.

"Someone has been messing with the runes around here." She looked at the magical formations. These higher level spell books were restricted to those with higher magical abilities. The mage's college didn't want students trying out spells that were well beyond their level and hurting themselves or others. Fire wasn't the best at runes, but the warm sun shone through a nearby window and she already wanted to take her mind off the fact that her lover and daughter were on the same island as her. It took awhile, but finally she found the issue. A rune had been altered slightly, making it look like another character. "Well, that's weird."

"So, these are the strongest Fire spells?" a female voice said behind her. "Oh, sorry, you okay?" someone asked, after bumping into Fire as they came around the corner.

"That's fine. I was just..." Fire stood up and looked at the others. There was Induca and Malsour, who gave her odd looks and sniffed the air. Oson'Mal was beside Deia, an amused smile on his face.

Her eyes thinned, seeing his expression. "Fixing something that *someone* broke." Fire dusted off her robe as she gave Deia a smile.

"Lady Fuego is one of the greatest librarians here. I bet that she could help you with whatever studies any of you wish to peruse," Mal volunteered. "Hah! Have you read the basics of their runing techniques? It's like using a hammer instead of an interface! Ugh, someone's going to need to re- write these." Dave walked to join up with the group. A High Elf trailed behind him and rolled her eyes.

"I just know where a few of the books that might help you can be located," Fire said, downplaying as she tried to think of a way to escape.

"She's also accepted my offer to dine with us tonight. That way, we might as well get the most out of your stay." Mal looked to the group and then Fire.

His eyes were serious and pulled at her very heartstrings. "It would be my pleasure," Fire said with a weak smile.

"Let's go and check out the arenas. I do know that you like to see magics at work," Mal said to Deia.

"Mind if I join?" Suzy asked. "Not at all." Mal smiled.

"I think I will stay here to catch up on some reading," Malsour said. "So will I," Induca said.

"If you want some alone time with your dad…" Dave trailed off.

"Play with your books as you wish." Deia smiled at Dave. That look made Fire remember how Mal had treated her.

"Like I don't even exist anymore." Suzy shook her head, still with an amused expression on her face.

Mal, Suzy, and Deia retreated. Mal shot Fire one last glance before they disappeared.

Dave closed his book with a thump. His cold eyes made Fire feel colder as he turned from beloved fiancé to protector.

"Who are you and why are you similar to Deia?" Dave's voice was low and filled with cold calculation.

"Grandmother." Induca nodded.

"She's Deia's mother," Malsour said to Dave. "What are you two saying?" Fire hissed.

"We trust him with our lives. Secrets are of little consequence to us." Malsour shrugged. "He is also to become Deia's husband."

"Ah, okay, so, why have you changed your body?" Dave tapped his book, becoming closer to how he'd acted when Deia had been there. "Wait, how do you two know her?" Dave looked to Malsour and Induca.

"That is complicated," Fire said, looking to the two of them. They held their tongues, giving Dave an apologetic look.

"And I look like this because others know my true appearance and I don't really like being the center of attention in my own college."

"Okay, so are you a Dragon or something else? Your aura makes me think you're a Dragon," Dave said.

"Something else," Fire said slowly.

"Okay." Dave sighed, sounding as if he really didn't want to know this all, but felt a need to. "Well, I'm going to go look at rune books."

"Are you going to tell Deia anything?" Fire asked, anxious. "If Deia asks me, I'll tell her." Dave wandered away.

Fire's eyes thinned, bringing power to her hands. She felt twin auras flare up. Her angry expression turned to surprise as she looked at Malsour and Induca. Before she could say anything, Malsour spoke.

"Do you wish that Deia's fiancé would lie to her for a woman he doesn't know?" Malsour asked.

Fire let her anger go, dissipating back down. "No, just…I don't know how she would handle it." Fire's anxiety returned.

"Well, it's about damned time you told her instead of her getting blindsided later," Induca said, her eyes level with Fire as if to challenge her.

Fire shook her head and let out a small chuckle. "Seems that you two have grown up while you've been gone. Shall we go somewhere more private to talk?"

26

SECRETS
AND
REVELATIONS

"How long did you know?" Fire asked as Mal walked into her office a few hours later.

"About the second day I was here. You might hide the strength of your aura, but I know it well, and even with those glasses and robes, I know when I find my little Fire." He moved across the room. Fire kept her arms crossed even as he moved closer and put his hands on her hips.

"Someone's moody." He lifted an eyebrow and pulled off her glasses. She wanted to remain angry at him, annoyed for the situation he had gotten her into. Deia and the others were good at aura suppression, but not as good at it or aura detection as Fire.

"Ignil." Mal's voice and the look in his eyes dissolved her barriers. She turned her face from him as he leaned in. Her cheeks heated up.

Why? What is stopping you? You've wanted to do this so bad for so long!
Mal pushed her against the wall gently, using a finger to guide her to look at him. His lips rose to hers.

Her anger fled as other emotions filled her: Happiness at seeing him. Fear that it would once again end or that the rest of the Pantheon would try to use her daughter and husband against her. Scared that it might be the last time and he would go and find another because of her constant pushing away. It was to protect him, but it hurt her so.

She gave herself into the kiss, grabbing at his shirt, drawing him closer as she wrapped her leg around him. After a few heated minutes, they pulled apart. Fire's body ached for more. To never let him go.

"That's my Fire." He smiled.

Fire looked over herself. She was taller!

"Dammit, how did you?" She had reverted into her natural form: Her rich red hair and eyes. Her leather pants and vest.

"I didn't do a thing. I guess I just have a secret way to break your magic." He grinned widely.

"Oh, shut up and kiss me." She pulled him in toward her. He didn't even try to resist, grabbing her thighs and pulling her up. He cleared her desk with a swipe of his arm. Flames started to appear around them, floating in the air, neither hot nor warm as they tore at each other's clothes.

"I liked that vest!" Fire complained as he threw it aside.

"I knew you couldn't stay angry at me for that long." He looked up from where his head lay on her chest.

She made a shuddering noise, a smile on her lips. Not deeming that statement worthy of a response.

Mal rolled over onto his back and pulled her onto him. She rolled over, cuddling his side, and wrapped her leg over his body.

The lights around them lessened in number, coming lower, keeping them warm.

Fire listened to his heart. Her fears once again started to fill her mind. Mal bopped her on the head, as if understanding them. "Now stop that.

Guess this is what I get for going out with a girl as smart as you. Always thinking, usually of the worst consequences." He gave her a hard look.

"I'm a girl, huh?" Fire smiled, happy to not think about her fears for a night.

"Prettiest girl I ever did fall in love with." Mal smiled.

She flicked his elven ears. "So, what other girls did you fall in love with?" She feared the response.

"Just this one called Ignil. She was quite the adventurer." Mal smiled mischievously.

"That doesn't count and you know it," Fire said.

Mal turned her over and looked down into her eyes. "There has only ever been one for me."

Tears welled up in Fire's eyes as she hit his chest. "You damned charmer," she said, trying to stop the tears.

"Would sound better if you did call me husband instead." He kissed her. "Because in my mind, you're already my wife."

Tears ran freely as Mal sat up, leaning against the desk and holding her in his arms.

"See what you did?" She took comfort in his arms as he rocked her and kissed the side of her head.

"Hopefully, it finally gets into that hard head of yours," Mal said.

Fire took a few minutes to calm down before they just sat there, happy to be in each other's arms again. "Husband," Fire said, as if testing how the word felt on her tongue. "Sounds pretty good."

Mal chuckled.

"So, what is the purpose of this dinner?" Fire asked. Trying to turn her thoughts away from becoming more than just Mal's lover, but to his partner. "To tell Deia who her mother is." Mal's arms tightened as she tried to distance herself, her emotions becoming erratic.

"There is a war coming; we both know it. You might not want her to know who you are, but she is her own woman and she deserves to know instead of getting blindsided with it later. She's going to be on the front lines of this war that's coming. It's something that she's always wanted to know. If we deny it to her now, then there might not be a time for us to tell her later." Mal's voice was calm and soothing.

"You make it sound so easy." Fire's mind conjured what the other lords and ladies might do if they were to find out about Deia. Already, they had tried to attack her Dragons multiple times, even changing them over to their side in rare circumstances.

"Deia has told me what she can in different messages, but this coming war looks like it could change everything that we know. She's said that the Stone Raiders are actually excited to confront the Dark Lord. Seems that they don't like him much and they want to go and kick his ass in the Pantheon," Mal said.

Fire's look turned incredulous before becoming thoughtful as she remembered Bob's messages and their recent conversations.

"I know that the Dwarves are going to be unlocking the vaults holding the Weapons of Power in that tournament in five months. The Dwarves are also making alliances with many of the races, offering their weapons and armor and opening up trade. Then there are the other things that are returning."

"Now is the time to meet with her." Mal kissed her head.

Fire felt nervousness in her stomach, scared at what Deia might do. "I'll be right beside you," Mal reassured her, again as if he knew what she was thinking.

She squeezed his arms tighter. "The Lady of Fire nervous to meet her daughter—some Lady of the Pantheon I am," she muttered. "Just the kind of lady I fell in love with." Mal smiled.

Fire couldn't resist smiling back as she rested her head on his shoulder.

Deia watched the Librarian Fuego and her father together in the small kitchen in the apartment her father had been loaned for his stay. Malsour and Induca were off on the balcony while she sat with Dave on one of the couches.

Looks like he's found someone else he likes. She smiled, seeing how nervous Fuego was. It was as if she were holding off having to talk to Deia in case she brought up anything to scare her off.

As long as she makes Dad happy, I'll be happy with that. Deia felt sad as she thought of her absent mother.

Mal and Fuego finally took the seats on the couch opposite.

"I'm just going to have a look out over Per'ush. I've heard that it's pretty at night," Suzy said, leaving them.

"Deia, we have something to tell you." Mal tried to hide his excitement and his smile but failed. He nudged Fuego, who seemed even more nervous than before.

"Deia, have you ever noticed that you have an abnormally high Affinity for Fire?" Fuego asked.

"Yes." Deia frowned. *This is not how I thought this conversation would be going.*

"That your Mana level is higher than it should be for someone your level?" Fuego took off her glasses and looked to Deia.

"Yes."

"Well, it's because you're not *totally* mortal." Fuego seemed to have trouble speaking the words. "You're a child of one Lady of the Pantheon and this dolt." Fuego jabbed her thumb at Mal, who looked amused.

"So, my mother is a Lady of the Pantheon? How do you know this?" Deia asked.

Fuego stood, a bundle of nerves, but resolute. Flames seemed to cover her body before someone else was revealed.

The same woman Deia had seen when she had reached her dad after the Earth sprites turned on the people around Boran-al's Citadel.

Deia's eyes went wide.

"I am the Lady of Fire, your mother," the woman said.

Deia saw her own red eyes, the same nose on the other woman. Her heart pounded in her chest. The Human half of her blood.

She stood up, as if in a daze, and stepped toward the Lady of Fire. She looked to her father, who rose as well. "Dad?" she asked, like a lost girl once again, the girl who had asked where her mother was again and again for years.

He gave her a nod.

She was far from a child now, but she still had a rolling storm of emotions running through her. Tears fell down her face. So many questions and emotions warred inside her, making her unable to talk.

"Why did you not say anything? Nothing for two hundred years. Was I that much of a burden?" Deia's face crumpled into tears and she buried her face in Dave's shoulder. He clearly had questions, but he kept them to himself.

Fire moved to hug her, but put her arms down, scared to hurt her. "No, of course not. I love you, but I didn't want to bring you into my world, where the Pantheon would do anything to get an advantage over me, like using you or your father as hostages." Fire's face fell as she fought emotions.

"You could have seen me once, just once as a child." Deia wiped her eyes.

"I wanted to so badly. I watched you with my familiars and different spells, and I even stood outside your tree many times, but every time I turned away," Fire admitted.

"She is pretty stubborn," Mal growled, giving a disapproving look to Fire. "But you must know that she did that to try to protect us. She loves us deeply and has always watched over us."

Deia wanted to hug Fire, but she didn't know whether that would be good or bad and she still wanted to appear strong and defiant.

"Well, are you going to hug her or mope on my shoulder?" Dave whispered into her ear, giving her a slight push.

It was what Deia needed. New tears flooded down her face as she wrapped her arms around Fire. Mal and Dave stood to the side, watching as Fire and Deia cried and shook together.

It took some time before they were able to separate from each other.

For hours, they talked; they laughed and they cried and Deia got to know the woman her father had adventured and learned beside, before falling in love with each other and making her. She learned of Fire's fears, why she had kept away from both Mal and Deia to protect them. How Malsour and Induca wanted to meet the daughter of Fire, practically their aunt, and had taken on the role of guardians and then friends.

By the time they left, Deia was mentally and emotionally drained. *She was the daughter of the Lady of Fire. Her half-sister was Denur, the mother of Dragons, and her mother created the mage's college and guild.*

Suzy was shocked but she'd learned so many crazy things since coming to Emerilia, it was just another Tuesday.

Malsour and Induca seemed relieved with not having to keep the secret anymore. Anna seemed to have figured it out, either on her own or by her father telling her.

Fire was nothing like what Deia had expected and so much of what she was hoping for. Deia fell asleep holding Dave, content in the knowledge she'd gained.

Mal felt a breeze from his open window. "You going to stand there or join me?" he asked sleepily.

"How did you know it was me?" Fire closed the door to his balcony. "Know you anywhere, even with a different face." Mal yawned and pulled the sheets back on his bed.

Fire got in as he pulled the sheets back over her and wrapped his arms over her.

Mal nearly fell back asleep before Fire turned over, her eyes looking into his.

"Mal, you awake?"

"No."

"So, what now, though? She knows about me and we talked, but what do we do now?"

Mal opened one eye, getting comfortable in the bed. "She is a grown woman. She has her own things she needs to do. Right now, all we can do is wish her luck. Think of her as just another college student at this point. Get to know her—her desires, wants, aspirations, talk about the future and your lives together. I raised her by treating her as I would like to be treated. Talk, don't dictate; you'd be surprised how well it goes."

"But I'm her mom, shouldn't I...I don't know? Do something?"

"Ignil, you are her mother, but she's her own woman. She's a couple of centuries old. She's seen some stuff in her time and she deserves your respect. Get to know her like you did last night; don't try to push yourself on her," Mal said.

"I thought that it would be such a big deal when it happened," Fire said into Mal's chest.

"She grew up, Ignil. She grew up much faster than I ever thought, that was for sure." Mal snorted, shaking his head.

"What?"

"I remember my mother and father telling me that children always grow up faster than you would ever think. One day, you're watching them crawl. The next, they're walking out your door and out into their own adventures."

Fire squeezed Mal's arm, reassuring him.

"The pain has lessened over the years, but I still haven't forgiven the Pantheon. Sure, some of you do good, but we shouldn't have them lording over us all the time. Down here on Emerilia, at least some rules are put into place against certain conduct. Where the Pantheon is concerned, they think they're above it all and try to destroy our rules just because they want more power." Mal sighed. "Your siblings are something else."

Fire snorted. "Yeah, I'll be happy as can be when they meet the people who they have lorded over face-to-face."

"I feel that it's coming." Mal's words sounded like a hopeful promise. "I do, too," Fire said, scared for what it would bring. The Pantheon was not going to fall easily.

27

PROGRESS

Dave touched the mirror, accessing its conferencing ability. He appeared in a simple room with two chairs facing a fireplace.

Kol, the old dwarf, waved him over. Even without eyes, he had the uncanny ability to know where everyone and everything was, usually even better than people with eyes because of a spell he used constantly, similar to Dave's Touch of the Land, that allowed him to sense everything around him and look through it.

"We've placed the order. We should have it soon," Kol said. "Good, good." Dave smiled.

"Are you sure about this? The amount of resources — it could give you an easy life until the end of your days."

"It could, but it wouldn't be as interesting as what might happen with connecting Cliff-Hill to the rest of Emerilia. I hope that we're ready for expansion." Dave rubbed his hands together.

"Always the...what was it? Industrialist, was it?"

"You listened to Suzy too much while she was there." Dave groaned. Kol cracked one of his rare smiles and clapped Dave on the shoulder.

The man was the grandfather and mentor that Dave had never had.

"We've got all of the smithies working on your order. They're of good steel and sturdy design, but they're by no means the best weapons we've made. We're coming out at above twenty percent production," Kol said.

"Awesome. I'll tell Suzy that. She's the one setting up this deal."

"Who are we arming with all of this? Those weapons and armor are much heavier than what a human might use. Not as graceful as what an Elf uses and too big for a Dwarf." Kol might not have eyes but his interest was clear.

"A month and a half and you'll see. Make sure that you've got the forge's emblem hammered into the middle of the shield and on every blade," Dave said.

"Almost makes me think that you're preparing for a war, boy." Kol dropped his voice lower.

"One is coming, but this—just think of it as a nice big surprise." He paused; a wide and cruel smile spread across his face. "One that the Dark Lord is going to lose his shit over."

"Well, I can get behind that." Kol clapped Dave on the back. "Now, I guess I better get this meeting started."

Dave followed Kol out of the eaves around the main table. The Dwarves pored over different plans that they had—arguing, looking thoughtful, making useful suggestions—or they might be just sitting down and talking with their friends.

As Kol walked in, they all finished up their different conversations and drifted toward the large table.

Kol took his time, so that everyone was seated.

"All right, calling this meeting of hammer-wielding vagabonds to session." Kol hit a hammer on the table. A few smiles and proud looks were on the Dwarves' faces around the tables.

"Okay, resources have been doled out. We also have a report from the forces that have been moved to Mithsia Mountains to train. The lord of the mountain, Fend, has thanked us for sending him the reinforcements he needs, so that he could switch his forces off and on the wall. We've been getting good reports from the training commanders in the area. Seems that there are some beasts in the area that are rather difficult to kill. The training has been good for our people. Also, a number of dungeons have been found in the area and are being farmed by different Dwarven warbands and warclans for training. The commanders believe that we will be able to extend deeper into the mountains with this new training. We will check on their progress in two weeks, at which time Rola will be running this seat." Kol actually sounded excited for once.

He really hates leading this all, Dave thought with a snort.

"We also have news from Dave, regarding the new materials that he has been processing for us." Kol waved to Dave.

"Thanks, Kol. Okay, so, production is slowing down. The refineries I had access to are moving to other resources that the owners need. It will mean that there will be less of the materials to go around. That said, there still will be shipments. Also, the Stone Raiders' first priority is to get refineries going for the sole purpose of refining out multiple materials. I was wondering if there was anyone who had designed a refinery to separate out any and all different metals and then smelt them down into ingots?" Dave looked around. He had an idea, but it would be hard to do.

No one seemed to have a suggestion.

"I know that we're working on mass refineries that would be able to work with one metal, refining it out and turning it out into ingots and then the crud from that getting run into the other refineries to get out any other metals within it," Edmur said.

"Do you know what the power requirements and material requirements would be like to make one of those refinery plants?" Dave asked.

"I'm not sure, but I could find out," Edmur said.

"If you could, that would be awesome. In the meantime, I have another solution based off what I did back on Earth. I've patented it, but if anyone needs a refiner to just throw all their raw ores into and have it separated out by category, let me know — I'll pass you a plan. It can be scaled up or down as needed." Dave took his seat.

"Any other announcements?" Kol looked around the table. Gonda put up her hand. Kol waved for her to talk.

"We have been experimenting with the new materials. Specifically, after a talk and the information from Jeeves, we've been able to start capturing large Mana charges through panels that have taken awhile to perfect. We've also been working with the material graphene extensively. We have found that a layer of graphene, while it cannot hold runes by itself, if combined into most materials it will allow for a new Magical Circuit or two to be added to the metal," Gonda said with some well-deserved pride.

The Dwarves clapped at their fellow Master Smith's achievement. Gonda took her seat. The Dwarves to either side congratulated her as Kol waited for the clapping to die down.

"Anything else?" Kol looked around. No one said anything. Dave raised his hand again.

"Dave?" Kol said, looking curious.

"It might be an idea for Aldamire to be on higher alert over the next two months. I trust you all, but this information was given to me with the condition it was not to be shared." Dave looked around the table. The happy expressions from earlier turned into frowns and beard tugging as they looked to Dave. "Hopefully, in less than three months, I will be able to tell you all."

"We will take it under advisement," Kol said. "Do you have any information on where this threat might come from?"

"Possibly the northwest."

"Understood. This information will not leave the council. I will inform clan commanders myself. Fren, make sure that the Aldamire warclans are ready for whatever might happen." Kol looked to the Master Smith who called Aldamire Mountain home.

"It will be done." Fren was not one for many words but when he did speak, it was not wasted breath.

"Good. Meeting adjourned." Kol hit his hammer down on the table.

"Wait, what?" Alkao asked Dwayne as he finished speaking.

"Josh wants to put a teleport pad in the middle of what you want to be your city. He will write up an agreement for you, like other businesses that have these teleport pads do. Give you part of the profits, a tax on it as well as certain rights to expedite stuff that you want to move. He is also willing to write up an agreement for a payment plan, at just plus five percent cost if you would like to purchase it from the Stone Raiders," Dwayne said.

Alkao laughed at what Dwayne was saying and Josh was proposing. A teleport pad was one of the greatest resources that a kingdom, let alone a town, had.

"While it is operating, what will the tax be?" Alkao asked. "Five percent on the total value of the goods," Dwayne said.

"That's robbery!" the trader leader for the Devil's Crater said. "We can do two percent tops!"

"Five percent and it stands. It would take you three weeks through forests to get to the next city. Who may want to trade with you or want to kill you. With the new teleport pad, we will also have traders who have recently joined our guild setting up a branch if you allow it. If they are allowed, they will buy goods for what the median price is on the market, no tax or anything on those transactions unless you place one. Also, the terminal is available for other transactions," Dwayne said.

Rather smart having him as the one doing this deal, Alkao thought, placating the trader leader with a wave of his hand. *Dwayne is one of the smartest and hardest commanders I know when fighting. When it comes to guild business, he's as strong as that shield he uses.*

"Okay, we are interested in it. That said, we will be losing money with this new tax and you know that we don't want to reveal who we are or where we come from until after we defeat the Demon Horde."

"With having a trading branch here, we can give you better prices. We were already adding a tax and then the cost of transporting materials. As for the war, Dave has an offer that he is willing to field. Suzy has made the condition be on the teleport pad." Dwayne's stoic features twisted into a grin. "She said if you took this deal, she wouldn't kick your ass."

Silence filled the room till Alkao laughed out loud.

"Very well. Please send over the contract and I will have a look over it. I believe that if it is everything that you have said, then we can come to an agreement."

Dwayne opened his interface and Alkao saw a message appear in his inbox.

"The deal that Suzy has is to arm the Devil's Crater Army and train your blacksmiths properly. Dave owns a smithy back in Cliff-Hill. He's increased his production to make weapons and shields for your forces: swords, pikes, all of it. He is ready to produce them at cost. She is also opening recruiting for the smithies up to your people so they can improve their skills. They would learn through working and making better items, also earning them room and board as well as a smith's wage for anything that they make above those two costs," Dwayne said, sounding as if he was having to remember it all.

"That is a generous offer." Alkao looked to the crafter's leader. "I think this is more in your realm."

"Yes, sir!" the crafter said with a grim look on his face. "What kind of learning will these blacksmiths receive?"

"Well, Dave is a Dwarven Master Smith, second tier. His master is the one who runs the forge. So, it will be the best in the world other than having them stuffed in a Dwarven mountain," Dwayne said.

Alkao hid a smile at the crafter leader's face, his look of shock apparent.

"I think that our blacksmiths would be eager to learn, but the issue comes down to payment," Alkao said.

"We are willing to extend a payment plan for four months after the Demon Horde is defeated. We do not think that we will be able to arm all of your forces. Suzy thinks that will take six months with the DCA rotating through Cliff-Hill to get sized and then the armor made. Well, unless our other friends are capable of doing it." Dwayne tapped his chin in thought, using the abbreviated version of Devil's Crater Army, much like how the People of Emerilia were called POEs.

Alkao wondered who these mysterious friends were that the Stone Raiders had been helping for so long. Dwayne and Kim had assured him that he would meet some of them soon enough.

"I think that will be something for the leader of the traders here to talk about with Suzy and Dave." Alkao looked to the leader.

The Beast Kin nodded, her expression guarded. Alkao was impressed with her skills and the way in which she held herself.

"So is that a yes for the teleport pad? I swear, Josh is messaging me more than a horny teenager in their first relationship," Dwayne grumbled.

"I think so." Alkao smiled. A few others in the room hid their amusement, primarily Alkao's brothers. They and their armies had seen or met the Stone Raiders and now had a rather interesting idea of who they were. In training, they were mad devils, but every other time, they were goofing off or going off to the dungeons for "fun."

"Good. Now I just have to deal with Kim complaining about walking all the way here." Dwayne shook his head and snorted as he pressed a command. His mouth moved, but Alkao couldn't make out words nor read his lips properly.

"He'll be here within twenty or so minutes. Suzy won't be here for another two days. Same for the trading branch coming from Verlun," Dwayne said. "I hope you don't mind if I say I am looking forward to checking out your dungeons and caves instead of constant meetings." Dwayne grinned.

"I know that the more risky of us think that way. Fortunately, we have much more level heads to keep us on course." Alkao smiled.

"Well, your councils are definitely less...*insane* than my fellow guild leaders."

The teleport pad disappeared from the storage room a few minutes ago. Now, all of the Stone Raiders who wanted to come stood in the teleport pad control room.

Josh tossed a fruit through the portal.

Dwayne kicked it; mush came back through the portal as Dwayne's pants were covered in pink fruit.

"Mmm, my favorite." Josh wiped his face, now covered in pulped fruit. He grabbed a towel from his bag of holding, walking through the teleport pad's event horizon and into the center of Devil's Crater.

"Dude! These are my comfy pants!"

"Mate, this was my clean face!" Josh said back. He pulled the towel from his face and noticed the Demons, Beast Kin, and the council members who led Devil's Crater standing off to the side.

"Pillock," Josh said to Dwayne, smiling to the Devil's Crater leadership. "Hi! Good to meet you. I'm Josh Giles. I heard that you've got a mission for us."

"Hello, Josh. It is good to finally put a face to the name." A large Demon walked out from the middle of the leadership group.

Alkao Travezar
Level 243
Aerial Demon

"Agreed," Josh said. The two of them shook hands. Stone Raiders were pouring out of the portal and headed off to meet with their friends who stood to the side of the teleport pad.

"So, shall we go and look over these plans of yours and check out just what kind of hell we're going to rain down on this Demon Horde?" Josh grinned.

"Straight to the point. Very well, come with me." Alkao flapped his wings. His guards and brothers took to the skies.

Josh and a group of Stone Raiders' leadership ran as fast as they flew, heading for Alkao's keep built into the cliffs around Devil's Crater.

28

HOMEWARD

Malsour was off in the libraries of Per'ush. He'd flashed a medallion that allowed him access to any college resources.

Dave was a bit jealous, but he was also excited to go and see Cliff-Hill. Suzy had been running the business side of things and keeping track of the minutiae of the businesses that Dave owned. Dave was excited to see the businesses, but he was more interested in seeing the people and getting to know what they needed.

All of them were interested to see how Cliff-Hill had changed.

"So, where are you off to?" the man who was selling tickets to different places asked.

"I have special coordinates, though I would prefer if I was the one to put them in." Dave passed over enough gold to make the ticket seller's eyes go wide.

"While it is not regular, with two teachers of the college backing your word, I think we can do that," the ticket seller said. The gold disappeared as four tickets replaced them.

"Thanks." Dave smiled and pocketed the tickets.

"Well, when you're done with the business your guild is up to, it would be nice to see you again," Fire, back in her disguise as Librarian Fuego, said to Deia.

Dave could sense the woman's nervousness. *Even the gods of this world got lonely and it seemed that they missed and cared about their kids deeply. Well, at least Fire.* Dave wasn't sure that Light or Dark would give much of a hell about any children they brought into the world.

Bob did not paint a flattering picture when talking about them. "I'd like that." Deia smiled.

Fuego's face flared into a wide smile, growing more as Deia gave her a hug.

"Look after this lot. Seems like they're a good bunch. Dave's all right," Oson'Mal said.

"Thanks, father-in-law." Dave smiled back at the man.

Oson'Mal was fiercely protective of his daughter, but Dave and Mal had made a friendship, understanding that the other would do anything to protect Deia. Also, drinking together and talking freely didn't hurt.

"Next transport!" the controller of the teleport pad called.

Dave waved to Fuego and Oson'Mal and moved to the controller's booth.

"Okay, this is all rather complicated," the controller started.

"Ah, I've done this a few times. Your gain is too high, dude — wasting power on that." Dave pressed different keys on the control booth's control pad and turned a few levers.

The teleport pad in front of the control room shifted and changed, rotating in new runes and out old ones until they formed a new pattern. Dave pressed the power button as the runes started to glow with power, a portal connecting the teleport pad to its location.

"Damn, you trying to steal my job?" The controller laughed dryly. "Nah, thanks, I've got enough work as it is." Dave smiled and shook the man's hand in thanks. He walked back out of the control pad. He saw through the teleport pad and out into a large stone courtyard.

Kol and Wis'Zel, as well as some Dwarven shield bearers, were waiting on the other side. Dave waved at them as Deia released Fuego and Oson'Mal from a hug. Induca and Suzy walked through the teleport pad's portal.

Dave held out his hand; Deia grabbed it as they walked through the portal. They stepped out into one of the training squares that Dave remembered the tournament, from a year ago, being held on. The portal closed behind them as Dave looked at the teleport pad that was stuck into the ground. There was cracked stone around it, but that could be fixed easily enough.

"Damn, it's good to be home!" Dave saw Lox and Gurren with wide grins on their faces as he crossed to the waiting crowd. Kol and Wis'Zel descended on him.

"Dinner later?" Deia asked, knowing Dave was going to be wrapped up in business all too soon.

"Sounds good to me." Dave smiled. He waved to his Dwarven friends who had trained him and helped him come to know Emerilia and be able to defend himself.

Dave turned to face his two managers. "All right, let's get this business crap sorted out quick, then we can get down to relaxing!" Dave smiled.

"Good to see you again." Zel smiled and shook Dave's hand.

"Look to be going soft, I see. Not enough time in the forge," Kol said. "I've been preoccupied with other things, Mentor," Dave said, his voice dry.

Kol made a displeased snort to hide his smile.

"I guess I'll tag along and see what you three have been up to," Suzy said.

"Lead on, Zel," Dave said.

They passed through the crowd, Dave saying hello, giving a hug or handshake here and there. His worries seemed to fall away. He promised to see them later as they left the training square and headed up Cliff-Hill.

Dave paused, looking at it all. Cliff-Hill looked like the name sake. It was as if a hill had once rested there and someone had cut away the slopes of two-thirds of the hill, turning the sides into sheer cliffs, leaving just the southwestern side with a sloping hill.

What had been a wooden wall covering that gentle slope was now completely stone, wrapping around the base of the cliff. A trench ran in front of it, with a bridge toward Omal and another toward the Mithsia Mountains and Kufo'tel forest. The road looped up and through the village at the top of Cliff-Hill. It seemed to have multiplied in size since Dave had last seen it. There must have been ten or twenty stone buildings where there had only been a handful when Dave left.

Below the town, there was the biggest building: a four-story apartment building with a small fortified wall around it. It had been the Golden Sabre's base when they had come to Cliff-Hill. Since then, the Stone Raiders had bought it from them and was the home to around fifty Stone Raiders who trained with the Dwarven forces, worked in the smithy, or traded with the people in Cliff-Hill.

There was a massive open area around it, plenty of room for expansion as trees filled the area. Well below that, through the trees, were two growing complexes. Laid out in straight lines, there were smithies close to the road that led to Omal; factories were next to the road that led to Mithsia.

The ceramics factories were five hundred meters long and two stories tall. Rough clay headed into one side, and then ceramics came out the other side, piled onto carts and sent across the stone-paved roads between the factories and smithies to the roads leading to Mithsia and Omal. Dave noticed another main road between the two factories now extended out into the forest, headed right for the training square where the teleport pad was located.

Dave knew that his smithies and factories had grown, but he hadn't expected them to have grown so much. He felt a bit of nostalgia as he saw his portable smithy away a bit from the main smithies.

The roads through the city were complete, a work of Dwarven construction. Dave looked to where his house was. It was a simple cabin, tucked away from the road to Omal, overlooking the western side of Cliff- Hill. It overlooked the fields that grew around the cliff faces of Cliff-Hill and the river which had been diverted to weave around the hill to water their crops. There was more room for the town to expand, but its progress left Dave stunned for a few moments.

"You've certainly been busy," Dave said, proud of all his people had been able to accomplish.

"We've got plenty more plans now with the teleport pad here. Our biggest thing is resources right now. With the new teleport pad opened, we can ship across Emerilia at much cheaper prices. Also, we can get some more workers in here. We've got plenty of room to expand." Zel smiled.

"After purchasing the teleport pad, we're going to have to wait a bit before we do too much expanding or hiring. We haven't got too much in the way of coin to make much. With that weapons and shield order that you placed, for now we're just losing money all over the place with the time and resources we're putting into it," Kol said.

"Why don't we go to the bank first? It's been awhile since I was at one." Dave hid his smile. "Is Ukon still running the place?"

"Yeah, and doing a damned fine job of it," Wis'Zel said.

"It'll be good to see him. So, now, tell me, how are the new runed furnaces going for you both?" Dave asked as they got onto a wagon. The teleport pad was located lower down the hill, where the old dwarven warclan training area had been. A good thirty- or forty- minute walk from the smithies and factories.

As soon as they were sitting, it moved forward up Cliff-Hill. Kol told the driver where to go as Wis'Zel talked to Dave.

"They've been great. The materials cost is a bit much, and as you said, we've only made as many as we've absolutely needed. However, we're going to need more very soon. They're faster and cheaper than the regular wood-burning furnaces. People like not having smoke all over the place."

"Keeping the people around us is half the business — don't need them actively fighting us on everything," Dave said. "Also, I think I can get a few of those furnaces, especially the bigger ones you were talking about, done for you."

"That would be great. As Kol said, we don't have much in the way of wiggle room for money right now."

"I think we'll be able to sort that out soon enough." Suzy looked to Dave. "You thinking of investing?" Dave asked.

"Yes, though I know I'm not going to get much of the place, but even a few percent is good enough. With the teleport pad, your factories, smithies, and all those workers, you've got a growing company. Might be an idea to start looking for investors to take off some of the financial burdens and planning." Suzy turned the statement into a question.

Dave winced. "Right now, I think we're good. We've got the right people in the right places. Having too many people with different opinions who don't know what is going on inside the factories and smithies could really mess things up. They see numbers and figures, not people and circumstances."

"True. It was an idea, though I think the only people with the kind of capital we are thinking would be lords and ladies. Which usually doesn't make them that in touch with regular people's troubles."

"So, what about the workshop? How are things going there?" Dave asked.

"Good, better than I thought," Kol said.

"We've got around fifty people learning. It's slow going as the teachers are learning from your methods as they're teaching it. Right now, they're like one big smithy working on five different weapons. If you could go and talk to them, it would help out. Some of the stuff they've come up with has been turned into patents, which we're getting five percent from. Not much, but these patents are for things that people use every day, so it's a near constant stream of income. It's certainly making others interested in learning," Zel said with some pride.

"Damn, the place looks like it's changed, though it's only talking with you two that I'm realizing just how much it's changed." Dave shook his head, once again looking out at Cliff-Hill. They were almost at the city center.

"It's been a crazy year." Zel grinned and looked to Kol, who nodded in agreement.

"Oh, Kol, I almost forgot, you know I said I had that healer friend? I was wondering if you were interested in her helping you out?" Dave asked. "I've become used to not using my eyes at this point, lad. It's not worth getting my hopes up again." Kol's gruff voice cracked slightly.

"Well, even if it helps fix your messed-up nose, so I don't hear you snoring from half a mile away, I'd count that as a victory." Dave grinned.

"I can still kick your butt, you young whelp," Kol grumbled. The corners of his mouth flicked upward in amusement.

"I'll take that as a yes, and I think we're here," Dave said. The wagon rolled to a stop outside a large stone building, people moving in and out at a rapid pace.

Dave sent Jules a message before he jumped off the wagon. The others followed, Suzy asking Zel about the day-to-day running of his ceramics factory.

Dave walked into the bank. A line led up to tellers dealing in all manner of tradable goods and coins.

"That way, back right." Kol pointed to a hallway. Dave followed his directions, walking down the hallway and coming to a reception desk.

"Hello, I am here to see Ukon," Dave said to the Elven receptionist. "Who are you?" she asked.

"Dave Grahslagg." Dave smiled.

Her smile faltered as she studied him. "Right, and I'm Oson'Deia. You are the third person to say that this week. I need a piece of identification please or else I will call the Dwarven warband to collect you."

"Am I enough proof?" Kol stepped out from behind Dave.

"Master Kol? So, he's really *the* Dave?" The receptionist looked at Dave.

"As I know it." Dave smiled, a bit worried about the impersonators, but happy that the bank had made sure they were arrested instead of allowing them access to his accounts.

"Sorry. I thought you would be shorter and have a larger beard and not as muscled." She went bright red as she realized what she'd said. "Uh, sorry, umm, I'll get Mister Ukon." She opened her interface, her Elven features bright red.

"If you don't mind, me and Zel will hang out here to discuss things," Suzy said.

"Sure, this is just boring bank stuff." Dave shrugged.

"Here, tell me how much of a share that will get me." Suzy opened up her interface, holding a trade with Dave.

"You sure? Isn't this nearly all of your savings?" Dave asked.

"We'll either get it back through the holdings here, or we can make it up in our next raid. I'm not too bothered." Suzy shrugged.

"Where's the penny-pinching Suzy I knew?"

"She learned that money isn't really all that important and she can always make more. Now go on, don't keep Ukon waiting." She waved Dave on as the door behind the receptionist opened.

Ukon appeared, a large smile on his face. "Master Kol and Dave, I heard the good news from Benvari Mountain. Two Master Smiths calling Cliff-Hill home—I don't think there is any other city outside of the Dwarven mountains that can boast the same!" Ukon shook Kol's hand and then turned to Dave.

Dave smiled and grabbed the Dwarf's hand. There was something that always made Dave smile when he was around the man, a kind of friendly energy. "Ah, it was pretty fun." Dave shrugged.

"Makes it to the Master Dwarven Smith level and calls it 'pretty fun.'" Ukon laughed, a deep, bassy sound. "Come in, come in." He waved them through the door.

"When Kol came to me with your plans to purchase a teleport pad for the town, I was a little shocked. The second teleport pad in all of Opheir right in Cliff-Hill? I knew I settled in the right place when I heard that you were taking all of our resources and putting it into the pad. I've never heard anything quite like it! Most just want to horde it all away." They entered Ukon's office. "Please, have a seat." He waved to the chairs in front of his desk and closed the door behind them, before he took his own seat. "So, what can I do for you today?"

"Well, first I wanted to link together some patents that I've made. The accounts have been made and the patents filed, but I wasn't near a bank to connect them. Then, I've got a deposit to make into the company's accounts and then my good friend Suzy also wants a part of the company and she is willing to buy into it, so, going to have to find out how much her money equals out of the company shares. We can do that first before everything else," Dave said.

"Well, seems like you've got a long list of to-do's," Ukon said. "You sure you want to do the share before accumulating all the assets you're putting in? You'll own more of the company."

"She's like a sister to me and I wouldn't trust anyone more—other than Zel and Kol, of course." Dave smiled.

"Well then, let's get that sorted out for you."

A prompt appeared in front of Dave, asking for the amount Suzy was depositing against the worth of the company.

Dave put in Suzy's money, earning a surprised look from Ukon.

The deposit screen disappeared. A new one asked for Dave's deposit.

He put his in as Ukon shook his head.

"I should remember that you're a Player. But still—having this much money in your pocket instead of a bank, you must've been in the back end of nowhere."

"Something like that," Dave said with a cryptic smile.

"Fine. I won't ask more. Now, onto the patents and everything else."

Deia watched as Dave and Kol walked into the new tavern that had popped up in Cliff-Hill.

"Finally able to break way from work?" Lox asked, the members of Party Zero looking up from their mugs and food..

"Just about," Dave said as he and Kol approached the table. Deia passed him a tankard. While Kol smacked Gurren's shoulder and sat down next to him.

"What would I do without you, my dear?" Dave kissed Deia, his scruff tickling her cheeks.

"Not a whole heck of a lot." She smiled, looking back in his eyes as they danced in the restaurant's firelight.

He pulled her in for another kiss.

"Oh, come on, can't have you two stuck by the lips all night. You got yer own house for that!" Lox said.

Kol laughed as he grabbed a beer. Gurren grinned. Suzy and Induca kissed one another as well.

"Ugh, damn well surrounded by couples." Lox shook his head, as if it were a funeral to their single lives.

"Don't worry. We're not stuck by the lips—most of the time." Dave laughed. "I heard you two were out with some of the Stone Raiders who did some dungeon prospecting and such?"

"Yeah, found some right doozies. Had some close calls, but I'll tell you—you Players, you can damn well level up quick." Gurren looked to Lox, who nodded in agreement.

Dave looked to them. "Damn, you've both gained nearly a hundred levels." Gurren was at 121; Lox was at 125.

"Whereas, you've gained twelve," Gurren said.

"I think what Gurren is trying to ask is, when are you going to start using those damn stat points?" Lox said.

"I'm starting to use them now. I kind of figured out what I want to do, though, I want to do it slow or else, I'll start slamming into walls or have to figure out how to walk again. Ugh, jumping like thirty stat points is one hell of an experience." Dave shook his head.

"That was your own fault." Deia poked him, still not happy he'd knocked himself out from absorbing the information about the teleport pads.

Dave looked away, drinking from his tankard. Gurren and Lox laughed at the two's antics.

"So, how long until we head out to wherever the rest of the guild is?" Lox asked.

"Two days. We've got some guild business to attend to tomorrow night as well." Dave looked to Lox and Gurren, who had both joined the Stone Raiders, the patch proudly displayed on their shoulders.

"Just say the word and we'll do what we can to help," Gurren said.

Lox nodded.

"Aw, shucks, you're going to make me blush," Dave said. They fell into laughter and moved to less serious topics.

Deia watched them with a fond smile as they shared stories from their latest adventures and ate a meal together.

"See you in the morning." Dave waved to Induca and Suzy, who headed to their room above the tavern. Dave wrapped his arm around Deia, walking down the street, headed for their own home.

"I've missed Cliff-Hill. It isn't any Kufo'tel, but it is home." Deia squeezed his hand.

"That it is," Dave said. Even now, there was wagon traffic going through the town and between Omal and Mithsia. Dave and Deia jumped on the back of a wagon, looking at the growing town center.

Dave put his arm around Deia. "So much has happened in the time that we've been gone for, and we still have so much more to do."

"Our adventure has just started," Deia agreed.

It didn't take them long to reach their home and they jumped off. They walked through the familiar trees, passing the campfire area where they had stayed while Dave was making his house.

The smithy and the ceramics factories had been removed, leaving a large open area out front and to the sides of the house.

Dave opened the door for Deia. She walked in and checked out the closets for sheets and warm furs. The night was getting chilly quickly. Dave moved to the fireplace; logs were set in the fireplace, and a chill came down the chimney. He formed a small stream of fire, soaking the wood. It slowly came to life, lighting the room up some.

"Guess my night vision's improved some. Don't even need the torches anymore." Dave turned around, his lips finding hers.

She grabbed the discarded furs from the floor, pulling them onto herself and over Dave. She kissed him. "I love you," she said, stretching out over top of him.

"I love you too, you enchanting Elven seductress." Dave's hands cupped her butt.

She smiled, moving and getting comfortable on top of him.

Dave couldn't help but smile at the cuteness of it all. He kissed the top of her head, hitting her ass lightly and wrapping his arms around her.

They fell asleep like that, the flames of the fire flickering gently in the fireplace.

29

A GLANCE INTO THE FUTURE

"He's here!" Pete, Geswald's secretary, burst into his master's office. "Who's here?" Geswald demanded. *Pete better have a good reason for barging into his office.*

"Josh Giles, leader of the Stone Raiders. He and ten other Stone Raiders arrived from some unknown location. They arrived in Emaren just a few minutes ago. They're already leaving the city and heading for Verlun!"

"How long until they reach it?" Geswald asked.

"A few hours? They're running, but it is hard to describe just how fast they can run." Pete shook his head as if he was still in disbelief.

"It takes two days to get to Verlun by wagon," Geswald said, stunned by the revelation. Pete's expression made it clear that he wasn't going back on what he had said. "What are they up to? They bought up that large farm on the outskirts of town and they seem to be building a new headquarters there. It's driving people away from them as it's even farther from Emaren now. Maybe there is an issue with the traders in his guild? It would make sense, with him coming here, to tell them face-to-face what he thinks and see how badly they've messed up."

Geswald rubbed his hands together, thinking of the Stone Raiders splitting off with the Exdar's Traders they'd made a sub-guild out of.

If they fall apart, then it will be much easier to take down the Exdar's Traders.

"I want our people in Verlun to know what happened between Florence and Josh. We need to know if there are issues between the newly merged guilds. If so, then we can use it to our advantage."

"I will send word." Pete bowed and left his master's office.

Geswald rubbed his hands together. The Stone Raiders were the problem. Breaking them off from the Exdar's would make the Player guild open to be attacked and pressured if they wanted to keep trading in the area. No longer having protection from a guild famed in combat was a good way to get one's stores destroyed.

Josh and the Stone Raiders stopped, sensing the auras of the party in the middle of the road. They didn't have their weapons out; they just stood there.

"Can I help you with something?" Josh asked.

"Do you know how long it's taken waiting here to see if you lot would show up?" A man walked out in front of the others.

Josh shrugged.

"Well, my name is Jeremy. On behalf of the Fellox guild, we issue you, the Stone Raiders, a challenge to prove which is the best guild at raiding. We will record a massive raid that we do and you record a raid that you do, then we post it on the forums and the other Players of Emerilia decide which of the two clans is the better raiding guild." Jeremy crossed his arms.

Josh felt his competitive side come out as he walked up to Jeremy. "Is there a time limit?"

"One month real time," Jeremy said.

"So, three months in-game? I think we can do that. What do you want to bet on it?"

"Bet?" Jeremy looked confused.

"Well, look, if we win, we're still number one, but if everyone starts trying to challenge us without some kind of bet, then it's just going to get annoying. So, let's say, a hundred thousand gold? You win, you get a hundred thousand gold and the title of best raiding clan; if we win, we get one hundred thousand gold and keep our title."

"I'll ask my clan leader." Jeremy opened up his interface, using voice chat for a few minutes. "Very well, we agree," Jeremy said.

A Challenge Issued

The Stone Raiders and Fellox guilds challenge one another to complete a raid in three month's game time. Both sides will record their activities. The one with the most votes from the Emerilia community will be named Emerilia's best Player Raiding Guild.

Failure: Don't complete Raid, don't upload video in three months' Emerilia time.

Reward: Title of Best Player Raiding Guild, 100,000 Gold

Josh shook Jeremy's hand.

"Now, if you excuse me, we're headed off to Emaren to go meet up with the rest of our clan!" A wagon rolled out of the woods as the Fellox Raiders jumped on, eyeing their competition.

"Good luck!" Jeremy waved, moving to the wagon.

"You too." Josh waved back before turning to his Stone Raiders. They started running again, Verlun visible in the distance.

Florence logged into Emerilia, her home turning into the fields around Verlun and the walls that were forming the new headquarters.

Her eyes widened at the walls. They looked to be made of one piece and as smooth as a kitchen countertop. Not the rough rocks that it had been just a few hours ago. There were Earth and Dark mages walking around, holding up the blueprints, forming the ground according to what they saw. Basements seemed to form out of the ground as rock and metal grew into the rough forms, creating walls and rooms. Crafters were sizing windows, or fitting in amenities and rune carvings where they needed to.

Florence saw a familiar face in the middle of it all, talking to her people.

"I should have realized that you were in the middle of all this." Florence walked closer to him.

"Ah, Florence! They said that you were AFK for a bit. I didn't think that you would mind if we sped up the project a little bit. As much as I like running, it isn't all that fun." Josh smiled.

"So, what is going on here?" Florence waved to the growing headquarters.

"Well, we're building the main building for the guild. We've got a storefront going in, as detailed in the plans, on the lower levels. Offices and room for the guild on the upper floor. Tavern to the side right there, then stables beside that. On the left side, we're going to be putting in the teleport pad as you've indicated on the plans. Going to include barracks and defenses around it. Can't be too safe with those things. We're going to be starting a road from here toward Verlun actual. We won't complete it. We've got a day here before I need to head over to Markolm where the Golden Sabres are staying. We might be absorbing some of their members into the guild if all goes according to plan." Josh smiled.

"Well, you've been busy." Florence looked over the growing compound. It was literally growing from the ground in front of her. The traders were helping out where they could. The builders Florence had hired were clearing the area and putting the materials where the different buildings were supposed to be and talking to the mages about structural integrity and such.

Trees sprouted around two Earth mages. The branches of the trees wove together as they grew, forming into a roof and stalls.

"Wow." Florence watched as the stables formed out of a dozen trees, a living building like some of the Elven cities she'd seen on the forums.

"Magic, it's pretty damn crazy," Josh said. "Uh huh." Florence shook her head.

"Have you got the people needed for Cliff-Hill and the other location ready?" Josh asked, not risking speaking of Devil's Crater out loud. There was no telling whether someone had a listening spell on them.

"Yeah, they're all ready and good to go. Got some people also interested in being farmers, checking out the crafting side of things and such. They're hesitant to do it as they're part of the guild and scared they'll be kicked, though I think with time they'll come to understand the guild is more like a country. You are part of it no matter what and you can do as you want, but it reflects back on us. As long as they're happy and answer the guild's call when we need it, then they can do whatever they like. I know some people are interested to talk to you E-heads and make this their full-time life. Living three times longer than the rest of humanity and being part of a magical world like Emerilia has its draws," Florence said.

"Are you thinking of making the transition?" Josh asked.

"Not yet. There are things that I have to deal with back on Earth, but maybe in a few weeks I could." Florence's mind moved to her brother, who was on life support. She'd come to understand that soon enough, he would pass away. There was no one left back on Earth and Emerilia had paid for his bills as she had forged out a life for herself on Emerilia.

Maybe becoming an E-head would be a good way to just get away from it all. A fresh start in a new place that I enjoy and have a bunch of good friends around me. She knew that she couldn't leave her clan now. They had only just started. The possibilities of what they could do were intoxicating.

"With all of this done, we could have the teleport pad in place within the day," she said, looking at all of the work.

"Good. Then, we can start cycling Players in and out. Have you talked to the bank about a place here?" Josh asked.

"I have, but they haven't got back to me. Seems that they think we're still too small for their business. Was thinking that we make up our own bank if they keep being assholes about it." Florence growled.

Josh let out a barking laugh. "What?"

"Seems you really are becoming a Stone Raider. If someone doesn't give you a solution, then you're going to get out there and make one. I don't know about a bank, but it's hard to scam people in this game. I'll leave that up to you." Josh smiled. "Once we get the teleport pad up and running, then you can check out the guild hall and meet up with Lucy. She's still organizing everything. Once it's all set up, then we can start shipping supplies through here and other locations. How many other branches do we have up and running?"

"One in Opheir, which'll be two as soon as Cliff-Hill is connected; one in Markolm; three in Heval; then here in Verlun. We don't have any in Ashal right now. None of us are high enough levels for it to be safe for us there." Gaining levels by just being a trader was not the easiest thing to do. "Well, all the more reason for people to follow what they want to do.

Bring those levels up through some fun. Once Cliff-Hill is connected, then we're going to have people from Cliff-Hill come here to train people here and then a training camp in Cliff-Hill for forest-orientated lessons. Then, another camp in the other location to teach about open area warfare tactics. It won't be fun, but it means that everyone in the clan will know how to fight and work together no matter what." Josh looked to Florence.

"But we're traders—we don't need to know how to fight!"

"You're the Exdar's Traders of the Stone Raiders guild. We have a big target on our back simply because of who we are, which also means that you do as well. Better to have it and the levels that come with it and not need them, than being attacked and you could have been capable of defending yourself." Josh looked to Florence, his gaze hard and steady. He was doing it out of care for them, not out of a want to just show them how they weren't warriors. They'd faced many kinds of enemies since they had come to Emerilia. He wanted them to be ready to deal with anything and everything. "Okay, you make a good point. I know a few people won't be too happy with it, though they'll get over it."

"Good! In the meantime, I have this." Josh pulled out a box from his bag of holding.

Florence looked at it. *Stone Raiders' Treasury.* "Josh! What is this?"

"It is what it says it is, linked right to the one in the guild hall. Instead of having to send it all back and forth, this will allow us to be linked together, connected at all times."

"Thank you." Florence tucked it away in a pouch on her hip, a small bag of holding.

"We've got far to go, but this is a good start." Josh looked over the four large buildings that were forming.

"That it is." Florence looked to the main building. On the face of the building, the Stone Raiders emblem was engraved above the wide open doors that led into the storefront.

Ela-Dorn checked her sword once again. Ela-Gal shook his head; it was the fifth time she'd checked it. Around them, five fighter and three archer automatons looked for any threats to their charges.

"Are you sure about this?" Hamdir asked again.

"I am. Hamdir, you were the one who said that we need to get out there and start making friends and not keep on hiding down here. This is a step forward in that direction. Also, if we do get a portal, then it would be one hell of a find. Think of all we could learn!" Ela-Dorn's eyes lit up as she thought of the possibilities.

"There are a number of safeguards and other items on the portals that the Aleph had never been able to backward engineer."

"With an inactive portal, then those safeguards shouldn't be in place, allowing us to study them more than ever before!" Ela-Dorn reminded him.

"I know, but the risk is still rather high," Hamdir said. "Risk big to win big," Ela-Gal said.

"Fine. I know when I'm beat." Hamdir held up his hands in defeat. "Look after yourselves and let me know if anything goes wrong."

"We will, mother hen," Ela-Dorn teased.

Hamdir shook his head, looking to the Aleph standing in the controller room behind the teleport pad. They nodded; the teleport pad flared to life and a portal opened to Cliff-Hill.

Ela-Dorn took a deep breath and looked to Gal. "Well, let's go and see Emerilia."

"Sounds like an adventure." Gal grabbed her hand and started forward, forcing them both into motion.

Ela-Dorn felt the sun on her as she looked out over a large flat area made from stones. A bunch of armed and armored Dwarves looked at them from behind their shields. Their eyes thinned at the sight of the automatons.

Dave and Deia walked through the dwarves, hand-in-hand. "Welcome to our home, Cliff-Hill. We're not far from our home. We can go there to talk business. How fares things?" Dave asked.

"Shard sends his regards. Most of your people have moved off to their next event. The guild hall is expanding. You don't think small, do you?" Ela-Dorn said as Gal's hand rested on his blades, watching the Dwarves and the others with detached interest. Ready for anything. The archers and fighters spread out, ready to protect their masters at a moment's notice.

"Ah, thinking small just limits one's mind," Dave said.

The Dwarves started to walk off, seeing to their other tasks. Many were still eyeballing the automatons. They'd never seen anything like them. Dave held out his hand to shake Ela-Dorn's. She shook it and then Deia's. Ela-Gal repeated the gesture.

"I have seen a lot of your feats, Deia, though it has taken too long for us to meet," Ela-Gal said.

"You are too kind." Deia smiled at Gal. "I heard that you are interested in the spellsword fighting style that Anna and I use?"

"I have seen it. The combination of your magic and your blade makes for a truly inspiring fighting style." Gal smiled.

"Shall we move to our house? Deia and Gal can talk about fighting things," Dave said.

"You just want to show off your toys. Don't think I haven't forgotten about you not practicing much recently," Deia warned.

Ela-Dorn held in her laughter at Dave's expression. She smiled and looked to Gal, who was sizing her up.

"Yes, I think that we will have to test your fighting skills once again. Better to be ready, right?" Gal's studying eyes looked to Deia, who nodded seriously.

Right about that point, Ela-Dorn was thinking that her face looked really similar to Dave's.

"Yes, let's move this to your place." Ela-Dorn waved Dave on.

Ela-Dorn tried to form words, but she found she couldn't. Deia and Gal were out front of the house, sparring and talking different fighting techniques. Some Stone Raiders clan members were hanging around, including two of Dave and Deia's close Dwarven friends.

The fighters and archers had stayed outside, watching for threats and being studied by the Stone Raiders around the home.

They'd stepped into the middle of the house. Dave activated a spell that transported them somewhere else.

"What is this?" Ela-Dorn's hand rubbed the metal frame of the room they were in. It looked like a command center of some kind. The lights were similar to mage lights, but instead of runes, there was metallic string running to them.

"This is called a seeder, one of a whole bunch. They were made to change Emerilia from what it was, to what it is today. It comes with all you might need for changing a planet's ecosystem, including the bits that you need on Emerilia to make it like a game." Dave led the way to the back of the command room and to an elevator. Ela-Dorn got in. It was a short ride.

"So, how did you find this?" Ela-Dorn asked.

"Mostly it was just luck. I wanted to get away from everything, so I picked the most remote place I could. I also happened to find this thing. I didn't know it at the time. Bob thinks that because I'm a bleeder, that some of the things that should be restricted from my interface aren't. It's also how he laid the hint for the housing complex that we stumbled into."

The doors to the elevator opened; they stood on top of catwalks. "Turn on lights," Dave said out loud. "It's got a limited computer interface that recognizes me as the commander of this ship."

Dave was talking, but Ela-Dorn wasn't paying much attention. She moved to the edge of the catwalk, her mouth open as the lights came on row by row. Stacked on top of one another was portal after portal. It was a massive storage facility of some of the most advanced technology on Emerilia.

Dave gave her some time and opened his character sheet. He put in twenty stat points into his Intelligence attribute, ten into his Agility, so he didn't start falling all over the place, and five to his Vitality.

It was a rush as he moved around, getting used to the changes. *Bit by bit, add it all together and then see what happens. Hopefully, the Demons are worth lots of EXP to kill. And the quest will give us a nice EXP bounty.* He hadn't been watching his levels before, but now that he was focused on them, he was acutely aware how few quests he had completed.

He looked to his character sheet as Ela-Dorn wandered through the catwalks, looking down at the various items littering the seeder's warehouse- sized storage facilities.

Dave opened up his character sheet, a massive smile on his face.

CHARACTER SHEET			
Name:	David Grahslagg	Gender:	Male
Level:	23	Class:	Dwarven Master Smith, Friend of the Gray God, Bleeder, Librarian, Aleph Engineer, Weapons Master
Race:	Human/Dwarf	Alignment :	Chaotic Neutral
Unspent points: 501			
Health:	18,800	Regen:	6.14 /s
Mana:	3,980	Regen:	15.75 /s
Stamina:	2,480	Regen:	12.70 /s
Vitality:	188	Endurance :	307
Intelligence :	398	Willpower :	315
Strength:	248	Agility:	254

Level 124

You have reached level 124; you have **501** stat points to use.

Quest: Survival of the Fittest

Together, the races of Demon and Beast Kin have worked together, making a foothold in Devil's Crater. The Dark Lord, who sends his Demon Horde, hardened by a long journey and countless fights, sends them unknowingly into your home.

He wishes to use it to grow his forces stronger. Show him your newfound strength. Rise from the history books that you were cast into and LIVE!

Requirements: Defeat the Demon Horde
Failure: Death
Rewards: 1,000,000 gold to the Devil's Crater Treasury

Quest: Dwarven Master Smith Level 3

You must craft 10 weapons of S quality with your Smithing Art (Currently 3/10)

Rewards: Unlock Level 4 quest
Increase to stat gain

Quest: Friend of the Grey God Level 4

Complete the Quest: Survival of the Fittest
Rewards: Unlock Level 5 Quest
Increase to stats

Quest: Bleeder Level 3

Complete the Quest: Survival of the Fittest
Rewards: Unlock Level 4 Quest
Increase to stats
(???)

Quest: Librarian Level 3

Conduct research that allows you to understand how to create your own teleport pad.

Rewards: Unlock Level 4 Quest
Increase to stats

Quest: Weapons Master Level 2
Kill one hundred enemies with every weapon type. One handed and shield: 13/100
Two handed: 41/100
Dual wield: 46/100
Archery: 0/100
Rewards: Unlock Level 3 Quest
Increase to stats

Quest: Aleph Engineer Level 4
Help build 1 Aleph facility
Rewards: Unlock Level 5 Quest
Increase to stats
Increased access to Aleph College Knowledge

Thankfully, with my classes, I can keep gaining stats as long as I keep up with all the quests that it gives me. Making seven S quality weapons is going to be hard, but I could use the coin to back up the smithy and it would also show that we're not just any smithy.

Dave had found that with his higher Intelligence, he would frequently start thinking of his future and the plans he formed. Time didn't seem as rigid for him. Though, once getting stuck into his mental fugue state, he came out more tired. Before he fell in anymore, he shook his head to clear it.

Ela-Dorn was looking over a collection of portals just lying in wait, four stories of them stacked and ready.

"Quite the sight." Dave leaned on the banister beside her. "Huh, I guess Anna's training to get me over my fear of heights kind of worked."

"And we can take one of these?" Ela-Dorn asked. "Yes, though I have a favor to ask."

"What?" Ela-Dorn looked to Dave, anxious that Dave would take the portal away from her.

"Any information that you gain from these things, I want to know about it. I have plans for the future and these are a big part of it. I'm going to need to know a hell of a lot about them in the future to do what I want to." Dave's usually playful tone turned serious as he looked to Ela-Dorn.

"We're allies and I hope that we can become friends. I will share anything that I learn with you," Ela-Dorn promised.

"Thank you. Also, the first thing I'm at least going to try to play around with is dialing multiple, different locations. You've got it with the teleport pads, but these portals are hooked one-to-one with another. I want to see if we can't change that." Dave's smile returned.

"You've just learned part of how teleport pads work and now you want to not only bring portals online, but modify them?"

"Remember, got to think big!"

Ela-Dorn shook her head and looked over the facility. "How the hell am I going to be able to get one of these out of here?"

"Well, that is the first hurdle. I have no idea."

EPILOGUE:

HEAD OF THE SERPENT

Lezar looked over the Demon Horde as it progressed. They were highly resistant to most diseases and poison, but that didn't mean that they were unaffected by it.

The Demon Horde was slow, most of them dealing with cramps and stomach flus that they had seemed to catch over the last couple of weeks.

Lezar smiled as the afternoon turned to night. Among the Demon Horde were his own DCA soldiers. It had been easy for them to get into the camp.

The Demon Horde didn't care who walked beside them; they just weighed whether it was worth stabbing them for what they had or not. The Demon Horde was growing in strength, due to their uncaring murder of one another to take another's belongings and food or to eat them.

"Tonight's the night." Krenua stood beside Lezar.

"That it is," Lezar said. "I am surprised that it has taken the horde so long to start making leaders. If either of the plans are pulled off, then it will be the beginning of the end."

"It does feel good to have a purpose once again. When seeing the Demon Horde, I can understand why the trust that we've built up within the Devil's Crater Army is so useful. Without it, we wouldn't be much better than the rabble down there," Krenua said, a look of disgust on his face.

Lezar grunted in agreement, taking one more look at the advancing horde. Some were trying out their ability at flying, but it took time to understand how to do it properly. It also made beginner fliers vulnerable. It was easy to throw a rock at a new flier and bring them to the ground, stunned and weakened for another attack. Only the strongest Demons, those who had grouped together, or were just plain stupid, tried out flying.

"Without their aerial abilities, we're going to be able to bleed them on the ground. Their loss of mobility is going to be essential for completing this. Make sure that you target the winged ones first."

"There are only a third of them with wings, most of them with wounded wings. You can see the winged ones starting to group together as we had within our own horde when we crossed these plains. You and your brothers were the first of us to learn how to not only fly, but to fight while flying," Krenua said.

"Exactly. Wings give them mobility and advantages. Tonight, we'll take out the leaders among the Demon Horde. The more chaos within their ranks, the longer it will take them to reach Devil's Crater and the more we can bleed them." Lezar's stony features turned into a cold, *pleased* smile.

"I'll head down to the rest of the groups waiting. It will feel good to cut these ingrates down a bit." Krenua looked over the two million-strong Demon Horde. His heart beat fast, a mix of excitement of battle and the fear of death that followed it.

"Good luck, Krenua. Bring me their heads." Lezar held out his arm.

Krenua braced forearms with the general. "We'll sow the ground with their blood," Krenua promised.

Lezar nodded.

Krenua headed down the hill that they were using to watch the slowing Demon Horde getting ready to make camp for the night.

Krenua jogged through the forest, his footfalls light as he made nearly no sound in his movements.

It was only through his mini map that he was able to find the Demons assigned to the mission, every Demon from Lezar's brigade.

They had traded their service clothes for rags in most places. For this mission, the Beast Kin were held back, as a very last resort. For this to go off without a hitch, the Demon Horde would have to think that their leadership was killed from within.

Krenua waited, looking over his interface, checking the linked scouts that were updating the map constantly with where the Demon Horde's people were.

The Demons who had already inserted themselves into the Demon Horde camp also ran updates on certain high-value targets.

Dusk turned into night. Demons tried to hunt food down. Brawls started between the hungriest. With no meat to be found, the Demon Horde was not averse to killing their own and cooking them for sustenance.

Still, the DCA waited; the night came and the biggest fights came and went. Darkness descended as the Demon Horde started to fall asleep. The night's air smelled metallic, telling of the victims who had already fallen.

"Go," Lezar said over the brigade-wide channel.

The Devil's Crater Army started to stand up in groups, heading into the Demon Horde's camp. They looked like hunters who were just coming in late. There were around fifteen thousand of the DCA soldiers who were part of the operation. Facing over two million other Demons, it was hard to figure out that they were part of the same group.

Krenua waited for his group's turn. They moved forward, relaxed and muttering among themselves as they got closer to the camp.

"Hope that there's some damn meat to be had in the camp," Krenua said as they walked.

"Well, if there isn't, then we'll have to make some of our own," another said with a bloodthirsty smile.

"Look at these idiots—more scared of one another than of the creatures that should be in this area." Ilia shook her head.

The camp seemed to be formed into a sort of arena: Demons around the outside, with the interior empty except for those brawling. The Demon groups had their backs to the forest, watching their fellows they thought of as a larger threat than the natural beasts.

Krenua shook his head, agreeing with Ilia's observation.

"Easier for us," Krenua said, as they moved toward the marked targets. "Spread out, so we don't look like a group."

They moved apart. A Demon made a pass at Ilia, slapping her ass. Her sword took off their arm; their leering smile turned into a howl of pain before she slit their throat. He made choking noises, causing three other Demons to draw their crude stone weapons and move up to help.

Their faces showed looks of shock at the saw blades suddenly emerging from the Demons' chests.

The DCA left the dying Demons.

It's pretty messed up that we're kind of killing our younglings. They were made from the same base as us, though they're pure destruction. The Dark Lord's perfect tools: they're dumb, strong, and loyal as long as they're fed. Simple fact is that they're coming to destroy my home and do that sadistic fuck's dirty work.

"What are you doing?" a large Demon said as Krenua walked past him.

The Demon didn't feel anything as Ilia's blade cut out the tendons in his knee, dropping him down before she took his head off in a powerful blow.

"Killing you," Krenua said, not feeling an ounce of guilt as he moved into the sleeping area. Other groups of DCA moved into the area also.

Krenua walked under a low-hanging tree to see three demons wrapped in their wings, sleeping around a tree. One of them looked around, her hand on her weapon.

Krenua didn't give her time to react, putting his blade through her eye and into her skull.

She slumped to the ground. Krenua dispatched another Demon a second after; the third rustled in their sleep but didn't rise.

Krenua made sure they would never wake from their slumber.

The rusty smell of freshly spilled blood made Krenua's stoic expression turn into a grin similar to Lezar's.

DCA that had been with the Horde moved on their targets. Fifty thousand Demons died in a few short hours. Not a large number compared to the mass of Demons, yet nearly every one of them had been the strongest of the Horde. Potential leaders and groups were quashed in a night, while the most aggressive ones were left alive.

"Pull back. Good work," Lezar said. The DCA melted back into the forest.

Krenua stayed up the few hours left until morning, watching the Demon Horde camp. Before night turned into day, movement started to fill the camp. It seemed that word had been passed.

By the time that the sun had risen, the groups that were remaining, the bottom feeders and the more aggressive ones, were pulling themselves together.

Krenua watched as a battle played out in the middle of the camp. The open area in its center turned into a gladiator pit.

The Demons would probably level up but without leadership and their mistrust, it was like the first days they came to Emerilia. It was a free-for- all.

"We kill fifty thousand; they kill nearly two hundred thousand. That's what I call a strategic advantage." Lezar watched the scene with Krenua.

"What do we do now?" Krenua asked.

"Nightly raids; I want to fan the flames. The more time we hold them back here, the longer Efri gets with his traps. I want them disorganized, sleep deprived, and unwilling to trust one another when we hit them." Lezar looked to Krenua.

"I'll see to it." Krenua nodded and looked back to the camp one more time. *Once they clear Efri's traps, then they'll be at Devil's Crater and the real battle will start.*

Josh watched the interface in front of Florence disappear. For a few moments, there was nothing. Then, the drop pad's runes lit up. There was a flash of light as the drop pad had disappeared. In its place was a teleport pad. A control terminal sat on top of it.

Everyone looked around, as if stunned by what had just happened. It didn't seem as nearly ground-breaking as they'd thought.

Josh knew that with time, it wasn't having the teleport pad that would change Emerilia; it was what they did through the teleport pad.

"Get the control terminal off and put it in the control room," Florence said.

Two Stone Raiders grabbed the terminal, moving it off to the control room on one side. The entire area around the teleport pad had been made for speed and efficiency as well as defense. They wanted to be able to control what went through the teleport pad immediately.

The teleport pad hummed with power; the Stone Raiders' hands went to their blades.

A portal opened, showing Lucy on the other side.

"Well, it looks like it worked. Congratulations." Lucy smiled at Florence.

"I didn't think that it would there for a bit." Florence laughed.

Lucy stepped from the guild hall and out into Verlun. The portal closed behind her.

"Ah, just had to ramp up the excitement!" Josh said.

"Yeah, ramping up the excitement has nearly turned me into a nervous wreck," Lucy said dryly.

"Well, anyway, I have to get back to planning out a fight. I'll see you ladies later," Josh said, seeing that they were eager to catch up.

"Fine, go have fun. We'll get your supplies sorted out." Lucy waved Josh away like some annoying mosquito.

Josh grinned, headed for the control room where the teleport pad's controls were. As much as he was excited by the things going on in Verlun, when he thought about the impending war that was going to happen at Devil's Crater, he couldn't help but feel more excited.

Fellox's hundred grand is as good as mine! What the hell can they do that compares to an entire war between two different groups of Demons with Beast Kin thrown in? Bloody hell, it's nerve-wracking, it's nuts, and it's bloody brilliant!

"What?" Geswald said, his pipe in his numb hands.

"From the sources that we have, we're getting reports that the Stone Raiders have installed a teleport pad at their new headquarters in Verlun. They are starting to talk to local businesses. We believe that it was put into place a few days ago. With their standing treaties with other nations for fighting on their behalf, their network is expanding rapidly," Pete said.

Geswald looked at the man blankly. His eyes moved around the office he sat in, but didn't settle on anything. "What kind of monsters are they that they can buy a teleport pad? Where did they even get the drop pad from?"

Pete cleared his throat. Geswald's eyes focused on him again.

"We have heard rumors of a member of the Stone Raiders being a Dwarven Master Smith. I think that is how they were able to make it. Three days ago, there was another teleport pad connected. This one in a town called Cliff-Hill. It's an insignificant place, but the only place in Opheir other than Nadorf. They are connected to a human city, Omal, as well as an Elven forest, Kufo'tel, and the Mithsia Mountains. Trade goes through the village, where they have large smithies and a ceramics factory. I have been looking into these factories and the smithies through the connections in the trader's guild. They're owned by the same person, Dave Grahslagg, the reported Dwarven Master Smith. He has multiple patents on different items and it seems that he is responsible for using all of the smithy and ceramics factories' income to buy a teleport pad," Pete said.

"So, the Stone Raiders basically bought *two* teleport pads in as many days. They call a Dwarven Master Smith one of their people and they can somehow get goods from somewhere on a near constant basis?" Geswald sat back in his chair, feeling much older.

The guildmaster was right. I've never seen a guild have this kind of power before.

"We need to cancel all plans that we have with the Stone Raiders. They are not a group we want to anger. We can maybe pressure them in some way, but direct confrontation will lead to nothing," Geswald said firmly, relieved that he had been held back from his hasty attack plan he'd made just a few weeks ago.

"Yes, master," Pete bowed, wincing as he said the next sentence. "Lord Esamael received the same information as us a few hours before. He sent a message for you."

"Well, out with it." Geswald frowned.

"Lord Esamael, upon hearing that there is a second teleport pad held within fifty miles of his own teleport pad, has expressed his *displeasure* at the current situation. He wants us to do something about them. If we do not, then he will increase the cost of using the teleport pad, as well as taxes, while doing his best to interfere in our businesses. He said it in more flowery language."

"Did he send his message to just us?" Geswald asked darkly. His mind worked to try to figure a way to balance himself between the Stone Raiders and Lord Esamael.

"No, he sent it to a number of merchants and traders. We have already received complaints from a few of them."

"Esamael is a powerful man. His family has owned this town and its teleport pad for many generations. They're more powerful than most kings. Their power is only beaten by the actual king of Gudalo on this continent. Even with no standing army, their ties make them strong indeed. With the new information about the Stone Raiders, we're going to have to tread very carefully," Geswald warned.

"Yes, master," Pete said.

"Send word to the council in town that we need to discuss these latest developments."

"I will see to it personally." Pete bowed before he left the room.

Geswald looked around his office. He had been excited with the thrill of the hunt and his opportunity to show others his real power and crush a group of Players. It would have been *perfect*. Now that he knew of their true strength and pulled back his plans, he was getting forced from another direction to try to carry them out.

I need time to figure it all out, to see a way of keeping Esamael happy while not angering the Stone Raiders too much.

Lord Esamael drank wine from his ornate glass. It was handcrafted straight from Markolm. It was worth a small village's income for a year. He didn't really taste the wine that was worth more than a farmer's yearly expenses. Opulence wasn't an acquired taste; it was a standard to him.

He had silver hair and bright blue eyes. His jawline and well-groomed hair would make many girls swoon for him. He was well-built, the physique of a man who took his physical training seriously.

He let out an angry breath as he drank from his glass again. His eyes were fixed on the horizon. In the direction of his gaze lay Verlun. The Esamael family had not gotten to their seat of power through sitting back and letting others walk all over them. They were well versed in the art of backroom deals and non-physical arm twisting.

Anyone who didn't fall in line, they put them in place with force. They might not have a big standing army, but they controlled the gangs and crime in the region. Accidents weren't all that uncommon.

I will have that teleport pad and I will get those Players to either leave or submit. They might be immortals, but they're still weaker than my own forces and I know where they respawn.

He drank deeply from his cup.

He had issued his orders out to the traders and other groups to start the discrete pressure. If the Stone Raiders didn't take the hint, then Esamael would be forced to take things into his own hands. He was the law here. No one liked being in a cell for months; even the immortal Players usually changed their bodies after a few months.

Esamael turned from the balcony and headed into his castle.

Emerilia will be continued in <u>*This is Our Land*</u>.

The Emerilia Series will continue in Book 5: This is Our Land Michael Chatfield's Amazon Page: https://utm.guru/embmmc Thank you so much for reading and for your support. I hope you enjoyed the book as much as I enjoyed writing it.

As a self-published author, I live for reviews! It is the best way to let others know about the book (other than recommending it). Please consider leaving us one and letting others know about the book.

If you're looking to chat more about the series with fellow readers, check out these places:

TikTok @authormichaelchatfield
Instagram @authormichaelchatfield
Patreon: patreon.com/authormichaelchatfield

THE CHATFIELD CONNECTION NEWSLETTER

Sign up for exclusive offers, original stories, events, and more.

https://michaelchatfield.com/pages/newsletter

If you're looking for more books,
you can find me through the QR Code below!

I always love hearing from fans — want to send me a note to connect about this book or another one? Reach out to me at info@michaelchatfield.com!

Thanks again for reading! ☺
Hope you have a great day!

CHARACTER GUIDE

In Alphabetical Order

Ankol (Dwarf)

Dwarven Master Smith. Smithing Art: Metal Spinner. Lives in Grorart Mountain.

Boran-Al (Lich)
One of the Dark Lord's Champions. Works directly under the Dark Lord. Creates Creatures of Power and carry's out the Dark Lord's orders. His Citadel was destroyed.

Alastair Montgoa (Arch Lich)
aka former Lord Vailyn. Gave up his fellow Aleph to have everlasting life; used the centuries to build strength and knowledge

Barry (Dwarf)
Dwarven Master Smith. Smithing Art-Unknown. Wandering smith.

Cassie (Elf/Human Halfling)
Holy warrior. Leader of the Golden Sabres. In a relationship with Josh Giles.

Dark Lord (God)
Embodiment of the Dark affinity. Created Demons. Normally an ally with the Earth Lord. Always looking a way to tip the power balance of Emerilia in his favor.

Dasano (Dwarf)

Dwarven Master Smith. Smithing Art: Metal Press. Lives in Grorart Mountain.

Akatol Dracul (Dragon)
Water Mage. Was the second Dragon, Denur's husband. Went mad and started a genocide, disappeared.

Denur Dracul (Dragon)
Fire Mage Hailed as 'Mother of Dragons'. First of her race, a creature of power created by the Lady of Fire. Seen as her daughter. Sister to Oson' Deia.

Gelimah Dracul (Dragon)
Dark Mage. Brother to Induca, Louna and Malsour

Fornau Dracul (Dragon)
Earth Mage. Quindar's mate Malsour and Induca's grandnephew.

Induca Dracul (Dragon)
Fire Mage. One of the youngest from the first generation of Dragons. Sister to Malsour, daughter of Denur, aunt to Quindar, great aunt to Fornau. Member of the Stone Raiders and Party Zero.

Kinal Dracul (Dragon)

Louna Dracul (Dragon)
Induca, Gelimah and Malsour's sister.

Malsour Dracul (Dragon)
Dark Mage. One of the oldest Dragons in existence, first born of Denur. Deia and Induca's Guardian, Stone Raider and Party Zero member. Brother to Induca. Great Uncle to Fornau Dracul and Uncle to Quindar Dracul.

Quindar Dracul (Dragon)
Wind Mage, wife to Fornau, Niece to Induca and Malsour.

Wokui Dracul (Dragon) Water Mage

Xednai Dracul (Dragon)
One of the first Dragons, had several Dragons. Her son is Fornau.

Gorpal Dunsk (Dwarf)
Dwarven Master Smith, lives in Aldamire Mountain, created 3 Weapons of Power - Mace of Fury, Tower Shield, Boots of Smash. Smithing Art: Paint Copy

Earth Lord (God)
Embodiment of the Dark affinity. Created Earth Sprites.

Edmur (Dwarf)
Dwarven Master Smith. Had been in the Dwarven War Bands as a Shield Bearer. Former pupil of Quino's Brother to Endur. Smithing Art: Metal's Song

Edwards (Human)
Military scientist within the Deq'ual System. Friend of Sato's

Edwin (Beast Kin)
Beast Kin representative on ruling council.

Endur (Dwarf)

Dwarven Master Smith. Had been in the Dwarven War Bands as a Shield Bearer. Former pupil of Quino's, brother to Edmur, lives in Zolu Mountain. Smithing Art Hammer Blows

Esa (Human)
Melee fighter. Member of Mikal and Jule's party. Fought at Boranl-Al's Citadel. Member of the Stone Raiders. Going out with Jules. Works under Dwayne as a fighter. Being trained for a leadership position under Dwayne.

Lord Esamael (Human)
Lord of Emaren within the Gudalo Kingdom.

Ela-Gal (High Elf)
Warrior living in Aleph, married to Ela'Dorn. Persectued by high elves as heretic.

Ela-Dorn (Orc)
Researcher and professor at Aleph College. Aleph Council Member. Married to Ela-Gal

Fend (Dwarf)
Lord Under the Mithsia Mountains.

Geswald (Human)
Trader's Guild Chapter head in Emaren.

David Grahslagg (Dwarf/Human Halfling)
In-game character of Austin Zane. Dwarven Master Smith, Resident of Cliff Hill, member of Party Zero and the Stone Raider's Guild. Other names: Austin Zane

Josh Giles (Human)
Rogue. Leader of the Stone Raiders. Was a investment broker on Earth, became an E-head. In a relationship with Cassie from the Golden Sabres.

Gimel (Human)
Warrior. Fellox Guild Master.

Gorrund (Dwarf)
Dwarven Master Smith in Benvari Mountain with Jesal, teaching four apprentices. Smithing Art: Blood Bender.

Goula (Demon)
On the Ruling council for Devil's Crater.

Gurren (Dwarf)
Shield bearer, member of Dwarven War Band under Lox's command, sent to guide people to Cliff-Hill. Friend of David Grahslagg, Kol's Grandson. Member of the Stone Raiders.

Helick (Dwarf) Dwarven Master Smith.

Kim Isdola (Human)
Cleric/alchemist. Lieutenant in Stone Raiders.

Ishox (Demon)
On the Ruling council for Devil's Crater.

Arch-Mage Jekoni (Human/item)
Soul bound to Staff of Growing, over 2,000 years old; missing legs. Held within Dwarven Vaults with other Weapons of power.

Jeeves (AI)
Made by Bob to assist the Dwarven Master Smiths.

Jeremy (Human) Fellox Guild member.

Jesal (Dwarf)
Dwarven Master Smith, Dave's master smith trainer. Smithing art: Nature's Guide

Jules (Human)
Healer. Member of Mikal and Esa's party. Fought at Boranl-Al's Citadel. Member of the Stone Raiders. Used to be an army medic, E-head without legs IRL. Going out with Esa. Works under Lucy as support, leads the healers of the Stone Raiders.

Joko (Dwarf)
Shield bearer, member of Dwarven War Band under Lox's command, sent to guide people to Cliff-Hill. Friend and trainer of David Grahslagg. *Deceased.*

Anna'Kal (Wolf Beast Kin/Administrator AI24681)

Air mage. Originally a program meant to assist Lo'kal with the running of Emerilia. Anna was uploaded to a Player body and inserted into Emerilia. She became emotionally attached with her charges. When the Beast Kin people were wiped out from Emerilia she went into cold storage, waiting for her father to awake her when a chance came to fight against the prison they had created.

Member of the Stone Raiders and Party Zero. Daughter of Bob.

Lo'kal (Jukal)
Scientist, created Emerilia. Awarded the position of the Gray God, maintains Emerilia, its people and Players. Other names: Bob, Bobby McMahnon, The Balancer, Gray God.

Kino (Demon)
On the Ruling Council for Devil's Crater.

Kol (Dwarf)
Dwarven Master Smith. Gurren's grandfather. Resides in Cliff-Hill. Taught Dave how to Smith. Runs his Smithies. Smithing art: Blind Man's Touch

Lady of Air (Goddess)
Embodiment of the affinity Air. Known for causing mischief. Her Champions act as spies and information brokers, tilting the balance of Emerilia.

Lady of Fire (Goddess)
Created Dragons, Mages Guild and College. Gave gift of 'knowledge' to the people of Emerilia. Mother to Deia, Lover of Oson'Mal and best friend with Bob.

Other Names: Ignil

Lady of Light (Goddess)
Sent Players to kill/capture Dragons to make her own Creatures of Power. Created the race known as Angels. Large rivalry with the Dark Lord.

Lena (Demon)
On the Ruling Council of Devil's Crater. Wife to Vrexu.

Lovan (Dwarf)
Mithsia Mountain Warclan leader **Lox** (Dwarf)
Shield bearer. Was the commander of the War Band sent to guide people to Cliff-Hill. Friend of David Grahslagg. Member of the Stone Raiders.

Suzy Markell (Human (IRL)/High Elf (Emerilia))
Austin Zane's secretary and best friend. David Grahslagg's best friend and assistant with running Cliff Hill Smithy and Factory. Summoning Mage. Steven's contractor, member of Party Zero and the Stone Raiders.

Max (Dwarf)
Shield bearer, member of Dwarven War Band under Lox's command, sent to guide people to Cliff-Hill. Friend of David Grahslagg. *Deceased.*

Meda (Dwarf/Elf)
Aleph Council member. Deals with the food within Aleph cities and facilities

Melanie (Human)
Arch Mage Alamos' Wife.

Melhoun (Water snake)
Made by the Water Lord. Sealed away.

Mikal (Human)
Rogue. Jules and Esa's party member. Member of the Stone Raiders. Friends with Party Zero.

Oson'Deia (Elf/Demi God Halfling)
Elven Ranger and Fire Mage. Daughter of Oson'Mal and Lady Fire of the Affinity Pantheon. Resident of Cliff Hill and member of the Stone Raider's Guild, Leader of Party Zero.

Other names: Ouluv'Deia

Penelope (Human) Fellox Guild member.
Pete (Human) Geswald's secretary.

Queen Farun (High Elf) Queen of Raolor.

Queen Mendari Selhi (Human) Queen of Selhi.

Quino (Dwarf)
Dwarven Master Smith, lives in Zolu Mountain. Trained the brothers Endur and Edmur. Smithing Art: Internal cutting.

Rola (Dwarf)
Dwarven Master Smith. Smithing Art Puppeteer. Lives in Aldamire Mountain.

Sato/Communications officer Sato (Human)
Lives in De'qual system. Communications Officer, becomes Vice commander of Deq'ual military forces. Grandfather original settler.

Emperor Talis (Human)
Ruler of the Xeugrera Empire, located in the Ashal Continent.

Tounk (Dwarf)
Shield bearer, member of Dwarven War Band under Lox's command, sent to guide people to Cliff-Hill. Friend of David Grahslagg. *Deceased.*

Demon Prince Alkao/Alkao Travezar (Aerial Demon)
Melee fighter. Commander of the Third Demon Horde and leader of Xerzit lands. Oldest of the five remaining Demon Prince's of Devil's Crater.

Dwayne Trebault (Human)
Melee fighter. Lieutenant in Stone Raiders. Leads and trains the melee fighters in the Stone Raiders.

Venfik (Elf)
Lady Air's advisor.

Lucy Vernia (Wood Elf/Human)
Lieutenant in Stone Raiders. Spy master, deals with supporting the Stone Raiders and paperwork.

Vrexu (Demon)
One of the seven Demon Princes. General in the Devil's Crater Army. Married to Lena, the youngest of the five remaining Demon Princes.

Water Lord (God)
Embodiment of the Water Affinity. Created the Mer-People and water creatures. Created the Water Serpent Melhoun. Rival to the Lady of Fire.

Austin Zane (Human)
CEO of Rock Breaker's Corporation. Engineer specializing in space vehicles. Background in Astro physics. Other names: David Grahslagg

Wis'Zel (Wood Elf)
Bard. Works for David Grahslagg, managing his Ceramics factories in Cliff Hill.

www.ingramcontent.com/pod-product-compliance
Lightning Source LLC
Chambersburg PA
CBHW060927030726
47503CB00003B/508